Young Americans

Young Americans

A Novel

Peter S. Rush

Prior Manor Press
355 Lexington Ave
New York, NY 10017

ISBN: 978-0-9990665-6-0 (hardcover)
978-0-9990665-7-7 (paperback)
978-0-9990665-8-4 (ebook)

Printed in the United States of America

To my brothers

for all we have been through

Prologue

Bogotá, Colombia 1977

The stench of unwashed humans enveloped Tommy Logan as a thick guard led him into La Modelo, the fortress prison in Bogotá. The prison housed over ten thousand prisoners. Across all the concrete walls, *Viva* la revolución was spray-painted in red.

Where was Sandy? How was she? Why did he bring her with him to Colombia this time? She had insisted, but he thought it would be dangerous. He had to get word to someone.

The charges against him were vague. *For suspicion.* It had something to do with trafficking emeralds. He and Harry didn't have any emeralds or coke when the apartment was raided. There was a little pot, the cash, and Harry's diamond rings and snorter. The soldiers found the pistols, but guns were a normal precaution in Colombia for anyone with property.

A short solider pushed Tommy into a ten-foot-long and four-foot-wide cage made out of screen mesh and bars. At the end was a tiny hatch, like a lion's cage in the circus, so that he had to crawl to enter and leave. Two barbers in the center of the room were giving complimentary haircuts.

The prison officers wore black uniforms with Maltese crosses. A dead-on Nazi design: black boots, black pants, black caps, and black sashes with gold insignias. Short on pay, but their uniforms were flashy, Tommy thought.

As a short, stocky peasant guard led him from the cage after his haircut, Tommy asked a lieutenant if he could use one of the pay phones by the door. He had to get word to the outside. He didn't want to get lost among the thousands of prisoners. "After you are processed," was the answer.

After being fingerprinted, the peasant guard led him into the reception area, infested with *gamines*. They were the street urchins of Bogotá who ran in wild packs, growing up on the street, learning to survive the best they could in the world. Hustling, pickpocketing, thieving—staying alive. The Oliver Twists of Colombia.

Where was Harry? He wasn't in the same wagon when Tommy had arrived. Now he wasn't in the processing area. What did they do with him? Did they get the shipment? Was he out three hundred thousand dollars?

When the *gamines* saw Tommy, a gringo, twenty of the children descended upon him, selling cigarettes, food, and paper as little pairs of hands were trying to go through his clothes. Tommy slapped them away and moved to a captain standing near the door who was giving orders.

"What happened to the girls?" Tommy asked the officer, the aches from his beating still reminding him of his stupidity. He'd fought for Sandy, but it hadn't been enough. Did he cause more harm? "Can you find out?"

The officer's eyes traced the blood on Tommy's face and the welts on his arms but said nothing. Now he had to get out. Could he make it to the American Embassy? They hadn't done anything wrong, and he could get help for Sandy. He had five thousand pesos stuffed in his sock.

"*Por favor,*" Tommy said to the captain, showing him some pesos. A message? The officer looked around quickly and gave him a sheet of paper and a pencil. Tommy quickly wrote. It simply read:

Mr. Jamison Carlton
Senior Vice President
Second National Bank of Georgia
Sandy is being held without charges by Colombian authorities. You need a lawyer who can be trusted.

The message cost him two thousand pesos to smuggle out to the American Embassy.

The guards began separating the prisoners.

"Patio 5 with the gringos?" the guard asked the captain as he led Tommy by the arm. The captain looked down at the paper in front of him and shook his head. "*Nada. Peligroso,*" the captain said. "Patio 4."

Tommy remembered *peligroso* meant dangerous. So they weren't putting him with the gringos. Harry would be there. He'd find a way to get there.

Walking along the balcony of Patio 4, Tommy saw clothes, bedding, and underwear tied to the railings as an outdoor clothesline. The steady noise of thousands of caged voices beat on his ears like a tropical downpour on a tin roof. It was night by the time Tommy got to his cell, a six-foot by eight-foot room with a toilet that didn't work and a concrete slab for a bed. The cell held four other prisoners. The *gamines* on the cellblock lived ten or more to a cell.

The cool night air chilled Tommy. One man, with a pockmarked face, was lying under his woolen *ruana* on a thin cotton mattress on the slab. He exchanged greetings with Tommy. He said his name was

Pepe, and he was in for hacking up five people with a machete. He was deferential to Tommy but didn't offer the sleeping slab. Disoriented, cold, and in pain, Tommy hadn't thought to buy a blanket at reception. He huddled under the concrete slab for warmth and pulled his arms around himself, but the cold stone absorbed his body heat.

Defeated, Tommy searched his mind for a way to get out. It was stumbling and dazed by the events of the day. Cosmic forces were playing with him—retribution for his life. Maybe it was payback: George reaching out from the dead to punish him. Fuck. George deserved it. Tommy knew he would pay in Hell. For now, he would have to fight to stay alive in here, and he would need money. Where would that come from?

If only he could find out about Sandy. Was she all right? Was he in love, or was it guilt? He remembered the soldiers dragging her into the bedroom. It would keep until morning; everything would keep. Surrendering to the pain and exhaustion, Tommy cried himself to sleep for the first time since he was seven years old, the night he was raped by a priest.

Chapter 1

Tampa 1975

Tommy was tired of waiting. He had been up since 2:00 a.m. and his body was aching with fatigue. Sandy Carlton was dozing across the room from him, her strong legs tucked under her on the green velour of the chair. Tommy flexed his shoulders, rolling them forward and ruffling his dark brown hair. It hung to his neck in long, natural curls. He flexed his hands against each other, extending the isometric pressure along his arms, up his shoulders, and down into his back. Breathing deeply, he tried to relieve the fatigue of his will, an exercise he practiced at the tae kwon do school he attended three times a week. He didn't like sitting, just sitting. He wanted Harry Burr to arrive. Harry was the connection that would bring him to the big time and closer to a million dollars.

"What time did he say he would get here?" Tommy asked again.

"Six o'clock. He said he didn't want to miss dinner." Sandy lifted her head from the soft chair. Her black silk dress from the party last night was thrown into a ball on the floor next to the chair, and she only wore black panties. "He's busy. He's an important man in Atlanta," she said in her own defense.

"How'd you know each other again? Oh yeah, you're his little schoolgirl, aren't ya?" Tommy smiled at his joke. Sandy said she had met Harry when she was in high school.

As Tommy looked at Sandy, he thought her breasts looked too small for her body, just one size, to throw off her otherwise perfect symmetry. Tommy didn't care; he loved the way she moved her hips when she was under him. All karate movement begins at the center of gravity, the pit of the gut, which moves, as does the force of life, from the pelvis up and out through the hands and feet.

Sex came from that center. When he and Sandy gripped bellies, holding tight with their abdomens, swinging with the easy sway of the hips, he was engulfed with joy at her body. His mind was clear of all other life, and the world would shrink into the ten feet surrounding them. Sex was the first pure pleasure he ever understood. He doubted that neither of his parents, Angela and Kevin, ever had any idea of how good it was. Did they repent every time they had sex?

Discovering sex had replaced much of Tommy's pain. There were always available women. Sandy had begun as one of them, but that was four months ago, and now he wasn't seeing the others. They weren't as good as Sandy.

He couldn't figure her out. She had everything she could want. Her father was senior vice president of a Georgia bank, her brother was a lawyer, and her grandfather owned a carpet company in Dalton. She had all the money she needed, a cabin in the Smokey Mountains, a condominium in Daytona, and a sailboat in Savannah. Yet, she wanted to be heavy.

Tommy looked at his diver's watch—ten o'clock. He didn't think this Harry Burr would show.

When Sandy first had bragged about her connections in Atlanta, he laughed. He couldn't tell how much of her talk was bluff and how much was fact. Then she told him about Harry Burr, her connection, and offered to make the introductions.

"He'll be here. He's got a lot of things to do. He's an important man," she had insisted. "He'll come because *I* asked him to."

"You have him by the balls."

"Oh, Tommy, you're so crude. He's a friend of my father's. That's how I met him. He's at least thirty-eight."

"Doing it with the old-timers too? I guess they go out of their way for the young cunt as sexy as you. I know you didn't learn to screw by reading a book."

"Stop it, Tommy. If you can't talk right…"

"Oh, for a piece of your virginity," he mocked. She swung at him, but he blocked it easily. "Don't start something you can't finish, sweetheart." He smiled.

The loud knock on the door surprised them. Tommy felt his stomach tighten, and he tucked into his pants pocket the small container of coke he'd been holding. He was ready, ready as he'd ever be.

He felt safe because Tampa was his town. He knew people here, and, at least, Sal, his sometimes partner, would find where he was. Touching the small of his back, he felt for the handle of the Smith & Wesson to be certain it would be a quick draw—just in case. Sandy quickly slipped on her dress. He nodded to her to answer the door while he stepped back by the patio door.

"Harry! Oh, Harry, it's good to see you." Tommy could see Sandy's legs in the air as she was lifted from her feet. He moved closer to the sliding glass doors.

"I told you I'd come." Harry's voice boomed in a deep baritone. "Did you think I'd break my word? Just had a little business to finish in Miami."

When he stepped into the room, Tommy thought he might be hallucinating. The uneasiness of his stomach began to churn, and he fought it down. He didn't have words; his mind was trying to comprehend what his eyes saw, but that made it more nightmare than reality. Maybe the coke was cut with acid, but it wasn't because he'd cut it himself. A friend of her father's? Friend?

Harry Burr moved into the living room, dwarfing the furniture. He was the biggest, fattest person Tommy had ever seen. His head was the size of a soccer ball, his skin porcelain white, hairy, and fleshy. Each arm was the size of a thigh.

"Is this the kid you were telling me about?" Harry said loudly in Tommy's direction. His dark, bushy black beard and long, oily black hair made Harry seem a man-relic from the age of the dinosaurs. Though Harry was a little taller than Tommy, he weighed over four hundred pounds.

Tommy floated backward into a karate fight stance as the fat man approached. Harry seemed to sense his readiness and stopped in the middle of the room. "Is this punk giving you a hard time, baby?" He again addressed Sandy, who was smiling at Tommy's discomfort. Next to Sandy, and behind Harry, was a tall platinum blonde whose huge breasts were straining to break free from the confines of her thin silk halter.

"Yeah, old man. What are you gonna do about it?" Tommy fell easily into his natural New York accent.

"Oh, he's a sassy one." Harry turned around to Sandy. "But he's good looking." He turned back to Tommy, eyeing him with his silver-dollar-sized eyes.

With the balls of his feet firmly planted on the floor, Tommy squared his shoulders with deliberate nonchalance, meaning it as a demonstration of equality. The fat man loomed in the room. The girls were quiet, almost invisible. The action was between Tommy and Harry. Tommy wanted it that way. All was uncertain, everything blind. It was that way going into any new situation. The feeling multiplied in the fibers of his muscles: Tommy flexed and unflexed slowly. The muscles must behave.

"Well, Sandy," Harry spun gracefully on his back leg, breaking the tension, "you have anything in this house for a growing boy to eat?" He tapped his midsection and walked directly into the kitchen. Returning to the dining room, Harry sat at the head of the wooden table and opened a jar of whole kosher dill pickles.

"The dill pickle is good for your sex life. Gives you longer stamina and the sperm a farther trajectory—titillating!" Puckering his lips, he lifted a whole dill from the jar and inhaled it. His eyes bulged with satisfaction as he rolled his cheeks with definite sexuality. "Anyone want one?" He glanced at the three frozen people before eating another in the same way.

He couldn't be real, Tommy thought. *There must be acid in the cut.* Harry let out a deafening belch. "That's Japanese for *thank you*."

"Harry, I thought you were going to teach him a lesson?" Sandy asked.

"You wouldn't want me to do anything on an empty stomach?" he said patiently like a father.

"Well, I might as well sit down," Tommy said, casually sitting at the opposite end of the table from Harry. "It's gonna take a while, I can tell." Everyone laughed.

"I like you, kid. You got some spunk." The blonde quietly walked over to Harry and began nuzzling at his cheek like a child. "Not now, Elsie. Sit down." Her flat face dropped, and she sulked around the table to sit at his right. "Here. Eat one of these; good for your sex life."

"You're good for my sex life." It sounded like Harry had pulled the magic ring behind her neck.

"I know I am. Now get me something to drink. Fruit juice would be fine." Elsie disappeared into the kitchen.

This was heavy. He was heavy, and he wasn't from the country club.

With a flourish, Harry raised his right hand and pulled back his sleeve. "Nothing up my sleeve." He wore two large gold rings on each of his hands, set with several clusters of diamonds. One on his index finger had four stones in it, all equal in size. From his neck hung a large teardrop-shaped pendant embedded with numerous diamonds, rubies, and emeralds. "Would you care to smoke?" He looked at Tommy, then Sandy, before turning the back of his hand to them and instantly producing a plastic bag, which he laid on the table, and then a pipe.

Unfolding the baggie, his thick fingers retrieved a flat, golden piece of hashish. "Have you ever seen anything so beautiful?" he said reverently. His voice was mellow and cultivated. "It's the finest Lebanese blond, not too light, not too wet. The finest blend of the best pollen those Arab hands could produce. Do you have a knife?"

"There's a razor on the table." Tommy motioned to the living room. He didn't like the pot high, so he would be careful with the hash.

"Sandy..." Harry said, and she got it.

The flat, hand-carved hash pipe was passed around the table. The thick, sweet odor scented the room like incense. The hash was very good. Tommy knew quality; the fat man had it. Tommy was proud of his knowledge and ability to judge pot.

"The olfactory sense is the least developed sense," Harry continued, "though people use it more than they realize. You don't taste food. You smell it. Animals, for instance, can tell people apart by their smell. People have the same senses, but we don't use them. I have this huge apparatus here," he pointed to his wedge-shaped nose, "and unlike ordinary people, I have taken the time to develop it. I can distinguish Lebanese hash from Moroccan or Afghani hash just by the smell. I don't even need to see it."

"Right," Tommy said.

"An unbeliever. You're going to have to learn the hard way, aren't you, kid?"

"There isn't an easy way to learn."

"A skeptic. I'll demonstrate for you." Extending his arms over his head, he brought them to his chest like a priest consecrating a host. Raising his right hand to a point in space, he produced a plastic bag. He repeated the action at another point in space. Laying the two bags on the table, he motioned Sandy to open them. In the first was a black, gooey substance like the resin from a pipe, and in the second was a firm, dry brick with a delicate odor.

"Do you know the difference between the two, *kid?*"

Tommy bridled. He didn't like the tone or the context. He didn't need or want a father; he was equal to Harry. He wasn't a kid. He had learned from the street and his own life how to stay alive. "Yeah, the first one is from Lebanon, and the other is from Morocco."

"Wrong. The first one is from Afghanistan. You know where that is?"

"Yeah. On the other side of the ocean."

"You're a sassy one."

"Just being accurate." He smiled at the business, all a bunch of bullshit but necessary. If Harry was going to give him shit, he was going to shove it right back. "It doesn't matter where it's from—maybe Morocco, maybe Micanopy. It only matters how it smokes. If it's good, I don't care where it came from. I can tell people it's very rare, handmade by Tibetan monks in secret laboratories in Hoboken and jack the price one hundred percent."

Harry was fondling the soft piece.

"You gonna play with it or smoke it?"

"I'm about to demonstrate, for your skeptical mind, the excellent sense of smell I have."

"Don't bother. Anything that big has *got* to smell," Tommy quipped as Sandy and Elsie laughed.

Harry smiled and shrugged. "Oh well."

Tommy had made his point. One for the kid. He tried to figure out where Harry was coming from. Not a cop. That was evident by his size and his connection with Sandy. But who? Tommy's scene in Tampa had taken two years to get together, but it wasn't sacred or unchanging. Dealing in reefer and a little coke was working well -- though he had to do too much volume and take too many chances— but what wasn't risky?

The pipe kept coming around, but Tommy passed it without inhaling. Hash made him lazy, relaxed, and spacey; he didn't want that feeling now. Getting up to stretch his body as well as break the spell of the table, Tommy went into Sandy's bedroom for her makeup mirror. Her bed wasn't made: jeans, halters, and panties were carelessly thrown around the room. She was a slob for a girl. She didn't really care about things. She had so many of them.

He didn't either; it mattered, but it didn't. Sandy had lived in her little girl's fantasyland supported by Daddy for most of her life. Tommy never had that and didn't want it. He was fortunate, he thought, that the world had become real when he was young. His father had prayed himself to death, the only one of his prayers God ever answered. It was all in the mind—just the mind. The bullshit of religion, the bullshit of government, the bullshit of Harry Burr, the bullshit of Tommy Logan. He wondered what bullshit actually looked like.

This was a game, movie, episode—whatever the name was—it was a segment that promised to be interesting. Harry was a trip, and he had good jewelry. Tommy figured Harry would be looking to gain the advantage. They'd see who was smarter, the man or the kid. Tommy took the mirror and returned to the dining room, where everyone was still smoking. Placing the mirror in front of him, Tommy smoothly took the brown bottle from his pants, opened it, and poured some coke into a pile in the corner. Harry stopped smoking; Tommy saw he had his attention. The coke was personal stash—guaranteed to knock his lights out.

Almost carelessly, Tommy chopped the rocks into powder. His hand was practiced. Drawing eight lines, Tommy took a hundred-dollar bill, re-rolled it, and snorted the first row. He passed the mirror and the bill to Sandy. She did two, then Harry, and finally Elsie. Tommy drew eight more, and the mirror went around again.

"Not bad," Harry said. His snorts were loud and rumbled like a storm.

Tommy smiled confidently. "It's not too bad."

Sandy and Elsie exchanged private glances from which the men were excluded. Tommy felt relieved, reconstituted, not only because he had received the appropriate response—*not bad* in drug parlance easily meant *wow*—but it confirmed his opinion and what he had learned. He was not stupid. Ignorant at times, but not stupid. If Harry wanted to think of him as a chump that was fine — as long as it went his way.

"Can you get this stuff regularly?" Harry asked distantly.

"Sure."

"How much an ounce?"

"Small time?"

"Just tasting."

"Fourteen." Tommy took a chance and went two hundred high. It was that good.

"Can I get some?"

"When can I see the money?"

Harry reached into his front pocket and brought out a roll of hundred-dollar bills. He counted off fourteen. "Satisfied?"

It was time to put on a show for Harry. Tommy dialed the phone. "Sal, yeah. I'm at Sandy's. Bring me my briefcase from my apartment. Get dressed before you come. Yeah, it's important. Do it right now. I don't care if you're eating dinner. Tell Terry it's an emergency. Anyway, pasta is better warmed over. Not on the phone. Ten minutes. *Ciao.*"

If Sal could keep himself together, Tommy wanted to be partners again, but the dumb Lombardi kept fucking up. Human nature.

Tommy sat back at the table. Elsie relit the pipe. Slowly, the insane world was holding together, pieces at a time—no large picture, but pieces that he could see as fragments. It was better than he had ever imagined it would be. The street teaches by necessity and example.

"Have any luck, kid?" Harry smiled a broad, toothy grin. His teeth were flat and even from years of eating.

"What's luck? Luck's when your best friend gets hit by the bullet meant for you."

Harry nodded. "You have some smarts, but you don't have any class. Got to have style, kid. Without style, you're just like the other million hustlers. Think you're good?"

"I know."

"Maybe you know, but I haven't seen anything."

"Neither have I." That's where it was. What's upfront counts. Always—until it comes to call the bluff. Most of the time, people can just get by on a bluff. Isn't it always the same? If I say and you believe, then I know, and you don't. Who knows anything for sure? Tommy didn't, but knowing he didn't was the first major lesson he had learned. Dealing with it wasn't as easy. For some people, in some worlds maybe but on the street, your life is on each roll. He was frightened much of the time, but he didn't mind it as much.

Harry rolled back both his sleeves and held his hands in front of him again. "The hand is quicker than the eye. A skeptic like you might not believe that, but you aren't the first." Slowly lowering his left hand, he turned it over quickly, producing a twenty-dollar gold piece—an old double eagle.

"Ever see one this shiny?" he asked, holding the coin between his thumb and forefinger. With a quick motion of his wrist, the coin disappeared.

Tommy was impressed, letting the side of his mouth turn up in a smile. It was a good act, but there was more to this than parlor room magic.

The fat man held his finger up to his nose and trumpeted like an elephant. The gold piece fell from his nose. Elsie clapped—Sandy started to but looked at Tommy.

"Let me see that thing, Houdini," Tommy said insolently. He no longer felt threatened, and the Smith & Wesson was still in the small of his back. Harry threw the gold piece across the table. Tommy made a one-handed grab. Turning it over in his hand, Tommy tossed it back. "If I know you a year from now, it'll be mine."

"You're welcome to try."

There was a loud knock on the door. Tommy sprang instantly to the front window. A long black Cadillac Brougham was illegally parked in front of the building. Sandy stood beside him.

"Open it," Tommy said. "It's Sal."

Dressed in a black suit, black shirt, white tie, dark sunglasses, and a wide-brimmed black hat, Sal Lombardi and Mike Broski entered the room. Sal was Italian; there was no room for doubt.

Tommy had retreated to the dining room table. Sal silently walked up to him with a black briefcase in his hand. Harry's eyes followed the newcomer. Sal didn't take off his sunglasses. Broski stood by the door, hands clasped like a Secret Service agent.

Sal had a bowl of black hair cut to his collar. His droopy black mustache, round baby face, and stocky build gave him the menacing appearance of a movie heavy. Sal was playing his part for effect tonight. Tommy took the briefcase and nodded to Sal. "I'll call you later."

Sal still said nothing but eyed Harry and Elsie without changing his facial expression. Then he sauntered back to the door, gave a parting nod to Tommy, and he and Broski exited.

"Let's see that money," Tommy said again. Whenever he sold, he ran the show. Always, no exceptions. He had trusted other people when he was starting, but not now. It wasn't worth the risk.

Harry counted out the fourteen bills again, while Tommy unlocked the combination. Inside were a kitchen strainer and aluminum foil, and in the top snap pocket were two bags of white powder. The one closed with masking tape was 28 grams, one ounce. Tommy had measured it earlier. This was his personal stash; he hadn't intended on selling it, but… If he had had time, he'd have stepped on this bag a little because it was too good to sell. But he didn't know how much Harry really knew. Tommy stood and exchanged the bag for the cash. Pulling out his money clip, he added the fourteen hundreds to the twenties he had. Tommy saw Harry glance from the coke to the money—that was the idea.

Laying the bag on the table, Harry opened it slowly, allowing all the powder to fall to the bottom. He dipped his finger into the bag and tasted before rubbing some on his gums. His nose wrinkled from the acid—it was good.

"Pretty clean."

"I only deal in quality."

"Why don't you come to Atlanta this weekend? Bring Sandy; she knows where I live. I can show you a thing or two."

"Like what?"

"You're young—whether you admit it or not. And you're going too fast. But don't let that fool you; you're still a boy in the real world. Ever been busted?"

"What's it to ya?"

"If you haven't, then you have no idea how the justice system works. And if you haven't done the whole trip in coke from start to finish, then you're a virgin. Controlled, not the controller. You have to rely on someone else, not yourself. Placing your fate in the hands of another man can be fatal. I can tell you want to be your own man. You understand, kid?"

"I'm listening." Tommy bridled again but wanted to hear. There was the street, and there was the office. Both profitable. One safer, the other way more fun.

With an actor's sweeping hand gesture, Harry brushed the conversation aside. "You know that I know what I'm talking about. I didn't get these," he held up the rings, "by being stupid. I want to see where you're coming from. Come to Atlanta. I'll show you what a big-time is about."

Tommy smiled in mocking sweetness at Sandy. "Want to take me to meet Daddy this weekend? We might even go shopping." He was usually good for an outfit or two whenever they went.

"I don't know if I want you to meet my father yet, but I'll always go to Atlanta."

"Settled, nice and simple. Harry, we'll see you in Atlanta."

"Great, kid. Sandy remembers where I live." Harry looked at her and winked.

"Yes," she said, looking away.

Harry took two large spoons of coke from the bag and inhaled.

"Hey, Harry," Tommy snapped, "don't be so stingy with the coke. I gave you a deal at fourteen. I should have charged you eighteen." Harry nodded a *get fucked* gesture. Tommy drew some lines on the mirror. Sell it first, then snort.

Harry rose with imperial authority, signaling the end of the meeting. He gathered up his toys as Elsie quickly put the drugs in a case. "Okay, kid. I had some really important business in Miami. Major score. Think about it: are you ready for the big time?"

After he closed the door, Tommy could feel how tired he was from the running around. His Tampa business was good, making twenty thousand a week for his crew, and he had just completed a deal for one pound of pot. He was concerned with the logistics: pot was big, smelly, and hard to carry. Coke was small, easier to conceal, and more lucrative. Sal wanted to stick with pot though his nose was becoming fond of the white lady. The quality of coke in Tampa wasn't very good. The Cubans, who brought it in from Miami, cut it with too much junk. There was a market for quality.

Sandy was lying on the king bed, watching television as he stripped. Her cat finally emerged from its hiding spot and jumped on the bed. The tension of the day and night translated into physical exhaustion. He wanted to curl up with her and sleep for two days.

The television was background noise. "*Today, a jewelry dealer was found dead in his room at the Fontainebleau Hotel in Miami Beach. Police are treating it as a robbery/homicide because over two million dollars' worth of diamonds may have been stolen. In other news, Hurricane Betsy is gaining strength in the Atlantic...*"

"Turn that shit off," Tommy said, collapsing on the pillow as Sandy drew the room into darkness.

Chapter 2

Tommy had twenty thousand dollars in hundred-dollar bills in a black leather messenger bag over the shoulder of his black silk jumpsuit as he got off the plane in Atlanta. He also had another ounce of coke in his bag. Sandy wore a thin nylon summer dress with spaghetti straps. It clung to the curves of her body.

Harry told him to call when he arrived, but Tommy decided to get a car and a room at the Hyatt first. It was better when he had his own transportation, and Sandy grew up in the city.

From the airport, Tommy took I-285 northwest, exiting at Doraville. The Olds 88 that he had rented drove like a boat. He wanted a Cadillac, but he couldn't rent one without a credit card. He had to get one.

The red brick houses seemed stamped from the same machine, America's 1950s identity crisis, no one wanting to be different. There was no life on the street—mysterious, monotonous houses differentiated by the color of shutters or a door. The houses stared inscrutably at the street behind moats of mowed grass. Tommy occasionally glanced into the rearview mirror to see if they were being followed. Habit.

"That's the one." Sandy pointed. Tommy parked in front of the house with black shutters. The Venetian blinds were drawn tightly. In the driveway was a new 1974 cream-colored Cadillac.

Sandy rang the bell, moving from foot to foot. Tommy opened the screen door and knocked loudly. Bells don't always work.

Elsie opened the door, braless, in a tight t-shirt and crotch-high cut-offs.

"Sandy, it's so good to see you," she squealed. Tommy recognized her horse face and her very fine body. He pushed his way past the hugging girls into a dimly lit living room with a large stereo system at the far end. Light came from the swinging door at the end of the room. Tommy quickly covered the distance.

Behind a large thick oak table, in a broad captain's chair, sat Harry Burr, cutting a deck of cards in the thick fingers of his left hand. He looked up at Tommy but continued to cut the cards.

"Glad you made it." Harry nodded his greeting. In front of him, on the table, was a large mirror with a pile of coke on it. "I'm trying to lose weight, so I'm having this for dinner. Dr. Bentley told me that cocaine decreases hunger. Here. He lent me this." He showed a thick book to Tommy. Harry read:

"… Here in Dr. H. Gold Mortimer's study, *the early writers of Andean travel indicated that Coca has a phenomenal effect upon endurance, so great, indeed, that many of these accounts have been regarded as simply fabulous; but as we have considered the possibilities of Coca through the potential energy hidden in its leaf, it is very easy to trace the foundation of truth from these stories. The Indians are described as relying upon Coca for food and drink, with no other resource. If you ask them why they venerate it, they will answer you that it is used to prevent the feeling of hunger, thirst, and the loss of strength, as well as preserves them in health.*

"The early church sought to discontinue the use of Coca, whether it contained food properties or not, because of its superstitious associations. Its use was to be prohibited because it was a substance which is connected with the work of idolatry and sorcery and strengthening the wicked in their delusions."

Harry handed the book to Tommy. "See? The Spanish Jesuits thought coke was something heathen, connected with the old Incan religion and beliefs. So like good Jesuits, they immediately made it sinful, like anything that was native, and made the Indians slaves of the Spanish empire. Coca-Cola used to have cocaine in it; that's what made it so popular. In the South, crackers still say *have a dope*. Cigarettes were once illegal in many states, and they put hundreds of thousands of people in jail during prohibition for wanting a drink after work."

Tommy nodded his agreement. He had read that Sherlock Holmes used coke because he had read the stories growing up. Cops and robbers.

"Now that the history lesson is over, why don't you invite me to join you?" Tommy said. Sandy and Elsie joined them while Harry drew some lines on the mirror.

"I'll show you where class is, kid," Harry said, removing a large jeweled ornament that hung from a thick gold chain around his neck. He offered it to Tommy. It consisted of two cylinders, one hollow and one solid, connected by a half-inch-wide thin flat piece. The whole pendant was gold, four fingers wide, and heavy. In the center of the flat piece of gold was a large diamond surrounded by a ring of small rubies. Around the wide end of the hollow cylinder was a ring of small diamonds. A loop of diamonds and rubies ringed each cylinder. Tommy didn't know much about jewels, but this piece looked impressive. He had to study up so he could keep up with Harry.

"The large diamond is three carats; those rubies on the tubes are one carat each. The other diamonds are half a carat each. The whole piece is eighteen-karat gold. Here, give it to me; I'll show you how a man uses it."

Harry curled the thumb, index, and middle fingers of his right hand around the solid cylinder. Closing off his left nostril with the ring finger of his left, he put the larger end of the hollow piece into his nose and snorted a six-inch line of coke. Harry did another long line before settling back into the captain's chair.

"I haven't even gotten to the entrées." His smile developed as his lips parted like the biblical sea to reveal his thick, fat cow teeth. "I call this the Enterprise," he held up the cylinder, "because it boldly goes where no man has gone before. It is truly a starship. It looks like the real one too." Harry handed it to Tommy.

Trying to imitate Harry, Tommy found his hand was too small. He needed all five of his fingers to hold it. He closed off his left nostril with his left forefinger. He passed the Enterprise to Sandy, who used it like Tommy. Tommy could see Harry was successful: a house, jewelry, and a Cadillac. If he did any business with Sandy's old man, who was the senior vice president of the Second National Bank, then he was the kind of people Tommy wanted to know. He could see possibilities with Harry. Maybe Harry needed a connection.

"Hey, Kippi, come in here," Harry bellowed, surprising everyone in the room. A cute nine-year-old girl with long, unwashed brown hair ran into the room. Outlined in sequins on her green t-shirt were three singing frogs. She wore blue jeans and red tennis shoes.

"What do you want, Daddy?" she asked, running up to Harry and leaping onto his lap like it was a swimming pool.

"Ow." Harry snorted, sneezed, and snorted again. Then he smiled as she gave him a kiss on the mouth. "Tommy here wanted to meet a foxy lady."

"He did?" Her eyes opened wide, and she turned her head, cocking her chin. "Are you him?"

"Am I who?" Tommy said.

"Is that him, Daddy?"

"Is that who, sweetheart?"

"Is that who wanted to meet me?"

Tommy gave her the coy expression he used in bars. "I wanted to meet a fox. Are you a fox?"

Tipping her head back, looking down at him, she said in an affected voice, "What else would you call me?"

"A punk."

"Daddy…"

"What, sweetheart?"

"He called me a punk."

"Don't tell me. Tell him."

"I'm not a punk. You are."

"No, you've got it wrong. Punks wear red tennis shoes and shirts with frogs on them."

Kippi looked at her tennis shoes and her shirt. "Daddy, I'm not a punk, am I?"

"Yeah, you're still a punk, but so is he." He motioned to Tommy. Kippi smiled and turned to Tommy.

"We're both punks."

Tommy caught her eyes with his, but it was hard—like she was avoiding the teacher's stare. He liked the kid. Her eyes smiled with the gaiety of childhood. He wished he was a child again, but that was the past. Someday he would have a child and would watch as he explored and experienced life. Sal's boy was only two and a sharp little kid. He called him, "Uncle Tommy." It had a pleasant sound, but he was content to stay only an uncle for now. There were still too many things to do, to see, to experience.

Harry cleared his throat. "Kippi Burr, I'd like to introduce you to Mr. Tommy Logan. Mr. Logan, Miss Burr."

"Why, I'm delighted to make your acquaintance," Kippi said, mocking a Southern belle voice and batting her eyes coquettishly.

"You should be." Tommy turned up his nose and looked away from her.

"Is that so," she continued. "And why is that?"

"Because I'm the meanest mother you'll ever meet."

Her eyes went wide, and she turned to Harry, her mouth opening and closing without a sound. "What should I say?" she whispered to Harry.

"Tell him that he's as tough as a pimple on a horse's ass."

She pulled away. "You're as tough as a horse on a pimple's ass," she said confidently. The whole room burst into laughter. Harry's mouth was wide open, and Kippi rocked on his belly. She looked confused but happy that her remark brought so much laughter.

Tommy liked the kid. She was cute and another part of Harry Burr. He had a family, so Tommy trusted him that much more.

Tommy and Harry went to pick up lunch while the girls cleaned the kitchen. In his new 1976 Cadillac, cream with black leather interior, Harry controlled his world with one finger on the complete instrument panel: seats, windows, locks, mirrors, speakers, and the sunroof. Before the machine age, Harry could not have survived without servants. Tommy believed he could have this and more if he played his cards right. He needed to control himself—not get too far in front—because he wasn't sure of Harry. It was a dangerous game.

"You're a cocky kid. I'd hate for you to learn your lessons the hard way, especially when there are other ways to learn." Harry spoke with a fatherly patience as they pulled into McDonald's. "All I can tell you is what I know. If you learn, then you don't make the same mistakes. That's good for you. If not, it's your life. Fuck it up if you want."

Tommy was trying to maintain distance from the seductive voice. If there was a deal to be made, he wanted it. The kids he was doing business with in Tampa were dead ends. Only there for the minute. Harry Burr had been around. "I hear you."

"The power of this country doesn't stop for punks. You're a small fry, a pesky gnat. When the powers want you, squish. You may be the toughest guy in the bar, but what can you do about ten cops? Or the FBI? Can you fight your way out of a prison? You're nobody; you know nothing. Mr. Tommy Logan, Mr. Nobody from Tampa, Florida. Who do you know? It's a matter of connections."

When they entered McDonald's, a thin, acned girl, her hair tied in pigtails, stepped back from the register as Harry approached. "I'm hungry," he bellowed at her. "Give me food." He pounded his fist on the counter. A black boy peeked from behind the grill, but when he saw Harry, he quickly retreated. "Hamburgers, juicy hamburgers. Give me one of them. No, give me twenty of them. The big ones— Big Macs. And twenty French fries and two of every kind of shake."

The girl remained transfixed. A mother and her teenage daughter entered, but on seeing Harry, they quickly changed their minds. The cashier piled all of the food into bags that lined the entire counter. Tommy shook his head as he picked up several bags. Harry was a glutton—something to be careful of. Could he keep the balance of power between them, or would Harry want to devour everything?

"Will that be all?" she asked meekly.

Harry spoke gently to her. "This is breakfast. I'll be back later for dinner. What time do you get off?" The girl's eyes popped wide as she shrank back in fear. Harry loudly laughed the whole way to the car. Tommy saw how he enjoyed the intimidation factor. Another point to watch: he had to manipulate a situation to his advantage.

"My uncle is a manager out at the Dunes Casino in Vegas. He's a front man for the syndicate. They're the ones with the judges, lawyers, politicians, and the *money*. They don't have to use muscle because they have the system working for them. That's why no one can touch them." Harry ingested an entire burger in one bite, the juices running down his beard.

Tommy was small and felt afraid sometimes. He watched the people in Tampa—loan sharks, pimps, hookers. Street people. Cash money draws all types. The magazine article said the government was involved in the drug business just like they were in Vietnam. It didn't take a crystal ball to figure out. Why should they have a monopoly? Tommy didn't want to take it over. Just a couple of runs, and he'd be rich and out of the business.

"You ever do time, Harry?" Tommy asked.

"A good question, grasshopper. That's what you are, still the apprentice. I like you. And I love Sandy like a daughter. So I'll give you a break. I've got a load of coke coming in next week. I'll give you first crack at it. As much as you want, up to a pound."

"Did you ever do time?" Tommy asked again, leaning forward and trying to pin Harry with his gaze. He didn't like the evasion.

"I did time until I learned. I bought wisdom with the time."

"What for?"

"Not being smart enough."

"That's what they all say after they're caught. What did you get caught doing?"

"They tried to pin an assault with a deadly weapon, ADW, for hitting a guy with a tire iron. They couldn't prove it; besides, he had a knife. I was hotheaded and young like you, grasshopper. My uncle was working for the mob in Cleveland, and I thought I was a hot ticket. We had a scam going with motorcycles, stripping them and

22

selling parts. It was good profit. We got too cocky. The judge took one look at my juvenile record and sent me up for possession of stolen property. One to five. It scared the shit out of me." His voice lost its detachment, and Harry seemed to speak with a tremble. "I learned—I learned the hard way. Never again." He regained his normal tone. "If you'd only listen to a little wiser counsel, grasshopper, you might save yourself some hard knocks."

"You say that, but I don't see any reason I should trust you with any of my money. You haven't shown me a thing."

"In time, grasshopper. Patience is a virtue which…"

"Oh shut the fuck up with that grasshopper bullshit. I'm not a kid. I've been out there. So what did you do when you got out of the joint?"

"It was the late fifties, and gun-running to Cuba and Castro was big money. A friend of mine from Cleveland, Joey DeVito—he's now an agent for the Alcohol, Tobacco, and Firearms—hitched up with a guy named Alan Smedly, who was and still is a big gun dealer. He's one of the few people with a permit to deal machine guns."

He looked over at Tommy. "When Castro took over, the business went to hell. The mob and foreigners were out, and the rich Cubans started heading to Miami. I set up an operation pimping blond American girls to the Cubans. I had a nice stable of girls then." He smiled a satisfied smile at the memory.

"I hear you," Tommy said, his eyes narrowed to slits. Harry sounded like con man. A good con man and Tommy had to doubt. Maybe it's true? That's the art of the good con, mixing enough truth into the scam to make it believable. How much? It's like buying coke. You know the stuff has been cut, but the good dealer can tell how much and with what. That way, you know what you're getting, and you don't get burned. He wasn't certain what Harry was cut with yet, and he was in no hurry to get burned.

The other side is always working too. If the deal is there, then he had to make it, because he could never be certain about the next one. If he and Harry could work out a way to bring the coke in direct—pure—profits would triple. He didn't want to get burned on a stupidity rap.

"So what do you do now, *pimp*?" Tommy asked with a snarky tone.

"I'm an ordinary entrepreneur trying to make a living."

"Can you do weight?"

"Of course. But I'm going to let you in on a good thing."

"What's that?"

"Because I like you, grasshopper. I can see that daring in you like I had at your age. You've got balls, but it isn't under control. You were scared the first time you met me, but you didn't let it show."

"What's in it for you? Be specific; I don't need your mumbo jumbo psychology. If you have a business proposition, make it."

"There you go being hasty again." Harry's voice was smooth and elegant. "When I met you, I knew you had potential. Now you're showing class. Some people will always be nickel and dime, but you have ambition. You don't want to deal with the middlemen; you want to go to the source."

"Yeah, yeah… I'm not hearing anything but wind from you. And I don't think I have the patience to wait till you run out of hot air." He looked at Harry's stomach. He wanted to see how badly Harry wanted him. Sixty-forty, no doubt.

"You're not listening. You can triple your profits on each ounce. I know the right people to get it from down there, and I have a way of getting it back in. To make it more profitable, I could use the right kind of partner. Why take the chance for a small profit when I can take the same chances for twice as much money. Right?"

"I'm still waiting to hear something. What's in it for you, and what's in it for me?" Tommy guessed Harry would get to money. Harry Burr was a smuggler—or so he said—not a nice guy trying to give poor little Tommy a chance. No, there was profit in it; Tommy was going to get his half. He wasn't working for anyone. "So you smuggle, Harry. How come you are copping from me?"

"'Cause I was in Tampa and felt curious."

"So, what's in it for you?" Tommy examined the broad, heavy lines of Harry's face. The beard covered a great deal, but it was a mask covering the calculating mind of a con man. One who was good enough not to answer Tommy, no matter what angle he came at Harry from. By the time he left that night, he was both ready to forget the whole thing and make one more attempt at making it work. The morning would tell all.

* * *

The next morning, Tommy wanted to be on his way home to Tampa. It would be a quick stop at Harry's before heading to the airport.

"Ah, the young lion," Harry said. He had a plate with eight eggs, twelve strips of bacon, a pile of sausages, and a stack of pancakes in front of him. Kippi was in the chair next to him. She cut around her single pancake face, leaving just the whipped cream mouth and nose uneaten. "Hungry?" he asked as he downed a large glass of orange juice.

"If I wanted breakfast, I would have stopped at Hardee's," Tommy said. If it was bullshit Harry was serving this morning, he wanted none of it.

"Sit down," Harry ordered.

"Tommy, breakfast is the most important meal of the day," Kippi lectured.

"Right, little momma." Tommy smiled at her sincere face but paced around the room, too wired to sit still. He wanted to get the deal in place and then get some sleep back in Tampa.

Harry released a giant belch, a foghorn announcing the approach of a giant ship. He wiped his mouth with his cloth napkin, then each finger individually. He pushed the plate to the side, and Elsie emerged from the kitchen and quickly cleared it without acknowledging Tommy. *What the fuck*, he thought.

"Now, my young partner, I am ready for a good day's work."

"I'm doing all the work; you're just sitting there getting fatter."

"Some work with the body. Others work with the mind."

"Yeah, right. I've got a deal to do—are you in or out? You've been fucking around with it long enough."

"Let's get down to business. Kippi, go into the closet in my bedroom. On the top shelf is a brown hatbox. Bring it to me. While she gets it, let's go over the deal you're proposing."

"I've got two hundred pounds of weed coming into Tampa. Twenty grand—great price. Are you in for half? Cash up-front. I'll have your half delivered in two days."

"And I'm trusting you with my money?" Harry raised his hand in the air. Kippi returned with the hatbox and dropped it on the table.

"It's a heavy hat," she said.

Harry lifted the lid and put a steel strongbox on the table. With a twist of his wrist, Harry produced a key to open the box.

Tommy moved over to the table and sat in the chair next to Harry.

"I have a deal for you." He unfolded a black felt about the size of a dinner napkin onto the table. He reached into the box and set four paper envelopes on the table. "Now, listen and learn."

He opened the first envelope and spilled a line of diamonds on the felt. With his fingernail, he separated them so each would reflect the light from the overhead chandelier. He repeated the action until four lines of diamonds covered the cloth. Kippi's eyes went wide, and she got on her knees on the chair, trying to get a better look. She reached for the glistening stones, but Harry cut her off with a slap on the hand.

"Ow, that hurt," she said, little droplets appearing in her eyes.

"Look with your eyes, not with your hands," Harry said. "You have to understand your diamonds."

"What'd you do, knock off a jewelry store?" Tommy asked. Harry shifted in this seat, his eyes darting to the ceiling and back to Tommy.

"No, no—nothing like that. I do some deals with my contacts. All cash business."

Tommy was impressed. He didn't know anything about diamonds, but the stones in front of him made him want to know more. He was sure Sandy would like a nice pair of earrings or a tennis bracelet.

"To understand diamonds, you have to remember your four C's: carat, clarity, color, and cut." Harry produced a jeweler's loupe from his pocket and picked up a stone, examining it slowly. "One-point-two-five carats, maybe a VS2 clarity, D to F in color, and a good cut. What do you see?"

He gave the diamond and loupe to Tommy. He was out of his league, but he dutifully used the loupe to get a close-up of the stone. It was beautiful.

"I don't know anything about diamonds." Tommy shrugged.

"You should learn. Untraceable, valuable, and easily concealed. In our line of work, a good investment." Harry took the loupe and described several other diamonds to Tommy. The only difference Tommy noticed were some lines in the stones. He thought he could see some color variation but didn't trust the light.

"Now, I'm going to make a deal with you that is better for you than for me." Harry began returning the stones to their envelopes. "It's to show what type of partner I am and how much trust I have in you. I'm in on this deal, but I'm not giving you any cash."

"I knew it. Fuck you, Harry." Tommy pushed his chair back from the table.

"Hold on, young partner. I said it would be better for you than me." He put two of the envelopes full of diamonds in front of Tommy. "You hold these two as collateral. Each is worth twenty grand. Put them in some safe place. When I see my half of the load, I will give you the twenty grand, and you can give me back the diamonds. You can't lose."

Tommy didn't know the price of the diamonds, but the deal sounded okay. Harry was cash poor and probably looking to fence the other diamonds, but he wasn't asking any questions. Harry was up to something, so Tommy would have to watch him. Sure, he could afford to front the money on this deal, and if Harry tried to screw him—well, he couldn't—he was protected. Tommy put the two envelopes in his pocket and held out his hand.

"Sure, Harry. We've got a deal. See you in a week."

"Grasshopper, you have made a wise choice."

Harry wanted the money, but what else could he want? Tommy was cash rich—that always drew opportunities. Tommy had a sense about people. Harry would want to make a deal.

"You drive a hard bargain." Harry shrugged. "Remember, I know more than you do. Remember that, it could prove important. It's a deal. Thirty-five cash against me and fifty-fifty on the coke. It's a deal."

"And I hold the jewels."

Harry nodded.

"I'll think about it." Tommy touched the diamonds in his pocket. Harry smiled.

"I've got to get back to Tampa now and deal with the real thing— not just this talk. I'll let you know." Tommy touched his finger to his forehead in farewell.

He put his arm around Sandy as they drove to the airport. He would show her that he was going to make it. She nibbled at his ear as they drove. Yeah, it was going to be a home run.

"Can we stay another night in Atlanta?" she asked. "We can stay at the Hyatt."

He cut across three lanes to the first exit to downtown. "Sure, babe."

Chapter 3

WHEN SANDY MET TOMMY A year ago, she was a freshman at the University of South Florida. On that day, it was the afternoon before she was ready to get out of bed. Classes were so unimportant. What did she care about tariffs, dead poets, or term papers? It wasn't going to make any difference, and besides, the teachers were boring. If they couldn't make the courses interesting, she decided she wasn't going to go.

Her assignments wouldn't get done, and she'd get a D or F for the course. She'd rather be water skiing.

Her apartment was in a new luxury complex set back in a small cluster of tall Florida pines, tinseled with brown Spanish moss. The exterior was constructed of green treated wood siding to blend quietly with the forest colors. It was a quarter-mile from school and appropriately named In the Pines.

Her large Persian cat, white with charcoal boots, leaped softly onto the bed and treaded daintily across the yellow cotton sheet to Sandy's naked breast. She stopped and sat quietly on Sandy's chest.

"Hello, Coke," Sandy said, stroking the cat between the ears. "Don't you look content?" She stacked three of the pillows from the king bed up against the wooden headboard and stroked the cat, who purred softly in unbroken bliss. A year ago, she had bought it as a kitten. Her mother hated the name. Sandy had felt the delight of defiance when she told it to her mother. It was something her mother could not change.

"Oh, like Coca-Cola?" her trim, gin-drinking, bridge-playing mother had asked.

"No, Mother. Like cocaine." Sandy had smiled at the blanching of her mother's neck. "That's horrible. Don't say that in front of any of my friends."

"If they ask, I'll tell them." That ended most of the arm-twisting about afternoon bridge at the country club when she went home, and the on-display routine for the old women's drinking society. Gin and tonic in the sun—the British do it—genteel.

Coke reflexively moved her paws against Sandy's neck, extending the claws ever so slightly. Sandy let her do it. "Softly." She stroked the ears and then down the back of the cat. She felt like buying something today. Maybe some halters; she was tired of her tops.

Tommy was coming over "after dark," as he said. She didn't know when. She never knew when—no one ever did. Only Tommy decided what he was doing. He always did. When Jennifer Scott, her roommate, brought him home the first night, Sandy thought of him as crude, arrogant, and very sexy. Tanned and tight, his dark chest hairs looked soft to the touch, to brush, to feel against her neck. His eyes were a sharp, clear blue—diamond enticing, dangerous. Not like the children who were in her classes, the jocks and fraternity types— middle class and boring. His accent sounded strange—almost dominant, with fast words. All of his movements were graceful and firm. Strong-arms, tight, round ass, and that gorgeous chest. On a thick, short-linked golden chain around his neck was a golden coke spoon with a cross handle, a flat Catholic cross. It drew her eye to his chest, a sign on his soft brown fur.

Sandy had taken a Quaalude and was watching *Serpico* on television. She wasn't following it, but Al Pacino was a dream.

"Who are you?" Tommy said when he arrived with Jen, who leaned against the couch. She teetered before falling over the arm, hiking her dress to her waist. Tommy reached over and pulled it down to her knees. "You don't have to lead with your pussy. I know where it is. Be cool. You didn't answer my question."

"Sandy." She felt a little naked in her thin knit halter and high cut-offs. She wasn't wearing any underwear.

"You the one from Atlanta?"

"Yes."

"Always so talkative?" He smiled quickly, and then turned his attention to the movie. "*Serpico*, dynamite flick. That dude was a heavy number. Did you know that he really was a New York cop, but he was honest? Didn't take money, so the other cops had him shot in the head. But he didn't die. Pissed them off. Cops are always on the take. The government is about taking other people's money. It's just another big syndicate."

She didn't know what he was talking about. "Who's on the take? I wasn't paying attention; I'm a bit wasted tonight."

"Got something to straighten you right up." He reached into the pocket of his stitched jeans and returned with a small glass bottle of cocaine. He took the spoon from his neck, opened the bottle, and dipped the gold into the gentle snow. He held the spoon to her nose.

"Cover your left nostril and inhale quickly when I say now."

Sandy pressed her left forefinger against her left nostril.

"Go."

She inhaled quickly and felt the numbing of the tiny flakes hitting the membrane of her nose. He reached into the bottle and brought out another spoon. She repeated the actions. The taste ran along her throat, particularly tart. Tommy then did two and looked at Jen, who was trying unsuccessfully to sit up.

"Me, me too," was all Sandy could make out.

"If you can sit still and snort, I'll give you some."

Tommy pulled the girl to the edge of the green couch. Sandy was leaning at the other end. Jen fell slightly forward, staying erect but swaying gently to her own tune.

"Forget it," Tommy said, smiling. "You'll blow it."

Jen's round dimpled face lost the smile, and she turned her thick, sensuous lips into a pout.

"Well…" Tommy said as he looked around the coffee table. "You have any cigarettes?"

"Give her one of mine. She'll never find hers."

"Good thinking." Tommy smiled at Sandy. "How do you do that while looking so good."

"I do a lot of things while looking so good."

Sandy met his eyes straight on. There were dangerous eyes, soft eyes. There was some terror in the directness she felt from him. The absence of clumsy children or the politeness of society.

"I'm sure you do. We'll have to check it out some time."

They both smiled. Jen was leaning on Tommy, trying to get the cigarettes. He held them away with his left hand.

They talked for a bit before Tommy carried Jen in his arms to the bedroom.

Sandy remained in the chair, listening more to their lovemaking than to the television. Lighting a joint for herself, she leaned back into the soft chair, angling her head so she could hear. Tommy's presence left disturbed energies in the room, a physical effect on her body, a mushroom touch running in scattered paths under her skin. For a moment, she thought she was afraid of him—then she was certain it would happen with them. It was like driving the Camaro on a Colorado road, ski jumping, or… Jen moaned between the sounds of flesh slapping, echoing like waves against a cliff. Feeling wet, Sandy touched her clitoris with her index finger. Yes, she had to be with him. He didn't have any choice in the matter.

The next day, he came back to see her. They had been seeing each other since.

* * *

For most of the day at Clearwater Beach, she thought about Atlanta. She and Tommy were going up on Friday. As long as they didn't go near her parents' house, it would be all right. She'd rather be at Harry's.

Harry Burr was her high school dope connection. She had seen him at her house several times before actually meeting him. He was sitting in the living room, waiting to see her father about some diamonds he had bought on the black market in Antwerp. Even in a grey suit and tailored blue shirt, Harry was frightening.

"When's your father getting home?" he startled her with his deep, rumbling voice. His size at close range made her not want to speak.

"About seven. Who let you in?"

"Your housekeeper said I could wait for Mr. Carlton. I think I frightened her half to death. Give her my apologies." Harry wore two diamond pinky rings, and his beard and his hair were neatly trimmed. She began talking about the weather, but Harry took charge.

"How old are you?"

"Seventeen."

"Is this your final year of high school?"

"Yes."

"Going to college? Ever smoke hash?"

Though she smoked grass with the kids at school, she had never done hash. "Sure. Lots of times."

"Ever hear of the hash genie?"

"What's a hash genie?"

"It's stories. He was a first cousin to Aladdin's genie. He was a wise man who solved problems. He'd get all the arguing people together in a room and light a pipe full of hash. No one had discovered what hash was then. They'd sit in the room smoking until they got mellow and agreed. He didn't think people should be fighting—it was the original peace pipe. He liked loving. In fact, he had a harem of one hundred and fifty wives. Did they ever have parties?"

"One hundred and fifty wives?" Sandy was entranced by his voice. "What would they all do?"

"My favorite thing—devote the human body to pleasure: eating, smoking, and screwing. And when the genie passed into the next world, his spirit stayed behind." Harry chuckled as he reached under Sandy's left ear. "He leaves presents to keep the world mellow."

A small piece of hash wrapped in aluminum foil fell from her ear. He dropped it in her hand. Amused, she felt more relaxed until she heard her father open the front door. Bolting to her feet, she went to the door. Harry winked at her. "Enjoy."

The next day, after smoking the hash, she found Harry's number in her father's Rolodex. Two weeks later, she bought two grams and set a new style at Chamblee High School. For most of high school, she was one of the trendsetters. That moment became her first pocket of power, a power that would never be lost.

High school days had been forgotten in the immediacy of living near Tommy. At fifteen, she had taken the best boy at Chamblee High School to bed on her first try. He was a boy. Tommy was a man, an alien, from spaceship New York, and who took his life in much larger doses than she could handle.

When she was with him, she wasn't as afraid of the world. Yet the sensation of slipping, of not being able to keep up, dragged on her spirit. She didn't always enjoy the ride. She was better now, not as afraid of being hurt by the fall. Freedom was essential.

With Tommy, rules she learned as a child were meaningless; he was too free. Harry Burr was already a bizarre nightmare that she could neither deny not confirm.

With Tommy, life was constant turmoil, filled with conflicting energies, many unfamiliar. When he was angry, it penetrated her with a pulsing rock rhythm, convincing her of his power. She didn't understand and wanted to, but it seemed too complicated. If only Tommy could understand that she was falling in love with him.

Somewhere, she believed in patience. That was the ingrained Southern womanhood of her mother. Men are always boys, and they lie, drink, and cheat.

Tommy arrived before midnight, ebullient with success.

"Ready to go, beautiful? You were going to cut classes tomorrow anyway." His arms reached her sides, sliding up to her shoulders as he kissed her.

"Tomorrow, sure. I've got nothing to do." She felt a slight twinge of shame. Looking into Tommy's strong eyes, she could count it away. His thin brown mustache made him look older, and the soft natural curls in his hair made him cuddly. Tommy took delicate cat steps around the apartment, the movement of his muscles flowing in patterns. She wanted to bring him to her, the energy and exhilaration. "I want to go on a deal with you." She blurted it out, overcoming her final reluctance.

"Sure you do. And I want to be the Shah of Iran. And what would you do on a deal except get in the way?" He smiled cynically yet playfully.

"I can take care of myself. I'm just as tough as you are."

"What do you know about tough? Daddy Jamison sure made it tough on you, didn't he, princess? What the fuck do you know but fancy clothes and *so boring* expressions? You're just looking for kicks to get off on. You don't know what it means to lay everything on the line. You're daddy's little girl, angel, and he'll bail you out of any shit you're in. Dope dealing is *real* and dangerous."

She cringed at the accusation and her vulnerability. "I've dealt before," she said bravely but felt a little girl's guilt at the lie.

"This isn't high school."

"I know that." She wanted to be angry, felt obliged to be angry, but she felt childish embarrassment. She persisted. "Harry would let me. I've dealt with Harry before."

"Sure you have, Mata Hari. Those old men just can't resist your ass, can they, baby?"

His words stung. Lowering her eyes, she backed off with guilt. Tommy wasn't a boy. He sensed more, the things she felt, the thoughts she couldn't express. He kept growing, getting stronger each day. She didn't know if she was part of his life yet and found herself sometimes withdrawing into a detached movie pose. "Can't you be nice for a while? I'd rather be with you. And I can do anything Sal does."

"You don't know much about the *real* world, dear." Tommy's voice was matter-of-fact. Not looking right into her, nor looking away, he was in her presence, but she understood him to be sorting through the streets. "Because you have standing in society doesn't make you immune to bullets, knives, or insults. Taking care, survival, getting by—that's what the man is taking out in the street."

"I'm not naïve. I've been around too." She hustled up close to him, feeling confident and leading with the inside of her right thigh. "And I know what I'm doing, don't I?"

"You ready for the big time?" He smiled as he entered into her kiss.

Chapter 4

IN THE ROOM AT THE Hyatt in Atlanta, the phone rang with a metallic clang. Tommy, gaining cognition, tried to locate the sound. On the fourth ring, he reached over Sandy and found the phone.

"Yeah," he said abruptly.

"Tommy, Tommy, it's Sal."

Tommy recognized the voice. He didn't want to be bothered with the Tampa business while he was still in Atlanta. It was unnecessary.

"Yeah, what's the matter?"

"Mike is in jail."

Mike Broski had arrived weeks ago from Providence, a boyhood friend of Sal's. Sal let him join the crew—he needed help with the weed. Tommy was certain he was trouble.

"What did he get popped for?"

"Possession of coke, carrying a concealed weapon, and possession of Quaaludes."

"Shit." Tommy didn't owe Mike anything. The kid was loud, arrogant, and dumb. A punk. "I leave you in charge for a week, and you fuck it up."

"You gotta get down here right away," Sal said.

"If you tell me again that I've got to do something, I'm gonna bust your face the next time I see you." Sal had inflated his ego a hundred times because he could afford a new Cadillac. He was confident when he was working with Tommy, but on his own, he was still too careless.

"Tommy," Sal blurted, "Mike got busted in your Monte Carlo. The ludes were in the trunk."

Letting the phone hang on his shoulder, Tommy sat up against the headboard of the bed. The car was just material property that could be replaced, but ludes? Where did they come from? Mike Broski? That piece of shit. Having his name cross a police desk in Tampa was not what he wanted right now.

"How?"

"I'm not sure. It happened last night, and he called me this morning. He didn't tell me much except he got popped."

"What the fuck were you doing?" Tommy shouted at the phone, wishing Sal was in front of him. "I told you to watch him, didn't I? Can't you handle business?"

"I didn't think that anything…"

"That's right; you didn't think. You fucked up. You fucked up big time. The expenses for your buddy—your boyhood buddy—are coming out of your share of the next deal. Understand?"

"Tommy, it wasn't my fault."

"Do you understand, Sal? Out of your share. You and that idiot Mike fucked up, and you're going to pay for it. I'm not."

"Listen; there was nothing I could do about…"

"Understand? I ain't brooking no discussions."

"Yeah," Sal's voice was subdued like a child's.

Tommy let the phone hang away from his ear, ignoring Sal's voice. For two years, he had slowly built a little business in Tampa, staying strictly around the university and not messing with the big people downtown or the Cubans in Ybor City. He was clean. Nothing more than a disorderly conduct charge against him.

"Did they confiscate the car?"

"I don't know, Tommy. I've told you everything…"

"Find out what you can. Get your cousin to watch the house. I'll be on the late flight, so make sure you are waiting."

Tommy hung the phone heavily on the base and looked at his watch. Eleven-thirty. It was too early in the day to handle this shit. The conversation had cleared his mind, but the grogginess of the short night remained. He had to get a lawyer—a good criminal one. Another fucking expense.

Reaching under the table next to the bed, he pulled off a piece of tin foil that he had taped under it when he had arrived. Unfolding the first layer, he tapped the package with his finger so that the coke would fall to the bottom. Then he opened the top like a blind man with an envelope of diamonds and dipped his spoon into it. Tapping it gently against the side, he snorted the coke with a sharp inhalation. He did another and closed the foil but didn't put it away.

He could feel the coke working its way through his system. The fatigue was less pronounced, and the heaviness was lifting, allowing a breath of the new day to revive him. Mike was busted in Tampa in the Monte Carlo—but ludes. Not his. Now the Tampa detectives had his name. He hadn't done anything, but the car was his. Mistakes. Stupid mistakes caused by Mike, the punk from Federal Hill.

He didn't need this kind of aggravation. Things were going well, and they probably would go better. Harry Burr was the man he wanted to do business with, and he was sure it would be very profitable for both of them. Sal was fucking up in Tampa, although he had made things good for Sal. Since Tommy bought him the Caddy, the Italian was riding around town in the shiny black machine, dressed to kill. They had been together for more than two years, and Tommy was fond of him. Things were changing, though, and Sal was getting reckless and heady. He wasn't smart enough for that. Tommy wished he were.

Tommy swung his legs from the bed and headed for the shower. He could smell the stale Brut deodorant in his armpits and felt tiny particles of grit on his hairline. The water would feel good, and everything would disappear for a few minutes under the warm water.

Tampa Airport was quiet. Tommy had booked the last flight from Atlanta, so he could spend the day with Sandy. It was better if she stayed in Atlanta at her parents' until he had the situation under control. The effort all day to forget the bust left him tired. There wasn't anything he could do now but continue. He didn't want problems with his Tampa business. Harry Burr was the new connection. To go firsthand, to import. That's where the real profit was. Harry was there. The house, jewels, car; he had a few assets.

Mike Broski was small-time—nothing—not even worth the time to bail him out.

Getting off the robot train at the terminal side, Tommy walked directly to the Sky View Lounge, which was open on two sides, facing the concourse in the center of the cylindrical terminal.

Sal was waiting. His short frame fitted into black flares and a billowy silk shirt open at the neck. His mustache drooped, untrimmed, over his lips to the lines of his chin. He wore sunglasses and a black leather hat even though it was ten o'clock at night, and he was indoors. He nodded to Tommy.

"What else do you know about Mike?" Tommy asked.

"Nothing much. He called me and said he gave them an alias when he was booked," Sal said with his little poor boy look. Tommy looked away.

"Scared, right. What was he doing when he got popped?"

"He said he was at the Ramada Inn off Busch when…"

"What was he doing with the Monte Carlo? I gave the keys to you."

"He wanted to go out, and I was…"

"What were you doing all this time?" Tommy snapped.

"I was at my apartment. I wasn't anywhere…" His tone was touched with little girl insolence.

"What did you say?" Tommy didn't move, but his voice changed as if he had gotten up. "How much coke did he have?"

"Not much—a couple of grams. The ludes were in the trunk." Sal looked at the ground.

"I don't do ludes, so where did they come from?" Tommy was disgusted with them all. Sal was covering his ass even though he was the one directly responsible for all the shit. Sal gave Mike the car keys and the coke. Mike took the gun on his own to be a tough guy. Tommy really didn't want to lose the car because getting a new one would be a hassle and lots of paperwork. What a circus.

"When they pulled him over, they asked if Mike was Tommy Logan."

* * *

"Are you Tommy Logan?" the police sergeant said, looking bored behind the long counter.

"Yeah," Tommy said. He was wearing his sunglasses.

"You're going to have to go up to the Detective Bureau to get this release. Do you know how to get there?"

"No."

"Go through that door there," he pointed to his left, "up to the second floor. You'll see the sign."

"Thanks," Tommy said and pulled the door when the buzzer sounded. He turned to see the sergeant watching him. He felt contempt for him but filed it away. He hated bullies more than ever.

The stairs were worn and shabby like the station and the whole of downtown Tampa. At the top of the stairs were two signs, *Criminal*

Identification and *Detective Bureau*, with the arrow to the latter pointing right. Tommy turned and followed the corridor to a door with an opaque window. Stenciled across it was *Detective Bureau*, and underneath was a place where a name had been scraped off. Opening the door without knocking, Tommy entered without removing his shades. The room was full of desks piled high with folders, papers, Chinese take-out containers, and coffee cups. It looked like a pigsty. Tommy smiled at his pun.

A middle-aged detective sat at the second desk. His coat was on the chair beside him, and a .38 hung in a shoulder holster under his left arm. His face was round, his jaw square, but his nose was flattened and twisted like a second-rate boxer. He put his bologna sandwich on top of a folder.

"Yeah, what can I do for you?" the detective asked, raising his voice like an accusation.

Tommy took in the feeling of a room full of cops. He wanted to cut and run. He didn't want to be here. The fear of the police state grabbed at the center of his courage and yanked with every bit of unreason it could muster. The detective was looking at him with an animal sullenness that made Tommy angry. He wasn't going to take any shit from these guys because he hadn't done anything wrong.

"I want to pick up my car. They told me downstairs I had to come up here for it."

"What's your name?"

"Tommy Logan."

"When did we get your car?"

"I'm not sure. I wasn't here," Tommy said. The detective winced at the tone.

"Take off those sunglasses and sit down," he said, raising his voice.

"They're prescription. I can't see without them," Tommy lied and sauntered over to a chair against the wall. The detective wrote something on a piece of paper, got up, and went through a door at the end of the room. It was half-glass, half-wood like the entrance, but it had *Capt. Lawson* stenciled on it. Tommy heard the monotone of an old man. The detective came back to his desk, sat down, and looked fiercely at Tommy.

"You a drug dealer, punk?" he snarled.

"No, sir." Tommy hunched his shoulders and dropped his head a bit. "I just go to school."

"Shit and I'm a minister."

"Really?" Tommy said mildly. "I thought you were a police officer."

The detective ripped a piece of his bologna sandwich with his teeth and chewed loudly.

A tall, red-haired detective entered by the same door Tommy had used. He was wearing a Colt Python. Tommy wondered if it was the gun that was in his trunk.

"You Logan?"

"Yeah." Tommy half smiled.

"Over here." The detective motioned Tommy to follow him to one of the rear desks. "I'm Jim Burdine, Florida Bureau of Investigation." He smiled and extended his hand. Tommy took it. "Sit down."

The cop was too friendly; Tommy didn't trust him. He was familiar with the police trick: one guy's the badass; the next guy tries to be your friend. They try to get your trust so they can screw you. Tommy wanted out, but the game was just beginning to get interesting.

"Nice weapon you have there," Tommy said.

"Yeah," Burdine said, returning the smile. "Now what can I do for you?"

Bait. They didn't think he was that dumb. "Downstairs, they told me I had to come up here to get my car. Here I am."

"Car, hmmm… what kind of car?"

"1974 Monte Carlo. Grey with a black vinyl top. License plate 3D-6723."

Burdine opened his drawer and shuffled through some folders. "Can't seem to find it here. Wait a second. Let me find out about it." Burdine exited by the back door.

A few seconds later, another cop, middle-aged and flabby like Karl Malden, came in, looked at him, and left. Two more cops, one with long hair and a beard, the other in a denim jacket, came in for a few seconds and left. Tommy sat back in his chair. At first, he didn't know what the game was, but when Burdine returned, it fell into place. It was a guided tour, everyone coming through to get a look at him.

"Who's this Mike Broski who was driving your car?"

"Didn't he tell you?"

"Yeah, but he gave us this alias, Peter Towers. Who do you know him as, Towers or Broski?"

"Neither." Tommy wasn't going to admit to anything. He had worked it out on the way over. They were going to try to get as much information as possible from him. Mike hadn't told them anything coherent, so Tommy had nothing to deny. He was going to be cool and really dumb.

"Neither. What do you know him by?"

"I don't know him."

"He was driving your car. There is an outstanding warrant for him from Rhode Island."

"Yeah, well, without my permission. I was out of town and left my keys with a friend. When I got back yesterday, my friend told me the car was down here. I thought it was illegally parked and got towed."

"Do you expect me to believe that, Logan?"

"Believe what you want. That's the truth."

"We had a suspicion of a stolen car; that's why we stopped him. Did you report the car stolen?" The detective looked down at his papers and made some notation.

"I didn't know it was gone until this morning. Maybe my friend reported it stolen when it was gone." This didn't make sense to Tommy. Sal wouldn't have called it in. So they deliberately stopped the car, hoping for what—hoping for Tommy to be in it?

"And what about the Quaaludes? Are they yours?"

"What's a Quaalude?"

Two more detectives came in and sat on the desks directly behind Burdine. They stared at Tommy.

"Come on, Logan. We're not that dumb. We know you're pushing narcotics, and we're going to get you. It's just a matter of time. So why don't you smarten up and cooperate with us? We don't want you; we're after the big fish."

Tommy had to contain his laughter. It was like TV. Maybe they expected him to break down sobbing and give them the names of all the underworld kingpins who ran the narcotics business in Tampa. What a crock of shit. He didn't know if they were dumb enough to believe that just a few people were behind it. Shit, if he had enough money, he'd run some weed in himself. Florida was great for smuggling—the coast was long, with lots of inlets and coves.

"Officer, I really don't know what you are referring to." Tommy took off his sunglasses and lowered his eyes. "I know I haven't done anything wrong. I just came here to get my car. That's it." Tommy kept his chin tucked because he didn't want to laugh at his performance.

"Listen, kid. You could end up doing time in Raiford. Think about it and smarten up, 'cause we'll get you." Burdine smiled confidently. He handed Tommy some papers. "Sign here and here."

Tommy read the documents. He wasn't about to sign anything in the police station without understanding it and getting a copy, but it was a simple release for the keys. Still, someone had set him up. Here in Tampa? It was probably a good time to get out of town—to deal with Harry in Atlanta.

"You'll have to pay the tow truck company for towing and storage," Burdine said.

Tommy was going to ask about the pistol, looking at the Python in Burdine's holster, but held his tongue.

"Where is this ABC Towing Company?" Tommy turned back to Burdine as he was leaving.

"Don't know."

"Didn't think you would." Tommy turned to the door.

"I'll see you again, tough guy. You can count on it."

"Can't count on anything but dying," Tommy said, looking straight into Burdine's eyes. He wasn't as afraid as when he had entered the office. It was over, and he was on his way out. Closing the door, he bounced down the stairs, tearing the door open with a lightning blow.

"Sergeant," he snapped like talking to a headwaiter, "where's ABC Towing?"

The man looked at Tommy, who was standing erect and proud in the center of the floor. He was a free man, and no one could tell him what to think or do.

"West on Hillsborough Avenue about two blocks before Westgate," he answered quickly.

Probably thinks I'm DEA, Tommy thought. The thought pleased him. He'd be a good cop—the kind of guy who was tough, but his word was always good. If he only had a badge and enough connections. His brother had tried being a cop, and they almost killed him. Maybe it wasn't so smart.

He walked out of the station into the blinding sun. The change from the air-conditioned building brought beads of sweat instantly to his forehead. Tommy was glad to be back in the sunlight even though he hated the sun when it made things too clear.

* * *

Back at his apartment, Tommy could feel the anger rising and wanted to drink to let it all come out. Mike was trouble; trouble he neither wanted nor deserved. It was pointless to reason with him. What was done was done—it had no reason. Why did the cop say the car was stolen? Why did they think he was driving? Where did they get that information, or was it just an excuse? Sal sat, looking at the floor.

"You're a dumb fucker," Tommy began in a low, cold voice. He could feel a glaze covering his eyes as his facial muscles tightened. Everyone born has lessons to learn. Some are easy; most are hard. Tommy had learned the hard way. "You have no idea what's riding on this or what you fucked up." The words were building. He had been careful up to now and was ready to make the next big step with Harry. He wasn't going to let this dumb kid fuck it up. Why was he even in Tommy's life? Tommy took another long drink. "That was my car..."

"Tommy, it wasn't his fault..." Sal began.

"It was your fault. I haven't forgotten that." Tommy turned to him. "You two-bit jailbird. You bring this idiot down here, and I'm dumb enough to let him in on a good thing. And what does he do? He fucked it up for you too."

The anger built within, pressing against the wall of his stomach and chest until it ached for release. It was no good thinking about it; it didn't do any good to reason with anger. There was no place for it to go but out.

Sal jumped to his feet, trying to block Tommy's left arm. Tommy turned instantly and sank a strong right into his gut just below the rib cage. Sal doubled with pain, his eyes pleading.

The anger was passing into control, slowing down and loosening its grip on him. It wouldn't do any good. No good at all. He inhaled through his nose, forcing the air into his diaphragm. It was the anger from all those beatings he took at the hands of the bigger kids on the playground. No more. He looked at Sal, who was still on the floor, and was content.

"You don't understand what you fucked up." Tommy was helpless; there was nothing he could do to recover what was lost. The cops knew who he was. If he could work out things with Harry, Tampa would soon be history.

Sal slowly leaned against the chair, still clutching his stomach. Tommy felt sorry for him but didn't move to help. Mike was fucking him as well. Since his arrival, Sal was out more, and Terry, his wife, and the kid were afraid. Mike had tracks on his arm, and now Tommy saw some on Sal's arms—they were popping. Tommy felt truly sorry for him but more for Terry and little Sal. He had problems of his own. He fixed a Bacardi and Coke, sat down on the couch, and dialed the phone.

"Sal, if they let him out, get rid of him," Tommy said as he waited for the call to go through. "Back to Providence or off to Miami. He can't stay here if you want to work with me." Maybe they were setting him up—ludes? Broski may have done him a favor. He needed to get things in motion fast before something else happened.

"Hello, I'd like to make a reservation on the morning flight to Atlanta. Six-fifty? Fine. Logan, Tommy."

Chapter 5

SANDY WAS WAITING AT THE gate when Tommy arrived. Her eyes were still crusted from the night, and she wasn't wearing any makeup. The three days he was away in Tampa, she, Harry, and Elsie had stayed up snorting and waiting for Tommy to call. Each night, she returned to her hotel room, hoping he would call there. After he called her, the mental strain of the past two days of not knowing fell away. Though her body felt like it was still sleeping, Sandy felt a larger crash coming.

They didn't discuss the feelings of fear she had. Tommy never seemed afraid. Since she met him, there were more things to be afraid of—more dangers than she ever thought existed in the world. Was it a deal? The police? Either way, Mommy had never prepared her for this.

It was like a coke taste, alluring nectar sliding through her saliva. The moment's taste that reasserts its cravings with the insistence of a child. The danger of life with Tommy; the surroundings of his murky world were never spoken of at the bridge club. Never mentioned or imagined except as the abstract of somewhere else. Her parents denied the existence of danger, reducing their lives to the non-existence of real physical danger, the gamble of being alive. Now she was afraid. She wondered if Tommy would always be cool and confident. She wanted part of it—to feel the strength of confidence, self-reliance, and danger.

When Tommy met Harry, she felt certain there would be blood. Before she met Tommy, Harry was her way to shock her friends. Life had suddenly lost frivolity as her hunger developed for Tommy. Was this finally it? Love?

Now, with Tommy returning, she was afraid to ask what had happened. She wasn't certain that she wanted to know—or, for that matter, if Tommy would tell her. She thought she could help him, but the days of anticipation, the gnawing silence, not knowing what or how bad it was, had created doubt. After that call from Sal, his statement was simple. "I'm going to Tampa. I'll be back as quickly as I can." Then they made love, and she thought she felt his fear. He was hiding something that she needed to know. He left her silently, without inviting any sympathy, support, or question.

Tommy was wearing tight denim pants and a light pink nylon shirt open at the neck. Sandy saw him as he cleared the exit. A group, twenty women and grade school children, was congregated near the entrance, holding signs of welcome that were in French. They were giggling in anticipation, while Sandy stood silently behind them, obscured from Tommy's view, moving from foot to foot.

She was frozen when their eyes met, waiting for the signal, hoping she was right—that he wanted her. She stood hanging on for an instant, wondering why she should care, why she was here. He was a foreigner, an alien. His intrusion into her life was toppling her pedestal. She had always been in charge, but he had changed it for her.

His brown curly hair hung down to his collar; the gold coke spoon and ivory ram pendant lay quietly against his chest. A tired, warm smile leaped the remaining distance, and they flew into each other's arms. A thunderous cheer erupted for the gathered group and the lounge broke into pandemonium. Tommy and Sandy glanced quickly at the arriving French students, in blue pants and white blouses, who were mingling with the American families. Their laughter was contagious. Sandy and Tommy broke out giggling.

"Hey beautiful, you wanna go to bed?" Tommy turned her toward him as they walked toward baggage claim. She had never felt so wanted.

"Take me. I'm yours," she said, falling into his arms.

He scooped her body from the ground and walked boldly toward the exit. Sandy burrowed into his shoulder, nibbling at his neck.

"Are people staring at us?" she whispered, afraid to look up.

"Yeah, everyone in the airport. Every one of them envy us."

She looked up into his eyes, which were again defiant. She didn't care what anyone thought. Who were they to have opinions? Tommy was the only one touching her. What else mattered?

* * *

Sandy, sitting cross-legged against the headboard in pink bikini briefs and a sheer negligee, stared at him from across the bed. Her long brown hair spread across her round cheerleader's shoulders.

"Everything's alright then? The cops don't want you?" She had disliked Broski the first time she met him in Tampa. Low class, white trash.

"Sure. You want me on the outside." He smiled as he dropped onto the gold-white Hyatt bedspread. "Look, it's just an irritation, like a mosquito bite." He pointed to her thigh. "It'll be over with. I have other things to think about that are more important." He slid his hand gently across the top of her thigh, his fingertips exploring the soft inner flesh.

Despite his smile, Sandy felt afraid for Tommy. The police could get him for dealing. She was beginning to love him. Her nipples were erect from his touch. He lay propped on his left elbow, his chest naked and brown while he stroked her legs and stomach with a boyish wonder.

"You were afraid? Worried?" He touched her neck and cheek.

Sandy bent gently to his touch. She was certain there was no-where else she wanted to be, no one else to be with. "Yes, I didn't know what was happening. I was useless; I didn't know what to do." She imagined he was in jail, or that he'd walked into a trap, or that Broski or Sal turned on him or got pissed off and did something stupid. He was here, free and wonderful.

"Was there trouble? Tell me." She wanted and didn't want to know. The ambivalence of knowledge, getting more than she wanted. Sandy wanted to know more about Tommy. She needed to be a part of his total world. She was certain she would worry more, feel more miserable at times, but she wanted more of him, more of his life, his adventure. It was intoxicating, excruciating, addictive. He was so certain in public, but here, he was a boy who needed her love.

"Tell me." She poked him in the ribs, making him start.

"What, hey…" He shook his head, smiling. "Ya really want to know?"

"Yes." She was firm and compelling.

"If I talk to you, your lips can't hear. It doesn't go anywhere. You forget. Don't tell anyone—girlfriend, priest, or even your guardian angel. Understand?"

"Of course." She was insulted that he should ask.

Tommy reacted to her tone. "It's that important, Sandy. I wouldn't ask you otherwise. I'll share things with you, but it has to stay between us. It can't be shared anywhere or with anyone." He felt he was on the verge of letting her in, allowing her to get closer, and the thought almost froze him.

"I understand." She shook her head, then leaned across and firmly kissed him. Stroking his neck, she wanted to calm him, make him feel peaceful and content. She wanted to make love.

He reached up under her negligee, gently massaging her nipples between his fingers. She felt shivers down her body to her lower back.

Digging deeper with her tongue, she wanted him to be weaker, yet needed his strength. This was her illusion, her dream, but she was sharing the terror of his life. Her body was forcing her closer and closer to him. The craving for satisfaction in the touch of his flesh. She had to know; she had to know now. It was important because… Because it was him and because it was her life.

"Tell me first…" She forced herself away from him. Tommy followed. She parried half-heartedly. "Please, Tommy… I really want to know."

He stopped and looked deeply into her eyes. "You really do, don't you?"

"That's what I said and what I mean." She imitated Tommy's street tone. They laughed intimately.

"Broski got popped," Tommy said.

"That's not it. I want the whole story. What happened when you went to Tampa?"

"It doesn't leave this room."

"It doesn't leave this room," she repeated.

"Broski got popped in the Monte Carlo. He was carrying coke, and someone planted ludes. The cops confiscated the car. I had to go bail it out." Tommy furrowed his forehead. "There was this cop from the state who took too much interest in a low-level stop." He tightened his lips. "He asked simple questions. It just didn't feel right—like it was a setup."

"Why would they do that? It wasn't your fault he was carrying coke. I can't believe those dumb pigs." She thought about how she'd get stopped for speeding, and sometimes the cop would hit on her. "I was afraid they arrested you. If they ever do…" She stopped herself with the thought.

"Then you go right on living. Right?" Tommy was still smiling his half smile at her. "The decision would be up to you. It's all very simple. Do what you want. No one's gonna do it for you. It's not easy, babe. I was scared when I went down to the station. Those things went through my mind. What is there to lose in life except life? I don't want you to be frightened or scared, but I'm going to live my life. If you want to leave, goodbye. Have a good time. If you want to stay, it's gonna be an interesting time. I can't make any more promises than that. That's all I know. I'm stupid, y'know—no college education. I've got to be me. I can't live as anyone else."

Smiling too, she rubbed the soft hairs of his chest. "And I have to be me." She moved into his arms, sinking her mouth against his, her senses assaulted with a sweet, salty, breathable fragrance.

Stripping away her panties and his, she reached for his hips and turned him on top of her. "I love you, Tommy. I really do."

"I know, Sandy. I love you too." He slipped into her. Their breathing increased as their bodies slapped softly together like small Gulf waves against the shore.

When it came time, she would know.

* * *

They arrived at Harry's at about noon. Elsie let them in immediately. Tommy wanted to see if Harry could put together the deal. Walking into the kitchen, he felt good, cocky, and strong. He had money and was working on making more. He would be an equal partner in any big gig with Harry. He looked around the large, modern kitchen, but there was no sign of Harry.

"Hi," Kippi said shyly from the doorway to the TV room next to the kitchen.

"Hey, foxy lady. Come here and give me a hug."

She eyed him carefully; Tommy waited for a second, then turned away from her. "Your loss."

Kippi instantly sprang across the room into his arms. Tommy felt her small hands grip tightly around his neck, innocent hands, child's hands. Lifting her off the ground, she tightened herself to him like it was the last time anyone would hold her.

"That was good, little lady." She was learning the tricks of her sex young, learning to tempt. "Where's your father at?"

"Still sleeping. He'll get up in a while. He usually does." She shrugged her shoulders.

"Which door?"

"The one at the end." She pointed.

What is danger; what is taking chances about? Gambling, reducing the odds as low as you can get them to go, then putting down your wager: money or your life. He didn't need a reason for what he did as long as it got done. "Hey, fat man, get out of bed. I want to talk to you." Tommy pounded on the door with his fist. He heard some groans. Tommy hit the door several times more with his hand. "I don't like to be kept waiting," he shouted, then returned to the kitchen. He wanted to get Harry moving—he was ready with his money and was ready to see if there was real opportunity in Atlanta. It was the joy of fucking the system again that would make the trip a blast. Live by the rules; feed that to anyone who'll believe it. Then make the rules.

Elsie made some coffee for Sandy. Tommy sat with a glass of orange juice. He never dealt in the long run; it was now that mattered. If he sat on his ass and watched the tube, that would be what life was about—someone else's world. No, that wasn't what he wanted. It didn't make sense, so why try and understand why people watched instead of lived.

"You know, Sandy," Elsie said in a voice that squeaked like chalk across a blackboard, "When I was dancing at Harry's club in Miami, this guy was really good to me. He said he was the president of the company that makes Always Dry—you know, the diapers? He told me about all these tests they had to do to make sure they didn't leak. He told me they even sell them in England. Can you imagine English babies in Always Dry? He was good to me, always at least a five-hundred-dollar tip."

Tommy had to know more about Harry, so he could stay ahead of him even if it meant listening to Elsie babble. Balance of power, as they say.

"Harry decided to sell the club. I think there was some trouble." She tilted her head. "Harry said he had an opportunity in Atlanta. So I said, 'What about me?' Harry said, 'Do you want to come?' So what am I supposed to do? Harry's always good to me like no one else—and he gave me Kippi as well." Her face was wide with a smile as she bounced up from the chair.

Tommy heard him before he saw him. A half-naked Harry Burr stood hulking like a bald gorilla. His tangled black hair hung to his shoulders from only the sides of his head; his dome was clean and shiny. His eyes were half-opened, his beard tousled, and the skin from his neck drooped like an old basset hound.

"Kid, what happened?" His voice was slow from sleep.

Tommy busted out laughing, the laughter coming from deep in his stomach. A bare roof with layers of fat-like shingles on a house, contained by blue boxer shorts. Every time he looked up, the laughter came back as Harry slowly woke up. Harry touched his head and felt his hairpiece missing. He looked down at himself, and his face darkened.

"What the fuck is so funny?" he demanded. "Why the fuck did you get me out of bed?"

Tommy's laughter subsided as he leaned back in the chair. Sandy and Elsie sat smiling quietly. "What happened? I just saw the funniest sight I've ever seen. You better not walk around Georgia like that, or someone's gonna declare you obscene and put you away." Tommy smiled broadly. "You're a trip."

"Isn't there anything wrong? You mean... You wise-assed son of a bitch." He started to move forward, but Tommy rose from his chair into a fighting stance. Harry stopped to reconsider when Kippi appeared in the doorway.

"Daddy, you're up," she shrieked as she sprinted across the floor and launched into Harry's midsection, her arms outspread.

"Ooooo!" Harry cried as she caught him unprepared, tipping him backward. Clawing frantically at the air, Harry finally grabbed the side of his captain's chair and fell heavily into it. Kippi hung on for the ride.

"Kippi..." he gasped.

"I'm glad you finally got up."

"Kippi, please," he groaned. "It's too early."

"No, it's not, Daddy," she scolded. "I've been up for hours watching cartoons. Early to bed, early to rise."

"Have you been going to school again? I was up late."

"So was Mommy," she continued, pointing her finger at him. "You shouldn't go to bed so late."

Laughter returned to Tommy, doubling him up in pleasure. He liked having the kid around. Maybe he and Sandy would have a couple once he was done with this business.

Harry sighed again, looked at Kippi with pleading eyes, and then bellowed, "Elsie!"

Elsie had slipped away the second Kippi appeared. "Did you call me?" she asked gingerly from the doorway.

"Yes, I called you," Harry said, looking tired from the exertion. She skipped across the room and joined Kippi in Harry's lap.

"Ooooo," he groaned. Elsie began kissing his left ear, while Kippi punched him in the stomach. "Stop it. Stop it. Who wants to be Queen for the Day?"

"What's that?" Kippi asked.

"Just answer the question. Do you want to be Queen for the Day?"

"Yes."

"Well, go into my bedroom and get the brown case next to the bed. Go quick." She disappeared.

"Which one, Daddy?" she yelled.

"Elsie, go show her," he said gently. Elsie disappeared too. Harry sighed with relief. "Lord, what did I do to deserve this?"

"What's the matter, Harry? Just hop out of bed and go," Tommy taunted.

"You've got a lot of balls, kid. Not brains, but a lot of balls. I would kill a man for less than what you just did."

"Only if you could, big man."

"I could. Don't worry about it."

"Do I look worried?"

Kippi and Elsie returned with the case. Harry opened it, removed a jar of coke and a spoon, and took two quick hits, then two more. The sounds of keys turning the lock to the outside door in the kitchen galvanized Tommy. He went tense like a cat, waiting to spring. Pushing his chair away from the table, he watched the door open. Harry yawned as he leaned back in his chair as if the show was about to begin.

"Hi, I'm George." A giant grinned at him. "Come on, girls." He leaned out the door and said coaxingly, "Come on." Two cowardly grey German shepherds meekly walked into the room. Closing and locking the door, George walked across the room and extended his hand to Tommy. The hand was huge, and Tommy hoped it wouldn't crush his.

George was in his mid-thirties and even bigger than Harry. Over six-two, he had two ham-shaped forearms and thick tree stump legs that Tommy could barely see under his enormous potbelly. His hair was brown and thinning, and there was an anchor with a snake coiled around it tattooed on his left forearm.

George made Tommy think about looking for the nearest exit, just in case. The man was missing the two smallest digits of his left hand.

"Tommy?" George asked.

Tommy nodded, not certain of his next step. He hadn't thought about who was in Harry's crew. George eyed him for a moment, then went directly to the refrigerator, drew a frosted mug from the freezer, and opened a bottle of Budweiser. He emptied the glass directly and, without pausing for air, opened another bottle. With his glass refilled, he joined Harry and Tommy at the table. The two dogs lay at his feet.

"When I was at my father's today, the lady next door was having some problems with her car. She couldn't get it started, and she kept grinding and grinding. Now, I don't know her too well; she didn't live there when I lived there. That was a long time ago, and there isn't any reason why she should have. I didn't have my tools because they were all here, but I couldn't stand hearing her grinding and grinding, especially since she was pumping the gas too. I could smell the flooded engine from where I was, and I was in the house. So I decided I was going to go out and tell her to just let it sit for a while." He got up and returned to the refrigerator for another Bud.

Tommy looked at Harry for some explanation, but Harry was inscrutable, his eyes watching Tommy while George was talking.

"But the phone rang, and I went to answer it. By the time I got back, the lady had already given up, so I didn't have to go over and do anything. Which is just as well," he paused and drained the glass, "'cause I really didn't feel like talking to her." He got up and returned with another Bud.

"That was like the time in the navy when me and this petty officer were on shore leave in Subic Bay—that's in the Philippines—pretty little girls over there—and we were down at this club, drinking. It served really good clams. Do you like clams? I love clams. Never had one till I was in the navy." Elsie and Sandy sat at the far end of the table, talking quietly. Kippi had disappeared. "They'd serve two dozen big ones—raw, right on the shell. It always amazed me how tender they were."

Tommy couldn't believe that the dude just kept talking. Leaning across the table, Tommy asked, "Is he always like this?"

"Yeah, give George a few beers and an audience, and he'll talk the ears off a brass monkey."

George sat, grinning, and silent for a moment. Harry did another hit of coke.

"It takes more than a few beers to get me going," George said to Tommy. "I'm a sailor, Merchant Marine now, engineer second class. I can outdrink any man around and still stay on my feet."

"That may sound like a boast, kid," Harry said. "I've seen him do it. The man is an incredible drinker. Now, me. I can't drink."

"That's for sure." George shook his massive head for emphasis. "The smell of beer gets Harry sleepy. He likes the hard stuff."

"That's right."

"Yeah, well." Tommy couldn't let the opportunity go by. "Some time, we'll have a little contest, you and me, and with something other than beer. Can you drink bourbon?" He issued it as a challenge.

He could drink bourbon, and when there was money on it, he could drink as much as necessary.

"'Course I can." George sounded insulted. "I can drink any man under the table with any drink." His Southern accent was bastardized from his time in the navy.

"Any time. We'll put a little something on it just to keep it interesting."

"You talk a good game, kid." Harry's wide eyes were focused on him, and Tommy just rolled his eyes. Wrinkling the fat on his nose, Harry yawned.

"Harry, have you shown Tommy the bikes?" George asked.

"No," he said, turning to Tommy. "Like to see some dynamite machines?"

Tommy followed George down steep steps to the garage under the house. Harry followed heavily.

"Did you ever see such a beauty? I've had this guy working on it for two years," Harry said, pointing to the gleaming motorcycle that was chopped and glistening like a trophy in the sun. The gas tank was cream white and shaped like a Maltese cross. Three smaller crosses were delicately outlined twice, first in green, then in red.

"All of this is chrome," he said, pointing to the exhaust system. "Each of these nuts is a solid brass alloy. There are two carbs, and George bored it out to twelve-hundred cc." George had gotten out a rag and was dusting the long white banana seat. The seat was set low in the bottom of a U, and the front end was chopped, so the handlebars extended from the driver's seat.

"It's got a low center of gravity, so it will handle well," George said, crouching beside the bike and shining the exhaust manifold. The engine block was a bright red, and the joints were silver.

"Ray, the guy who is building it for me, is a funny guy. Really great mechanic, but he paces himself. Can't hurry a real Southern boy." Harry walked over to a big black Honda that had two red tail-lights shaped like Maltese crosses, as well as two mirrors of the same design. "But I need a new mechanic; Ray got ten to twenty for knock-ing over a bank." Harry picked his teeth with a nail.

After dressing, Harry showed Tommy both bikes in detail. Tommy had never seen Harry move so much. He thought nothing that big and fat could move, but Harry was light like a balloon instead of a tub of lard. Sandy had mentioned the bikes, but it hadn't meant any-thing to him. Now he understood.

"That one, I'm building for show. This one—this one is Zorro, and he'll outrun anything on the street."

It was a 750 Honda that was bored out. It had two large footrests, wide crash bars, and a tremendous saddle seat. Everything was black except the exhaust system and crash bars, which were chrome. Harry swung his right leg over the seat and settled into it like a king mount-ing his favorite steed. The heavy suspension sank under his weight.

"Open the garage, George," Harry bellowed over the roar from the black machine. It carried the minimum muffler allowed by Georgia law.

The motorcycle bolted from the garage to the end of the driveway with a burst of mind-splitting noise. Harry paused, then gunned the bike into the street. Tommy walked to the end of the driveway and could almost see a tail of noise as Harry streaked around the corner. Seconds later, George came roaring from the garage on a blue 750 street bike.

As Harry roared back down the street, not a single window opened or person came out. The motorcycle looked like a bicycle in his hands. Like a little boy, Tommy stood on the curb, admiring the bikes and the riders. He had never understood bike gangs aside from their plain meanness. He was going to learn to ride a bike.

"You want to go for a ride or are you frightened?" Harry posed the challenge.

"Sure, let's go," Tommy said without hesitating.

Harry revved the engine and popped the clutch. They took off as if they were shot from a gun. The sudden momentum caused Tommy to grab tightly at Harry's waist. Finding ready-made handholds in the rubbery flesh, Tommy held handfuls of the moving meat like a skier holding onto a towrope. Slowing the bike for a moment at the stop sign, Harry had the big bike spring on the road. Tommy had never felt so much power responding to such a touch. Driving as fast as he could, Harry got onto the interstate and opened Zorro up. The cars and the road zipped by, and Tommy felt himself getting sick like he did when he was a kid. The motion was becoming too much—he wasn't in control of it. His stomach began to churn and fought to escape through his mouth. He tried to look over Harry's shoulder, but the force of the wind was too great.

Despite his great bulk, Harry controlled the bike fluidly like a walrus in water. The bike tilted and wove to the calculated rhythm of Harry Burr. With the slightest movement of weight, the bike sliced through the traffic unencumbered. The steady flow of traffic soothed the initial shock of entry into the world of machines. Tommy tightened his stomach and made up his mind to hold on. Closing his eyes, he held on tightly.

As they came off the interstate back to Doraville, the bike seemed to slow to a visible speed. As the ride ended, Tommy thought he could feel every dip in the road from the trip. He was afraid and felt it. It was a different fear, one from the power and the danger. He'd like to learn to control that power.

"How'd you like it?" Harry asked, flushed from the wind against his cheeks.

"Looks easy." Tommy smiled bravely.

"For a Florida boy, you don't have much color." Harry laughed. "You don't ever give in, do you?"

"Do you?" As soon as Tommy felt his feet back on the ground, the nausea dissipated. "I want to learn to ride one of those things."

"You do?" Harry climbed the stairs to the house. "If you are around awhile, I will teach you that and other things. I think I will keep calling you grasshopper because you have a lot to learn."

"Right."

"We'll see."

* * *

Inside the grey concrete blocks of the mall, lush palms, fountains, benches, and soft music lifted Sandy's spirits. Festooned in finery, fantasyland beckoned in light, softness, and safety. The vaulted ceiling of the modern cathedral was hidden in the myriad of shops, reflections, and colors. Silent escalators whisked shoppers from level to level.

Middle-aged women, bodies abandoned for the kids, searched for youth and beauty. Hordes of blue-jean-clad prepubescent children reveled in the pure, calculated exhibit of American materialism.

Rich's, J.C. Penney, Casual Corner, Zales, and the food court circulated strands of enticement, luring the milling shoppers with promises of satisfaction. Piped music soothed the strains of decisions and the flow of plastic money. The world of shopping was desirable and fulfilling. All was well and good in the village.

Sandy saw the old men sitting on wooden benches in the non-shade of the non-palm trees. There was no air, no breeze, no sun, no shade—rain never falls, and rainbows never appear. Elsie tried on fifteen different tops at Chantilly Lace before buying five of them.

Sandy bought a pair of black silk pants and a top. Elsie paid with a credit card; Sandy used hundred-dollar bills. They had been shopping for hours and had already made one trip to the car.

"Isn't Harry going to be pissed at all the money you're charging?" Sandy had spent nearly three hundred dollars that Tommy had given her. Elsie was above one thousand and counting.

"It's alright; the credit cards aren't mine," Elsie said, looking into the next shop window.

"Won't Harry be pissed?"

"They aren't Harry's either." Elsie gaily smiled as they entered Rich's.

"Whose are they?" Sandy wasn't certain she understood what she was hearing.

"I don't know. I just sign the name that's on them. That's what Harry told me to do. I only go shopping once with them, and then Harry takes them away. That's why I spend a lot when I get a good one." She held up an American Express card.

The offhand expression shocked Sandy for a second and then worried her. Stealing credit cards offended her because she was brought up with them. Her father gave her an American Express card for her trip to Europe after her junior year in high school. Her mother always let her have the Rich's card.

"Elsie, how did you meet Harry? I've wanted to ask you for months," Sandy asked as they bought ice cream cones.

"In Cleveland the first time. I was fourteen and wanting to hang out with the guys who had motorcycles. Harry had one, a big one; he was skinny then. We would ride along the lake at night, the wind keeping my hair up. It was really long then, down to the middle of my back. I used to stay at Harry's 'cause my old man was always beating me with the birch rod he brought from Jessup, Kentucky, where he was from. If I wasn't around, he didn't notice 'cause he was drunk. He probably liked it better." After a lick of her ice cream, she continued. "When Harry went into the army rather than go to jail, I had to go back and live with that son of a bitch. That didn't last long, so I took off again."

"When did you have Kippi?"

"I didn't have Kippi," Elsie laughed, showing her flat teeth. "One of Harry's girls had a baby—I don't know who her father is. I told Harry I wanted a baby, so he let me keep her. Harry is so sweet."

Sandy felt her inquiries were bordering on stupid questions, but she wanted to know more. "When, where did that happen?"

"That was in Miami. After Harry got thrown out of the army, he went back to Cleveland but got caught with some stolen stuff and got sent to prison. In prison, he met these guys who worked with people in Miami. I was with this loser in Cleveland, and one night, two guys came to the apartment and told me to scram before they cut off my tits. I'm sometimes a little slow, but not when I'm scared. I called Harry's sister and then just showed up at his door."

"Why did he get thrown out of the army?"

"I think he killed somebody but isn't that the reason you are in the army? I don't really know, but he had this really nice place in Miami and had three girls. I was the fourth. Harry would get us trips with these rich guys, judges and like mafia types, to the Bahamas. We'd go for the weekend, and it was really nice."

Sandy didn't need to ask more. Harry had bragged he was a pimp in Miami. She should have guessed about Elsie.

"I thought he went to jail," Sandy said.

"Oh, that too, but Harry didn't do anything wrong." She stopped to look at a pair of black platform shoes studded with rhinestones. "He knows all these important people. People ask him to fix things for them and he does. He's very smart, and he's good to me."

Walking next to Elsie felt like traveling with a neon sign. Her large breasts, probably implants, were only partially covered. Her tight shorts even attracted the attention of women and children.

That was attention Sandy neither needed nor desired. Elsie seemed to provoke crude comments wherever she went but never seemed to hear them. Their lives were totally different, yet Sandy liked how Elsie totally accepted her life, rolling with the waves as they approached. Sandy felt they were threatened by the forces that Harry was getting Tommy involved in. She wanted to impress Tommy, but she was afraid that Harry might get him killed.

Sandy was torn between the world of the mall with its brightly colored tile, all-weather carpet, and opulence and the seedy bars Tommy found in every city. Harry could frighten her, and she feared for Tommy's safety. She experienced the hypnotic power of Harry and his ability to control. Each time she looked back at that first night with Harry and Elsie when they seduced her, she wanted to warn Tommy. She didn't want to speak about that night, so she said nothing. Fantasies swirled through her life, and she had to be quick enough to catch pieces as they rushed by. Many had ended, but this adventure was just beginning.

Chapter 6

SINCE COMING BACK TO TAMPA, Sandy had been asking more questions about Tommy's deals. He was sitting on the bed with ten stacks of bills, each containing fifty hundred-dollar bills. Fifty thousand in cash. Tommy was buying half of a thousand pounds of pot that was being flown into Gainesville that night. If he turned it quickly, he could make another fifty grand, enough to do another deal with Harry. He had wanted Sal as backup muscle because of the size of the deal, but he was too strung out to be of any use.

"Give me that blue and white flight bag," Tommy said, wanting to give her something to do. She disappeared into the walk-in closet and rummaged through the bags and shoes. She wanted to go, especially since Sal couldn't. Tommy thought the deal would go smoothly because they always had with Clay Sorrel, who ran his show like a military operation.

"This one," she said, slouching on one hip with an Eastern flight bag in her hand. "You can't go alone. Not with this much money. You're going to need someone to cover you."

"Are you that someone?"

"You can't do better," she said, firing the bag in a line drive, hitting him in the shoulder.

"Spunky tonight." He faked a lunge as she danced out of the way. "Can you keep it together?" She nodded. "This isn't a game. This is the real thing, you understand? No time-outs, no do-overs. You have to be alert."

"You watch out for you, and I'll watch out for both of us." She smiled coyly but with a hard turn of her top lip in an imitation of Tommy. So Sandy was his wingman.

"Shit, I can't win with you. Let's get in gear." He hoped the deal wouldn't go too late because, at three in the morning, there wasn't much of a crowd to get lost in if something went wrong. The plane would come when it came—but it never came early.

Tommy put the money into the case and zippered it. He put the case on the floor next to him. "Here. This one's yours." He gave Sandy a .25 automatic from his pocket. It was a small gun with a five-shot clip. "Put it in your purse, or somewhere you can get at it quickly."

Sandy let the pistol rest in the palm of her hand. She looked at it while bouncing her hand slightly as if feeling its weight. Tommy noted that the steel looked bluer against her skin. Holding it up in front of her, she sighted over the barrel and pointed the gun at the lamp. "Click," she said.

He smiled at her. After they had returned from Atlanta, Tommy taught her the correct way to shoot. She seemed to like carrying a gun. Now she could be *bad* if need be. He wasn't certain if she would use it, but she might. He wasn't counting on needing it, not this trip. This trip should be smooth.

"Okay, Annie Oakley. Put it away and let's hit the road. Did you have the scheduled service on the car today?"

"It's all set. So am I." She put the pistol in her purse. "You ready yet or are you going to sit on your ass all night?"

"Whoo, the lady is cooking tonight. I'm coming, woman. I jest gots to get me organized." They both laughed as Tommy shuffled. Sandy would have to feel the vibes of a deal on this trip. A deal—the fear and the uncertainty. To know is to do. Making the score, passing the case, waiting, wondering. Do the cops know? A rip-off? Can't sue the man. It has to be settled right away.

He checked his Smith & Wesson, making certain the cylinder was full. He returned it to the shoulder holster under his left arm. The pistol was cleaned, oiled, and ready. The sample of pot he had seen looked good—a golden brown with compressed buds. It looked good, but he had to see the actual product. Tommy had done pot deals with Clay for over a year, so he had a certain amount of trust—but only believe what you can see.

In the case was fifty thousand dollars of his own money. It had taken him time and too many risks and much effort to get it. No one was going to take it away from him.

Going down to the car, Tommy carried the bag easily on his shoulder. Sandy almost skipped with agitation. Tommy figured her adrenaline would keep her high all night. There was no more all-encompassing body and head high than danger. It's terrifying, crippling, cruel, unreasoned, exhilarating, liberating. It stirred every force in the human body. Survival, when it comes down to it, that's all we want.

Sandy became quiet in the car. She seemed to be fully occupied as if she were running movie scripts and TV plots through her mind. He could sense her anxiety. He understood. He still felt the anticipation and adrenaline in his system when the deal was ready to happen. It was still early. He patted her hand, and she turned with a smile.

"By the way, where are we going?" she asked.

"Gainesville. You didn't have anything to do tonight, did you?"

"No."

He felt she would be enough backup on the deal. He didn't expect anything to get jammed up with Sorrel. It never had.

Gainesville was one hundred and thirty miles north of Tampa on I-75. When he was in a hurry, he could make it in an hour and a half, but this night, it would take more than two hours. He used the cruise control on Sandy's Camaro so he wouldn't exceed the speed limit. While he was dealing, he didn't want to get caught for petty shit. What he was doing could put him away for a long time. He would call Clay when he got in. Tommy had decided on the Waffle House; it was usually crowded, and he could watch everyone coming through the glass windows. Easier to spot if anything was getting squirrelly.

As they approached Micanopy, the exit before Gainesville, Tommy took it. Since his brother Steve had returned from Africa, Tommy wanted to re-establish a relationship. They had a few extra hours, and he didn't want to hang around for too long. Now, if he could find the place, since his brother wanted to live with the peace of the country. The shit that happened when he was a cop in Providence fucked him up a bit. His time in the Peace Corps should have chilled him out.

It was the second dirt road past the intersection with 441, and the Camaro kicked up a cloud. At the small frame house with a tar paper roof raised on cement blocks, Tommy saw the green Volkswagen Beetle. *He hasn't gotten rid of that piece of junk yet,* he thought.

The noise of their arrival brought Steve Logan to the screen door. Taller than Tommy, his athletic body was tanned from two years in the tropics. His hair was to his shoulders, and his beard was long, giving him the appearance of the medieval paintings of Jesus Christ.

"Holy shit! What did I do to deserve the honor?" Steve said as he wrapped Tommy in his arms.

"Was in the neighborhood. Didn't think it would be right to pass you by. This is Sandy. My brother Steve."

Sandy smiled a country club smile, but Steve wrapped his arms around her.

"Welcome to country living," Steve said. "I've got beer or iced tea."

Tommy looked around the room. Two folding chairs, a crate for a table, pillows on the floor, and nothing on the walls or the windows. There were three shelves of books on cement blocks—always books with him—classic and contemporary.

"You really outdid yourself on the decorating," Tommy said as Steve returned with the beers.

"It's a roof over my head, indoor plumbing, and screens on the windows," Steve said.

"There's much, and there's shit." Tommy turned up his mouth. Sandy laughed as Tommy went around the room, touching surfaces with the tip of his finger like a white-glove inspection. "How can you live like this?" Tommy dusted off a chair before he sat in his white linen pants.

"Better than the last place in Africa. These walls are wood, not mud," Steve laughed. "Here on business?"

"Of course."

"You were in Africa?" Sandy asked, moving forward to the edge of the folding chair.

"Yeah, Peace Corps," Steve said, handing Sandy an iced tea before sitting on the pillow. "What kind of deal this time or do I not want to know?" he asked Tommy.

"I'm gonna buy five hundred pounds here, and I'll turn it in Tampa. Easy score. You should come in. I could use your muscle. And I'm working on a big deal in Atlanta."

"Not my scene, man."

"Good money." Tommy waved his arm at the room.

"Got everything I need. You need to get out before they get you." Steve shook his head, looking like a yogi on the pillow he'd chosen to sit on.

"I'm very careful." Tommy paced around the small room. No way in hell could he live like this. Steve was smart, back in school for another degree, but he was wasting his life. "Come on, man—just for a bit. I could use the help."

"Sandy is your muscle tonight?"

She smiled and shook her head, dabbing the sweat from her forehead. "Don't you believe in AC?"

"I haven't had it for years. And it's not as hot here as it was there." Steve stretched his arms over his head and placed them flat on the floor.

"Listen, I met this guy. Real big time." Tommy moved closer. "We're talking about import—no middlemen. I'll cut you in for some help."

"Tommy, moving a little weed is one thing. Fucking smuggling— you're out of your fucking mind. That'll get you big time jail. And your connection, I'm sure he's a real honest citizen who won't sell you down the river."

"I don't know why the fuck I talk to you. So you killed somebody as a cop. It's done. I'm offering you a chance of a lifetime. Get out of this shithole. Have some real money. Be somebody."

Steve pulled his long hair into a ponytail and wrapped it with a hairband. Slowly standing, he faced Tommy. "I know who I am and who I was. But do you? How much money will it take to make you happy? What will it buy you if you're doing twenty years in prison? You already got more than you need."

"I've got a number. One million and I'm out. It's easy money."

"Yeah, sure. It's always easy money until it isn't."

"Right, have it your way." Tommy pulled on the front of his silk shirt to let some air into the clinging shirt. "Sandy's right. No AC? You're out of your fucking mind. There's an offer on the table. It won't last long." Tommy walked to the door.

"It will still be no. You're always welcome wherever I am." Steve clenched him close. "I hope I won't have to bail you out. Be careful. Sandy, nice to meet you. Don't let him get a big head. I'm always here for a dose of sanity."

Sandy gave Steve a kiss on the cheek. "Thanks."

* * *

As they left, Tommy thought about the deal. He would feel better if Steve was with him but... but... he didn't understand where his brother's head was. Money was power. Why didn't Steve understand that? Maybe he did, but just didn't care? Tonight would double his money, which he'd turn into a million. A nice, round number.

Clay had to do a minimum of five hundred pounds of grass on the deal, but with Tommy, they could go for a thousand and get the high-volume price cut. The sellers needed his cash. Tommy would pay C.O.D. Clay's suppliers were cool enough to wait. They would front to him because he had the sure, quick sale. Clay had been a Green Beret in Vietnam; he was a professional.

The timing of the deal was the most beautiful thing of all. He was getting the grass for two hundred dollars, and he could still set it at three hundred, so the profit on five hundred pounds was fifty thousand dollars on one deal.

* * *

Putting on the right signal, he let the Camaro gear down before the car surged around the wide exit ramp. It was time to wait. Sandy pulled out the Allman Brothers tape and pushed in ZZ Top.

The Waffle House was practically empty. They sat down at a booth near the phone. Sandy ordered coffee while Tommy ordered orange juice. He called the pay phone number, but there was no answer. He hung up and sat next to Sandy. The money was in the trunk of the car, which he could see from where he was sitting. He left his gun in the car but put Sandy's purse between them.

At first, dealing was an adventure, fun like cutting class or smoking in the bathroom. Then the money came, more money than he ever imagined. It's what you shouldn't see too young because it makes you hungry. Everyone respects a man with money, whether he's respectable or not. No one asks where it came from; they're looking to get a piece for themselves. Neither really appealed to him anymore, not in the same way. He had gone beyond, into a way of life, a conscious revolt done almost with compulsion. He needed the adrenaline to keep him alive. He'd die if he was forced to experience life through a television.

He got up and called again. Still no answer. He didn't like it. Sandy ordered more coffee, but he didn't want anything.

This deal had to come off smoothly. He was aware of his lazy preparations and not having proper backup. He was tired from running around the past two nights. He was using coke to keep him awake, his muscles responsive. Any fight had to be a short one, or he wouldn't make it.

The chances of getting ripped off were close to zero, but he had thought that two years ago when it had happened to him here in Gainesville. He had just started his partnership with Sal, and they had been stone-sure of their first big deal. Sal was still leading the deals and had bought from this guy Sid on two occasions.

"Let's go, Sal," Tommy had said in a hurried whisper. The air was colder than he thought it would be, and he had pulled his blue jean jacket closed.

Sal lifted his compact body out of the ripped bucket seat of Tommy's GTO and hurried across the parking lot after him. As they got into the backseat of an old black Continental, Sid, a dark-haired, oval-faced Midwesterner, turned to greet them.

"Hey, Sid." Sal spoke first. "You have the stuff?"

"Sure do." Sid smiled jovially and passed Tommy a plastic bag containing a pound of Colombian pot, slightly red in color and with firm, aromatic buds. Tommy reached in and raised a handful to his nose. He breathed deeply, savoring the rich-bodied fullness of the dried buds. He always believed that fine reefer, when dried correctly, was more aromatic than hash. Southerners always disagreed with him.

"It's not bad," Tommy said and held up a bud. He passed the bag to Sal. "You have more of this?"

"Sure. Like I told Sal before, I can do up to one hundred."

"Is it all these many buds?" Sal asked.

"It's the exact same stuff. I just scooped that off the top when I came out." Sid's head bobbed like it was attached to his shoulders with a spring. Tommy thought his grin was nervous and tense. He thought the dude was a little afraid of him.

"Okay, Sid. What price?"

"What size?"

Tommy and Sal exchanged glances. If it looked good, they would go in with all of their money and some fronted from other folks.

"Well?"

"Two sixty-five a pound."

"And for quantity?" Tommy asked. Sid looked from Sal to Tommy, trying to figure who was making the decisions.

"Two forty-five. You're making too much profit," Sal said.

"Listen," Sid began to protest but stopped when Tommy and Sal sat up. "Two fifty-five if you do over twenty-five pounds."

Tommy leaned closer to Sid. "We'll do sixty at two-fifty if you can do that much."

Sid sat back, and his smile fell from jovial to gloating before returning to the Midwestern grin. Tommy wasn't sure what it meant.

"Okay," Sid said. "You guys bring the cash to the Sky Hill Motel, Room 7. You know where it is? When I have the money, we'll go get the pot."

"Is it gonna be just you, Sid?" Sal asked.

"Mind if we take some of this to test?" Tommy asked, pocketing a handful of the pot from the bag as he handed it back.

"Course not," Sid said, taking the bag from Tommy. "See you fellas tonight."

Tommy had shivered again as he re-crossed the parking lot.

"That's fifteen grand," Sal said. "Can we get that much together?"

"I think so," Tommy said confidently. "Ernie, Tom, and Rob make five. You're in for…"

"Twenty-five hundred."

"Good, that's seventy-five hundred. I've got fifty-five, so that leaves us needing two thousand."

"Great," Sal said, picking up the open Michelob he had left on the floor of the car. "Know where we can get that much in the next four hours?"

"Yup," Tommy smiled. He borrowed two thousand dollars at ten percent a week from a loan shark. That was twenty-two hundred by Wednesday.

Tommy and Sal sat at the dining room table; the money spread out in little piles before them.

"Seventy-five hundred here," Tommy said, arranging the bills, so they all faced in one direction. The loan shark had given him twenties, probably from some bookie operation. The rest of the money was in fifties and hundreds.

"I've got the same." Sal laughed. His laugh came from deep in his stomach, but he tried to muffle the force of it, so it came out like a staccato giggle. "We're all set tonight."

"Yeah, but I wish we didn't have to rush for cash like this. I'm tired of trying to put together fifteen grand. I want that kind of cash to do it right." Tommy got up and took two bottles of Michelob, handing one to Sal. "Y'know, if we only had that kind of capital, we could get in and out of deals with a lot of profit. If it's our money, we can do what we want. Tampa isn't that big of a place, and we know the area around USF really good. Between you and me, we know most of the people who deal. Once we get set up, we can run the wholesaling end of it. This selling on the street sucks and is too dangerous. We should only be dealing in quantity. We've got to have the money to do it. As long as we're not greedy, no one's going to mind us having a piece of the pie."

Sal gently placed the money into the backpack on the table. Tommy turned away. He realized that Sal got squeamish when he began to talk like that. Sometimes the wop from Providence was just as cocky. Sometimes. But not with the same ferocity Tommy felt within, his own private devil.

He was nineteen when he dropped out of University of South Florida. It was too much trouble. Books didn't make money, hustling did. Tommy preferred the money. He started winter quarter with good intentions. Sitting in a marketing class, a half-assed adjunct professor told him to take off his sunglasses and hat. Tommy refused, and the teacher became adamant and tried to take them off for him. Tommy almost broke his arm when he tried to grab him. That was the last class Tommy attended.

"I don't know about trying to run a monopoly around this school. It's gotten pretty hot recently," Sal said.

Tommy waved the argument away with his hand. "What monopoly? All I'm talking about is that if we get enough money together, we can run this smoothly. You've got a brother up north and friends. So do I. A pound of the shit we're buying tonight goes for three sixty a pound in Boston. The profit's good."

"Yeah, I know we can make a lot of money if we give it half a try. It ain't that hard." Sal zippered the case. "I'd like to make this money tonight best of all. We ought to get moving if we want to get out to that motel by eight-thirty."

"What's Sid's last name?" Tommy grabbed the backpack and the beer.

"Lloyd."

"You've got a damn good memory."

"Got it from my mom. She never forgot a damn thing my father ever did in his life. And neither did he." They both laughed. "She made him take out all sorts of insurance policies just in case. Then she nagged the hell out of him for all his faults, mostly other women, until one day he was just tired of the whole thing and dropped dead at the racetrack with a winning ticket. I think he died with a smile on his face. I sure would have."

"I see you've got a woman just like your mom." Sal grimaced. "I think I'm gonna bring the thirty-eight," Tommy said, tucking the snub nose into his belt.

"We won't need that. Sid isn't that tough. It's only him and us. We can take him if he tries anything."

"Yeah, it's not worth the risk. I'll take this gravity knife just in case." Tommy slid the folding knife into his right boot. Putting on the denim jacket, he pulled the keys from his pocket and opened the door.

The meet was at the Sky Hill Motel at I-75 and University. There were three motels and three gas stations at the exit along with a place that sold pecan stuff—too sweet for Tommy.

"It must be the last room," Sal said as Tommy inched along the motel's deserted parking lot.

"There's his car," Tommy said and pulled in next to the Continental. Tommy slung the money around his shoulder and knocked on number 7. Sal stood to his left.

"Yeah," Sid said through the door.

"It's Sal and Tommy."

"It's open. Come in."

Tommy opened the door. They quickly walked into a small hallway and closed the door. Sid was sitting at the far end of the L-shaped room on a bed. The bathroom was on his left with the door closed.

"You got the money?" Sid grinned.

"Right here," Tommy said, tapping the case. Sid's face suddenly filled with a gloating smile traced with cruelty, as if he enjoyed butchering animals on the farm.

"Then don't move, pretty boy, or your head will be across that wall." Tommy looked at the man who opened the bathroom door. He had them covered with a sawed-off double-barreled shotgun. He held the weapon like he was ready to use it. Tommy felt his bowels loosen, so he consciously tightened every muscle in his body like he was ready to enter an arena. He began looking for a mistake. Then a big-boned kid emerged from the bathroom with a revolver.

"Sit down on the bed," the man with the shotgun said with a Chicago twang. It wasn't going to happen. Tommy refused to believe it could happen.

"Why don't you drop the money, pretty boy," Sid said, and the malicious smile Tommy had seen earlier covered his face.

There were two beds in the room. Tommy was between them and the man with the shotgun. Sid was on the other side of the bed near the back of the room. They couldn't shoot. Well, they could. Tommy thought that in an out-of-the-way motel like this one, no one would check until the maid came in the morning. It was a gamble. Everything was a gamble, but the money wasn't his.

"Hey, listen. You don't really want to do this." Tommy kept the flight bag over his shoulder. They were going to have to take it off him physically because if they thought he was just going to hand it over without a fight, they were living in a dream world.

"The money, Tommy," Sid said, raising a pistol to him.

"Man, you guys sure have a lot of firepower," Tommy said lightly.

"Give 'em the money," Sal whispered.

"That's right. Listen to your buddy," the man with the shotgun said.

"It's right here," Tommy said, putting it at his feet.

"Get it, Frank," Sid said. The big-boned kid pushed Sal onto the bed and advanced to Tommy.

Tommy waited, sucking his breath deeply into his diaphragm and tensing all his muscles for one explosion.

"Get away," Frank rumbled, pushing Tommy back with a hand as he bent to pick up the flight bag.

Tommy felt the hand on his chest and wanted to explode, but he held his temper until Frank bent to pick up the bag. Swinging his right leg with the force of a pile driver, Tommy shot a front snap kick to Frank's head just as he began to say something. He let out a savage blood-curdling scream at the same time. The kick struck Frank low, right at the base of the chin. Frank didn't stand but went from a forward crouch to a fully extended position on his back as he flew up and across the bed toward Sid.

Tommy leaped across the bed at the man with the shotgun. He had to deflect the weapon before the other man realized what was happening. The cold steel rewarded his hands, and the man fought for control. Tommy saw him take his finger from the trigger as they fell to the floor against the wall. The man was stronger than Tommy had thought, so he had to get a punch in quickly. Taking his left hand from the barrel, Tommy began savagely beating the man around the head. One, two, three. Tommy tried to crush the man's skull but didn't have a good angle.

A hard blow to the back of his head caused a cold sensation to run down Tommy's spine. It tingled with an almost refreshing feeling until it reached his hands—and it left him without the sense of touch. He could no longer grip the gun barrel, and a sharp, numbing pain was throbbing along the base of his neck. He swung hard again at the man with the shotgun, but the blow had no power.

Tommy felt another blow strike him near the head. Half-turning, he put his left hand up to ward off another. He saw Sid winding up again with the butt of the gun. Tommy tried to duck, but the last blow had slowed him. He saw Sid's fist containing the .357 magnum come crashing down at his face. His left arm was of no use, and all Tommy could do was try and get his head out of the path. The gun barrel caught him on the chin and snapped him back against the wall. He suddenly felt nauseous, and his head ruptured and imploded until his mind became scrambled, then blank.

"Tommy, Tommy…" His name sounded very vague, and he wasn't certain he was the one who was being called. The pain in his head, the sharp throbbing of his neck, assured him that it was. Sal was holding a wet washcloth against Tommy's chin and face to stop the bleeding.

"Do you have the money?" Tommy muttered through his swollen tongue. He thought he had kept his mouth closed during the fight so he wouldn't bite his tongue, but the force of the gun barrel had been too much.

"No, they got away with it," Sal said. He had a large area of pulverized flesh over his left eye.

"Damn," Tommy said. "Which way did they go?" He tried to get to his feet, but the nauseous feeling returned. "Whew, they really hit me."

"They carried out the big guy. He never got up."

"I knew I hit that sucker. As soon as he bent over..." Tommy tried to smile the best he could. "We better get out of here before they charge us for the damages." He waved his hand over the demolished motel room. Both lamps were broken, a table had been smashed, and blood was on the carpet, linens, and chair.

Trying to walk normally, he felt like he was in a planetarium. The stars were whizzing wildly, some of them nebula clouds and comets. He was the outer container of the universe; it all swirled in his head and made him feel like vomiting, but he couldn't.

"I think I better drive," Sal said, putting his hand out for the keys. "You took a pretty good beating in there."

"Yeah," Tommy said, handing him the keys. He didn't want to drive anyway. "What were you doing, by the way, while I was taking the beating? The big guy didn't get up; I had the other stooge on the ground." He stopped and looked disappointedly at Sal. "You let Sidney take you?"

"He had a gun, man."

"The other one had a shotgun. So what?"

"So..."

"Oh, so you figured you'd rather give up the money than get killed. Shit, those guys wouldn't have used those pieces. Not for fifteen grand."

"What makes you so sure?"

"I'm alive." Tommy shook his head, disgusted with the outcome. "But they got the money." He rubbed the back of his head and then his jaw. "We're gonna have to get it back."

"How?"

"The way they took it from us."

"I don't know, Tommy."

"I'm open to suggestions. You know of a better way?"

"No."

* * *

That was two years ago. He was just nineteen then. It wouldn't happen again.

"Waitress." Tommy snapped his fingers in the air. "Bring me another orange juice."

"You okay, Tommy?" Sandy asked. "You haven't said much tonight."

"A little tired," he said and got up to use the phone. He didn't know what the delay was. Possibly in the transport or someone wanted to weigh things in advance.

"Clay?"

"Yeah."

"Tommy. What's going on?"

"Just a lot of delays. Why don't you get a place off the highway. Make it a first-floor room. Call me in another hour."

"Everything cool?"

"Yeah, everything's cool."

Tommy pulled into the Ramada Inn right off I-75. The room was a standard motel room: two double beds with identical plain cotton bedspreads. Registering under Jimmy Russo, he wasn't worried about anyone finding him to rip him off.

Waiting. If he only had a dime for every minute spent waiting for a deal to come down. He liked the hours, though, and that was important in choosing a career. When he began doing deals, at least three fell through for every one that happened. Waiting was a part of the business. It would never be run on appointed times or in regular offices; it was much too dangerous for that. Tommy felt a little depressed about things in Tampa. It didn't make any difference to him. He'd survive it all. He was certain of that, but the potential was there for so much more. If only Sal and his wife could get their shit together, then Sal wouldn't act so crazy. It wasn't the time to deal with that.

Dialing Clay's number again, Tommy wanted to get back to Tampa as soon as he could. Once this deal was completed, he was going back to Atlanta and Harry Burr. He was the big time, and there were things that could be done.

"Clay?"

"Yeah, it's set, Tommy. What number are you in?"

"Ramada. One twenty-seven."

"Be there in an hour."

He had known Clay for over a year. They were never friends as such but dealt with each other over that time period some twenty times. Once a month was fairly regular, but they had been small deals. Both being in Tampa, they knew many of the same people.

"Get ready; Clay will be here in an hour," Tommy said to Sandy, walking to the sink in the bathroom. His eyes were burning from the strain. Covering his face with a wet washcloth, he wished all of the pain would evaporate. He wished, he wished. Taking the cloth off his face, he ran it again under cold water. Maybe a shower would do better. He went back, got the bag, carried it to the bathroom, and put it behind the toilet.

"What are you doing?" Sandy asked,

"We're taking a shower," he said. "You're going to have to stay awake for a while."

They had sex in the shower, which woke them more than the water did. Tommy shook the water from his hair, feeling refreshed. He sat on the edge of the bed and divided the coke he had in a small cylinder into six lines. Two were larger than the rest. Tommy snorted first and did the two big lines. "Here, beautiful," he said, smiling. "Got to keep you on your toes."

"You keep me on my toes," Sandy said, kissing Tommy before snorting two lines.

Yawning, Tommy offered the bill to her. "The rest is for you, darling." She smiled sheepishly and snorted.

Tommy took the towel and wiped the table clean of any coke crumbs. He stashed the bottle in his coat, slipped the holster back on under his arm, and adjusted it so it was just at his left kidney.

A sharp knock on the door broke the silence that had descended on the room. Tommy grabbed the flight bag and was across the bed and against the front window in a flash. He looked between the curtains and saw the long brown hair of Clay resting on a New Harvest Restaurant t-shirt.

"Sandy, open the door," he said. Tommy stayed in the corner just in case it went bad. Sandy opened the door, and Clay brushed past her. "Close the door."

Clay looked to see Tommy against the wall. "Man, I thought you might've split," he said half-jokingly.

Tommy saw the surprise on Clay's face when he realized that he had been covered with the pistol until the door was closed. That was the knowledge that kept people honest. When they know that you always go somewhere prepared for the worst, they won't try and fuck around with you.

"I wasn't sure if you were ever going to show up." Tommy smiled and advanced to shake hands with Clay in a power grip.

"Yeah, well, the plane was late, and they wanted to get everything stored away first. Now we're ready to go."

Tommy hated having other people control the show. Someday he would make those decisions. "So, how is it happening?"

"Real simple. Give me the keys to your car. I'm going to put half in your trunk, half in mine. That way, neither car will ride low. I'll come back and give you your keys. Then we'll meet at my place in Tampa, where you can look at it and pay for your share. Okay?"

"Yeah, why not." It sounded good, and he still had the money with him. These people must really want the stuff out of the area quickly. It was cool. "How long to getting the cars filled and back here?"

"Twenty minutes, tops," Clay shrugged. He had very long hair and a dark beard and was well-built. Tommy heard he was wounded in Vietnam but didn't know much else. Clay didn't talk about the war.

"Get moving. I didn't come up here for the great nightlife."

Everyone laughed. "See you in twenty."

* * *

The drive back to Tampa was uneventful. Clay's house was on a back road facing the Hillsborough River. It was already seven, and the early dawn was cleaning the street. Tommy backed the car into the garage and waited for the door to close before he exited.

After opening the trunk, Tommy threw one of the three burlap sacks of pot over his shoulder. He squatted to make it rest comfortably. He walked through the door from the garage into a Florida room that was windows on three walls. Brown drapes that extended to the floor protected the room from outside view. There were two burlap bags already standing against the wall that opened into the kitchen. Clay followed him in with another sack. Sandy had the flight bag and Tommy's jacket. Tommy went out and got the last bag. Clay ripped one open with his hunting knife. "It's all that nice gold tops," he said, scooping a handful of the compressed flower buds in his hand. The room was filled with the richly aromatic odor of good marijuana. Even in his coked left nostril, Tommy could smell it.

"Looks good," Tommy said, bending over the bag. He flipped his gravity knife open and stuck the blade deeply into the pot. Pushing the blade down into it, he turned the pot to check the consistency of the quality. He stabbed the bale several times, going lower with each thrust. He shook the bale; there was no sand, so it was solid weight.

Clay retrieved a three-foot-high Toledo scale. It had on weight on the bottom arm and a fine balance on the top arm. He flipped the weights to zero and balanced the beam. "All set," he said.

"These should be a hundred apiece, but I know they aren't," Tommy said, putting the first bag on the scale. "One fifteen." Clay wrote it down. "Ninety-six." Tommy threw the second bale aside. "Do you have a saw to split this bale and a couple of trash bags?"

"Yeah, sure thing," Clay said. The pot must be good because he was forgetful tonight. Clay was a pothead; it slowed him down sometimes. That was one of the things Tommy didn't like about pot. Coke kept him right on his toes and kept him from feeling tired. He could get a lot more done. It wasn't like speed. Meth was a killer; you could feel it rush through the body, racing the body's organs like in a motocross, the wild rampaging action of hills and holes. Coke was a settled-back high. The mind and body were active and controlled. You didn't feel it until you had to move. It was a good feeling until it went over the edge, and the paranoia began. Tommy tried to stop before the edge.

Clay returned with a Bowie knife and four black heavy-duty trash bags. His arms were tanned, and his mustache drooped over his mouth, completely hiding his top teeth except when he smiled. Then, the gleaming whiteness from beneath the brown hair made his smile friendly. He cut the bale in roughly half. "Try that," he said, putting the larger of the two on the scale.

"Two fifty-two," Tommy said. "That ought to do it, counting these bags. My five hundred and yours." He dumped the remaining half bale into one of the trash bags. Tommy double-bagged his, sealing one, then the other in the opposite direction to seal the odor.

"Want coffee or anything?" Clay asked as they sat down at the kitchen table.

"Orange juice if you got any. Do you know how many people don't drink orange juice in this state?" Tommy shook his head in disgust. "It's excellent for you and if you ain't got your health, what have you got?" He swung the flight bag onto the table and unzipped it. Laying out the stacks of hundreds, he formed two rows of five bundles each. "There's five grand in each stack. That's fifty hundreds for a total of fifty grand. Count it."

Clay selected packs at random and counted them. When he was satisfied that the cash was correct, he put it into a leather briefcase he had brought out for that purpose.

"Give me a hand with this stuff," Tommy said. Clay nodded and followed Tommy out to the car, carrying two sacks. Tommy leaned over and gently kissed Sandy on the cheek. "It's all over," he said softly into her ear. "It's time to go home."

She raised her head and smiled with satisfaction. "We did it."

"Yeah, we did it. Let's go." He kissed her again while he ran his arm across her smooth shoulders.

* * *

Tommy unlocked the door to Sandy's apartment and kicked the door shut behind him. He carried Sandy straight into her bedroom and placed her softly on the bed the way a father would his daughter. His shoulders and neck were tight with exhaustion and coke, and his eyes were stinging. He began to undress her but then thought better of it and stopped. Sitting at the end of the bed, he leaned back and closed his eyes. His feet were still on the floor. Sandy curled up next to him, and as soon as she touched him, he flinched suddenly. "What's the matter?" she asked.

"I got to go," he said without opening his eyes. Sandy ran her fingers lightly over his chest. It caused goosebumps to appear on his stomach and arms. This summer, he was going to do some fishing or water skiing like he did in high school. Maybe see some high school friends or go to Gainesville and chill with his brother.

He couldn't sleep. Not now. Not yet. There were too many things that he still had to do, people he had to… Sandy's hand began to tickle, and he put his hand on top of hers to stop.

"What's the matter?" she asked, her eyes fluttering.

"I've got to go."

"Why?" She held on tighter.

"I've got to go. You sleep." He wanted to get up, but his body enjoyed the supine position. Sandy moved her head to his chest and reached around his neck with her left arm. She was breathing deeply and regularly.

He had to swim; if he remained motionless, he would sink. It was treacherous, a fool's gold of delight. Sandy jerked with a spasmodic muscle contraction, causing a wave of the emotion to inundate him. The shock of the movement brought back consciousness, and he opened his eyes quickly. The white plaster ceiling had no place for him to focus, and he wasn't certain he was awake. His eyes found a squashed mosquito, and he concentrated on it to assure himself that he was awake. He had to get up. Pulling Sandy's arm from his neck, he rolled out from underneath her.

"Where are you going?" she asked.

"I told you, I'm leaving." The sound of those words and the finality of the tone woke her.

"Don't go. Not now," she begged. "Can't you stay for a while and get some sleep?"

"No. I've got work to do."

"It can wait. Everything can wait." Her shirt was open, and her delicately round breasts heaved in supplication. "Tommy, please stay. We made it. Now we can just be together for a while."

"Yeah." He wanted to, but it didn't change anything. There were five hundred pounds of pot in the trunk of his car. He didn't like leaving it there.

She unzipped his pants, her hands groping for his penis. He was too tired for that. Sex didn't matter right now. Sandy used her mouth, but Tommy was thinking about the rest of the day ahead. First, he was going to divide the stuff into fifty-pound lots. Sal could deliver the fifty to Greg. He would call on Sam Dougherty. Mike from Miami wanted reefer. He wasn't going to front anything to anyone. Whatever wasn't gone by six o'clock tonight, he was going to sit on.

"I've got to go," he said, pulling Sandy up to his chest. "I might be back later."

"Well, I might just not be here," Sandy said in a hurt voice. Tommy realized how she hated it when he was indifferent to her sexually. "I'll go back to Atlanta, then."

"Have a good time," he said, getting up. She was trying to threaten him, and he didn't like it. It didn't make that much of a difference. He walked to the bathroom to wash his face. Sandy followed.

"Damn it, Tommy." She raised her voice. "Why won't you do this one thing for me? You..." She stopped short at his look.

"Listen, woman. I could give you a hundred reasons why I have to go. No. Five hundred. I don't have to give you any. I'm leaving. If I don't see you again, have a good life." Tommy brushed past her into the bedroom and took the container of coke from his jacket pocket. Sitting, he dipped in and took two spoonfuls. Sandy glowered at him from the doorway.

"You rich girls are all alike. Do this. I want. Gimme," he mocked. "You think your body can get you anything. Well, it can't." He took another spoonful, knowing the edge was very near. He shouldn't talk to her like that. The coke was making him brittle.

"I hope I never see you again," she hissed at him.

"Maybe you won't." He shrugged and put on his jacket. He ducked under her arm as she stood in the doorway. He reached the couch in the living room. He had to get things set up so he could move the pot. He didn't want to be holding so much quantity. "Greg," he spoke abruptly into the phone.

"Yeah." The reply was sleepy. It was only seven-thirty a.m.

"Wake up," he said harshly. "Are you still interested, or are you going to sleep away your opportunity?"

"Yeah, yeah—I'm interested," Greg said.

"Do you know what you're saying, or are you just agreeing out of habit?" Tommy felt a smile coming but suppressed it. When Greg was just waking up, he would agree to anything. Tommy knew from experience. "Shake it off and get whatever bitch you have there to leave you alone for a few seconds. Are you focused yet?"

"Yeah, I got it," Greg said.

"Right. Get your ass out of bed and make sure you are. See everyone you have to and make the arrangements. Capisce? I know it's only seven-thirty, but I don't give a fuck if it's Howdy Doody Time. Wake them up. Remember, the early hippie gets the herbs. I'll be by in an hour." He hung up without waiting for an answer. Greg was lazy; that was a major point against him. Not dumb, just lazy. He didn't bullshit when he said he could do something. And Tommy thought the market was dry.

"Tommy, I'm sorry," Sandy said, sitting next to him.

He was going to call Sal but figured he might as well just go by his place. He didn't like making any more calls than necessary to that phone. He didn't trust it.

"Yeah, I'm too." He pulled her closer. Sandy was a together chick. Sometimes she took a while to understand, but she did understand. He didn't really want to leave. With Greg committed to buying half the load, he felt some tension ease. He picked her up and carried her back to the bedroom. As he was getting dressed, he felt warm from their lovemaking.

Crawling to the end of the bed, she hugged him tightly, then let go. "You're crazy. You know that. I'm in love with you. There isn't anything that's going to change that." Her voice echoed with a lucidity and a certainty that penetrated Tommy. He believed her more than he believed anything, yet he felt a dull ache of cynicism that sprang from the dark side of his life. He had trusted, believed the priests in black robes when they taught, but they left him dirty and ashamed. Now, she was here, confessing her love. Was it something to depend upon, to trust, the word love? It was borne out in action, not a word. To do, not say. He had to trust.

Since meeting her last year, the times had been good. She was stubborn, willful—and she was enriching with her charm and strength. He had thought she was just another rich bitch with no ability to survive, to initiate, to create. It took him a day to learn differently. Endings were like beginnings with her, unexpected yet inevitable and significant. He'd see her tomorrow—maybe. Or the next day. Soon, when the work was done, the deal completed. How could he tell? Why worry about it? He experienced tonight; tomorrow will do its own thing.

"Got to go. Understand? It's the way. I'll see you later." He pressed her close to his chest and inhaled the soft fragrance of her skin. "We'll go back to Atlanta this weekend. No business."

She smiled and reached for a kiss, her tongue twisting his before letting go. Then Tommy turned quickly and left. It was Wednesday morning: he wanted to get back to Atlanta. Harry had talked about plans for bringing coke directly from Colombia. Now he was ready to hear the details. He was going to check everything; nothing could go wrong. He was tired now, beat and dragged down. He tooted two more spoons from the jar.

In the next two days, he moved most of the reefer. He still had one hundred pounds he was delivering to Harry. He had to make certain the man could do the deal. He would drive it to Atlanta tomorrow. The coke wasn't doing much good anymore. Tommy was numb all over, and he could feel his teeth grind unconsciously. He was checking his rearview mirror often too. Was he getting paranoid about that cop from Tampa, or was it just the coke? The road absorbed the automobile, the machine propelling him through space. The power was important, but he just wanted it to be done. For two days, he had bounced like a ricocheting bullet, but he was on the home stretch.

His profit was fifty grand—that plus his operating capital came to nearly one hundred and fifty big ones. The first thing in the morning, he'd put most of it in safety deposit boxes.

He stopped in Gainesville on his way to Atlanta and was happy when Steve agreed to spend the weekend with him. The drive allowed Tommy and Steve to relive memories of growing up—baseball cards, snow forts, and crab apple fights. He didn't tell his brother he had one hundred pounds of pot in the trunk.

"When you meet my partner, you'll, you'll... you'll see for your-self." Tommy was going to explain Harry but wanted Steve's opinion. Steve had enough street experience even if he had turned his back on it.

"So, what are you and this partner up to these days?" Steve was dressed in shorts and a grey t-shirt.

"We've got big plans. Just need to build the capital a bit more. Got to spend money to make money."

"I wouldn't know," Steve said. "And how much risk—that's the big question."

"You know I'm always careful." Tommy snapped.

"Until you're not. That's how everyone's caught." Tommy and Steve held each other's eyes.

At Doraville, Tommy parked the car in the driveway next to Harry's Cadillac.

"Ready for a show?" Tommy smiled as they walked to the front door.

Elsie answered the door in a too-tight halter top and form-fitting jeans. She kissed Tommy and then placed a wet kiss directly on Steve's lips. "So glad to see you."

"Ah, grasshopper. What do we have here? You've brought the elu-sive brother," Harry intoned from his captain's chair.

The room was dark as usual, with the window blinds drawn tight. There was a floor lamp on behind Harry, casting a shadow upon his face. He was dressed in a flowing guayabera shirt Tommy had purchased for him.

"Harry, this is my brother Steve." Tommy said, ignoring the grasshopper bullshit. He didn't need to start that way.

Steve advanced to Harry, and Tommy watched as his brother's eyes methodically surveyed the room before he moved forward. Always the careful one. Steve extended his hand, and Tommy guessed that Harry was putting a little extra pressure on the handshake. He smiled because he believed his brother was made of steel. He counted off the seconds in his head.

"Nice to make your acquaintance," Steve said, holding firm. Tommy guessed he was applying a bit of his own pressure now.

"Yeah, welcome to Georgia," Harry said, releasing his hand without lowering his gaze. "How was the trip?"

"I-75 was as boring as ever."

"Elsie," Harry bellowed. "Get these boys some beers. And bring me some chips and dip."

"This isn't a social trip," Tommy said, opening a beer and pushing his chair back from the table. Steve walked around the room, looking at the stereo, the assortment of cut glass figurines of naked women in various sexual poses, and a large tree stump coffee table. "Are you ready for the deal?"

"Grasshopper, I was born for the deal. That's who I am."

"Interesting collection," Steve said, pointing at the glass women.

"I had them in the entrance of my bordello in Miami in case we had guys who no speaka the English. Like they did in Pompeii," Harry said.

"Interesting concept," Steve said as he sat at the far end of the table, away from Harry and Tommy.

"It did the trick."

"Forget the trick. Can you do the weight, or do I need to find other buyers?" Tommy said. He really wanted to cut this visit short. Sandy was back in Tampa, and he wanted to be on the road by nightfall.

"How much?"

"Three hundred a pound if you take it all. Sixty thousand."

"Quality?"

"Best Colombian—all buds. Nicely packed."

"If it's what you say, I can do it. Let's see the merchandise."

"Give me a hand," Tommy said to Steve, and they walked to the front door. They returned with four army duffle bags. Tommy set one next to Harry's chair and opened it. The smell of the pot instantly filled the room.

"Nice aroma," Harry said as he grabbed a handful of buds and laid them on a dish in front of him. From inside his shirt, he produced a package of rolling papers and rolled a big joint. He lit it and took a big hit. "Nice and smooth." He passed it to Tommy, who took a hit. Steve passed as he returned the joint to Harry.

"I'll take it at two hundred a pound."

"Fuck, I didn't drive all this way to get nickel and dimed. You find this quality in Atlanta?" Tommy stood up and grabbed the bag from Harry.

"Calm down, grasshopper. This is the Atlanta bazaar. Got to keep your cool. What can you do on the price?"

"Not much, asshole. I told you the price before I came up."

"Yeah, but now you're here. Do you really want to drive this stuff all the way back to Tampa?" Harry sat back and toked on the joint.

Harry was right, and Tommy was pissed that he didn't start higher. With Harry, he needed to remember everything is a negotiation. "Two seventy-five is my best," Tommy said.

Harry toked again. "Elsie, what time does Kippi come home from school?"

"Three o'clock like every day." Her head appeared from the kitchen. "An hour from now."

Harry swiveled his massive head around on his neck, cracking it loudly. "Two hundred fifty and you have a deal."

Tommy let the words sit silently for a few minutes as he looked at Harry intently, then glanced at Steve, whose stare was full of daggers. "Let's get this done. I've got other business to do."

Steve followed Elsie to the basement, carrying the bags of pot, while Tommy counted the money. Steve shook hands with Harry and managed to duck, so Elsie's kiss landed on his forehead.

"Soon, brother." Tommy said.

As they re-entered I-75 south, Steve said, "Don't ever do that to me again."

"What, brother? It was cool."

"The fuck it was. Two hundred pounds in the trunk, and you didn't tell me."

"If I told you, you wouldn't come."

"Damn straight."

Tommy peeled off five-hundred-dollar bills. "For your company."

"I don't want your money," Steve said, looking straight ahead. "I don't like being taken for a fool."

"You weren't. I just wanted a second opinion. What did you think?"

"Of Harry?"

Tommy nodded.

"He's trouble. You know that. He's smooth, but I'd be very careful because he will probably play everyone. But then again, I wouldn't be doing any of this—because it never ends well."

"Harry's a con, but I think I've got this covered. I'm holding twenty thousand dollars of his diamonds," Tommy said as he smiled. Still, he better be extra careful. Steve was a good judge of people.

After dropping Steve in Gainesville, Tommy felt guilty about ignoring Sandy. She had to understand; it was business. He had to do it when it was there. It wasn't a nine-to-five job. Tomorrow, they could hop on a flight to Atlanta. He'd make it up to her. He had the cash now, and a bigger profit was waiting. He was even too tired to think much about that.

After unlocking the main lock to his apartment, Tommy dropped the keys as he worked on the security chain. He put it on so that the landlord couldn't get in and look around. After locking the door, he threw the safety bolt.

He took about half the money from the flight bag, wrapped it in aluminum foil, and put it in the freezer with the steaks and ice cream. He left the rest in the bag and hung it inside a shirt in his closet. Everything was done, finished. A broad smile covered his face when he saw his drawn, tired face in the mirror.

"Man, go to bed. You look horrible," he said to the mirror. He put the Smith & Wesson under his pillow and unplugged the phone. Stripping quickly, he was asleep as soon as his head touched the pillow.

Chapter 7

TWO WEEKS LATER, TOMMY BOARDED the flight to Atlanta on Saturday morning, having slept all day Friday. Sandy wanted to stay in Tampa to withdraw from college. He felt confined in Tampa, caught among small crustaceans and insects. There was more opportunity to grow in Atlanta, more room to move. Since meeting Harry, he thought he could reach one million in a year. With coke directly from Colombia, the markup would be one thousand percent and still be better than the Cuban stuff.

Taking an aisle seat in first class, Tommy watched the auburn-haired stewardess demonstrate how to put on the oxygen mask without damaging her makeup. Tommy caught her eye for a moment, and she flashed her eyes at him.

The fat man said he was making arrangements to score coke in Colombia and bring it back directly. Tommy had his doubts. He hadn't heard the details yet. Harry was forever saying, talking, telling stories. Tommy wanted the specifics. He figured to get in on the ground floor, to know all the risks before his ass was on the line—or his money. It was time for Harry to show him what and who he knew.

Moving forward with Harry and this deal was the best thing he could do now. In Tampa, he would definitely get angry at Sal. The dumb wop was getting worse on coke. He was running every day with Broski, who was out on bail for drug possession. The last two grand Sal made went into their arms. And Terry, Sal's wife, tried to keep the pressure on. Sal wanted out of the marriage and she didn't. Pop, pop, pop. He was popping to forget that living ain't easy.

With Harry Burr, life was just beginning to get interesting. Tommy would make sure real arrangements were firm, not just fantasies. He didn't know what he didn't know. Taking chances was a matter of business, a matter of life. Avoiding the risks was rejecting the realities of life. They were all going to end in the same place: six feet under. Sooner? Later? His father was a failure in life; how much could Tommy know? What did he gain with the faith? Not one more day of life. When his lottery ticket said *now*, he was gone.

Harry was in his captain's chair in the same position Tommy had last seen him—immovable, massive, more of a mountain than a human. His cragged features, overly large, protruded like a Gahan Wilson cartoon. He wasn't human—no one in the real world would ever believe that Harry Burr existed. But he did. He was sitting right there before Tommy, snorting coke.

"Look at you; you haven't moved in two weeks." Tommy walked into the room, making a quick fake toward Harry. Harry reacted with a block, but Tommy never threw the punch. "Always this jumpy?" Tommy scoffed, sitting across the table.

Harry rolled his lips outward, showing a wad of pink flesh. Then he darted the tip of his tongue between his pink lips so that it just peeked through. He wiggled his tongue, so it appeared to quiver. "Want to eat some pussy, grasshopper?" Harry asked, resuming his facial contortions, his tongue quivering more excitedly.

"They must have taught you that in prison. They must of loved getting a piece of your fat ass in there." Tommy wanted to test his vulnerability.

Harry's face lost its comic feature. There was a flash of anger mixed with pain in his eyes. The mask of detached serenity had been broken. Tommy guessed why: prison. He had no desire to experience it. Every time Sal heard the word, Tommy could hear him clutch inside. The word elicited terror. "*HELL!*" the priest would scream from the pulpit, but for Tommy, Hell was serving mass with Father Byrne, who insisted Tommy return to the rectory with him. Thick wooden blinds drawn tight against light, cigar butts in the ashtrays—it started the same way every time. He was the smallest in his second-grade class, with bright blue eyes and curly brown hair. He sat in the first pew with his class, where Father Byrne noticed him. He was asked to be an altar boy, an honor, his parents said. Who could you tell?

Father Byrne had a big booming voice that seemed to ricochet off the side altars, repeating eternal pain from the shadows of the saints. Tommy always wondered if churches were designed to create those unearthly echoes. He guessed very little was left to chance.

Religion, government, military—all organized and refined over the years into grand piles of shit. Rules, laws, interpretations, contradictions—all conveniences of power. Keep the people down; by third grade, it happened again and again. There was no one who would believe him. Tommy now refused to obey. When Father Byrne began asking for him to come out of class to help at the church, it was enough. He created so much havoc in class; the principal's office became his refuge, until he went to public school the following year.

With the knowledge he had of his own life, he had to fight. The only language he understood was power. When he heard the peace freaks with ideals and big words, he could see ignorance surrounding their frail excuses. Who made laws? Right; rules of war—who made the rules for war in Nam? B-52s against pajama-clad peasants. Some rules. If I lose, I lose my way, on my terms, fighting for what I want.

"Kid, one of these days, you're gonna say the wrong thing to the wrong person." Harry's voice was subdued.

"One of these days. Make me laugh. I do it every day. Jest my way. What you say," Tommy began in a mocking cadence. "Shit, when the man tells me to move, I say why? Don't make me happy, whore. I don't move 'cause some jive-ass honky tells me to move my sweet behind. All I can say is move it baby or lose it." Tommy looked straight into Harry's eyes. "Ain't it the truth and as the Almighty is above us, that's the way it comes down." He laughed, but Harry sat glumly, his eyes still traced with resentment.

"Here, *kid*," Tommy said as he threw a bag of Lebanese hash on the table. "Brought you a present since you love the stuff so much." Tommy calculated the words to change the mood, the point having been made. "Prison fucked your mind, didn't it? They made it hurt." Tommy wanted to know more.

"They fuck your body and your mind there, grasshopper. It's out of control. Nothing you can do but try and get out of the way. That's pretty tough when you're a big guy like me. And I was tough," Harry said. His massive shoulders heaved with a sigh, and he sat back onto the broad wooden chair and lit the hash pipe.

"When you hear the clink of the gate behind you, the world changes. Life doesn't have the same rules. The walls swallow you, and you become part of the garbage it feeds on. I was big, fat, young, and hot-tempered. The scum fed on fear. After the first trouble, I learned real quick to shut up and get along. You haven't learned that. The idea of prison is to break the spirit, to hobble you like they do a horse. It's not Miami Beach. From the moment you walk in, the stupidity of the system hits you in the face like a bag of piss. And they keep making you eat shit. The dregs of society, the dumbest, most ignorant part of America. The government keeps them in massive structures so that *good* society doesn't have to deal with the idea of them. Mental cripples, defects, law avoiders, and idiots—once they walked the village green until the proper people were thoroughly disgusted. So they built bins and closed the doors. It works. It's a system that forces you to bend over and spread your cheeks while they stick it to you. That's what happens when they get you. And if you stay a wise-ass, dumb kid, you'll have to learn the hard way like me. You're not dumb."

"You're becoming perceptive in your old age."

"I'm not fucking around, grasshopper. You can either learn from the master or make the mistakes yourself. Prison is an acid trip. Eat a pound and go away for years without any fucking say. Get up, eat, work, go outside, sleep. The same thing every day—no choice. And they keep you in constant fear, using the big stick." Harry put the mirror and the opaque pill bottle filled with coke on the table.

There was fear in Harry, emanating like the smell of burned flesh. It was struggling to swallow the thick, fleshy body; it crawled from the layers of his fat, oozing drops of sweat onto his shirt. Tommy watched, surprised at its visibility. The weakness of Harry's character was evoked by his memory of prison. The smell frightened Tommy deep in the recesses where the animal fear occurs. Now it was under control in him. No sweat bead, no tight lips or trembling hands— under control, cool and smooth.

Harry did a quarter-inch-thick line of coke with his Enterprise tooter. Then he did another, inhaling with a massive breath. Cutting the pile of coke into two lines, he did two more. Tommy figured Harry did a whole gram in four snorts. Harry tipped his melon head back onto his shoulders; his torso didn't move. Sucking air through his nostrils, he made the honking sound of a truck horn.

"There she blows," Tommy said, standing at the table. Harry snapped his head forward with a huge grin.

"You slimy son of a bitch punk." He stared at Tommy but didn't move from his chair. "Can't you behave like a civilized human? I thought you wanted to do business, make money."

"You're hogging the coke like it's a pizza. Let's get one thing straight, big man. Any deals come down, even up, or I'm not in." Tommy's eyes were hard. "Make no mistake about it."

"Well, grasshopper, why should I trust you?" Harry's voice began climbing. Tommy did two lines. The coke was good, but Tommy was pacing himself. He could feel his body, his consciousness stepping outside his body while still controlling it. He felt from the outside as well as in. He could touch his skin and feel the touch. Really laid back, but… his mind was working.

"Listen, Harry. Did you get me up here just to talk my ear off, or do you have something? I keep hearing a lot of hot air from that tank you're carrying there. If you ain't got a deal, then stop wasting my time."

"When I was your age, I was just as hungry and impatient." Harry nodded. "But I'm not in a hurry. I've got plenty from the last trip. This one will happen when I say it will."

"What last time? You bought that weed from me."

"I just wanted to see what you could do. When I do things, I go and do first class. I don't deal with the pimps and whores anymore." Harry was coasting under the momentum of his words. "Three months ago, I did a plane from Colombia," he began, his fleshy cheeks undulating with the cadence of his deep voice. "Who do I get but the chairman of the board of the National Drug Abuse Research Center here in Atlanta? Dr. Ollie Bentley, Stanford, Harvard, Princeton, —and a plane, twin-engine Cessna that I have stenciled with the NDARC logo.

"I send them down to Ft. Lauderdale's ADIZ zone, the Air Force thing that tells them when planes are coming in. He went down because it was the only thing we didn't know. Dr. Bentley gets off on beating the system. He's as looney as a 'luded spic. So he went down there and found out how to beat it. Ollie went to the Air Force colonel and told him they were writing a book and would like to use his name, blah, blah. And the colonel got so friendly that he said, 'Don't quote me, but if I were a smuggler, you know how I'd do it,' and he told him how to fly over and under in the ADIZ zone, so it looked like a high wave. Sometimes the radar picks up waves. And that's how we did it." Harry paused to sip on a glass of tonic water. Tommy settled in his chair, trying to make sense of the story.

"Then we loaded up for Bogotá. Quintana, who you'll meet one of these days, made the connection. I set it up and made the buy. Dr. Bentley brought this dumb Mexican broad, his latest tamale, on the trip to make it look like a vacation. She bought a stuffed alligator from a street vendor, and when the cops ask to see it, the broad freaks out. The DAS, Colombia's secret gestapo, blew up and searched everything. They tore the fucking airplane from stem to stern. They ripped the alligator up and unstuffed him. And they checked out the broad; looked in her ears, eyes, nose, snatch, and up her ass. They assumed Dr. Bentley was okay so didn't bother to search him.

"A sergeant grabbed the survival kit, which the FAA demands for over-water flights, and went to pull the ripcord. Quintana said quickly, '*Momento, señor*.' The cop had the stuff. Quintana explained to him about the survival kit, the CO_2 cartridges, the flare gun, the inflatable life raft, the rations, and how it couldn't be put back together. They should have looked. Everything looked right with the kit, but there were twenty keys of *el cokoritoo* inside that Quintana talked those fuckers out of looking for. By the time the plane taxied to the end of the runway, someone at DAS had figured out what happened. By the way, Ollie has a pound and a half insurance between his legs in a woman's long line girdle. The police came running down, yelling for them to stop. The pilot freaked, but Quintana just leaned forward on the throttle with him. That was all it took. The pilot was having a Vietnam flashback, but he snapped out of it and stomped on that mother.

"Sailor George was waiting with a rented cabin cruiser forty-five miles from Palm Beach. He had a green tablecloth and a red one. The green one was out, and they made the drop. The survival kit bobbed on the surface, and George swung the boat around." Harry drew a large arch in the air. "George is heading back toward it when this nuclear submarine breaks the surface. George thought a monster was surfacing to eat his boat. The thing looked as big as Stone Mountain. He couldn't see the front and rear at the same time, so he knew it was time to go. He turned that cruiser and ran it flat out. It got so hot, he burned out one of the fucking diesel engines, flat fucking out. He slowed the boat to a crawl to conserve fuel and radioed me and said if I wanted the stuff, I'd have to get it myself. " Tommy could see Harry calculating his reaction. He was controlling the flow, spinning the web, setting the stage.

"The moral of the story—there wasn't anything in the one we dropped. There were two survival kits on board. Quintana switched the life preservers.

"If anyone was following us, they thought it sunk, and it was sunk, whether the sub had come up or not. The package was gone. I have the kind of luck where a nuclear sub picks that spot for a walk-on, adding to the element of doubt. So Ollie went home with his pound and a half. He didn't even think of sharing it with me.

"I met Quintana in Lauderdale and got back on the plane with the life preserver under my arm. I had everyone scared the plane was going to crash into the ocean. The captain came on the intercom and told everyone we weren't even flying over water, but it was a cloudy day, and I had a life preserver with me. What a fucking trip—twenty kilos of pure Colombian snow. Ain't bad." Sneezing in a loud, puttering display, he shook his nose and lips. "I'm ready to do it again, kid. I'm willing to make you my partner."

"Sure, for one hundred thousand dollars. You want me to trust *you* with that kind of bread?" Tommy stood, walked behind the chair, and flexed his back. He couldn't do it. "I trust you only as far as I can throw you."

"It's just money, kid. Can't put too much value on it. It ain't real. Some dude in Washington runs the printing presses, and the government accepts the paper."

"Well, I don't have any printing press, and I don't want any submarines getting into the deal." Their smiles met halfway across the table.

"It's cool, grasshopper. The deal is simple and direct this time. I'm going down to take care of it myself. All the plans are made. I'm offering you an opportunity, a once-in-a-lifetime chance."

"Sure you are. The once-in-a lifetime-sting. What's the plan?"

Harry's eyelids contracted, and his neck retracted into the fat like a giant tortoise. They hadn't discussed details. The fat man did know the big time. If he could meet Dr. Bentley and some of the other people Harry knew. Grasshopper. He was it. There was much to learn. Harry understood impatience and violence.

"I can't tell you everything."

Tommy nodded.

"I have a specially designed bag. Designed by an ex-army intelligence colonel. His son will be carrying it through. Quintana and I will go down and make the score. You'll be there to meet it when it comes in. Simple, direct, uncomplicated."

"Tomorrow, I want to meet these people, then I want to go over some details. The time is getting ripe, and I like my fruit ripe on the vine."

"Yeah, we'll see what the weather's like tomorrow." Harry rose from his chair, and Tommy saw the submarine breaking the surface of the ocean. His gigantic proportions still amazed Tommy. He didn't have any comprehension of how someone could get that large.

"See you in the afternoon, grasshopper." Harry's voice was fatigued, flat. "Don't do all the coke, or you'll never sleep."

The house was asleep except for Tommy. All the shades and drapes were drawn. He had no idea of the time. He didn't live on that basis; it was an irrelevant piece of measurement. Grams, ounces, pounds, and kilos were more significant divisions.

Tommy didn't feel greedy. That gets you in trouble, but to be smart and demand your share—that's where it's at.

Harry kept saying he was the same when he was young. Tommy didn't really believe that it was meant literally, but Harry did know. When people began giving him shit, the rage for being beaten and abused built inside, forcing reason and free will aside. Authority was meant to abuse the innocent and helpless. Obey, obey—that was Father Byrne. Harry was teaching him to control it. Coke could fuel his anger, and it could destroy him.

He was a package of high explosives. Dynamite with the potential for destruction was always present. All he needed was the right blasting cap and boom! The Tampa scene had made him worse.

Both Sal and Mike Broski were skimming reefer and coke. He had become more suspicious. Especially about Sal—it really bothered him. They were almost like brothers sharing the good and the bad, but Sal couldn't handle the pressure. He couldn't see beyond his immediate pleasure. Terry had taken their son, little Sal, and left, causing Sal to fall apart more. With Broski around, Sal's life was following the morning trail to oblivion.

After this deal, he would clear out of Tampa. Move to Atlanta and work out of a real city. The city was larger, faster, classier. Tampa was a dead end; it was time to move on.

Harry had such big plans, which worried Tommy some. Harry was a cool con man, but in Tommy laid a nagging feeling that it was more show than substance. There hadn't been any reason to lie. Harry now talked about the big score and branching out into nightclubs like he did in Miami. Just money—it just takes money. Tommy had some money and was not letting it go.

Sitting in the captain's chair, Tommy put his feet on Harry's table. The furniture designed for the big man dwarfed Tommy's dimensions. He turned the jeweled Enterprise over in his hands. There was a difference in the size of their bodies, but not their minds.

Harry wanted to arrange everything. Tommy wasn't buying it. The deal had to be his too, or he wasn't interested. One hundred grand would do a lot of running. It would come together—Harry had talked long enough. He didn't think Harry wasn't setting him up. He just had to watch carefully—no submarines or Mexican girlfriends. Nice and smooth. The house in Doraville was growing comfortable. Kippi was its light and the link through which Tommy trusted Harry. The child was the universal link.

* * *

He awoke in a cold sweat, his heart pounding against his chest, trying to escape. His childhood nightmare had returned. Tommy shook his head to clear the images from his drowsy mind. The dream was a regular after it first happened. The chill of the sweat and the trembling of his fingers, then he would whimper for his mother, muffling the sound. There was no one to hear him. The priest behind him, pounding away.

Pulling the blanket over his shoulder, Tommy propped himself up on one elbow on the couch. He felt confused and was uncertain of the room he was in. In the dream, he was in a large old bathroom with a white porcelain tub propped up on paw-shaped legs. The sink was made of porcelain, and it was large and pear-shaped. It had two faucets and a black rubber stopper on a chain. It was the bathroom in the rectory. Tommy was hiding from the priest who was teaching him a way to heaven. Tommy could hear the crashing sound of the water when he pulled the chain for the toilet. It cascaded in a deafening but cleansing harmony. He needed to clean the sticky mass in his ass. He needed to be clean.

He stood on a stool and put one knee on the edge of the sink to reach the hot water. When he turned on the water, a white gas, smelling sweet like his grandmother's perfume, billowed out and clung to his head in a cloud. It would clean him, cleanse the filth from his body, his mind, and all the places he had been touched. The sweetness began to choke him as he tried to duck away from the cloud. As he pulled away, he looked up as the cloud spilled over the edge of the sink and onto the black and white tile floor, coming to kill him.

He pulled hard to get away from the cloud and felt himself becoming smaller and smaller. The sink grew into an enormous edifice, a giant rock overhang. The legs of the wooden stool were as thick as he was, and he was shrinking, getting smaller. He cried out, but his voice shrank more quickly than his body before being drowned out by the chatter of crickets.

He tried to wish himself back into the cloud—it had turned black and hung over the sink, casting darkness on the floor. He grabbed the stool with both arms and hung onto the leg with all his strength, determined not to let go. His arms were growing shorter and shorter until that last remnant of his former self was only as wide as the stool leg. His mightiest screams brought no one, stirred nothing, echoed nowhere. The water in which he stood, once insignificant to even a child, was becoming his grave. He felt he would drown. The sink threatened to collapse and bury him in an avalanche of porcelain. He wanted it to; he wanted it to end.

He would drown—a tiny speck of dust that no one would ever find. They wouldn't have to bury him or cry for him. No one would know where he disappeared. He would be too small for Father Byrne's heaven, and the angels would sweep him out with the other dust, and he would fall, forever nauseous from the motion. With one final cry of his insignificant voice, he would awake, dazed, in a cold sweat.

Once, the dream had come frequently, but that was years ago. Tommy rolled to his back and stared at the plaster ceiling. The dream hadn't changed; it was as he remembered it. He wished Sandy was lying beside him, quietly and completely his.

Bolting upright, he shook his head violently from side to side. Had to face the thing, shake it loose so it could go back to where it came from, fight it so it wouldn't want to come again. Flexing his body, he concentrated on a kata movement, trying to clear his mind. Forcing, forcing—fighting the waves at the beach and knowing the battle is unwinnable. The fight is the important, the purifying action. It is the only reason when all else fails.

* * *

"Tommy, Tommy. Wake up." The voice was small like in the dream. Tommy grunted and groped with his hand to shoo it away without opening his eyes. Small hands caught his and began pulling him toward the edge of the sofa. His senses became aware instantly like a switch had been turned, and he pulled the little hands to him.

"Where are you going with me?" he snorted at Kippi, who was now on his stomach.

She giggled and wiggled some to get away, but Tommy had a firm grip on her. "Daddy told me to wake you up," she said defensively. Sitting up, she said in a more defiant, scolding tone, "And I tried calling and calling, but you didn't move. I didn't think I'd ever wake you up."

"What's the matter—doesn't anyone around here ever read you fairy tales?" A puzzled expression darkened her face. "If you read fairy tales, then you wouldn't have had any trouble."

"Why? What would I do?"

"You would have walked quietly over to me," Tommy lowered his voice, causing Kippi to lean closer, "and you would have given me a big kiss." With that, he surprised the child with a kiss to the lips. Her eyes widened, and her expression stayed frozen for seconds.

"Is that how I should do it?"

"With me, that's the only way. The story's called *Sleeping Beauty*." Tommy smiled. "And that's me."

"Oh no, it's not. I know Sleeping Beauty was a girl like me."

"How do you know? You've never read the book."

"I saw the movie on Walt Disney," she protested. "And Sleeping Beauty was a girl, and the Prince was the one who kissed her."

"That's the Walt Disney version. That's not the way it is in the book. Don't forget women's lib. All that's changed." Tommy couldn't contain his laughter. "Now beat it, punk," he lifted her off the sofa as he stood up, "before I beat you."

"You can't catch me," she said and danced toward him, challenging him to move. Tommy faked once, then caught her with a light tap to the cheek.

"That's for nothing. Wait until you do something."

* * *

Harry was propped in his chair at the table. Two boys were sitting to his left, facing the door when Tommy arrived.

"So you finally made it, grasshopper."

"Cut that shit out. I ain't in the mood for it." He wasn't about to let Harry assume the role of boss in front of the two kids. The dream had passed, and he was back in today. Tommy guessed that the slim kid with black curly hair and olive skin was Quintana, and the dimpled, innocent-looking one with blond hair was Boulton.

"At least you got your ass out of bed," Harry continued in a lubricous voice. "It's two o'clock in the afternoon."

"Since when did you learn to tell time?"

"Before you were born, kid."

"Did you learn on an hourglass?" Tommy looked hard at Harry. He wanted no mistake about how this was going to be divided. Though they had talked it out, Harry would agree with anything, then try and change the terms to his advantage as things moved along. Tommy was still holding the diamonds, so he had some collateral. A deal was a deal with Tommy, and Harry had better understand it. "Are you going to make the introductions, or do I have to do it myself?"

Harry waved one arm in a theatrical gesture, "Mr. Boulton, Mr..."

"You're Quintana, and you're Boulton," Tommy said quickly to the two who sat silently at the end of the table. "Don't let this barrel of lard fool you. I'm making the decisions. Wally the Walrus here jumps, flaps his jaws, and toots on his tooter. Don't you?" Tommy smiled at Harry.

"Whatever you say, boss," Harry mocked, and everyone laughed.

Harry's plan was simple. Harry would go to Bogotá, Colombia with Quintana as an interpreter and meet his people for the deal. Boulton would meet them later with false-bottom cases made by his father. Harry would install coke in the concealed pockets, and

Boulton would walk it back through customs in Puerto Rico, where Tommy would be waiting.

Tommy eyed Quintana, who returned the gaze with a trembling eye. He was good looking, with long black curly hair that fell to his collar, offsetting his wide, dark eyes. His hands were long with the slender fingers of a woman. His olive skin added to the sexuality that made him seductive to either sex. Tommy sensed a confused worldliness about Quintana. The body didn't know where he was from—a Puerto Rican who grew up in a Southern white town. He was looking for kicks and running away from something.

Boulton was leaning forward in his chair, obviously wanting attention, but neither Tommy nor Harry had given him recognition. "I'm going to do another line." Boulton's voice was pitched too high for his age. Harry rotated his head toward him and slowly pushed the mirror with the coke to him.

"Sure, kid. Go to it." Harry held out the huge jeweled Enterprise to him. The boy turned it over in his hands with a look of puzzlement. The hollow part of the tube was nearly as large as one of his fingers.

"Do you know what that is, Boulton?" Harry half smiled.

"Some kind of jewelry, like a pendant."

Tommy let out a howl, and Harry rumbled deeply. Quintana joined without conviction; Tommy could see he was puzzled as well.

"You take the narrow end of the hollow one," Harry continued, "and insert it into the end of your prick." Both Boulton and Quintana winced. "Then you drop a spoonful of coke into the other end. It really gets you off."

Tommy was determined to keep a straight face no matter what Harry said. Quintana shook his head in utter disgust. Boulton blanched. "Does it hurt?"

"Maybe a little the first time 'cause you're a virgin. After that, you're like a chick and can't ever get enough." Boulton's dimples changed from white to red. Harry was leaning back in the captain's chair, his head weaving like a snake dancing on his shoulders. He spoke with the detachment of a guru.

"Sigmund Freud, the great psychiatrist, is the one who devised the method. He was really into coke back around nineteen hundred. He told all his friends about it and prescribed it for those people who were hooked on morphine. He invented speedballing." He chuckled. "He'd try anything. He put the coke in suppositories and stuck them up his ass, in his ear. He made a coke eye drop solution. Back in those days, they had drinks made out of coke—like Coca-Cola. Why else do you think it got so popular? They made it right here in Atlanta."

"God, I didn't know that." Boulton shook his head in amazement. Tommy turned his head to the wall to hide his laugh and spotted Elsie. She was wearing a red miniskirt and a tight white t-shirt that fought to contain her breasts. She brushed Harry's neck with her red-tipped fingers before sitting on the edge of the table, allowing the boys a peek at her panties.

"It doesn't matter how you get the coke into your body as long as you get it in. A doctor friend of mine designed this instrument. It allows maximum penetration into the sperm tubes, so the coke gets absorbed right into your balls. There isn't anything like it."

Boulton's eyes were now huge; he was aghast at the idea. Tommy saw the whimpering need for acceptance cross the young brown eyes. Harry was leading with just enough fact and fantasy to bewitch the kid. If Harry could, he'd probably get him to do it.

It was sad to watch how the kid had no sense of getting fucked over. That innocent naiveté, babes of the American middle class, bored to death of the safe, sterile, dull life that their parents so thoughtfully provided.

Harry was a different sort. He got off on the guru trip, the band of followers. Why not? The kids had no direction. They were ignorant because their parents and society wanted them that way. The world is big and full of equally acceptable realities. Harry was just kinkier.

Business transactions never come out even. Someone usually controls more of the profit. There was no tangible way of accounting for taste. This kid might dig the hell out of it. No matter what, Harry was already loving it.

Boulton turned the jeweled instrument over in his hands. He kept testing the weight and looking at the thick silver tube and the bright-jeweled settings.

"Go ahead and try it. The experience is like nothing else you've ever felt." His voice was mellow with a distant reverence for a higher authority. "It's best if you stand up. I'll help you. I'll put the coke in." Harry filled a spoon from his private bottle and snorted it with a loud honk. "This stuff is one hundred percent—the only way to do it.

"Stand up on the chair," he ordered. Boulton looked down at the floor, then back at Harry. Tommy could see that Harry had the boy on the string. Boulton was not aware of the other people in the room.

"Go ahead. You want to." Harry was smooth and soothingly sexual, the resonance of his voice filling the room. Elsie sat silently, looking like she was in awe of Harry. Quintana was wide-eyed and frozen in his chair. His eyes filled with amazement, then terror, as Boulton unzipped his pants. Suddenly, a spark of modesty broke the trance.

"With her here?"

"She's sucked more cocks than you've ever seen. Go ahead."

Boulton let his jeans drop and then his white Jockey sorts. His penis was adolescent pink and shrunken.

"You've got to get it up," Harry said matter-of-factly. "Would you like some help?" Harry turned to Elsie, whose eyes were on the exposed virginal genitals of the boy. Harry tapped her on the arm, and she quickly went around the table. Quintana's mouth opened. Harry gloated with smug assurance as Elsie expertly took the boy's penis into her mouth. With a practiced rhythm, she coaxed the member into a full salute.

Tommy sat back and watched the show. The kids would do as they were told, conditioned like robots not to think.

"Those dogs; I just can't believe them sometimes. Here, look." George burst into the room, holding up a bloody rabbit. Dressed in dirty jeans and a plaid shirt, he looked like Jed Clampett, only he was the same 5XL size as Harry. "I went out back after working on the bike just to check on the girls. And don't you know it, as I came around the side of the house, this here hare tries to make it across the yard. No way. Those dogs were on it in a second. Caught it before the critter could go either way. It died confused. Thing never had a chance." The two German shepherds sat nervously at his feet. They smelled like they had been rolling around in cow shit. George looked at Boulton, standing on the chair with his pants at his ankles. Elsie had her hands on his ass.

A dull but interested look came across George's face. "What's she doing?"

"The kid thought he might have crabs, so Elsie's checking him out," Harry said.

"Crabs? Kid, I hope you don't. When I was in Korea, some oriental meat gave me a case so bad, I nearly volunteered for the front. She looked young but must have had too many pongs. I like the ones with less mileage." He waved the bloody rabbit in his big paws.

"That rabbit looks very dead and chewed up," Harry said, lifting his eyebrows.

"So I got to figuring," George continued, "those little critters are just like humans. All they really want is to eat and fuck. And the way they spread; I knew they were getting plenty of fucking. So I figured I'd introduce them to drinking since I've always found it better than eating. So I started them off at five a.m. with a shot of one-twenty proof corn mash from this still some of the country boys set up. Figured to get 'em right before they went to work for the day. Every time I had a drink, I'd give 'em some lightning. Two days, I went to this two hundred proof grain mountain lightning. Blind a man if he were to drink it straight, but it gives a nice punch to lemonade. One shot of that, every critter there jest plain up died."

"George, you shouldn't have taken it away from the dogs," Harry said as Tommy watched George drop his arm. "You oughta bring the rabbit out and let them eat it. Then they'll like the taste of blood and will want to catch them all the time. You might turn them into real good hunting dogs."

So this would be the crew for Colombia. What a collection. Harry wanted Tommy to trust him with his money—not likely. He would have to be very careful, he decided as he looked around the room.

George beamed. "Yeah, yeah. That's a good idea. Bet they'd be really good hunting dogs too. Wouldn't you girls?" He waved the rabbit at them. "Come on, girls. Look what I've got for you."

Everyone in the room roared in laughter. As it subsided, Harry turned to Tommy. "Sometimes, he's pretty simple. Booze and cunt."

"Just remember the difference." Tommy looked steadily at Harry, feeling uncertain but determined. It was the only way he could be.

Chapter 8

BOGOTÁ WAS LOUD, DIRTY, AND congested. The high altitude and thick brown pollution gave Tommy a heady feeling—light and spacey, like sniffing glue—soon after arrival. He wasn't letting Harry go alone with his money, so he was reading up about the city. It was placed between two mountain ranges at 8,000 feet and had been founded in 1538 by Sebastián de Belalcázar. It was rich in history and in blood, a city cast in the tradition of European cities. No American city had such a history of violence. A city of turmoil and contrast, there were struggling entrepreneurs, a ruling elite, and human excess all merged into a city of two million people, where the dogs fight with the Indians for survival.

As he walked toward customs, Tommy felt a twinge of nervousness race along his spine. He tried to ignore it. He had to be cool. He was dressed in a tailored black suit, a light blue shirt that was open at the neck, and sunglasses. He wasn't wearing his spoon—no need to advertise.

Harry's plan sounded pretty good. All except one part. There was no way he was allowing his money to leave the States with Harry. No way. So he went along and would see a foreign country for the first time.

On the other side of the turnstile barrier that separated him from the country, a small, greasy-haired boy with wide, dark eyes had his nose pressed up against the railing. Suddenly the boy's eyes sparked as he shouted, "Mama, Mama" to the middle-aged woman behind Tommy.

An expression of relief crossed the woman's lined face as the boy darted through the fence and hugged her bosom. The guard smiled.

Harry was carrying half the money. Tommy was carrying twenty thousand dollars. Neither of them had any traveler's checks.

Harry had made reservations at the Hotel Tequendama, which was supposed to be the best hotel in the city. Harry was with Elsie and Kippi. Tommy traveled alone. Boulton was arriving in three days for a two-day stopover with a Georgia Baptist tour group.

Tommy watched the customs man rummaging through the bags of a family who was in line in front of him. Everyone was arguing and shouting. The language sounded incredibly fast. Tommy understood nothing and hid behind his shades. Alone, he was detached from all that was around him. Harry was already through customs and had disappeared into the terminal. Lines of chattering people were still grabbing and jostling bags at the customs table, where heated discussions raged.

In this world, Tommy was a stranger. In the States, he was an outsider because he chose to do as he wanted. That was always his decision, and it was enough to set him apart. He struggled to keep going, to keep believing in himself. There was no way he could avoid it. As an altar boy, the world didn't give a fuck about him—he was nobody, and he knew it. Given a chance, social justice would screw him to the wall. Anyone with any sense knew it too. He was on the outside because he refused to follow the dumb-ass rules and rulers. He was dangerous because he was willing to fight for his own freedom.

As he realized he wasn't going to talk himself out of anything here, a feeling of loss edged along his lower ribs. This was big time. They had a plan and a way to get out. Tommy would swim home if he had to.

The customs man said something, but Tommy had no idea what. A sense of panic began filling his lungs. He shook his head. "I don't understand." The man said several things before finally hitting the word *turistica*.

"Yeah*, tourist*." Tommy nodded, and the customs man quickly stamped the passport without looking inside his bags. A small, dark-skinned porter with a red cap was next to him immediately.

"Señor," he said, picking up the bags, "taxi?"

Tommy wondered how the good ladies of DeKalb County would like the ferocity of Colombian life. He had read that after Simón Bolívar, the George Washington of South America, freed the country in 1819, the winners broke into factions and drove Bolívar out. Since its creation, Colombians had fought civil wars nearly every twenty years. And the civil wars weren't over yet. Tommy realized it when he saw the truckload of combat troops combing the national park in the center of the city. He couldn't tell if they were doing maneuvers or searching for someone. He didn't want to find out.

Harry and his entourage settled into a suite on the nineteenth floor of the Hotel Tequendama. Quintana and George, who had arrived on an earlier flight, were seated in two pale green chairs when Tommy entered.

"Hey kid, what's happening? How does it feel to be abroad?" Harry laughed at the pun, and everyone joined in. Harry filled the sofa, his loud Hawaiian shirt open to his belly. "We is here."

"You bet your ass, fat man." Tommy smiled confidently. He was glad to be in Bogotá. It was a trip, a different country, a different head. The smells were strange, intriguing. The noise was a new, rhythmic music. He had made it. Customs was nothing. He just hoped it would be that easy going the other way.

The taxi ride into the city had been frantic, the traffic thick. Horns screamed. Tires screeched. When he opened the window, the automobile fumes slapped him in the face. And there were policemen—many police of different sorts. Some had sticks, some just pistols, but what disturbed Tommy was that many of the cops were armed with M-16s.

Walking over to the window, Tommy looked toward Monserrate, which was in the eastern section of Bogotá. There was what looked like a football stadium below, but its shape was odd.

"Hey, what's that big stadium over there?"

"Which one?" Quintana replied, coming over to the window.

"There." Tommy pointed.

"That's the Plaza de Toros, where they have the bullfights."

"Really?"

"*Si.*"

"Out of sight. I have to go to one of them. Real bullfights." Yeah. To stand up and challenge a bull with just a sword and a cape. A picture flashed through Tommy's mind of himself as a matador and Harry as the bull.

The city spread from downtown into a cloud of smog. Most of the world's supply of cocaine came through Bogotá, and many people were getting rich on the trade. Very rich. It was a duty to take the opportunity when it presented itself. Nothing happens in life; it is caused.

The room felt like a Holiday Inn room except that the television was black and white. This was the best.

He was a criminal now. Right, and Nixon became the president. Tommy would always be an outlaw. A large black cockroach emerged from behind a fine champagne bottle. From Thunderbird to Dom *Pérignon*. Blond Colombian pot to pure Colombian lady, more valuable than gold. The cock and the roach—no wonder society liked hard drugs, making kids into that ugly, obnoxious insect.

Kippi came to the window beside him, looking at the insect. "Ooh, it's dead, isn't it?"

"Yes," Tommy said as he smashed it.

"Good. I don't like them. What's that, Tommy?" she asked, pointing to the arena.

"That's where they have bullfights."

"Oh." She was silent. "They have bulls fight each other there?"

Tommy smiled at the idea. Not any more absurd than having a man fight a bull or two gladiators fighting. "No, a guy called a matador fights the bull. He usually kills the bull."

"Oh." Her voice dropped. "Why don't they let the bulls fight each other?"

"The bulls are too smart for that. They'd just stand around and talk about it."

She looked at him, then back at the stadium. "I guess I'd do the same thing if I was a bull."

"You're right." There were too many ways you can get fucked over, though. Got to be careful, got to be cool.

* * *

On the second day, Quintana suggested that they change hotels. "This one isn't cool, Harry," he said. Tommy thought he looked more at ease in Bogotá than he did in Atlanta. He was taller than the average Colombian and not addicted to the Brylcreem look.

"No one knows we're here," Harry said. He was now in repose on the green couch in the living room of the suite. Tommy could see that Harry didn't want to move. Last night, Quintana had scored some coke, and Harry was enjoying it. But that wasn't the reason they were here. The Tequendama wasn't cool. He had to agree with Quintana—he had been offered coke three times in the lobby and on the street in front. If the Colombians offered it to every gringo they saw, the cops had to be keeping an eye on the place. This was where the amateurs stayed.

"I think we should move too," Tommy said.

"There's no reason. We're fine here." Harry snorted as he did another hit of coke. "No one knows we're here."

"Wrong. Didn't you see the way everyone turned when you walked through the lobby?" Quintana asked. "They know the big gringo, and the police, they are watching too. My contact said this was a bad place. Too many police."

"What does he know?" Harry snorted again.

"I like this room, and I don't think there is any reason to move either," Elsie said. She was sitting on a chair, reading a comic book.

Quintana looked frustrated as he walked through the door into the adjoining room. Tommy followed.

"What's the story?" Tommy asked. "What exactly did the guy say about this hotel?"

Quintana threw his head back in relief now that Tommy was paying attention.

"He said this place wasn't good. There are too many police here."

"Did he seem nervous? Will he bring the stuff here?"

"No. Tommy, I don't think he will. He didn't want to give me the taste the first time. He said it was bad to stay in the hotel. Sometimes the police just come up into your room. They don't need warrants here."

It was time to move. If the place wasn't cool, Tommy didn't want to be there. Who could he trust? That was the major question. He had heard stories about the Colombians who would sell you coke, then sell the information to the police, who would arrest you, sell the first dudes their coke back, and then make you pay out the ass to get out of jail. Everyone made money but you.

Harry didn't want to move because he didn't like moving. It was that simple. Tommy wasn't going to leave *his* ass exposed. Harry was going to come down and do this deal alone? Right.

"Do you know of another place that isn't so hot?"

"Yes. He told me about a hotel called Cardinal; it's on the other side of the city. He said there's never police there."

"How much is Harry paying you?"

Quintana looked at the floor. "Five thousand."

"We make it through, I'll double it. Go get us some rooms there." Tommy handed Quintana four thousand pesos. "Bring the keys back here. Then we'll leave in small groups."

"Yeah, right, Tommy. Good plan." Quintana beamed. He sat back in his chair, and Tommy could see the sense of importance growing in him, until his whole being took on that aura of importance that little people needed.

"I didn't give you the money to fondle. If this place is hot, I want to move *now*."

Quintana's face dropped a second, but then he got up quickly. "*Si*, you're right, Tommy. I'll be back quick."

"Yeah, good." He nodded to Quintana, acknowledging his confidence that the job would get done correctly and quickly. He was going to have to keep a close eye on everything. Harry wasn't looking at what might and could go wrong. Since he got the first bag of coke, he hadn't been looking at anything. Tommy was uneasy; the stakes were too high. He didn't want to make a mistake that would cost him years of his life or get him killed.

The rest of the plan was unclear. Harry had told him the basics, but not all the details. Boulton was to arrive soon with the case, which had a false bottom. He hadn't seen it yet. Customs could tell a false-bottom case right away, couldn't they?

The deal wasn't going like it was supposed to. Harry wasn't all there; nothing was ready. Quintana was making street connections. Harry didn't have anything set up. Nervous, Tommy realized he didn't have a pistol. And the cops carried M-16s. Not much of a battle. It was the Colombians who worried him. He had packed and unpacked the Smith & Wesson twice before deciding not to bring it. With that much cash, the gun was too much risk. He didn't know Colombian customs. Now he wished he had brought it.

Next time, he wouldn't trust Harry as much. Now, though, there were too many things to think about. From here on, he couldn't leave anything to chance.

* * *

By ten o'clock that evening, they were all installed in the Hotel Cardinal, a small, family-run building on the other side of the city. They had arrived separately, with Harry and Elsie taking the only suite on the second floor. George and Kippi were next door. Tommy and Quintana were on the third floor, in front, where Tommy could watch the street. The money was still divided. Harry wanted the connection to come to the hotel. The high altitude and coke had reduced Harry to low gear.

Tommy sent Quintana to meet the Colombian and bring him back to the hotel. This way, Quintana would know where the dude hung out if anything went wrong. The police thing at the Tequendama still had him edgy. If he knew what he knew now… There wasn't time to think. Stupid little things can fuck up the whole deal. Were they hot? Was Harry hot? Getting room service from a shady Colombian? In this business, there was a certain amount of trust necessary, like in combat. There are enough enemies around so that you *have to* trust your so-called friends. Take it or leave it; there was no other way.

"That was a dumb mistake to have us in that fucking hotel," Tommy said, his voice tense. Harry sat uncomfortably on the small bed.

"It isn't anything important. We're just more American tourists. Who knows anything different?"

"Do you think anyone could forget you?"

Harry smiled, but Tommy could see he was self-conscious. Harry liked to think he wasn't bizarre, but he was. He used it to his advantage most of the time, but this wasn't one of those times.

"Grasshopper, be patient. I know what I'm doing."

"The hell you do. Since we've been here, you haven't done a damn thing but snort coke. I'm here to make money, not fuck around. You do understand that."

Harry looked at him with a cold eye. "I *have* done this before, and it has worked. If you could do it yourself, I'm sure you would. But you can't. I've set the whole thing up, and it's working beautifully so far. Right?" His motions were languid but controlled. He wasn't as fucked up as he was the day before when he had done five grams of coke.

"When is the dude coming with the stuff? Do you know how long of a ride it is from across town?"

"It won't take long."

"He's bringing the stuff or just another sample?" Tommy tapped his fingers on the table. "And if it's good, we're taking it, right?'

"Yeah." Harry moved as if he heard something.

"Don't worry. I told George to watch the front of the hotel from his window. He'll call when they pull up." Tommy shifted the fourteen-inch switchblade that he had bought with Quintana's help. It was on his hip, the same place he wore the Smith & Wesson.

He would have felt safer having a gun. The difficulty of the language caused Tommy to feel awkward and not recognize his normal self. He wondered if it was affecting his judgment. Probably not, but he couldn't be certain. Nothing was certain, but then again, that's where the profit was.

Harry seemed unconcerned about getting ripped off down here. He acted like it was a law-abiding country. If the cops needed to carry M-16s to enforce the law, he could imagine what firepower the criminals had. Quintana and Tommy had seen truckloads of troops patrolling the city at night.

Knocking on the door, George called, "They're here."

"Keep awake and watching," Tommy said through the thin door. He turned to Harry. "I'll be in the bathroom until we know it's cool."

Harry nodded. "Don't get jumpy on me."

Harry said fifteen thousand a kilo for pure. Good price.

The country was beginning to make Tommy nervous and edgy. Harry's lack of planning compounded the uncertainty. Tommy wanted to get it over with and back to the States. He hated his inability to understand the language.

There was a knock on the door. Tommy and Harry exchanged glances. He slid into the bathroom, keeping the door open a crack.

Harry bellowed, "Come in."

Quintana opened the door and walked in. Behind him were two Colombians in their early twenties. Harry was sitting on the bed, and he looked up at them slowly. He marked the expression of surprise in their eyes when they saw his size.

"Come in and close the door," Harry commanded. Quintana ushered the two into the room.

The Colombians spoke quietly to each other. One was a darkskinned Indian with oval eyes and straight black hair. He looked fierce and had a scar on the left side of his neck that extended into his shirt. The other was a little shorter and was lighter in complexion and overweight. They walked forward to Harry and sat on the other bed.

Tommy stepped from the bathroom and locked the door to the room. The Colombians turned quickly at the sound of the latch. Tommy eyed each carefully, and they returned in kind.

The Indian bristled like a dog whose territory was invaded. Tommy was unexpected and had crept up on them with stealth. Their suspicion was evident. Tommy enjoyed having the edge—a demonstration in case anyone had any notions.

Walking with careful karate steps, Tommy skated across the floor like Castadena in power gear. His eyes never left the Indian. The other Colombian just smiled. Harry had narrowed his eyes behind his upraised cheeks.

"*Buenos dias*" Tommy said as he stopped at the foot of the beds.

"*Buenos dias*," the chubby one said. The Indian only nodded.

"Who are they?" Tommy asked Quintana.

"He is Jose," he said, pointing to the chubby one. "And he is Rodrigo." The Indian smiled. His teeth were black and rotten.

"Let's see what they have," Harry said impatiently. He cleared the table next to his bed and placed a large mirror on it.

Quintana asked, and the Indian produced a paper bag from his shirt. The coke was inside in a plastic bag. The Indian also produced a large knife from inside his shirt and quickly opened the plastic bag and set it on the mirror. The Indian looked practiced with the blade.

"It's very good," Jose said.

"We'll see," Harry said, spooning out the largest rock in the bag. Using a razor blade, he intently chopped the solid piece of cocaine into particles. He did it with the affection of a cook, preparing a meal.

"How much for this?" Tommy asked.

"Fifteen a gram," Jose said.

"What?"

"Fifteen dollars a gram," Quintana said.

Tommy thought for a moment. Thirty grams to a Colombian ounce, so $450 for an ounce and a kilo is one thousand grams, so fifteen grand for a kilo. The price was right.

Harry picked up the Enterprise snorter, and the two Colombians sat up with interest. "You like this, huh?" Harry asked.

"*Si*. It is very nice," Jose said.

Harry made a line with the coke the length of the mirror, which was nearly twenty-four inches long. He exhaled slightly then, lowering his head like a charging bull, he inhaled the entire line. The Colombians' mouths fell slightly open. Harry sat back against the bedpost, his face showing no expression. He put his large thumb to his left nostril and inhaled with a bellow. Then he rolled the fat on his nose and puckered his lips.

"It is good, no?" Jose beamed.

"It's not bad," Harry conceded.

Tommy got up and went to the table to examine the coke. Harry had been snorting so much that he didn't have the sense to tell. Tommy wasn't taking any chances of getting burned. There was always the possibility, but he was going to minimize it. Looking at the Colombians, they seemed on the level. Why not? They would make good money on this deal, and if it worked right, they could make more. That's why everyone was in it. He had to be careful because it was their country. They knew it, and he was the stranger.

"How good is it?" Tommy motioned to Jose.

The Indian said a few short words, looked at Tommy, pointed to the coke, and said a few more phrases.

"He said his cousin made it himself up in the mountains. He says that it is all pure, the best there is."

Tommy nodded, went to the table, and touched his finger to the white powder. He rubbed it gently on his gums, which began numbing immediately. Cocaine was a good anesthetic. He took Harry's razor and separated a small pile of coke into a corner of the mirror. Then he pricked his pinky with the blade. A drop of blood appeared, and Tommy dropped it on the coke. The coke slowly turned bright red. Tommy was pleased. Coke is a coagulant when it is close to pure. It turns a bright red; if it's too dark, it can cause a blood clot to the heart. Tommy had seen junkies run it into their veins to test it. Stupid. If it's bad shit, it's too late once it's in. He preferred letting his blood come out to meet the southern snow.

The Colombians watched with interest. Tommy was certain to let them know that he knew what he was doing. If they don't think they can beat you, they won't even bother trying. It saves time and hassle. Always stay on guard.

"You and your technical shit," Harry said. "It's good. My nose can tell." He reached for the razor, but Tommy held it away. He said quietly, "Later."

Harry's face froze, and his eyebrows drew narrow around his massive nose.

"How much is here?" Tommy nodded to the bag.

"Fifteen grams."

"We want two kilos. Today." Tommy looked at Jose to make sure he understood. Quintana translated anyhow.

"*Si*. It is possible," Jose said. "We want dollars."

"Yeah, you'll see dollars when we see the coke."

"Please, *señor*, it's toot. Other word very bad."

Tommy understood and nodded in agreement. "Tonight?"

"It is possible."

The two got up, and the Indian began to reach for the coke on the table.

"Leave that here," Harry said. "Then we know you are coming back."

The Indian looked at Quintana, smiled his rotten smile at the fat man, and said something to Quintana as he turned to leave.

"What did he say?" Harry demanded.

"He said the big one has a nose for it," Quintana said.

Tommy unlocked the door. "Tell them to call when it's arranged. Set a place to meet them. Make it public. Then you can bring them back here. Understood?"

Quintana nodded and spoke to the Colombians. "They understand."

"*Fresco*," Tommy said to the Indian. He had learned the word for *everything's cool* earlier, and it was useful.

"*Si, fresco*." The Indian eyed Tommy as he backed out through the door.

For the next four hours, they waited. Tommy was drinking a Coca-Cola. He wanted to be sharp. Harry wanted more coke, but Tommy brought it back to his room. He didn't need the big man strung out at this point. He had George keep watch from Harry's room. Quintana was with him. Elsie and Kippi were out of the way in George's room. The waiting was the worst. Tommy looked for an escape route if it was a rip-off. He had counted the money again. Twenty thousand was with Harry. He had the other twenty. He paced.

The call came, and Quintana left to meet the Colombians. Tommy wanted to make certain that only two came—he could handle two. Were they on the level? Distrust kept him alive. He watched from the window until the car pulled up, and he could see the Colombians exit. He sprinted downstairs to Harry's room.

"George, take the back stairs and come around the front of the building and wait. If anything goes wrong, you can grab them before they get into the car." Harry was still seated on the bed when the two Colombians returned. Tommy stayed near the bathroom until they sat, and he locked the door.

The Indian reached under his poncho and produced a large knitted bag. "Dollars," he said. Harry leaned forward and pulled a flight bag from under the bed. He counted out the packs of cash. "Fourteen, Fifteen. Let's see it."

The Indian produced one compressed bag of white powder. Tommy snapped the switchblade open, catching everyone's attention, and cut a small slit in the bag, extracting enough sample to blood test. It was bright red. He then produced the second bag of cash, and they repeated the process, with Jose counting the money. Tommy kept listening for footsteps or car doors. He didn't know where he was, but he felt he wasn't secure.

The Indian's eyes constantly scanned the room as if the jungle would come alive. The Indian produced two more bags, and Tommy gave him the cash. After counting it, he stuffed the money into the knitted bag, and it disappeared under the poncho. Everyone stood, and Tommy unlocked the door. There was less suspicion in the Indian's eyes. Tommy thought it was respect, but he wasn't certain. The cultural difference was too hard to read. He had to keep it together. Now, if only they don't go to the police.

"I'll take the coke to my room since they know you are here," Tommy said, reaching for the two bags.

"It stays right here," Harry said, narrowing his eyes into reptilian slits.

"No way. If they're coming back, they'll come right here."

"It's staying here," Harry repeated, his voice deepening.

"Fuck you. I'll take my half." Tommy moved to take one bag.

"All of it stays." Harry moved to his feet as George entered the room. Tommy was pissed. He wasn't going to take orders.

"Get out of my way," he said, his voice carrying the words like small daggers. He reached for the bag, but Harry clamped his giant paw over his hand, looking him in the eye.

"Don't do something stupid, grasshopper."

"Fuck you," Tommy said, raising his arm violently against Harry's thumb, freeing his arm. "I'll take what's mine."

"It stays here. It's yours when we get it back to the States." Harry moved close to Tommy, his face inches away, his lizard tongue darting between his fat lips. "Now, go to your room."

"Fuck you," Tommy said, pushing Harry's chest but not moving him. He stepped back into fighting position, but George pinned him in his thick arms.

"Let me go, you ape," Tommy said, stamping his right heel into George's instep, creating a howl of pain and his release. Spinning to face George, he launched a front kick, but he was too close for it to do damage. George bull rushed him to the wall like a defensive lineman, flattening him against the cheap sheetrock. The force knocked some of the wind out of Tommy. George followed with two powerful gut punches, and Tommy sank to his knees.

"Now go to your room. I'll take care of the merchandise till tomorrow," Harry said as George pushed Tommy to the door.

"You motherfucker," Tommy said, feeling the bruise spreading across his ribs. It wasn't over. If he had his pistol, it would be. The gorilla had surprised him; it wouldn't happen again. And Harry, he would deal with Harry. But not now. He stumbled up the steps, options turning over in his mind until he lay in his bed. There would be time.

* * *

The next day, Boulton arrived with the First Calvary Baptist mission group. They were on a weeklong tour of missions in Lima and Bogotá before returning home via Puerto Rico.

The coke was good. Harry packed the bags with the skill of a surgeon. Now it was time. Tommy would have to wait and trust. There was nothing more he could do. Frightened and elated, he was certain they had it together. He would know in San Juan. Then he would deal with Harry.

Chapter 9

SANDY'S ANGER SUBSIDED AFTER THE first day Tommy went away. She had a sense of loss when she woke alone. She shook it away, but it returned when she watched television alone that night. The next morning, she was better. She was pissed at being treated like a thing—a chair or the bed. Tommy didn't tell her anything. He only said, "I'm going away. I'll be back in a week." Kippi told her they were going to Colombia.

Love was like that, and she was afraid for Tommy. They were going to smuggle; she was sure of it. Harry and Tommy were doing it. She was responsible for introducing him to Harry.

She brushed her hair and walked from the vanity to the square bedroom. The sun bathed her in reflected light off the bright yellow sheets. Coke, her cat, scampered into the closet, her furry impression still on Sandy's pillow.

"Coke, tttt-tttt." She sat her naked body on the thick shag carpet and dragged her long hair along the floor. The cat looked once, then scampered playfully after it. If he had invited her, would she have gone? Yes, yes, she wanted to say, but she couldn't be certain. If Tommy had just asked her, she would have gone. They would have looked better as a young couple.

She felt a wave of guilt swallow her in a heavy gulp, stripping her of her will, her decisiveness, and she fell to the floor. Would she have gone? Did she know? Again and again, she wanted to say yes, but she was afraid it was a lie. There wasn't an answer because there wasn't the question, but if… Was it her fault if he got caught in Colombia? What would she do? Call her father at the bank? Fat chance.

Her head was still bobbing from the hash she had just smoked. The guilt was present, coming from her mother's Presbyterian meddling, always wanting to know. Guilt served like ice cream in the summer.

Grabbing the cat's white fur behind the neck, Sandy lifted it to her face. The cat sniffed at her nose, then licked it. Jennifer, her friend, had gladly taken the cat while she was in Atlanta. It was nice to have her back for now.

"Thanks, Coke. I needed that." She swung the animal in her cradled arms. Coke first rumbled, then broke into an easy, fluid purr. Sandy sat up and leaned back against the bed, the cat's long white fur covering her breasts. The guilt was more of an afterthought. Breaking away didn't come if she was around any of that safety. Her father was the orderly bank executive, clean-cut, decisive, cold. He measured people according to his standards of success. She never felt inclined to enforce those standards, and he constantly scolded her for it. Why bother? He was always on business trips.

As she stroked the Persian across its stomach, Coke extended her legs until they were straight. Sandy's lips turned up in a smile, then went limp. Sandy wanted to be with Tommy. Yet she was too afraid of what might happen. Guns were too loud. They weren't television guns. The smell of real gunpowder was acrid.

For the deal in Gainesville, he had trusted her enough. Why not in Colombia? Harry was much older than Tommy. He would let Tommy take all the chances. And she didn't know what was happening. That just got her pissed off all over again. Damn.

Could she trust Harry? He used people. Harry was smart. As smart as her father? There wouldn't be any problems. Why wouldn't Tommy let her come? He didn't care. Was he using her? Her thoughts ran through the fears like a stick on a picket fence until they blurred. She was going to shake free, free of the thoughts, free of him. Time to figure a way to get it out and gone. Was he coming back, or would he get busted there? She couldn't live like this.

Placing the cat on the bed, she went into the living room. Putting on Steely Dan, she hung limply at the waist, allowing her hair to fall forward. She emerged from the position like a blooming flower and danced to the rhythmic music in twirls and sweeps. Her body needed to let go. That was freedom. Swirling in a moment of delight, stepping and spinning with the precision of perfect control and perfect abandon. Her feet touched the rug. It had the softness of the cat as she propelled herself wildly around the room, her hair trailing like a tail. Her blood oxidized with her brain, bringing headiness beyond the hash. Her hunger had to be satisfied. Why was Tommy so self-sufficient? Was he ever weak? He didn't always seem real, yet he touched her.

Throwing her hair over her shoulder, she thrust her hips forward aggressively. She danced at an imaginary audience of men. She spun the erotic dance to tease them, knowing that none would ever touch her. Falling to her knees, she spread her legs and fluidly caressed the inside of her thighs, finally dipping her index finger into her moistened vagina. Holding it up in front of her, she beckoned the ghostly hordes; she smiled in complete security, smiled at their salivating desperation, and took the taste herself. It was the helpless look in their eyes, the vulnerability that fascinated her. Salacious, whining animals from afar, coarse but terrified of her up close. Where did Tommy come from? What did he want? There was a shudder of uncertainty as if the hands of those faces were ants crawling across her skin. Her body shuddered and the reverie crashed at the ringing of the phone.

"Is Tommy gone? Are you alone?" Jennifer, her friend, spoke gaily. "What are you doing now?"

"I'm just hanging out, practicing to be a topless dancer. I hear the money is great." They both laughed, having discussed the possibilities of trying it in the past. Then the fantasies began. "Tommy left two days ago. He should be getting back soon."

"Well, if he isn't around, you might as well enjoy yourself. Come on over; we'll play tonight. Go out catting."

Her first impulse was to resist the invitation. Why? She had a life. Fuck Tommy and his macho bullshit. She was going out with Jennifer to see what was available.

"Yeah, sure. I've got some blow, so we're in gear." She laughed at her mocking of Tommy's rhythm, surprised at the intensity of her delight. "It's only seven. I'll be over in a while."

The apartment felt strange to her. It had been months since she had been back to Tampa. The gypsy life was hers now, moving from city to city.

Jennifer's greeting was sassy and effervescent—the out-of-control feeling when all games were fair to play. Stepping out, catting around town, chasing and being chased. A feeling her mother never had or ever would. It was sad in some ways, never experiencing the hilarity of life.

After smoking a joint, they went to the Connection. It was still early, and the bar was only half-full.

"Evening, beautiful ladies. Getting an early start on your evening?" Hank, the manager, was behind the bar.

"The evening's already begun, big boy," Jennifer said with a trace of glee. The girls smiled secretly at each other and giggled. Hank looked perplexed and gave up trying to understand.

"What can I get you, Sandy?"

"Black Russian and a Tequila Sunrise," Sandy said quickly. So many people recognized her because of Tommy.

Jennifer wore her high school queen look of detachment and disappointment. Hank was still looking at Sandy's white silk halter, which perfectly outlined her breasts.

"Jennifer, there's one for you." Sandy pointed with her head to a tall blond surfer type. His hair was long and straight, his chest tapering to a smooth stomach. Jennifer smiled.

"You know my type. Surfers are usually good fucks—lots of body control—but they can't talk. I went out with a guy from Daytona for three months. As soon as we saw each other, we'd strip and fuck for a half hour. Then we'd smoke some grass, suck for another hour, then fuck again. He'd usually leave or put on some headphones and listen to surfing music. I would get high or water ski—what a life. It ended when his surfboard gave him a hernia. If he wasn't good in bed, he wasn't good for anything." Both of them laughed easily. Hank returned with the drinks.

"Put them on the tab," Sandy said, her laughter subsiding. It was good to be loose. "And put five on for yourself."

"I thank you, ma'am." Hank bowed slightly and smiled at her.

She could see longing in his eyes. Most of Tommy's friends looked her over, yet with a certain amount of respect. "Jennifer, how do you get yourself involved with these losers? You pick 'em just for their bodies?"

"None of them have money, so the body better be good. I don't know where all the good men are these days." Jennifer was nearly two inches taller than Sandy. Her light hair was thick and windblown on her shoulders. With a light complexion turned a roasted almond, her freckles tinged her face with innocence. "Don't talk to me, sweetheart. You were going to marry that guy from Emory Med School."

"No, I wasn't. My parents wanted me to—that's as far as it got. Nothing more." Actually, Sandy had wanted to get married. Looking back, it was the desire to get away from home that made her so desperate. High school seniors should be forbidden to get married. Then came Tampa.

"You're not doing bad. Tommy doesn't beat up on you, and he doesn't want a mother."

"He's all man with me." She smiled coyly.

"I hear you. But he's still a man." Jennifer gave a disgusted look, then cracked up in laughter. Then she quieted quickly. "Here comes surfer boy. Act mature."

The blond boy walked slowly around the bar, his eyes on Sandy, who didn't return the look. Jennifer sipped her Sunrise with anticipation.

He placed his freckled blond arm on the bar between them. "Gimme a Bud," he shouted. Hank was talking to a full-breasted girl wearing a yellow Harley Davidson t-shirt.

"How do you get a beer around here?" The surfer leaned over to Sandy, trying to look down her halter.

"Try talking to the bartender." Her voice was playful. Maybe a fling would do her good—get her mind off the danger Tommy was in. "Hank, get this guy a drink," she shouted.

The surfer took the beer. "You're a woman of influence."

"I know my way around." Sandy arched her back.

"You come here often?" he asked.

Oh, God, how lame. Sandy realized this wasn't going to happen. Jennifer saw the opening and quickly had control of the situation as she led the surfer to the dance floor. Sandy felt a sense of relief, but the dread crept back in. She centered her attention on the stained glass that separated the sides of the bar.

A thin, straight-haired girl slid into the chair next to Sandy. Her face was shadowed with gauntness, giving her a foreign appearance. Thickly clad in beads and bracelets, she moved like a dancer. A wide pink and black scarf was tied on her head, falling with her dark hair to her shoulders. On her right hand were a large opal ring and several small gold ones. On her left, she wore turquoise and silver.

After ordering an anisette and looking over the bar, the girl turned to Sandy, eyeing her slowly. "Your troubles won't be for long," she said confidently in a deep, sexy voice.

"What makes you think I have trouble?" Sandy leaned a little closer. She didn't know she was showing that she couldn't stop thinking about Tommy in Colombia. She forced her country club smile on her face.

"I can see these kinds of things. Your conflicts will soon be resolved. My name is Carla."

"I'm Sandy." She felt a bit shy revealing herself quickly, though the trust felt strong and genuine.

"When were you born?"

"March."

"An Aries? Your face shows fire, and so does the mood you're in. You will always have a strong will and strong desires. It is destined for you, and there's nothing you can do to change it. You must accept your fate as it has been written."

"What fate? I'm not following you." There was a huskiness to Carla's voice that didn't fit with her thin face or body. Carla seemed possessed by another being, and its voice was in control. Sandy felt a female bond and a sense of the outrageous.

Crossing her right leg over her left, Carla spun the barstool around to look at the rest of the crowd. Her long skirt fell open, revealing a tattoo on her thigh of two female figures holding hands wrapped by two snakes. There was a bed of flowers framing the scene. Sandy's mouth opened in surprise. The green snakes were almost docile in appearance and had glassy eyes. Each long, narrow, female figure was stepping forward, and their fingers met in a bridge between them. Carla followed Sandy's eyes.

"They're the twins: pleasure and pain. While the snakes fertilize the soil for the flowers, the twins express the differences we all have. In conjunction, there is harmony. That is why they smile—the symmetry of life, the focal point of balance is the point where their fingers meet. The edges constantly change, but the point can always be found." Carla sighed for a moment. "The trouble is, the search continues forever."

The figures came to life as Carla flexed her leg, having them dance on her skin. Her soft, white flesh focused attention on the colors of the tattoo.

"Did it hurt?" Sandy asked.

"Hurt? Life always hurts; can't avoid it. Oh, this? No. An old fortuneteller down near the docks did it. It wasn't expensive, either. Here." She took Sandy's hand and brought it to her thigh. "See, it feels like regular flesh, but it tells a story. Now I live in the artist colony at Cassadaga. You want to meet her? She's an old lady who traveled all around the Caribbean and even went to Samoa, where she learned tattooing. She reads Tarot and palms. Do you have a car? It's only a few minutes away."

Sandy was trying to get a hold of everything. The girl was exotic, something new. The exquisite detail of the tattoo fascinated her, and her frankness was intriguing. Carla's nails were long and polished red; her lipstick was thick red. In the long, dark gaze she gave Sandy was an earthen security of knowing and a supernatural ability to foresee.

How was she able to move with the freedom of spirit? Sandy was apprehensive of going with her, with the tattooed woman. The fear tugged at her throat until she answered, "I can't. I'm with a friend."

"The blond." Carla gestured to Jennifer, dancing with the surfer. Sandy nodded in surprise—Carla knew too much. "Wait here a minute." Carla snaked onto the dance floor in languid, exotic movements but in time to the Southern rock. She danced up to Jennifer, and after some animated words and laughter, Carla returned.

"It's all set. Jennifer will stay here until you get back, or she will get a ride. So don't worry. See how easy life is to settle? Most problems are the same. Come on; I think you'll find Madame Doucard fascinating." Her giggle filled Sandy with undisguised girlhood glee. It felt so good to let go of the strings that held everything in place. She could stop worrying about Tommy for a few hours.

* * *

Madame Doucard's parlor was furnished in thick, overstuffed furniture from the early part of the century. A salmon and violet pattern covered the short black couch. A thick curtain of blood red velvet hung from the doorway, obscuring any view into the rest of the house. Carla had disappeared behind the curtain, leaving Sandy alone with her unease in the Gothic surroundings. A copper-colored pole lamp with a Tiffany-type shade cast a singular shadow from the illuminated light in its base. The house smelled of incense and garlic. On the mantle were delicately painted Oriental vases and a crystal unicorn. One round wooden table surrounded by four chairs dominated the center of the room. It was covered with a dark red material. She felt she was in a foreign country just like Tommy, and maybe in some danger.

"Welcome, my dear. Sit and be comfortable," Madame Doucard, a plump woman in her early seventies, said, entering slowly through the curtains. Carla entered behind her. The woman's face was lean and wrinkled, with angular features that were incongruous with the round lines of the rest of her body. Large gold earrings hung to her shoulders against grey hair that was brushed back from the front. Her white tunic blouse was tied at the waist with a thick sash of red velvet. Her long, pleated skirt was the same blood red as the curtains.

Sandy didn't move, afraid to do the wrong thing. She was still near the door, thinking which way to move before she joined the woman at the table.

The woman chuckled. "Relax, sweetie. Diogenes, my boa constrictor, is fast asleep. You're here for a reading, right?"

"*Yes.* Yes, for a reading." She said it too loudly and felt embarrassed. Carla's smile caught her, refilling her with calm and security. There was no reason to be afraid of these women. It was her own psyche that doubted, doubted her ability to cross the gap that separated her from Tommy. He told her she would leap her chasm of fear when she was ready. She wouldn't look down; she would just jump. Her mother refused to recognize its existence. While Jennifer breezed through men with naïve gaiety, never straying from her high school boys, Sandy saw more, wanted more, and expected to receive it. All of her life, she had dared, from her first lover to the insanity of Tommy Logan. Hers wasn't Jennifer's life or her parents'. It was hers, first and always. Though she wanted to give it to Tommy, he wouldn't take it. And now this woman was going to see the future. To know the future. She was ambivalent and anxious. What was happening in Bogotá?

The old woman directed Carla to lower the lights. She brought a double globe table lamp from the corner and set it close to the table. She lit four candles in a brass candelabrum. "Now, this isn't just for fun, you understand," Madame Doucard said, smoothing the thick tablecloth with her purple-veined hands. "Twenty dollars for the reading. Ten more for your palm. Pay in advance."

Sandy flushed. "Certainly, I didn't mean to think... It sounds reasonable." She fumbled for the money. Carla remained very silent, blending into the over-decorated room, but her presence reassured Sandy.

Sweet Tibetan incense filled the room. After dimming the lights, in only candlelight, Doucard shuffled a deck of Tarot cards. "Separate them into two piles. Now, you must ask a question, one that you wish to be answered. The cards will help guide you. There are no answers in the cards; they draw from you, acting as a link to the eternal." She paused as if taking a long drink of water and drifted in silent thought.

The darkly furnished room became a labyrinth for Sandy, looking in from all sides but without a path to follow. What answer did she want? Thousands, thousands, but Tommy, what was he... No, she didn't want to ask that question. It wasn't his night. What was to happen with them? That was important to Sandy. It could free her. She thought it without relish. What was going to happen with them? That was the question she wanted to be answered.

Doucard was watching her when she looked up. "Ah, I see a troubled question in your mind. Don't speak it. The cards will know. I can feel them already." The old woman placed nine cards into three triangles with deliberation and hypnotic warmth. She placed the tenth one alone, away from the rest. The first isosceles triangle was pointed toward Sandy. The other two were pointing down to the lone card. Madame Doucard sucked air with each card, drawing energy from it. Sandy settled into the process with uncharacteristic resignation.

"This first place is your spirituality. It represents the metaphysical plane of life. Here lies the essence and substance. Your card is the Ace of Cups." Her voice dropped in tone and volume, ending all noise in the room.

A chalice overflowing with water, laying in a hand extending from a cloud, looked religious and medieval to Sandy. There was a dove dunking a wafer into the cup. Her feeling for the card was stronger than she wanted. The long, feminine fingers of the hand holding the cup were passive and tranquil.

Doucard's voice began as suddenly as it stopped. "Your ideal is great love, joy, contentment. Yes, my dear, your ideal of ideals is to fill your life with beauty and pleasure. It will be productive; bring you fertility and joy. Wanting the greatest joys when your cup is filled, joy will overflow to those around you. A noble ideal."

Sandy's eyes were engaged by the old, drooping hands, which seemed out of a Disney cartoon. Intrigued from the moment of movement, she watched each finger gingerly move with choreographed precision. Already Sandy was afraid for the rest of the cards and to continue. In the next row were the Eight of Cups, the Six of Pentacles, and at the apex was the Ace of Wands. The third triangle contained the Star, the Lovers, and the Fool.

"The lovers stand in harmony, in companionship as long as they share and create together. It is more than love. The angel insists upon the choice. And you know your struggle between that perfect inner love that you desire and the profane love you crave." Madame Doucard looked into Sandy's face for the first time during the reading. The lines of her face were the pieces of the incomprehensible puzzle.

"At this point," she pointed with a long red nail, "you are the Fool, in the unification of the spirit. The Tarot brings you choice, which resides only in yourself. The Fool is above the mundane life of the days. With no sense, there is no despair. He is coming to the choice where the dreamer must choose, the mystic must decide. It is a momentous occasion—all could be lost with one turn of the wheel."

The final card was the Tower, a card torn with conflict, fury, and confusion. Sandy felt the meaning without the words.

"It is the card of change, catastrophic, and the end of the old order. It was the card of Czarina Alexandra read by Rasputin." With a wide, crooked smile, Madame Doucard gathered the cards quickly into the deck and hobbled to the dark ebony sideboard and put them away and turned on the globe light.

The mystical spell was broken as Carla extinguished the candles in the cold white light. Sandy quickly came back to the present.

Doucard gently took Sandy's hand and turned the palm up. "Your life line is long, as is mine. You must see, feel, and know life before you become an old woman like me." She shook her head encouragingly; a smile of memory crossed her face.

"There will be a lot of sons of bitches along the way. I got my share. Been married seven times; three died. Three ran away, and a Chinaman in Rio was deported. He was an Oriental artist. He did this one." She pulled up her cotton skirt, revealing an intricately designed tattoo of a dragon sitting in a garden. She dropped her hem quickly, not giving Sandy much of a look.

Doucard explained how she became a tattooist to support herself in Rio. Sandy imagined the excitement of those moments and the exotic names. If only she could be half as brave... She began wishing for strength and courage, coolly walking through danger in control of the situation.

"Why do you put designs on your skin?" she asked simply.

"To add, illuminate, remember, because... Each one has reasons, dreams, problems. My reasons then were most important; today, I don't remember. I don't need to; I have the marks as part of me. I carry others in my heart and on my walls. The trick, my young sister, is to do anything at all. Your life is long—fill it with delights and doubts. It will all end sooner than you think." The old woman's bemusement was quizzical, unresolved, and calm.

Sandy envied her knowledge. The vision and knowing—mostly that—of what a woman had to be, could be. Not knowing where she was going or why. Hers was a reassuring voice.

"I will give you a present tonight; it's time for a celebration." She raised her voice in merriment. "The best of my ancient art. What would you like? A hummingbird?" She dropped the blouse from her left shoulder, exposing a faded, withered bird. "The dragon? A heart with his name? I even do battleships and anchors, but no one wanted one for twenty years. Good riddance too. What will it be, my dear Sandy?"

Carla spoke for the first time. "A symbol?"

Doucard tugged at the white hairs on her alligatored chin. She shuffled into the other room, returning with a sheet of designs, a needle, a pipe, and several small containers.

Sandy took the sheet, unsettled at the speed of events. There were birds, dragons, animals, exotic crosses, mythical symbols. In one corner, a tiny rose caught her eye and her thoughts.

"I think you should get the bed of roses," Carla said, putting her hand on Sandy's shoulder. "The others are too big for you." She smiled as if with a sisterly embrace.

"The roses… It might be right for you." Doucard shifted her long, pleated skirt while moving her chair closer to Sandy. "The rose is beauty and danger. The poets have written, the singers have sung, wars have been fought, but they can neither add nor detract from the beauty of the flower. And when it is dried and pressed, it will remain forever."

Panic crawled around her blood, circulating fear with every heartbeat. A tattoo? What was she doing? Sandy wanted to… But didn't want to admit. What would her mother think? Her mother… No, no. What would Tommy think? Fuck Tommy, banish him. His opinion didn't count, nor her mother's or anyone else's. It was her decision.

She looked quizzically at the old lady, then at Carla. Their eyes kept her calm; their presence radiated security. Why not? That was the only true question. What did it matter either way? Now was the moment to be dealt with; who cares about what might happen? Now, it was here, and soon it would not be. Peering at the two women, she had control and daring. In their eyes, she could see their confidence, and the reflection lifted her in waves of certainty.

"I want the rose." Sandy was surprised by the sound of her voice and at her decision. She wanted a tattoo and wasn't afraid—as much.

"Do the bed of roses—it is a bolder statement," said Carla.

"Yes, many flowers would be magnificent," Doucard added.

"No, a single rose," Sandy said, pointing to the spot. She wanted it to be clear, unique, and beautiful.

* * *

Madame Doucard busied herself with preparations and colors. "Which shoulder?"

"I don't want it there." A sudden giddiness of life filled Sandy with smiles. She lifted her leg onto the chair and pulled up her skirt. "I want it here." She pointed to the inner side of her thigh, inches from her crotch. "I want it pressed, so it will last forever." She was all the reason she needed.

With the deftness of an artist and the precision of a surgeon, Madame Doucard's agile fingers drew the outline of a rose on a thorny stem and edged it with needlepoints.

The white hairs stood straight on Sandy's exposed tanned thigh. Her thin veins were throbbing through the sensitive flesh. Her fear left her body limp as a child fearing needles, and here, she was certain of the pain. Resisting the trembling, fighting back tears, she knew it was going to hurt.

Carla took her hand, and Doucard radiated calm.

"Don't be tense. Relax. The pain is fleeting, as are our lives. Take a shot of this."

The mescal tequila was thick and strong, taking her back another step. From that safe distance, Sandy studied the colors as the woman created with joy. The red and green saluted her while the flower expressed tenderness. It was a part of her now... How about that, Scarlett O'Hara? What will Atlanta think? What will she do next?

As she left the house with Carla, the cool night air woke them both. The parlor and the old woman already seemed a dream by the time Sandy reached her car. She felt the pain when she touched the inside of her thigh as she sat in the seat to confirm the reality of the night. A sense of pride and exhilaration raced through her, and she sat up straight behind the wheel of the Camaro. Her heart was still rapidly beating as she continued her composed expression. Sandy's shivers were frequent, like mushroom body rushes.

Carla's presence was close as they passed a joint. The evening was cascading as the traffic zipped passed hundreds of unknown bedrooms. Calm had returned to the air, and she, for a moment, drifted off into the hazed marijuana smoke. The interior glow of the car light made her feel important. The realness of experience, actually in knowing, the first touched flame, cherry time belonging to her for once and always, even as it faded into memory.

Again, she touched her thigh. It was the reckless way of living she loved, the abandoned pleasure of doing life for its own sake. But years of trained responses don't fade quickly. She was the stumbling kid who got caught stealing cookies. Were secret moments stolen? Her mother taught her to believe it. Account for every minute, every one. There were always secret ones, not for anybody else—hidden away at the bottom of the heart so no one would know.

A year ago, she would never have been here tonight—or been ready for the next experience. The big world was still too frightening to her—her father's world. If Tommy had taken her... If—that's no way to live. Here and now. The experience and excitement.

Carla extended her arm gently over Sandy's shoulder and rested her head on it. Sandy could smell traces of perfume mixed with the incense of the house. Carla's cheek was warm against her naked shoulder, the flesh soft. Confusion began ringing inside again, the mixed signals of pleasure and fear. The center, the balance point of Carla's tattoo, was too far away to grasp. She was constantly tilted, falling from one side to the other until she wanted to vomit but only had dry heaves. Was the night too far gone to salvage? Was there any reason to hold on, which seemed to be too much trouble?

It was time to go home, put it away until tomorrow, set it down for a while, resume peace and... and what? Desire? Nothing seemed that simple anymore.

"Carla, Carla... Hey, wake up." She shook her gently. "Where are you staying? If you want, you can stay here. I'm too tired to drive."

Her dark eyes began focusing on Sandy's face, and recognition illuminated them. "Yeah, fine. I've got to hit the road early tomorrow. Going to Daytona."

What was Sandy going to do? Wait for Tommy again? This couldn't go on, not this way. It didn't make any sense to her. She didn't like it.

When they returned to Sandy's apartment, Carla removed her skirt and folded it on the chair. Besides the tattoo on her thigh, she had a butterfly on one knee and a daisy on the other. Sandy wondered who she was and how she came to be so free. Again, there was admiration, twice in one night for two women. She was surprised: she had never admired women. Not her mother, and not her relatives. Yet in one, fated evening, she had met two, and she knew it. Grown up; was she an adult yet? What did it mean besides the stuffy life? Eating dessert after dinner?

Watching, she felt tenderness for the dark, thin figure lying in composure on the soft pillow, a twig on a raft floating away down the brook. With an impulse, unable to find a middle ground, she bent down and kissed her.

Carla turned her head, returning the kiss. Decisions, always too many, too often. Carla touched her shoulder and ran her hand down over Sandy's now-erect nipples.

Sandy moved to the couch, touching the butterfly and the daisy before allowing her hand to explore the two females. Sandy felt Carla's fingers reach the rose and continue past it into her wetness. The night continued.

* * *

Bells were ringing in every direction. Sandy was certain the building was on fire. The bells were so loud, no one could hear her. No one would ever hear her... and she screamed, waking herself instantly. Rattled, she got it together to answer the phone.

"Hello?"

"Good morning, beautiful. Ready for a big day?"

It was Tommy, but his voice was very distant and filled with crackles and fuzz. She looked around, but Carla was gone.

"Yeah, where are you? I can hardly hear you. When are you…"

"Hang on, just listen a moment. Get a piece of paper." His voice was sweet. She fumbled through the top drawer until she found both paper and something to write with.

"Yeah, I'm ready. When are you coming…"

"Go to Delta and pick up a ticket to San Juan. It's pre-paid in your name. Check into the San Juan Hilton, also in your name. Bring my tan shoulder bag. It's all packed. Lock it and check it through with your bag."

"Yeah, but what am I supposed to bring? How long? What are we going to be doing?"

"Something pretty, something for swimming, but anything you bring, I'm going to take off you soon."

She was trying to read his voice, but the connection made it impossible. She didn't dare ask how things were going, and a surge of jealousy returned. "When is all this taking place?"

"What do you mean when? Now, of course. Get into gear, and you can be on the beach by sunset."

Life was happening too fast. Confusion was up and around. Today. This was happening today. San Juan by sunset. In a few hours—what time was it?

"Do you have it, yes or no? I don't want to repeat myself." Tommy was strained by her silence.

"Yes, yes, I do. Today? Are you going to be there? Oh, I don't have anything to wear. Do I need any…"

"Just bring yourself, beautiful, and the bag. I'll see you real soon. Ciao."

And he was gone. The receiver was again just plastic. It was another shock, one to perk up the day. The bubbling audacity of her life intoxicated her. She was going to San Juan today. Just like that, no obligation, nothing better to do. That was certain.

Going into the living room, she found her skirt neatly folded on the chair. On a piece of paper towel was the note: "Thanx, love Carla." And the evening was over. Sandy looked down at the rose on her inner thigh. It was there. She had done it.

In less than an hour, she showered and packed. Anticipation was rampant as she moved with purpose and order. Each thing, one at a time. Beach, dinner, shopping, boating… whatever.

When she took Tommy's bag from the closet, its weight surprised her. Why did he need so many clothes? She opened the bag. His Smith & Wesson was on top in the shoulder holster. A military .45 and a long-nose .38, each holstered, were wrapped in clothing. What was going on? Was she walking into trouble? She didn't like it when guns became involved. That could mean police, and she was terrified of that. She had to go with the feeling Tommy gave her, the direction to the end. She decided only to pack the Smith & Wesson.

Fear tightened as she arrived at the counter. Trembling, she held her hand as firmly as she could in front of the dowdy attendant. What world was awaiting her? With the incipient mischief of a child, she wanted to peek through the curtain at the next day. Tonight she would be with Tommy. That would be enough. She would wait for the rest to arrive. It couldn't be helped or pushed. Now it was beyond her control, and she would let go. The man put the bags onto the conveyor and handed her the ticket.

"Checked all the way to San Juan, Miss Carlton. Have a nice trip."

Chapter 10

TOMMY ARRIVED FIRST IN PUERTO Rico. All arriving passengers were channeled through a tightly partitioned room with only booths and uniformed guards at the end. He was asked to open his suitcase, but it was not searched.

The open-air humidity of the terminal greeted him with a wreath of dampness. His narrow Colombian shirt clung to his chest while beads of sweat formed over his eyebrows. The moisture was a surprise, even for a Florida boy.

Four Puerto Rican men in shorts casually pushed brooms in an empty fountain that bordered the departure lounge. He wondered if the fountain ever worked. At the far end of the L-shaped terminal was a small neon sign that said *Restaurant and Bar*. Tommy headed for it.

The middle-aged waiter took his order for pineapple juice and rum without uttering a sound. Tommy sat back, looking out through the large, dirty windows, thinking of Sandy. She was scheduled to arrive in an hour. Harry, Elsie, and Kippi were on a later flight. George and Quintana had gone directly back to Atlanta.

The tension of the last five days was embedded in his shoulders and neck like steel hooks. He wanted to be lying on the beach with Sandy with no place to go, to just be, with food catered and sweet drinks. When this was over, he'd take Sandy to Virgin Gorda—he had heard of a nice little place they could enjoy—when the deal was over.

In the past few days, things were becoming clearer in his life. He was concerned about the future. Harry had frightened him this time. There was the ninety proof Harry bullshit. The ten percent was coming through this time. George was on a short fuse—there were only so many times Tommy would let that ape touch him.

He thought as he sipped his breakfast punch that if Sandy had been along, he might have been cooler, not so uptight. This was the first time, his cherry. The aloneness of the foreign country and the inability to speak or understand had fractured his sense of security. It was bothering him then, but he couldn't deal with it until now. In passing moments, he caught himself thinking of her—she was becoming needed. Tommy smiled. *Looks like that woman's web is starting to fall. Better get my ass in gear before I get caught.*

He had known aloneness in Bogotá. Trusting himself, relying on his own instincts to get by. There wasn't ever a place to go for the answer. The decisions were internal, placed for survival. Ambivalent facts were jumbling his security, keeping certainty beyond his outstretched fingers. In Tampa, he always could feel how close fate was. A familiarity, like English, he had never appreciated before this trip. With one step, his movement broke the inertia of culture.

The terminal smelled of mildew and aviation exhaust. Seeing her skim through the crowd, lean and assured, with her head held back like a thoroughbred, he felt his heart twist with delight. He sauntered the shortest interception route to her. As their lips met, each quivered in mutual delight. Separately yet in perfect harmony, they let go of all thoughts except one. Their separation melted in the flesh.

* * *

The master suite of the San Juan Hilton was on the seventeenth floor. Since Tommy had made the reservations, he got the best room for them. Harry and family were staying on the sixteenth floor—a smaller room but a bigger bed.

After making love, Tommy and Sandy went into the main room, where the baggage had been dropped.

"Where you get these ideas, I'll never know," Tommy said grinning, with admiration. "I've never known a lady, and I emphasize the word, who was so spunky. I was shocked as shit when I saw it. Even didn't believe it for a moment. God damn, a tattoo."

"I didn't do it to shock you," Sandy said, casually tossing her hair while enjoying the attention. She wanted to attack him again. "I did it because I liked it, and I wanted it." She cocked her head slightly to one side.

"Where is my suitcase?" Tommy asked.

She pointed to the leather bag next to the large green couch. Tommy flipped it open on the table and retrieved the Smith & Wesson. From the side of the bag, he loaded the cylinder and popped it shut.

It felt good in his hand. So far, everything was on track, but he had a nagging in his confidence. Someone might know and want to take it away. He wasn't going to get ripped off, having come this far. He put the gun on the table and lustfully approached Sandy's white ass. She turned quickly and leaped at him, catching him off guard. He fell clumsily against the table. As the gun hit the floor, Tommy immediately shielded Sandy. As it struck the floor, there was a deafening explosion. The smell of gunpowder was clear and acrid. Then instantly Tommy came alive.

Grabbing the gun and holster, he quickly went to the balcony and placed it on the railing, where one quick kick would send it sailing into the Caribbean. He listened. There were no sounds, no footsteps. He exchanged glances with Sandy, who stood naked in the center of the room.

Tommy bent over the bullet hole that was next to the armoire. It seemed to have penetrated the gypsum into the next room. Tommy was not about to go see. Since there was no inquiry, he pulled the chest over several inches to cover the hole.

All the years he had owned guns, this was the first time one had ever discharged accidentally. One in a million. Was this an omen?

A huge grin crossed his face as he twirled Sandy around. She returned his puzzled grin. When else would a gun go off accidentally? At the wrong time. What does it mean? Murphy's Law? Didn't mean nothing. Done, and nothing happened. He remembered a story, the myth about three sisters, the Fates, who wove a fabric for each life. Each added her own thread. They like some fabrics and wove and wove before snipping off. But in others, a sister would dislike a thread and snip. That's all she wove.

Harry and family would arrive shortly. Boulton was due around six with the church group. Tonight was the moment of truth, the final inning, game point. After all the time, the fears of doing, risking, exploring the unknown, tonight he would know, for certain, the truth of action. No longer talk. Not the bullshit around the dorm, not the horseshit in Harry's dining room. It was here, tonight, in Technicolor. Did they fuck up or score. Stay tuned.

The anticipation was producing a light, merry feeling like the final day of school before summer vacation. No more nuns or faggot priests. One phase was finished; the better one about to begin. Looking out over the Caribbean from the hotel, Tommy's body was warm from the day of lovemaking.

"What do you want out of life?" Sandy put a *Vogue* magazine on the floor. She had shown Tommy the wedding invitation from some of her high school friends who were getting married. Tommy thought she was smart enough not to bring it up with him.

"I want to be rich," Tommy said, throwing his arms open. "A fucking millionaire, so I could do whatever I wanted."

"Like what? You can't just sit around and be rich." She sat on the arm of the chair next to him.

He patted her leg. "I don't know 'cause I'm not there yet. Soon, maybe." He smiled at her.

"You will be." She ran her hand through his hair. "You like kids. I see the way you are with Kippi."

"Yeah, she's a cute kid." He pulled her into his lap. "Don't be getting any ideas."

"What is it, Tommy? You have the strangest smile. What are you thinking?"

"I do? I was thinking what a bitchin' lady you are." He kissed her solidly on the mouth.

She pulled back momentarily. "I know there's more to it than that. You'll tell me later."

"I will?"

"Yes, you will." She pulled him down to the floor and made love to him.

* * *

"Give me that suitcase," Harry said in the officiating voice of a bishop. Boulton dutifully took the case to him.

The entry through customs was a Norman Rockwell piece of Americana. The good ladies of the Baptist Mission Inspection Tour arrived at the airport complaining about hotel dirt, disgusting bathrooms, noxious smells, and other inconveniences. Their testy, suppressed anxiousness to get home was quickly communicated to all the customs agents. Boulton, who had been adopted by four middle-aged women during the trip, remained quiet and bashful while the women kept the custom agents engaged. He was passed through without his bag being opened. It was cake.

Bolton brought the suitcase to the hotel. Harry laid it flat on the coffee table in the middle of the suite. The case was a standard Samsonite case, which blended in with all the others at the airport.

"Boulton, go into the other room and watch cartoons with Kippi."

"Why? No. I want to know what…"

"No, you don't. Then you will never have to lie. Now go." Harry's tone was firm and final. Boulton got up and walked to the door like a scolded puppy.

Tommy was sitting in the chair across from the table when Harry began removing the clothes. "Are you going to open it now?"

"Yeah, we should check the merchandise. And make Boulton back into the clean-cut young man that he is." Harry licked his lips and continued to unpack the suitcase. "Don't you agree?"

Harry had a slippery way of getting what he wanted without taking responsibility for the losses. The idiocy of the hotel and the first delivery of coke that he snorted himself. Tommy had to make decisions for him and them. He was still a partner and hadn't forgotten that Harry was a liability in Bogotá.

"We've gotten this far; Why take any chances? If we leave it where it is, no one will find it."

Harry stopped and looked at Tommy with the tolerant grasshopper look that pissed Tommy off.

Cool. He was determined to stay cool. Detachment was the form of resolve that would keep all things in their proper place.

"There aren't any more customs between here and the States. We can fly to Tampa, Atlanta, or anywhere you'd like, carrying the stuff in clear plastic bags. There are no more searches. Do you understand that? Can you get that through that stubborn guinea part of you?"

Tommy felt the power game Harry was playing. It was between the two of them, and Harry didn't have his pet gorilla around to protect him. Harry had a power thing; he wanted people to obey him.

"I understand that, but I think it would be better if we waited until we got back." He wondered where Harry would go with it. Actually, he wanted a taste of the coke too.

"You can keep your half anywhere you want it," Harry said cheerfully. Using a round-tipped knife, he removed the leather strip along the inside perimeter of the bag. The inside lining was one flat piece of soft leather. Harry rubbed his hands on the inner and outer sides of the bag. "Even knowing it's here, I can't feel a thing. This is a first-rate job."

Tommy walked around the table and leaned right over Harry's shoulder.

"You can get fucked, you rotten little punk. If you think I am going to just sit here with three kilos of one hundred percent Colombian cocaine in front of me after successfully beating the toughest customs in the world, you've got turkey turds for brains." He began to chuckle as he turned a wide smile to Tommy. All the arguments didn't mean anything now. They had done it. "We've got a sizable profit here. I think we're entitled to celebrate. Would you care to join me, partner?" Harry seemed like a little kid at Christmas. He paused. "Every package deserves to be unwrapped."

Tommy was feeling giddy again with the light, loose style of the world that can be no better. He gave Sandy a wink, and they both watched Harry as he lifted out the entire inner lining of leather.

The plastic bags of compressed white powder snugly fit into a grooved-out section of the leather. One of the great qualities of coke was its easy compressibility; the leather was only hollowed an eighth of an inch. Harry was holding one bag of coke with fatherly affection.

"I'll take out the rest," Tommy said, moving the suitcase off the table.

"A fine idea," Harry agreed, putting his mirror where the suitcase had been. Laying the bag on the table and carefully taking off the tape, Harry broke it open and gently brought it to his nose.

"Don't snort out of the..." Tommy said.

Harry inhaled with a loud snort. He tipped his head backward and snorted hard again, pulling the white specks from his mustache. He held the bag on his stomach.

"Ho, ho, ho. It must be Christmas because it's snowing in San Juan." They all laughed.

"Gimme that before you drop it on the floor," Tommy said, grabbing the bag from the jovial Harry. The coke would taste good, and he was certain he needed some. The last week had been hard on his nerves.

"Oh," Harry said, reaching for the bag, "don't take that too far."

"Shit, man. I'm just putting it on the mirror." Taking a playing card from a deck on the table, Tommy spooned the coke onto the mirror. He put about six grams into a pile, a little at a time, so no one would knock it over. Elsie sat at the table next to Harry, waiting for her share.

With a double-edged razor blade, Tommy drew eight lines using about half of the coke he had laid out. After looking for a second, he made four more, then four more, using all the coke. Now they were snorting size.

Tommy took a gold cylindrical tooter that Sandy brought him and did the first line. He inhaled again and did a second line. The coke was strong and coolingly numb. Dipping his finger into it and rubbing it on his gums, the numbness made his teeth stand on edge, bitter-tasting but fresh out front. The bittersweet taste dropped from his nose and through his throat in an acid-tasting lump of saliva. He swallowed again, savoring the taste of the coke. Like a fine wine, he let it live in his throat, all the way down. It was what he needed.

They made it. They fucking made it. It wasn't that hard. Time to celebrate. Harry's Enterprise fired up its engines, and the party was on.

* * *

Morning came quickly, and everyone was asleep except Kippi, who was sitting quietly on the couch watching cartoons when Tommy entered the suite. He sat beside her on the couch. Instead of cuddling, Kippi moved away to the other end.

"Morning, punk," Tommy said. He hadn't seen much of her since the first day in Colombia. And even there, she was mostly out of sight. Kippi made no response.

"I said morning, punk." Tommy moved over to tickle her, but Kippi began crying instead.

"What's the matter, baby." Tommy stopped trying to roughhouse with her. She didn't look at him, but the tears continued to flow. "Can I help?"

She shook her head no and still didn't make eye contact with him. He put his hand gently on her chin and turned her reddened face toward him. "Whatever it is, I can help."

She shook her head vigorously and didn't stop crying. Tommy was at a loss. He didn't know what to do. "Are you hurt? In pain? Tell me," he said.

"I can't," she said quietly.

"Why?" Now Tommy was determined to figure it out.

"Daddy said not to tell anyone. Elsie said not to tell anyone."

"I'm not anyone. I'm Tommy, your punk friend. Remember?" He smiled at her while feigning hurt.

"I know but…"

"But what, punk? You know your Daddy and I are partners. We share everything."

"It's not like that," she said and hid her head in the pillow.

"Like what? You can tell me."

"About Uncle George."

"What about Uncle George?"

"Stuff…"

"What kind of stuff?" Tommy realized that Kippi had stayed in George's room in Colombia. "Did he touch you? Did he make you touch him?" Kippi kept her head in the pillow while nodding.

"Your father and Elsie know? And they told you not to tell?" Her head continued to nod. That son of a bitch. Fucking gorilla. The reaction started in his stomach and moved electrically throughout his body. He could feel drops of sweat on his skin as Father Byrne's face loomed over him, pushing his head down on his cock. Fucking pedophiles. They needed to be castrated and killed. How the fuck could Harry let this happen? It was a good thing George wasn't here because he would never see the States again.

"It's okay, Kippi. It's not your fault. You didn't do anything wrong." He stroked her back as she buried her head deeper into his arm. He never had anyone to talk to, to tell him he didn't do anything wrong. He had to discover that himself, but by then it was too late. He'd kill the old pervert today if he thought it would do any good. He would talk to Harry; this was wrong. Perverted wrong. He stayed with her while she cried herself asleep on the pillow.

* * *

As they entered the casino with a flourish, all eyes turned to Harry and Elsie. From the dance floor with Sandy, Tommy could see he was high. Harry was walking easily, gracefully, with his stomach leading the way and opening a path for the rest of his body. His toupee was in place, and Elsie had trimmed his beard.

His shirt was silky, with large, billowy sleeves and large ruffles. His four-hundred-pound body dwarfed any two people in the room. His gold belt buckle was inset with three diamonds outlined in mother-of-pearl. On a thick golden chain hung the Enterprise, and on another chain was a golden teardrop pendant with three sapphires.

Elsie was hanging on his arm; her blond hair was raggedly cut, giving her a raw, wild German look. She wore a white crepe dress that just covered her ass and strained to keep her breasts inside. The back of the dress was open nearly to her waist. She cat-walked like a model next to Harry, allowing his bulk to lead the way. Tommy stopped dancing in the middle of the floor and held up his hands to the band. They looked at each other a moment and then at the massive figure of Harry Burr approaching the platform like Henry VIII. They stopped playing.

Tommy left the center of the floor to meet Harry.

"Good evening, *señor*," Tommy said loudly and bowing in the formal European manner. "It is a great honor to have your presence with us tonight. I hope you will find everything to your satisfaction."

"Indeed," Harry intoned. "Let the music continue."

Harry led the group to the restaurant, where he occupied an entire banquette. Hushed conversations floated from every corner of the room. Questions, speculation—but no answers. Harry and Tommy congratulated each other with their eyes.

After ordering oysters, shrimp, salad, soup, and five entrées, Harry said to the waitress, "That's for me. See what they want." Her mouth dropped in amazement, and Harry's rumbling laughter created a chorus of laughter that included the waitress and wine steward.

Halfway through the meal, Harry lowered his voice and leaned across the table to Tommy. "Have you noticed the two guys in the far corner in the dark suits? They've been watching us for ten minutes."

"Shit, not tonight. Spare me," Tommy said as he poured another glass of wine while taking a look. He caught the eye of the medium-sized man, who quickly looked away. It looked like the heat. There was nothing wrong—they were clean as far as the island was concerned.

"We're clean. If they knew anything, they would have taken us by now. We've had plenty of time to pass it," Harry said.

"What's this? All of a sudden, you care about the police. Hell, you acted like there weren't any in Bogotá. You have some warped realities," Tommy said. This wasn't the place to bring up Kippi.

"Listen, punk," Harry started but failed to finish. Tommy followed his eyes to the two men slowly leaving the room. "Let's enjoy. Sometimes the coke puts on a paranoid edge. The only bad side effect."

"That's what I've been told. Forget it. You're going to teach me to play blackjack like a pro."

Harry topped the meal with a flambé and a shot of cognac. Then they went to the casino.

The tall blackjack dealer had long, boney fingers and skinny wrists. He wore no jewelry, and his cuffs were tight against his arms. The green on the felt table was soothing. There were seats for six people, but Harry took up the two center ones. Tommy sat to his right, and Sandy was on Tommy's right. Elsie played the slots. Harry told Tommy to watch him, but there wasn't much to watch. Harry was down three hundred while Tommy was up two, and it reflected in the mood. Harry was not a graceful loser.

Sandy leaned and whispered to Tommy, "I'll be at the craps table. Don't let him get into trouble."

Tommy replied, disgusted at the prospect of being a nursemaid.

Harry drew double eights and split his hand, doubling down on his original hundred-dollar bet. He drew two face cards. The dealer showed thirteen. He drew a five. Harry muttered at the dealer, but it was too low for Tommy to hear. A crack was beginning to show in the façade of fat as irritation was visible along his forehead, and impatience ran from his nervous fingers. It was time to join Sandy at the craps table.

"I'm out," Tommy said, getting up from the table. Three hundred dollars up—not bad for an hour. "Come on, Harry. Let's play craps."

"You play. I'm just getting started," he growled, turning to the dealer.

Tommy shrugged. He didn't care where Harry lost his money. He joined Sandy at the craps table, winning on his first bet. Before he had a chance to get into the game, Harry's voice came bellowing across the room like a bull elephant. "Pay me. That card was from the bottom." A wave of motion swept Tommy toward the sound. Security men and pit bosses surrounded Harry while the slots kept ringing.

Tommy got close enough to listen but didn't try to see what was happening because he might start laughing.

"It was from the bottom of the deck." Harry's voice and size kept everyone at a distance for several moments before a thickly set pit boss yelled at the dealer.

"What's the problem?"

"He says I dealt from the bottom. I didn't."

Harry looked the square-jawed man in the face. The pit boss looked around at the crowd before turning to the dealer. "Pay him."

Then, turning to Harry, he said, "Now get out of here and don't play in my casino again."

Harry's eyes were slightly glassed as he passed by Tommy. Six security men escorted him. Only three had uniforms.

Tommy grabbed Sandy's hand and walked quickly to the elevators. He had to make sure all the shit was stashed. A stupid time to create a commotion while holding two keys of pure lady.

"Well, fuck you," he heard Harry roar as he came out of the casino. "I get thrown out because I catch you cheating me?" A small crowd of people began to gather as the security men tried to keep Harry moving. "Step right up and empty your pockets, folks. The odds are bad enough, but they cheat…" One of the uniformed guards jammed a billy club into Harry's side.

"Shut that fat motherfucking mouth if you know what's good for you."

"And who's gonna…"

Sandy and Tommy jumped into the elevator, and Tommy pushed fourteen, sixteen, seventeen, and all the higher floors. No one would know which floor he got off on, and it would take a while before returning to the first floor.

They got off on seventeen and took the stairs to sixteen. The handle on the fire door opened easily. Staying against the inner wall, Tommy cracked it just enough to see into the empty hall. He listened, but the hall was quiet. He turned to Sandy.

"If anything happens, take off." He handed her his money and stepped into the hall. With smooth karate steps, he crossed the empty space to the room.

He signaled to Sandy as he put the key into the door and turned it. The suite was too quiet and black. Tommy switched on the lights, the Smith & Wesson on his hip, his heart pumping hard. A figure rose from nowhere over the couch. Tommy dropped to a crouch, finger on the trigger before Sandy shouted, "Tommy! Don't!"

He froze while focusing his eyes on Boulton, who stood, terrified. Sandy came over to Tommy, who lowered the weapon and breathed deeply. "Thanks," Tommy said quietly to her. "Close the door."

The mirror was on the table, but there was no coke in sight. Thank the Lord. He picked it up and headed for the bathroom to wash it clean. In the leather shaving kit on the top of the counter was the open pouch of coke. Harry wasn't so dumb after all. Relieved, Tommy washed off the mirror and returned to the living room.

"If anyone comes to the door, get to the bathroom. The coke is on the shaving kit. If I shout, 'go to hell,' run water into the bag until it is clean."

Sandy nodded quickly.

"Of all the times to pull a super stunt, Harry pulls it now. Boulton, where is Kippi?" Tommy looked at the couch and into the small wet bar.

"Sleeping in the bedroom."

In two minutes, Tommy had everything put away and the room looking clean. Boulton's bag was closed and in a closet. Then a knock came at the door. Everyone froze for an instant. Sandy disappeared into the bathroom as Tommy went to the door.

Harry opened the door, his face ashen as he walked into the center of the room. Elsie was a step behind, followed by two security men.

"These gentlemen were kind enough to escort me to my suite," Harry said, his eyes darting around the room.

"Is there a problem, gentlemen?" Tommy asked. He assumed they were hotel security since they didn't push their way into the room. Paying customers had some rights.

One walked over to the dining room table and the window before turning back to the door.

"No problems as long as your friend stays out of the casino."

"Fuck you. I wouldn't go back into your…"

"He won't," Tommy said firmly. "Thanks for the help."

The two turned, still looking the place over, but Tommy had it looking like the cleaning lady was just there.

"What the fuck were you thinking?" Tommy said after they'd left the suite, keeping his voice low. He assumed the house cops were still at the door. He turned on the television to a loud Spanish channel and sat on the sofa, his adrenaline still pumping. "Next time, let me know where the coke is. Never mind. Let's not have a next time."

"I put it in…"

"Never mind. I found it. I'm going to take it all to my room. They know you now and may still be watching. We should split first thing in the morning." He was prepared for another fight with Harry, but this time the gorilla wasn't around.

"I want to keep my half."

"Right. Then in case the cops decide to search your room, you can ingest the whole thing. No way. You're hot."

Harry was defeated. "Whatever you say. Elsie, get the bag from my bathroom."

Sandy held up the bag.

"Here, take a gram for tonight," Tommy said, spooning out a small amount onto the mirror. "Do you think they called the cops? Did they ask anything else of you?" He needed options. What else could go wrong?

"We better get out of here tomorrow," Harry said absently. "Go to the other side of the island, where it's quiet."

"Great idea," Tommy said. "I'm going back to Tampa. I'll see you in Atlanta. Elsie, put him to bed."

"I can walk. I'm not a cripple," Harry snapped as Elsie and Tommy tried to lift him from his seat. "I'll see you in the morning. The other side of the island—it's cool there."

"Right, Harry. In the morning." Tommy took Boulton's suitcase from the closet and went to the elevator. Waiting for the elevator with Sandy, he tried to look relaxed, but his body was ready to explode. He wanted to tear the entire hotel apart. He felt ready, primed like a musket just waiting for a spark.

Closing the door to the room, Sandy huddled under his arm. "Hold me. Please hold me." She pulled herself nearer, snuggling for safety.

Her softness brought back the joys of the afternoon. "You okay? It's over."

"Oh, Tommy, Tommy, Tommy. Is it always going to be like this?"

* * *

Tommy was awake before dawn. He hadn't slept much; he didn't want to. This day had to be picture smooth. Boulton was set to leave on the 8:30 flight to Atlanta. Tommy would leave at eight to Tampa and take the suitcase with him. Harry and the rest would go back to Atlanta, and he would meet them there.

"Wake up." He slapped Sandy on her ivory ass. "It's time to go." Tommy got out of bed and pulled the covers off, exposing her tanned body. Only her ass was that delicate white that Tommy loved so much. Today was neither the time nor the place. He dialed Harry again.

"Get out of bed. We're leaving." There was a muffled groan. "Now."

"Yeah, yeah…"

The lobby was full of police and frantic-looking hotel staff. Dressed in khaki pants, a crew neck shirt, and Top-Siders he had bought in the casino clothing store, it was collegiate time for Tommy. It would be hard to recognize him as the guy from the previous night. He took Sandy by the arm, dropped the key into the deposit box, and walked casually to the exit.

Tonight they would be in Tampa.

Sandy was digging her fingers tightly into his arm. When they got back, he should throw a party. She would like that. Maybe in Atlanta, when everything was secure.

In Tampa, he would clear seventy-five thousand for the kilo. Not bad for two weeks' work. They were set and on the final run. Once he hit the States, everything would be smooth.

With the luggage in the back of the taxi, as he pulled away from the hotel, Tommy felt the same sense of relief as when he'd left Bogotá. Not that it wasn't fun, but it was definitely time to be moving on. The driver had the radio tuned to English language news.

"*Last night, in a daring holdup, five bandits robbed the Hilton casino of an undetermined amount of cash. Police are looking for one suspect who is accused of diverting the attention of security during the holdup. The suspect will be easy to recognize because he weighs over four hundred pounds.*"

Now it fell into place. He began to laugh. Of course, Harry was a suspect. No one forgot his performance last night. How absurd, how fucking absurd. Busted for robbery, shit. If they only knew. He would love to see Harry blustering and huffing when they brought him downtown. Robbery! How stupid. With all the other crimes they were committing. He smiled to himself. Were they waiting for him at the airport? If they were, he could pass by unnoticed better than

Harry. Robbery. At least they could beat that one, no sweat. Shit, Harry was going to be a show and a half when they hauled him away with his mouth flapping a mile a minute.

As they exited the taxi, Tommy said, "I'll check the bags. You wait here by the entrance. If there is any trouble, split. Understand?"

"And leave you? Forget it." Her tired voice had recovered its defiance.

"Just wait over there until I check the bag. Do that much for me." He wanted to shout his tension at her but remained calm. "Please."

Sandy pouted for a moment before sauntering away. Tommy grabbed the suitcase and walked directly to the Delta counter. In a few minutes, he would know if he made it.

Chapter 11

HOME WAS A VAGUE FEELING, but as the plane closed in on Tampa Bay, Tommy surrendered to the familiar as Sandy squeezed his hand. Rolling down the windows of the rented LTD as they crossed Courtney Campbell Causeway, the thick afternoon air gave him a sense of security. The warm Florida air was nostalgic with old songs and names. The coke was in the suitcase in the trunk. He had rented the car and headed west, so if anyone was watching or waiting for him at his place, they would have a long wait.

Clearwater was safe for Tommy. No one in town would recognize him, yet he was intimately familiar with the roads, beaches, and motels. He had all the coke, and it was time to cool it. The better part of valor is to know when it's time to split. Now was a good time to take a break in the action. Time out; catch his breath. What's the next play, Coach?

It didn't work like that. There wasn't anyone he could consult.

Was Harry in jail? What could they prove? Nothing. He had all the evidence in the trunk. Did Harry have any coke from last night? Tommy doubted that; Harry was too greedy about the stuff. He'd need a lawyer, but Harry had been down that road. Some of his friends were lawyers.

Right now, however, there was nothing Tommy could do. He wanted some rest and sun. Nothing more. A little time with Sandy to get things straight. If Harry was in jail, what then? Would he talk? No way. There was nothing he could do now. Later, when he had some information, but now it was time for them.

Reaching across the seat, he pulled Sandy closer to him. The strong perfume of the Bay washed over them in invisible droplets. For a few days, no one was going to intrude on his life. A few days. He deserved it.

In the morning, he would put the coke in a safety deposit box in Clearwater under the name of Brian Wilson. The Beach Boys, right. No one ever questioned it or batted an eye. It was one of his private stash places. He kept the key in a metal pill jar concealed in a tree in Dunedin Cemetery. It was that simple and secure.

The neon sign of Gulf to Bay Boulevard was the main drag, America's necklace of franchised neon to the Gulf—McDonald's, Arby's, Burger King, Shell, Exxon, Ponderosa, and Cracker Barrel. Three lanes of divided roadway teamed with traffic and huge car lots advertising the abundance of the good life. After dark, the hot rods and the Cadillacs took over the street. That was the nightlife of the town: kids and real estate men.

Crossing the bridge to the palm-lined causeway, he could see the beach, which lay ahead. He felt a tremendous letdown as he rounded the corner by the Clearwater Hilton. He was making it, and the sense of success brought the aching tiredness of struggling, hour by hour, with the tension and pressure of living. He looked forward to a double bourbon and a king-sized bed. Tonight he would leave the coke in the bag, not even bother to unpack. No one would find it. Tomorrow, first thing, he would go to the bank, then relax. The heaviness of the week wore on him like old clothes. Now was the time to get rid of it all, just throw the clothes away and buy a new outfit.

"Do you think Harry's in jail?" Sandy asked.

"I don't know. When I called George, there wasn't any word yet. After we check-in, George may know something."

He was guessing but really didn't want to know. Not now. Harry was in the system. Nothing he could do except follow the formula. In the clink? Harry would know what to do; he'd been in at least one time before. Tommy realized there was little he knew about Harry. It was hard to tell truth from stories. Harry was from Buffalo, but grew up in Cleveland after his father, in a matter of years, lost a hardware store, feed and grain shop, and auto supply house. Jumping into Lake Erie from the back of a ship in February ended the man's misery, as Harry told it.

He grew up in the poor section, chumming with the tough kids. By seventeen, he had a rap sheet for stealing cars and petty theft. He said he'd gotten smarter. Sandy told him about the army and killing someone. Tommy wondered. In the months since their meeting, Harry sometimes amazed him, but often, he didn't make much sense. Harry wanted money and to be high—and food. His presence in public was always a comic affair.

His role in Bogotá was totally without thought. Was he smart enough in Puerto Rico? Did he have any coke on him? That was the big question. If not, the robbery could be disproved. But coke would draw a charge. He didn't think he could go into a police station and put seventy-five thousand in cash on the table without raising a few heads. So send George?

Great idea. George would call the Puerto Rican police spics right to their faces. Then there would be two problems. For the first time, Tommy hoped the police would be efficient and catch the real dudes. They would take care of Harry's problem and his own dilemma.

"He'll need a lawyer. How do we get him a lawyer? He's got to speak Spanish too. Tommy, do you know any lawyers who speak Spanish?"

"Slow down. We don't even know if he's in jail. Don't start worrying about things you can't do anything about."

"We have to know what we're going to do."

"Only after we know the problem. Don't waste your energy thinking about solutions to imaginary problems." Maybe some time in jail would do him good. How could he do that to Kippi? Why would he do it?

He pulled into the Seabreeze Motel, which was right on the beach. The one-floor motel had rooms that faced the Gulf of Mexico. Tommy paid cash for three nights and carried the bags to the room. He called George, but there was still no word from Harry.

"We have to assume he's alright," Tommy told her. "He's scheduled to be in Miami around six. If George doesn't hear from him by then, we'll know something is wrong. We can worry about it then. Let's assume everything is on schedule." He was tired of the discussion even though he couldn't shake the same fears that were nagging Sandy. There was a helplessness in ignorance—he didn't enjoy it but couldn't change it.

"Tommy, there could have been two people like Harry in the Hilton last night." She looked tired as well.

He opened the door to the beach, and a breeze from the Gulf swept the room. The day was warm for February: the weather the tourists loved. Sandy came quickly to his side, putting her arms around his waist.

"Tommy, what would you do if you were in jail instead of Harry? Would you be scared?" she lowered her voice, and the husky emotion of her voice surprised him.

"Hey, it's not me. Look, it doesn't matter. Harry didn't rob the casino. We can prove that. This is life, and it ain't always fair. We could have been busted for the coke, but those little old Fate ladies like our crazy pattern. If it was you or me in there, there would be other choices. No, don't start crying. It's not me, and it's not going to be me. I know what I'm doing." Tommy said the words, not knowing if he believed them. He pulled Sandy closer until her lips were hugging his. Sandy trembled and drew even closer.

Curling her bronzed leg around the back of his calf, Sandy squeezed her stomach against him. She was part of him, at that moment, so that nothing could take her away from him. His lips were strong as he groped his way into her throat. She was alive, and he was instantly warm as they fell to the bed.

She touched the hairs of his chest in a swooping, caressing movement. He was frightened like a puppy or a little boy, but the softness of her flesh made him want to grip her for the rest of his life right there, in the fragrant softness of the white hairs of her neck. He lifted her t-shirt, sliding his hand across her erect nipples. He rolled the tip between his thumb and forefinger. Sandy shifted closer and moaned slightly. Like the first time, he was drifting into the unleashed passion of exploration and excitement. His body was drawing from her flesh, complete and unchecked satisfaction.

Wanting her, he wanted forever. Just one movement to forever. The rest wasn't going to matter then; this was the real meaning of life. He ran his left hand lightly down her right shoulder and under her skirt, across the rose. A phantom touch, angel touch, and little goosebumps appeared on her leg.

Dropping his hand to her crotch, he entered her panties, exploring the hair with his fingers. She touched his ear with her little finger, tracing circles on it and around the side of his neck.

He involuntarily moaned as she slipped her hand into his pants. It surprised him as much as it pleased him. His thoughts were on the soft wetness of her pussy, his fingers searching gently in time with her movements and groans. She was all around him, under, over, next to, and outside. He wanted to be part of her.

After pulling off her bottoms, she unbuttoned his pants. In an instant, they knelt naked on the bed, facing each other. He explored her breast and arms as she guided his hands with her body movements. Her eyes were moist and longing.

He was very much in love with her. When they first met, she was naïve and spoiled. Here on the bed, she was exquisitely the lady of his life, the woman of his dreams.

"Make love to me. I want you." Her voice was urgent with emotion. She pushed him to his back, mounting him with slick hips.

Tommy rose to her swaying motion. She sat upright, moving her body with her thighs. Arching his back, Tommy raised his hips to meet her while caressing her breasts with his fingers. Rhythm came as naturally as the touch, keeping time to the sexual orchestra of enjoyment. Clicking without trying, the rushes of pleasure built as she changed speed into a slow, gripping, rolling motion. He swung his hips as she tasted and tempted him with rapture. Leaning backward, she held his balls in her cupped hand.

Neither could hold down the mounting crescendo or urgent pleas of their bodies. Tommy began first, thrusting and exploring, staying high against her body. Sandy responded, instantly pushing Tommy deeper into her. Desire and energy enveloped them in a frenzy of muscle and magic. Striving for a final, last, culminating second, Sandy fell forward to his chest, groaning and panting. Tommy's hips retreated to the bed as they returned to lyric circles.

There was no other world for them while they were touching. They made love two more times with Tommy on top and from the rear. By four o'clock, they were exhausted and went to the beach to sleep.

There was no word from Atlanta. Harry had been busted. They had a quick dinner at the burger bar on the beach and retreated to the room, making love for most of the night.

In the morning, Tommy called again. George began going on about his dogs. Tommy cut him off.

"I didn't call to chit-chat about your fucking dogs."

There was a moment of silence.

"Have you heard from Harry?"

"Oh yeah," George said. "He said he would be back...back tomorrow. I guess that means today."

Tommy would have killed the pervert bastard if he was in front of him, but the relief spread instantly. Alleluia.

"Harry said the goddamn spic held him in jail overnight on the stupid robbery charges until they caught some other spic who worked at the hotel. Inside job. Harry threatened to buy the island and sell it to some A-rab oil sheik." George laughed. "Wished I could of seen it. Big ol' Harry with all those little spics running around. I wonder if their cells were big enough for him. When I was in the navy, there was this Korean place where they kept prisoners. The prison cells were so small..."

"Tell Harry, I'll be in touch with him tomorrow. What time is he getting there?" The news took the rough edge off the trip. Now they could all enjoy. "Tell Harry I'll be in touch after everything cools off."

"Yeah right, Tommy. I figure if he doesn't come in till the afternoon, I can take the dogs out to..." George continued about the dogs as Tommy hung up.

* * *

After talking with Harry once he was back in Atlanta, Tommy decided to move his coke. After two more days at the beach, they returned to Tampa. George was on his way down to pick up Harry's share.

Dropping Sandy at her place, Tommy took the suitcase to a furnished one-bedroom apartment concealed in an obscure complex. Tommy used it as his in-town stash. He thought he could turn both kilos in Tampa.

Tommy opened the suitcase. The bags of coke were intact—six-point-six pounds each. From the bedroom closet, Tommy retrieved a brown briefcase with a combination lock. The three-number combination was 327—Sandy's birthday.

Sitting at the kitchen table, he opened the briefcase. Inside was a large aluminum kitchen strainer, a square mirror, a teaspoon, and a pack of single-edged razor blades. From the kitchen, he brought aluminum foil, Glad bags, four bottles of powdered vitamin E, and four of Inositol—both good cuts and nutritious too. On the top shelf of the hall closet was a triple-beam Ohaus laboratory scale.

He locked and chained the front door, so he felt safe. With the teaspoon, Tommy dipped into the full bag of coke, which was powdery but had many good rocks. He gingerly dumped it into the strainer, holding it over the mirror. He shook the strainer gently until the powder was sifted. The solid pieces of coke, he dumped on one side of the mirror. He repeated the process three times, carefully building a mountain of rocks.

Opening the vitamin E, Tommy spooned it into the strainer and mixed it with the coke, which was too good. He had to step on it to make it palatable to the American senses. The E complex was a real fine cut, better than lactose, a sugar that would eat the coke. Lactose had so many impurities in it that after a while, the coke got a milky taste. If the buyer knew his shit, the coke would burn black with lactose rather than the oily red-yellow of good coke. Dextrose was a little better, but it was still a sugar. The vitamin E was the best—slightly bitter, and it burned clean.

The Cubans would put any shit in as long as it was white. Cornstarch, baking powder—they didn't care. Snort cornstarch a few times, and your nose would get so clogged, you couldn't breathe. Anyone with any sense would stop there—but not a lot of people had common sense. Continuing to cut the coke, he did two ounces in a one-to-one ratio. So now he had four ounces. The kilo would give him seventy cut ounces. Depending upon the price, it would earn him one hundred thousand on a fifteen-thousand investment. Not bad.

Tommy placed a piece of foil on the scale and weighed it to zero again. He set the scale to twenty-eight grams and began to sift the mix from the mirror onto the foil. It fell silently like flour, but the texture was finer and heavier. Finally, the scale tipped heavy. Tommy stopped and, using the end of a playing card, spooned off coke until the arrow on the swing arm stopped at the centerline. He took several rocks from the pile and placed them on the foil. The scale tipped heavy again. With the card, he once again removed some coke until the scale balanced.

He took a Glad bag from the box and emptied the contents of the foil into it. He closed and sealed it with masking tape. His business had started with the first pound of pot that he broke down into smaller lids for sale. With the coke, first, it wasn't his, and then sometimes he had a piece of the action, but it was already cut. Now, the supply was his, soup to nuts, and he was controlling his own show.

He cut the first pound and got thirty-five bags. He could get rid of half just by walking into the Connection, their favorite bar. First, he had to make some calls. He began putting everything away, then stopped and returned to the suitcase, which still contained Harry's kilo. Carefully undoing the lining, he took out one bag and laid it on the table. Opening it, he spooned twenty-eight onto the scale and put it into a separate bag. With twenty-eight grams of Vitamin E in the bag, he resealed it as a down payment on the beating he took. He resealed the suitcase.

He put one bag of pure coke into the air conditioner, and he slid two more under the plate in the oven. Putting cut ounces in the brown case, he locked it and put it in the crawl space above the closet. If anyone was going to rip him off, they'd think that was all of it.

He did two spoons before he slid it into a special pocket in the fold of his jacket. If anyone searched him, they'd never find it. The other ounces were in foil in brown paper, which he put into a grey tool kit that he snapped shut. He'd put that in the car trunk. The apartment was locked and looked unchanged from the time Tommy had walked in. It was cool.

* * *

"Who is it?" Sal said through the door.

"Open the fucking door. It's Santa Claus," Tommy said, half smiling to himself.

The door opened cautiously, then Sal flung it wide. "Tommy." His tone was half surprised but mostly filled with relief. "I didn't know you were back. You didn't let me know, and I thought something might of happened to you."

There were more tracks on Sal's arm—he'd been popping with Mike. The dumb shit. He couldn't believe Sal was becoming a junkie.

"Yeah, well, how are things going here? Make any money recently? Where is the four thousand from that reefer I fronted you to sell?"

"Well, you see, that deal didn't come off the way you wanted it to. Those people didn't want to spend that high, so rather than have the shit around, I sold it to them for less."

"Where's my money, Sal?"

"Well, I figured to turn the money on some coke. I figured I'd make a good profit. It wasn't as good as I thought."

"Oh shit. I don't want to hear it. Not now. Get me whatever money you have for me."

Sal stood there silently. "I'll get some tomorrow."

"Oh shit." Tommy shook his head. The guinea was all gone, wasted away. There was a small riding toy in the corner and some blocks on the floor, but there weren't any other signs of Terry or the kid.

"Make me something to eat. I have to go out later."

"Yeah, sure Tommy." Sal stomped into the kitchen. Tommy sat on the couch and dialed his phone.

"Hello, Tuna."

Tommy waited. "Tuna, it's Tommy, and I have a lovely lady for you to meet. You will like her. Yeah, it's near one. The night is as pure as a virgin's cunt. Sure, sounds good. I know you'll love to make her acquaintance. She's just your type. Yeah, yeah. Ciao."

One down. Tuna always wanted coke and had money. He was a credit card Jewish prince from Miami. Anything he wanted. Tommy made a few more calls and told people to meet him at the bar. He could see where they were coming from.

Sal brought out a bowl of minestrone soup. "It's all I could find." He sat down. "Maybe Terry didn't really take the kid back to Providence. Maybe she's somewhere down the beach." He slumped back in the chair.

"I figured." Tommy nodded.

"I've been so lost, Tommy. I don't even know which way is up or down. I still don't believe that she would really do that to me. She waited that whole year I was in jail, and I've been doing good by her here. Oh, sometimes I fuck up a little, but I always gave her what she wanted when I could." His voice broke as he bowed his head.

"You've been fucking around too much. Where's my money? In your arm? Look at you. What the fuck is the matter with you? Of course, she left. First, you're popping skin and running with other ladies. You know how jealous she is. It isn't that difficult to figure out. None of it really is. Terry wasn't fucking around when she threatened. You didn't believe your guinea wife was stubborn? You gotta dry out. Get into rehab before it's too late." Sal was a rising cost. This time, it was four grand. If he couldn't trust Sal with that much, he couldn't trust him to do deals alone. And Mike, who was out on bail with Tommy's money, was worse. He wasn't getting anything in return. Not even peace of mind. This town was a dead end for him, but he'll do one last round to sell the coke.

Sal sat in the green chair, leaning forward, his elbows on his knees. His shoulders heaved slightly but soundlessly. His grimace was comic in its sadness.

"Tommy man, what am I supposed to do? I want her back."

"Do you really? Look at you. Your arms look like you've been run over with golf shoes. You've been with the cheap whores downtown, popping. You don't want her—you want to run shit into your arm. And not only your stuff, but mine too."

If he had brought Sal on the trip to Colombia, which had crossed his mind for a moment, he would have been hopeless. He would have ODed on coke the first day. Tommy didn't have time to play nurse-maid to a junkie. If he could work, fine. Otherwise, he didn't cut it. He'd get him into a rehab program, but after that, he was on his own like every other creature.

"Listen, Tommy, I'll change. Really. I'll go to rehab or whatever. You have to convince her to come back. I don't want to live without her."

"Then get it together, Sal. You can't continue to fuck up."

Sal shook his head. "No, no. I don't care about her—I don't care if she ever comes back. I don't care about anything."

"So, you don't care about anything?" Tommy spit the words. "So what's new with life? You think you've got some special problem? It ain't new. There's nothing that's new—just the same old shit. If you don't care," Tommy pulled his Smith & Wesson and passed it to Sal, handle first, "go blow your brains out and stop worrying about it."

"But Tommy, don't you see it's… Well, I already lost her and the kid. Everything."

"So what are *you* gonna do? You want me to care for you? I've got problems of my own." Sal needed to face his life.

"Yeah, but…" Sal looked up at him. "You keep going. You have what you want."

"Shit, you're dumb." Tommy got up and walked around the room, shaking his head in amusement. He pulled the glass vial from his jacket and put six spoons of coke on the table. Flipping open his pocketknife, he began chopping the rocks. Sal leaned closer.

"Listen, you dumb motherfucker, it doesn't matter to anyone if you care or believe in anything. It ain't off their backs," Tommy said. "They only care when your shit gets in the way of their shit. You say, 'At least I believe in something.' Shit yeah! I believe in Tommy Logan, that's all. Why? 'Cause I'm all I got. I make money 'cause I like to spend money. That's pretty easy to understand. I'm telling you straight up. Nobody will care if I curl up on the floor and bitch and moan about how life is meaningless. Everyone knows that deep down inside, from junkies to good Christians."

"When we were in Catholic grammar school, those nuns in their big black outfits used to scare the shit out of us. Remember? I was a tiny kid, and the world was big. I was cute, and the nuns made me their pet before they pimped me out to the perverts who ruled from the rectory. School was a big con. Nobody cared if I learned."

Tommy did a line. Sal came and sat next to him. "I always wondered if the nuns got it on with each other. What do you think?" Tommy rolled up a hundred-dollar bill for Sal, who fumbled it anxiously.

"Yeah, I suppose. God isn't a good lay." Sal smiled for the first time as he put the Smith & Wesson on the table. "But how do I... I mean why..."

"No 'why' man; just do it. If you spend all your time thinking about why you're going to do something, you'll never get around to doing it. You're hung up on one chick who was your wife. Well, you fucked that up, and now she's gone. So pick something else. Anything—another chick, money, religion, it's all the same. When you got your reason, the rest of the questions aren't so hard to answer. Thinking doesn't get you across the street. You've got to walk.

"I get this hollow feeling in my gut, just like everyone else. So what? Have a drink, say a prayer—peace, love, brotherhood. 'Hey man, want some dope?' It's all a bunch of shit. People have got to believe. I stand up and say, 'fuck you.' I'm stupid. I'm crazy. So what? Who isn't? And that's too much for people to handle."

He took the gun from the table and offered it to Sal again. "Here, man, answer all your questions." Sal took the pistol. "Put it up to your head; feel the cold steel against your temple." Sal raised his hand until the barrel rested against the left side of his head at the hairline. "Now, just squeeze. It ain't hard. Five pounds of pressure, and that's it. All your questions will be answered—forever. Go on. That's what you want, isn't it? The answer. Find it the easy way --the quick way. No more bullshit. No more meaningless days and nights. Go on. Squeeze. Squeeze."

Sal looked at Tommy, his eyes wide and glazed. Tommy sat back, a half-smile on his lips. Sal didn't have the balls for it; he just wanted more coke and an easy scam. Maybe he could get right if he went cold turkey. When it came his time, Tommy would end it. That he was sure of. There were people who would be more than willing to oblige if he gave them the chance. Some of the youngbloods downtown would love the chance, but Tommy never wanted to give the man an easy target. He felt sorry for Sal because he was a long-term friend. He wasn't the bleeding-heart type, but maybe Sal could get his shit together—but would need intervention. Sal had been ripping him off for a while now, and who else? It had to stop. It doesn't pay to take any more punishment than necessary.

Sal was sitting frozen like a statue, the gun held against his head, drops of perspiration collecting around his forehead. His eyes were on Tommy, and his breathing was rapid. He looked like he would explode from the internal tension.

"Gimme that thing, you dumb motherfucker," Tommy said, pulling the gun roughly out of Sal's hand. "You'd probably miss anyhow, the way you're shaking."

Sal let out a gasp of air that hissed like a punctured balloon and put his head down in muffled sobs.

"Get up," Tommy snapped as he lightly hit Sal across the face with the back of his hand. "Don't cry in front of me. You want the pistol again?" He shoved it at Sal's hand. Sal looked at him with tear-filled eyes. Tommy hit him again with an open hand. Sal's head snapped back against the couch, and a trace of anger crossed his eyes. That was what Tommy was waiting for.

"Here, do some more." He gave him a rolled-up bill. "Now get your shit together and get dressed. We're going to do some business tonight."

Sal looked back, the anger still present, but then he smiled. "Yeah, I'll be ready."

Tommy would need him around for a while. He would help him straighten out; he wanted Harry to know that he still had backup when he needed it. He had to complete this deal with Harry. George was coming to Tampa to pick up Harry's portion of the coke. Tommy gave him Sal's address because he didn't want to compromise his place.

There was a pounding on the door that sounded like a sledge, so it had to be George. He was already two hours late, which generally pissed Tommy off. The fucking cracker couldn't tell time.

With his hair cropped short and blue overalls, George looked like he had just arrived from working at a sawmill. The black hair on his thick arms didn't quite cover the two anchor tattoos from his time in the navy. Harry had said that George still worked as a merchant seaman—a boilermaker handling the diesel engines.

"Get lost?" Tommy asked.

George screwed up his left eye. "I'm here, ain't I?" he asked and landed with a thump on the couch in the living room. Sal barely moved from the corner chair. "You got my package?"

Tommy waited because he wanted George to ask again. It was his game, not the gorilla's.

"Look, Harry said you would have a package for me. That's why I drove the fucking seven hours to get here."

"Sure, I've got the package." Tommy put the coke on the dining room table. "You have my package?"

"Harry said he'd give it to you in Atlanta." George moved forward on the sofa to launch himself to his feet. Tommy could see the bulge on the left side of George's overalls. He was packing.

"Not so fast," Tommy said, moving the package back into the bag on the floor. "This is cash and carry."

"Don't fuck with me. Harry said he'd give it to you in Atlanta. You don't trust him?"

"It ain't trust. It's business. No money, no merchandise." Tommy sat at the table as he watched George process his next step. *Don't do anything stupid*, he thought.

"Listen, I came for the package, and I'm leaving with it." George reached to his side for his pistol.

"I wouldn't," Sal said, putting the muzzle of his pistol to the back of George's head. "Just sit still, you fucking ape." George let his hand fall to his side. Sal came around the sofa, his eyes still glazed but burning. Tommy wanted to hurt someone, and George just might be the guy. "Now, careful. Put your piece on the table, butt end first." George moved slowly, placing the gun on the table without taking his eyes from Sal.

"You fucking slimy wop. You don't know who you're messing with. I won't forget this," George said.

Sal whacked George hard on the side of the face with the pistol, drawing a stream of blood. George shook off the hit and moved to get up, but Sal cocked the pistol. "Go ahead, you fucking cracker. Say something else."

George hesitated.

Tommy felt it was getting out of hand. He didn't need any bodies in the apartment.

"Okay, Sal. Calm. This is business."

Sal and George stayed locked in a stare down.

"I'll break you in half, you guinea toad. Big man now with the gun, but you'll see." George began to get up, but Sal blocked his way.

"Enough," Tommy said, slamming his hand on the table. "Let's get business done. George, call Harry."

The big man slowly pulled the phone but made a quick fake at Sal, who backed up a step and raised the gun.

"I'll get you. I always get them," George said as he dialed the phone. "He needs to speak with you."

"What the fuck. No money, no package," Tommy said.

"It's okay. I'll give you the flowers when you get back up here. Keep the baubles as collateral." Harry was using his sincere voice.

It didn't really matter; he had the diamonds. It was more to make the point. He would deal with Mister Burr when he got to Atlanta. Now he had other business to do. "Okay, Harry. I'll give you half now and the other when I see you," he said as he dropped the receiver back into its cradle. He put one bag on the table.

"Okay, George. Move before it gets out of hand," Tommy said.

George stood, and Sal moved back against the wall, the gun still pointed. Tommy picked up George's gun and popped out the magazine as he motioned him toward the door.

"I won't forget you, you little wop," George said as he spat on the floor.

"Go fuck a cow, Li'l Abner," Sal said.

Chapter 12

LATER THAT NIGHT, TOMMY SOLD six ounces to Tuna with no problems. Tuna had plenty of money and was scared to death of Tommy. The deal was done quickly, and everyone was happy.

Next, he drove downtown on I-75 to the spade bars. Tonight he was dressed in a black denim jacket and pants outlined with silver studs. His shirt was a crepe with long lapels that he could tie or throw around his neck. The car didn't handle the way Tommy liked—maybe tomorrow he would trade it in. After this delivery, he would meet Sal at the Connection.

The Hurry Back Café was on Nebraska Avenue down near the docks. Parked at the front door was a long red Cadillac with a white vinyl top and a television antenna on the rear fender. The interior was black leather and leopard fur. It belonged to Pee Wee.

Tommy was glad he was there in case there was trouble. Circling the block, Tommy parked his car on the street adjacent to the bar. He checked the Smith & Wesson tucked in the small of his back. He also had a .25 automatic slung inside his boot as a backup piece.

Coming around to the front of the bar, a large, wasted hooker wearing a blond wig, orange eye shadow, and red hot pants walked up to him. Tommy was wearing his shades so no one could see where his eyes were.

"How's business, Jezebel?" Tommy smiled. "Ain't it wonderful that God gave you something that won't wear out? Sure beats Detroit."

"Aw, go on, honky. You is police."

"If I was police, hooking wouldn't be a crime—you'd all be work-ing for me." Tommy didn't stop for a response but entered the bar. Business time.

He pushed his sunglasses to the top of his head. The bar was dark, very dark, and Tommy could feel the eyes of the place turn to him. He let the door close quickly so that he wasn't silhouetted and stepped to the side to let his eyes adjust. The bar, a large horseshoe, was to his right. A young black man dressed in a black cotton suit, black vest, and a white wide-brimmed hat stood up in the light, tak-ing a step toward him.

Removing his sunglasses, Tommy stopped him with a stare as another young man joined the hat man. The bar wasn't full. The juke-box played Smokey and the Miracles as Tommy spotted the derby at the back of the bar.

With a long, easy gait, Tommy walked to the back of the bar like he owned it. The tension was increasing as several more young men joined the hat man He wanted them to think he was The Man, not just an easy mark. The youngbloods were always out to prove something.

Sitting with his back to Tommy was Pee Wee, a black man in his mid-forties with his black derby hat, white shirt, and green suspend-ers. His head was shaved, as were his eyebrows. In his mouth was a stogie that seemed fixed like a permanent hair lip.

Across the table from Pee Wee was Cecil, a small man in his fifties with long grey hair and a twitch in his left eye. Tommy walked up be-hind Pee Wee and tipped the derby slightly forward. Pee Wee turned.

"Hee hee. How ya doing, kid?" He smiled, showing a large gold tooth. The young blacks stopped.

"Hey, Pee Wee. Saw your ride outside and thought I'd stop and see which way the wind was blowing."

"Hee hee, kid. My ladies say they haven't seen you for a while. Been in the big house?"

Pee Wee ran most of the people on the street. Sal met him first through an Italian booster from Providence who had been in Raiford with him. Tommy got to know Pocahontas, a tall, sultry vixen who worked in Pee Wee's stable. Tommy sold her coke, and she'd stop by the Connection on Thursday nights. He had only seen her twice since Sandy.

Tommy and Sal had bought their first pounds of pot from him in five-pound lots until they found a better connection. It was always low quality, not the good Rastafarian ganja. Tommy hadn't seen Pee Wee in nearly a year.

"I've got something to keep your ladies going all night."

"So kid, you've got the blow to make them go?" He smiled at Cecil and gave him a nod. The grey-haired man twitched in reply. Running a ring-covered hand through his straight hair, the man got up and walked over to the youngbloods, who were just within earshot.

"Let's go, niggers. Get you black asses back to where they belong." The first one, in the black linen suit, hung for a few extra seconds. Cecil looked at the bartender, who was six-four and two-sixty-plus, and the youngblood backed off.

Tommy could see what was happening 'cause it went down this way every time. The first time he had copped reefer down at the dock bar, he sat in the seat closest to the door with his hand on his pistol the entire time. Then, he was frightened and sweating like he was confessing his first mortal sin. Now he didn't keep his hand on this gun all the time but wore two instead.

When he sat down next to Pee Wee, Tommy kept the bar in front of him and the wall to his rear. No Wild Bill Hitchcock routines here. "I just said if you want your ladies to go, I got to know." This time, it was Tommy's turn to smile. He had the upper hand.

Pee Wee didn't have to run around to know what was going on. This was his bar, and he sat like an African chief, his retainers only bringing him the most important news. Pee Wee was cool and had nothing to lose.

The police knew Pee Wee, and he knew the police. The arrangement had been made years ago. Everyone had their price, and as long as payments were on time, no one got hassled too much. That and, of course, information when the police needed it.

Pee Wee raised his hand, and the bartender dimmed the lights in the rear, where they were. The man had style, and Tommy liked that. He kept his feet firmly planted and his right hand ready for the pistol. Though he had known the man for years, treachery was a part of human nature and accepted, especially in this business. Maybe he had just been ripped off, made a bad bet, or was just feeling mean. You never were sure. No one was going to take him easily.

"So you got the blow? Let me see it." Pee Wee leaned forward, taking off his sunglasses for the first time. Tommy held forward a spoonful of coke, and Pee Wee hit it. Then another. The black man returned his shades to his face and leaned slowly back into his chair. On his left arm was a large gold bracelet inlaid with pearls. Knowing Pee Wee, it was hot and from out of state. He snorted again to clear any remaining grains into his nostril, then swallowed.

Tommy could tell by the way Pee Wee laid back in his chair that the ounce was sold. Maybe two. When the enjoyment couldn't be concealed even by someone as practiced as this pimp, Tommy knew that bringing it in himself was the only way to go.

"When can I get some of this blow?" The black man's voice was deep like a kettledrum. He was wearing a gold coke spoon around his neck.

"When I see the bread, you can have the blow. Fifteen."

"Ain't no blow worth that kind of money, kid."

"You can get cheap shit, and at four in the morning, your ladies will be passing out like flies in the snow, or with mine, you'll have to pull them off like bitches in heat. This is Colombian pure, not that jumped-on shit the Cubans sell. You can still taste it."

Pee Wee showed his big gold tooth and reached into his right pocket to pull out a roll of hundreds. He counted thirteen on the table and smiled again.

Tommy placed the bag of coke on the table. Pee Wee moved forward and removed his shades again. He pushed the bag around a minute, then opened it. Tommy was certain the cut was right, and in this bag, he had put more rocks. Pee Wee liked the rocks.

"Who else can give you rocks like that?" Tommy was aloof, distant, cool. His feet were still ready, as was his gun hand, but Cecil and the bartender kept everyone away.

"Fourteen, kid. That's all it's worth."

"Take your fourteen and go buy it somewhere else." He reached to pick up the coke.

"Now, now. Why you want to be so hasty? A man's got a right to consider his business carefully," Pee Wee said.

"If you can get better for less, knock your lights out. This is straight from down south, no fucking middlemen stepping all over it. You can still taste it. And there's room for another step."

Pee Wee put his pinky in the bag and rubbed some coke on his gums. He waited before smiling again.

"Can you do two?" Pee Wee asked.

Tommy refused to smile, but he could see that Pee Wee was already thinking about how he could make four ounces out of this quality, less for any he kept for himself. He counted out the money, and Tommy put a second bag on the table. Pee Wee took two spoonfuls and let his head bob with pleasure. Tommy took the money and added it to his roll. He was taking a chance bringing that kind of money to the Hurry Back, since anyone might like the chance to take it off him. He wanted to keep Pee Wee on edge.

"See you later, old man. Stay out of trouble." Tommy rose and backed to the side door.

"Hee hee. See you later, kid."

Tommy quickly pushed the side door open and closed it just as quickly, making it difficult for anyone else to see. Walking rapidly to his car, he was smart to have parked on the side. Several youngbloods emerged from the rear door. Sliding into the front seat, he gunned the engine and bolted down the street.

* * *

When his brother showed up at his apartment, Tommy had been drinking since early afternoon. Tommy sat at the glass dining room table, the bottle of Southern Comfort and 7-Up next to the mirror with the razor on it.

"What do I owe this honor?" Tommy said as he inhaled a line of coke.

"Nice digs. Where'd all the furniture come from?" Steve looked around the apartment at the two plush couches and side chairs in matching blue fabric. The television was set on a stand surrounded by a reel-to-reel tape deck and two large KLH speakers. It was luxury. A green and blue shag carpet covered the floor, and Kmart copy art was on the walls.

"Rented. Easy as shit." Tommy pointed to the mirror. "Want some?"

"Not now." Steve was in shorts and a blue denim work shirt. His hair was to his shoulders, held back with a woven leather headband. "You shouldn't do so much."

"Fuck you, brother, giving advice again. Look around. I'm not living in that shithole you call a house."

"I just don't need stuff." Steve turned a side chair toward the table and draped his strong legs over the arm. "Stuff brings you trouble."

"You may have dropped out of the world because you killed that kid. But I didn't. I'm going to be a fucking millionaire. Nobody will ever touch me again." Tommy downed the remainder of his drink and made another. His eyes darted around the room, and he struggled to stand.

"It was a reaction. You know how… fuck it. No reason to go back there." Steve took Tommy's arm and led him to the couch.

"Yeah. I'd like to kill someone. That fucking priest." Tommy's voice thickened as he looked at the floor.

"What the fuck are you talking about?"

"Nobody did anything about that shit. They have the power. They have the collar—that makes them untouchable. And it is probably still going on." Tommy got up and opened the drawer next to the television. He took out his Smith & Wesson, waving it at Steve. "If I had it back then, back when I was seven, I would have blown his fucking head off."

"What the fuck are you talking about?" Steve took the gun and placed it on the table. "You sound crazy."

"Crazy." Tommy grabbed Steve's shirt. "That's what they said. No one would believe or even listen." His tongue had slowed as he put his head into Steve's shoulder and began to sob. "It wasn't right, but they wouldn't believe me."

"Who wouldn't believe you?" Steve patted him gently on the back.

"No one. No one." The alcohol and cocaine had taken over. "I couldn't talk to Mom. Dad was brainwashed by the priests. Not his own son. I hated it. He made me go back and serve mass with that fucking pedophile. Week after week. You remember how I always tried to pretend to be sick when he wanted me to go, but he would force me? And that fucking priest would tell me he was saving me from the devil. I believed all that shit back then."

Tommy's head bobbed like it was on a string. He went to the table and began chopping the cocaine harder than necessary. He snorted two lines and passed the rolled-up hundred-dollar bill to Steve. Steve looked at the bill and then at his brother whose eyes were still wet. He quickly snorted a line and sat at the table.

"Why me? Why not Tommy Delaney or Kevin McCarthy or Tommy O'Toole? Why me? Because I was small? Cute? Compliant? Believer?" He snorted two more lines. Was he coke paranoid? He couldn't stop. It had to come out.

"When did all this shit happen? Is this when you started to get in trouble at school?"

"Yeah, yeah. That was part of it." Tommy finished his drink before making another. "I couldn't tell you. I couldn't tell anyone. The priest said I would go to Hell. I tried to tell Dad that the priest was doing stuff, but he cut me off. *Priests are men of God. Do what they say.* Shit. That's parenting. Letting your seven-year-old be raped by a fucking priest. Who can you tell in a Catholic School? The nuns? Yeah, right." He took another long drink, lingering with it in his shaking hand. "If I only had a gun back then, I would have used it."

"That was then," Steve said, putting his hand on Tommy's. "I'm sorry that it happened."

"Sorry, fuck. No one cared. No one got punished for what happened to one little kid. I don't care. No one will ever fuck with me again. I promise you that, brother. He's been doing... he's a fucking pervert, pedophile..." Tommy's eyebrows were furrowed, and his lips drawn tightly. He reached for his Smith & Wesson. "I'll fuck him up so bad." He waved the gun at Steve. "I'm the bad ass now."

Chapter 13

AT THE CONNECTION TWO WEEKS later, Tommy didn't see Sal's Cadillac. He had better show; Tommy had to be able to depend upon him. He and Sandy had been laying low, going to the beach and spacing out. Now it was time for work.

"Hi, sweetheart," Tommy said to the blond girl at the door. The doorman said, "Hey T, how's it going? Hi, Sandy."

"Couldn't be better." They walked in without paying the cover charge.

There was a good crowd in the bar—some couples on the dance floor and more people at the tables beyond the railing. The seats at the oval bar to his left were almost filled. Smoke hung like a dirty window across the room. He sat at the end of the bar where he could see everyone who entered or left, as well as the whole bar.

He felt good tonight. The deals came easy, and despite the Sal problem, things were in good working order. The coke he was moving was primo. Now he had his lady and a business that was riding high.

He didn't need to apologize for his life. Drugs permit people to cope with the fucking hypocrisy of the system. Booze, the oldest and most universally enjoyed drug, has kept the violence of man primed and his pain numbed. Tommy Logan was a two-bit nobody. For the first time, he was on an international enterprise—a fucking multinational. If the government zeroed in on him, bang, over—destroyed.

He wasn't afraid to speak with action; he was willing to be that free. What could be taken from him but life? He would live his life, nothing more.

"Tommy, did everything go alright?" Sal asked, weaving slowly up to him. He was dressed in black with a dark red shirt and black wide-brimmed hat.

Glad to see you could make it." Tommy turned his attention to the honey blond Texas bartender. "Rum and coke, luv," he said, flashing her a smile. She was his favorite, a real lady. At Christmas, he had given her a gold bracelet just for the hell of it.

"I'll have a margarita," Sal said.

"I'll catch you in a bit," Sandy said as she shook her head, looking at Sal. "Sad."

Under the wide brim of the black hat, Sal's dark complexion gave him a sinister look. The droopy mustache made him look like a Mexican bandit, but his eyes were crazier and colder. This was the reason he and Tommy looked threatening together. As a pair, their presence frightened people into submission.

Something was wrong, seriously wrong. Sal didn't usually drink because he would pass out—especially with tequila. Tommy had to get Sal help. He wasn't going to do it on his own. When he turned everything into cash, he would get Sal into rehab—maybe next week. In the meantime, Tommy would be more careful watching his own back.

"Hey, Tommy. Good to see you're back," Mike Broski said drunkenly, leaning to put his hand on Tommy's back. Tommy blocked it with an inside forearm.

"Don't touch me."

"Yeah, sure, sure." Broski was wobbling on his white platform shoes, a vase waiting to crash to the floor. He leaned on Sal for balance.

"Why did you bring him out so fucked up?" Tommy asked Sal. "He's more trouble than he's worth."

"Trouble? Who's giving you trouble? I'll take care of them. Just show me who they are. Listen, motherfuckers..." Broski started to shout. Tommy grabbed him by the shirt and slammed him against the wall, applying extra force with the palm of his hand against Broski's sternum.

"I should revoke your bond, you dumb son of a bitch." He turned to Sal, who sipped on his drink.

"He took a bunch of downers. What could I do?" He shrugged.

"Park him in the back or put him out in the car. Just keep him quiet and out of trouble." Sal nodded but was looking at a tall brunette in black crepe, who was dancing with a Cuban.

"Do it now, Sal."

Sal nodded again and led Mike to a table at the back of the bar. The changes Sal was going through were only scrambled when he was around Broski. The kid had no common sense. None. He was a fuckup from the womb. Sal was going in that direction. Tommy hoped he could pull him back. There was a lot of violence behind that comic face. Tommy hoped Sal would find another lady, soon. Tonight, he couldn't worry about their problems. Tonight, the order of business was getting rid of another six ounces. That wouldn't be hard here.

Tommy ambled around the oval bar, checking out the clientele for familiar faces. Some of the regulars were in, but some he didn't care to know.

Willy, the head bartender, leaned over the bar as Tommy leaned in. "Been having some trouble with the Latins. They're into fighting, and they move in packs."

"I know."

"There's been some really bad blood between Sal and some of the Latins. I don't know what it's about for certain—women? Drugs? Don't know."

"Thanks for the heads-up. Another rum and coke. Put it on my tab, and one for you too."

"Thanks, Tommy. Watch yourself. We're here." Willy nodded at the other bartenders.

"Yeah," Tommy smiled. "And you know I'm with you. Is Hank in the office?"

"Think so. He was here a few minutes ago, so I think he went back."

Tommy walked defiantly around the bar, challenging any glance he met. This was his bar, and he could do what he wanted. One night when he was high and feeling bad, he had jumped on the bar and walked around, kicking drinks off it. Everyone was stunned silent. Tommy threw Willy a hundred and said, "Set them up again." He needed to be crazy sometimes, or he never really felt free.

Willy was right: there were more Latins, both Cuban and Tampan. The Tampan Latin was a mixture of Italian and Cuban, highly volatile and unstable. Extremely macho, they always wanted to fight. Tommy didn't mind a fight but would rather stay clear. They had their own customers for coke, and he had his—a matter of unofficial territories. Their customers never overlapped except for Pee Wee.

He rapped three times on the plain wooden door. "Hank." Tommy opened the door as Hank got up from his desk. "Hey, big man, what's happening." Tommy slapped him five.

"Tommy, good to see you. Where you been? What's new?" Hank smiled a grin as wide as his face. Tommy remembered the first time he had knocked on that door, and his fear. Time and business had made Hank a friend.

"Mainly the same old thing. Every now and then, I come across something special." Tommy locked the door. "Still have that mirror?"

Hank reached into the top left drawer of the cherry wood desk and brought out a plain round mirror. Tommy took a small brown bottle from his pocket and spooned coke onto the mirror. There were several small rocks, which Tommy separated from the rest. Taking his pocket knife, he began chopping them. Scratching the side of his nose, Hank got ready for the coke, which now laid in lines on the mirror.

"The Latins started coming over here in groups, looking for white pussy. Christ, if they'd bring some of their dark-eyed girls, there would be enough women to go around and not so many fights. Latin, green, ugly, or fat—the way most guys get by closing, it doesn't much matter. They're so drunk, they can't tell the difference."

Hank rolled a hundred-dollar bill and did a line, then another. He handed the bill to Tommy.

"I'm not making as much money, and I don't want to put up with the bullshit every night. I don't need the police coming in here to break things up. I'm going to keep things under control." He did another line. "Want a job? I'll make you chief of security. You get to hire your own staff."

"Shit, I take the beating while you make the profit? If I take the beating, I make the profit." Tommy smiled, appreciating the compliment.

"Yeah, I don't want the job either. That's why I offered. This is really fine coke. Any for sale?"

"How much do you have in mind?"

"If it's like this, at least four for now. What price are we talking?"

"Fourteen."

"That's high."

"So are you."

Hank sat back for a moment, his mouth involuntarily chewing. "Yeah, you're right."

"A deal?"

"You drive a hard bargain, T, but you have the best coke in town."

Tommy returned quickly from his car and put four ounces on the table, and Hank counted out forty-two hundred-dollar bills. Tommy added it to his roll. "I'm sure you're going to enjoy yourself."

Hank smiled his toothy grin. "Yeah, you're right, but it's business too."

"Got ya."

Hank still had buddies from his pro football days who liked coke. When they tasted what he had, Hank would be back for more. Maybe two or three. If he had any left, fine. If not, those were the breaks. Things were working smoothly, and Tommy was pleased with himself. He was making money, lots of money. Yeah, he was a capitalist; that's what the game was about. Why not? Let someone else make the profit? Somebody's got to make the money because the demand was there.

The bar was filled when Tommy came out of the office. The aisles were crowded with guys, Latins on one side, whites on the other. On the dance floor were some mixed couples. The whole white ass trip was so stupid. White girls didn't know how to fuck like the Latin girls. Pocahontas, Pee Wee's whore, had the little tricks and more body control than any woman he had ever met.

He could sense a battle brewing over women. If Harry was here, he'd want to run a stable for the Latins. Why give it away for free when you can make a living doing it?

The dance floor and the tables were three steps lower than the two bars, with a wrought iron railing separating the two levels. Tommy walked its length, eyeballing the lower level. He thought the two blacks in the silk suits were the same ones from the Hurry Back. He hadn't gotten a good look at them, but he remembered the gold chains.

There was going to be a fight tonight—that, he could tell. The air in the bar was warm, smoky, and dark. People were compressed, wanting room and crowding each other. Hank was doing a hell of a business tonight and had a whole crew of big boys on hand. The dance floor was alive with human energy fused with the electric current, cloaked in a cape of numbing sound. Dance to the music, going to war, all the savage little humans prepping their bodies for later— fighting or fucking. The band was playing "Honky Tonk Woman" and the lead singer was good.

There would be a fight tonight, so he better get some business done. Then he'd be glad to fight. He felt like punching someone—it would feel good. Sometimes people think they can push, as long as they didn't push him. The Latins were pushing tonight.

Tommy walked the length of the bar, squeezing by in the crowded room. With his last sale, the night was made. Tomorrow, he would unload the rest—some repeats like Hank. Sal was at the end of the bar, sweet-talking a dirty blond chick with too much makeup and too many pounds.

"Hey, Sal." He put his hands on Sal's shoulders. "Gumba, how's it going?" Sal's cheeks were puffed, his eyelids heavy, and his pupils shrunken. He looked drunk, which was unusual.

"Where's Mike?" Sal shrugged. "Around. This is my friend Suzy." He leaned over to kiss her but missed.

"Where's the Cadillac?"

"I traded it for a 240-Z. Straight up. Great deal." Sal smiled.

"You mean you traded my Cadillac without asking?" Tommy was incredulous, turning away from Sal to hide his rage.

Then a rumble began to run through the bar like the rain coming through live oaks until a fight broke out on the dance floor. The bartenders leaped over the bar with the precision of commandos, blackjacks in hand. Tommy jumped over the bar to protect their backs as he watched the bartenders smother the fight. He was on the outer ring, but the unrest was a bad odor that hung across the room as four participants were roughly forced to the door.

A thick Latino, dressed in red, snarled at Tommy, "We're gonna get your ass, *puta*." He was twenty pounds heavier than Tommy.

Tommy stepped forward, his hands at his side. "*Que es una puta?*"

The man turned slowly, removing his sunglass with his left hand as he reached into his coat for a ten-inch stiletto. Tommy stepped into a right roundhouse kick off his back leg, snapping the man's head to the left as the body followed it to the floor. He sidestepped into the next onrushing Cuban, doubling him up with a reverse punch to the midsection. Tommy could feel the solar plexus collapse under his fist as the man gasped, falling to the floor.

The whole area around him was an eruption of hands, feet, chairs, and bottles. A short, square guy charged him with a broken bottle, but Tommy quickly threw a chair into his path, and as the man looked down to move it, Tommy caught him on the cleft of the chin with a front snap kick. The man straightened out backward and landed hard on the wooden dance floor.

A crushing blow forced Tommy's head left, and he dropped into a low stance to hold his balance and face the attack. The man was already behind him, fighting to get a two-handed chokehold on Tommy.

Turning his head to the side, he realized that the man was larger and stronger than he was. Instantly, with all the force of his jaws, Tommy sank his teeth into the hand at his neck and stomped viciously at the instep, crushing the foot. There was a cry of pain, and Tommy was loose. He turned, leading with a crushing back fist to the head, then a sidekick, which doubled the man in half before he fell to the floor. Willy, the bartender, was about ten feet away with several bodies around him. Hank was driving several people out the door with a riot baton. The fight was gone from the room, and the silence of the room was an eerie calm as people, even the band, had stopped to watch the fights. The bartenders had the last group surrounded and began moving them to the door.

"I'll get you, *puta*," the man in the red suit yelled at Tommy as he was pushed toward the door. His face was bloody, but that didn't stop Tommy from swinging with a back fist, but the man was already out of reach.

Willy had a cut on one hand from a bottle; Hank was untouched. Tommy was bleeding from the mouth where he had been blindsided.

He felt better, clearer. The air was calmer, smoother, like it had just taken three seconds. Tommy tasted blood in his mouth and swallowed it. Nothing much hurt. In fact, he could go a few more rounds. He really had power in his punches tonight.

* * *

After last call, the bar cleared, and Tommy walked Sandy to her car and sent her home. He was going to get another bottle of champagne from Hank and make one more stop before returning to the apartment.

Sal was still in the corner of the bar, propped on his elbows like an old wino. He was drunk, but Tommy had been feeding him coke all night to keep him together—in case. He wasn't much use. His friend Suzy realized it and split.

"Let's go, Sal." Tommy hit him on the arm. He held out another spoon for Sal, who inhaled it quickly. "Can you drive?"

"Yeah, I can drive… Why did she leave, Tommy? I was trying. Sometimes I just broke down. I made mistakes. She should forgive.

The Lord says forgive your husband. And I'm her husband, and little Sal is my son." His eyes began filling with big watery tears that fell to his chest. Then he shook his head. "Fuck her, the rotten whore. I don't care if she don't care. What did she want? What did she ask for that I didn't give her?"

"Let's go, Sal." He wished he could drop him off at rehab right now. But tomorrow. Sal was shuffling his feet deliberately, like a little boy looking for a can to kick. His black hat was crushed and tilted, and his coat was rumpled in the shoulder from the way he was sitting. He looked more like an immigrant right off the boat than a cocaine dealer. His mustache hung heavier, and his eyes lacked the fierceness of the earlier Sal. Tommy picked up the bottle of champagne and walked to the front door, where Willy was waiting with the key to Sal's car.

"You sure can use those legs. I thought the first guy was going through the dance floor."

Tommy smiled. "You did a number on a few yourself."

"Take it easy, T. You too, Sal."

The night air was cool, not oppressive like the day. Tommy liked the night; it was when he was alive and ready to prowl. Tonight was his night, and he was ready to get home to Sandy.

"Where's your car?" Tommy asked. There were still some people hanging outside—guys and chicks, but Tommy didn't want any company.

"It's in the alley over here." Sal motioned.

"Can you drive?"

"Yeah, no problem, but give me some blow."

Tommy gave him a piece of foil with a dime of coke in it. He wanted Sal to sleep too. Tomorrow he'd look into rehab. "Don't do it all at once. And don't let that woman get you down."

Turning in the opposite direction, he walked across the street to the parking lot. One more stop and then to Sandy. As he unlocked the car, the night was shattered. *Bang. Bang.* Two shots in rapid succession. They came from the alley where Sal had disappeared.

The blood was pumping hard into his legs and arms as Tommy sprinted to the alley. The Smith & Wesson was in his hand as he tried hard to swallow. He didn't know if Sal was shot or had done the shooting.

Hugging the wall closely, Tommy slid down it and turned the corner at knee-level. The alley looked empty. Tommy looked back over his shoulder at a crowd of people coming his way. He walked silently down the dark alley, his stomach taut, perspiration forming on his forehead and in his armpits. He walked quickly, quietly, and close to the wall.

Near the end of the alley, Sal lay face down on the blacktop, his hat crushed to his head. Tommy felt nauseous but ran and knelt quickly at Sal's side. He touched him once, then ran out into the lot behind the bar. A huge figure in overalls waited a moment before he jumped into a blue pickup truck at the far side of the lot and gunned it toward the street. Tommy ran to the middle of the lot, stopped, and leveled the pistol. He squeezed the trigger as the rear window of the truck appeared in his cross sights. There was the sound of shattering glass, and the truck swerved before righting itself and speeding into the darkness. He was gone, but why did he wait? Did he want Tommy to see him?

Turning quickly, he ran back to Sal, who had not moved. Tommy felt for a pulse, but he wasn't sure where to find it. He held the wrist, then rolled Sal to his back and listened to his chest. Both shots had penetrated his guts. The smell of shit seeping through the holes filled the air with death. Tommy turned pale at the sight of Sal's death mask in a dark alley, quaking at the suddenness and finality of it. There were no more words, no more problems.

Why? Why? Despite the problems, Sal was his friend—his old friend. That was a rotten deal. Sal's wallet was still there; it wasn't a robbery. It had to be George. There couldn't be two big men like that. Was Harry behind it?

* * *

The old ladies of Fate finally got fed up with Sal's pattern. Snip, snip. That's all they wove. It was a quick way to go, dead in an alley, guts shredded by a few bullets. He left Terry and little Sal with nothing.

Human pride was wrapped in a bundle of shit and rages. Life was over, no score, no last words. Just over without any choice. Sal was gone, biting a piece from Tommy's flesh. They had shared dangers and pleasures. Tomorrow he was going to help him get straight. No, it was done, and nobody could undo it.

Everyone goes when the man is at the door. Open up. The order is unmistakable—it's a no-win situation. No reason to get upset, no reason to feel crazy with disgust of the living, disgust at the stupidity of the world, and total unfairness. Here reality was pungent and immediate. Sal was shredded, his guts oozing onto the asphalt alley. He was the first one to leave, to leave Terry and little Sal. He wanted his pleasures but couldn't see what he had. Grasping, scared, unable to conceptualize the world, Sal only saw Sal. He never foresaw each event in his life from birth to jail; separation and death came as a surprise to the guy. There wasn't anything that could be done about it. Maybe next time around.

Tommy made the sign of the cross. "Hey man, if you're there, you'll understand. He's my friend. He wasn't a saint, but he cared about his kid. I wanted to go on the record for him, in case no one else does."

The crowd was already down the alley. Hank was in the lead with a .44 magnum in his right hand. Tommy stood and holstered his Smith & Wesson.

"Tommy, what happened?" Hank was flushed from the run. He stopped the small group with a raised hand. Several of the bartenders behind him kept the crowd back.

He didn't want to talk; he wanted to explode, to hit someone, to scream. Why? So useless, so senseless. Tommy fought for control of his tongue. "Someone got Sal. Twice in the gut." He turned to the body while speaking to Hank. "It was a blue pickup. It's got a bullet hole in the back window. I'll get that mother…"

"Tommy, I'll handle this. You get out of here. The police will be here any minute."

"I don't give a fuck if a hundred cops are here. He was my friend, and I'm not leaving him here in this fucking alley. I don't give a fuck what anyone says." Tommy was shouting, the blood pounding in his neck. The crowd edged backward, sensing danger.

"Easy, Tommy. I understand what you're feeling…" Hank stepped forward warily.

"The fuck you do… What did Sal mean to you? You didn't…"

"Sal's dead, Tommy. You're not. Do everyone a favor: split. I'll take care of Sal. There's nothing else you can do for him. You'll only make it worse for everyone but the guy who did this." Hank put his hand on Tommy's shoulder.

Letting the anger lift with that touch, Tommy wanted to get out of there as quickly as he could. Useless. Ridiculous that there wasn't anything he could do. He wanted to make it right, make it better, to avenge.

The prostrate form of Sal looked like a small animal in the shadows, hiding from human light. Sal's face hung limply but serenely, all the tension finding its proper harmony. Maybe it was better for Sal now. He was on his way to junkiedom. What's death but another stage of living? Tommy reached into Sal's right pocket and took out the dime of coke in foil. Opening it, he poured it into the air.

"Here's for your spirit, my friend. You're on your own. If you need to get high, come visit." He said it aloud but to himself. "Call his mother. She lives in Providence. I'll call Terry." He slowly shook his head. "Talk to you later."

"Yeah, Tommy, go home. There's nothing you can do."

Tommy nodded. Maybe not now. There was a reason why, and he would find out. But not now. Not now. No emotions. Sal was only a poor little sucker who got in the way of heavy forces. And what was he? No emotions, not now. He walked through the crowd, which melted before him, no one meeting his gaze. He was alone, above, touched by grief and personal loss that no one else could feel. He alone heard the clanking of Sal's soul, dragging its chains, trying to find out where it was. Tommy hoped so. Life is trouble. Only death is not trouble. Someday a bullet would catch him. This wasn't his day—it was Sal's.

It was too late to go downtown; all the clubs were closed. Tommy drove on I-75 toward the Tampa skyline, luminous spotlights proclaiming the glory of civilized man. Right in front of him, institutionalized and fortified in respectability as the norm. Sal should have been there. A banker, not a stupid ex-con.

Drug dealing was wrong, but the insidious, ruthless methods of the boardroom were correct. They built the skyline of the city, but from whose pockets? No thanks. He would never do it. He didn't want to sit at a desk from nine to five and rip people off. He'd rather be face-to-face with life in the alley.

Sal was dead now. The first link to his beginning here was gone. When they met, Sal was a wannabe tough guy fresh out of prison, desperately wanting to be respected. He could never see himself, only the objects in his life. Time for him to move.

Tommy rolled down the window as he drove onto the Howard Franklin Bridge to cross the bay. The large bright moon whipped the clouds into a creamy whiteness. The cool night air was giving him a strong, lucid head. He took a step backward and realized he could never escape the man at the door. He understood how power worked. With enough money, he didn't have to step aside. When the man came, time was over.

Maybe he was crazy. Sal was dead. That was the sealer, the omen for departure. He would leave Tampa as soon as he could. Tomorrow?

Was Sal killed for fucking another man's old lady or ripping over a Cuban in a coke deal? Both were capital offenses on the street. But the big man—was it George? He was a stone killer. Did Harry know? Order it?

Tommy took the bridge toward the beach because it had no exits for seventeen miles. Once on it, there was no getting off, no turning around, straight through to the end. He pressed the pedal to the floor. The road was obscured by the morning fog as the car headlights refracted and scattered in the water vapor. He was driving into a wall that parted as he came nearer. The car glided effortlessly over the concrete as Tommy exited from the reality of his existence.

The ride back was smoother as the sun began to nudge the horizon. Tommy was leveled, all systems go. He chose Fletcher Avenue because, at daybreak, cops emerged from their nightly naps in time for morning coffee runs along Fowler Ave. He had done enough business; he didn't have to move the rest right now. He had a strong sense of disaster in Tampa. It was a low-life street hustle where little events were capital crimes. He wanted to be in Atlanta by tonight. He didn't want to get involved in a murder investigation. No way did he want any police investigating him. The police would come looking to talk to him. He hoped they found the killers quickly. In the meantime, he wanted to stay out of their way. Out of state was safer.

Sandy was the most important person to him. That's where he should be. He wanted her to get away from this sordidness, although it was part of his life. The filth made him afraid to get too close to her or allow her to see the ugliness of it all. If she had stayed last night, seen, smelled the… He shook the thoughts, throwing them away. The night was over; morning was a new time. He had to keep it together.

Sandy was lying asleep on the green overstuffed couch in the living room. Her light brown hair covered her breast carelessly. She was serene and extremely beautiful, a child in her innocence. He was convinced with all the certainty of death that they would be together. He was satisfied it would last—for a while.

He didn't want to wake her or disturb the tranquility she possessed with the horror of his reality. Lying there, her long brown legs—snaking from under the short silk shift—were smooth and inviting. The tattoo on the inside of her left thigh looked lighter.

Stirring when he shut off the television, she sat up. "Oh, Tommy, you're here. I tried to stay awake, but…"

"It's okay, baby. I didn't expect you to." It was enough to be with her, to have her waiting. She was his link with the dual worlds of Tampa and Atlanta, the street and respectability. She was part of the affluent, looking at the street from the limousine window—her daddy's little princess. She wanted to get out and walk the street. Did she understand Sal or Sal's death? How would she understand? The strength she brought to him was more than he could ever express.

"Tommy, what's wrong?" Sandy cleared her eyes, putting her arms around his waist and drawing him to the sofa. He offered no resistance. "Are you sick?"

"Yeah, I'm sick." He wanted to end the conversation and not talk.

"Is that it?" She touched his forehead. "No, something happened. The vein in your neck is twitching like you're mad at someone. And you're sweating. What's the matter?"

He tried to smile, but his facial muscles didn't respond. He didn't want to respond. He didn't want to be anywhere these memories could touch him or affect his judgment. He shrugged helplessly against her hug. She backed away.

"Tommy, something happened. It shows. Tell me—share it with me. That's part of what love is. Maybe I can help. It can't be that bad."

He glared at her presumption, venting puffs of anger. "Sal was killed tonight—two bullets in the gut. Help me out of this one. He died without time to cry. Just gone." He offered her a hit from his golden spoon.

"Dead? When, where… Tommy, my God… Were you… You're not hurt?" She examined him more closely. "I thought the fight was settled…" She began to shiver, and she wrapped her arms around herself.

"I put a bullet through the back window of the truck. It got away. Sal was lying in a lump, smelling like a load of shit, his hat squashed down on his head. All these people wanted to look at him." His voice choked.

"Tommy, stop. I don't want to hear anymore." She buried her head in his shoulder.

"What don't you want to hear about?" He pulled her directly in front of him. "You don't want to hear that people die; people kill. Is that what you don't want to hear? It's true, lady. And I don't like it any more than you. I've got to survive. When I die, then I won't worry about it anymore." His own fear refused to mask lines on his forehead. "All I know is that I'm getting out of this town. I don't want a murder investigation coming down around me. I can't move fast enough for that. I have more important things to do. You understand?"

Sandy was quiet and subdued in his hands. She didn't need to hear any more. It was no use to fight; she just wanted him to hold her. She saw it all moved on blind faith. He was the other side of life, the fast lane. The roller coaster excited him. The money, the frenzied excitement, and the danger kept him alive. The roller coaster was going too fast for her, and she couldn't scream.

She ran her left hand up his neck, her fingers entwined in his curly hair. Her hands explored his crown in a soft circular motion, forcing Tommy to close his eyes and float with the sensation. The coke urged him along. At each feeling, each try, his body surprised him. It was fantastic.

Always fighting. Life seemed to happen that way. He was looking to be better than the next guy. Not modesty. Fact. Look at where he was, so what did any of it mean? Tommy didn't use time units as a reference point. Grams and ounces were more certain.

Time was the limiting dimension. It limited Sal to twenty-five years and some months. How long for Tommy? What view of the world should he take? Get a steady job, wife, kids, mortgage? Trade fear for security. Was it much safer there? The school teacher dies just as dead as Sal. As our lives extend, we become greedier.

Sandy's eyes regained their tranquility. "I'm not sure I understand any of it. I don't know if I want to, either. I'm happy you're safe. I would have been... the fight was bad enough... you take too many chances." She stopped her motherly tone.

Tommy turned to her, taking a deep breath from between her breasts. She had a natural sweetness that put all other fragrances to shame. With his fingers, he traced the outline of her figure, from her breasts to the rose on her thigh. Her flesh was soft yet very firm, pleasing to touch. She was the reason for him to live. A woman is a reason, better than most, but as difficult to survive.

Sandy ran her hands down his chest and circled inside his pants with her forefingers. Closing in on him with her body, her tongue was soon in his mouth. The taste was salty, alive, and teasing. It darted about, seeking sensitive spots to brush against. Tommy ran his hand up her arm, then across to her neck before returning to her breast. Her nipple was firm and seemed to quiver as he touched her.

He couldn't remember a time when he wanted to be in the arms of a woman more than he did now. His feelings were primitive and deep, from the sinews of his masculine muscles. She was an end, the end of all existence. There was to be no more in any promises that were ever made.

Running his hand along her gently quivering thigh, his fingertips were vibrating in harmonic rhythm with the waves of her body. The asphalt alley and the rank smell of fresh shit were lost in the essential softness of her natural perfume. This was a different life, a different dimension. This was the better world. She wasn't part of any of the other, yet she was all of the others.

Sandy inched her way down his chest, smothering his body with warm little nibbles. Gooseflesh crawled along his side and in the small of his back, but he knelt, concentrating on the sensation of Sandy's mouth and fingers. Here, warmth penetrated him, giving strength. She was all for now; she was satiating.

He fell back to the couch and locked eyes with Sandy, watching the thin bones of her shoulders rise like wings as she reached to hold him. Her tanned skin was silken and damp from her perspiration and his. Smoothly, she slid over him, swallowing and surrounding him, raising and lowering her hips for her own pleasure.

"Oh, Tommy, Tommy," she began to pant. "Oh, Tommy, how do you do this to me? Oh, baby, come on. It's what it's all for. Oh, Tommy, I don't ever want to lose you." Moving faster and faster, her body strained like a runner reaching for her last ounce of energy. With a spasmodic cry of exhilaration, she slumped forward on his chest, burying her head in his neck.

For several minutes, they lay motionless—two morning glories, waiting for the sun to wake them again from slumber. Tommy was still strong inside her, filled with a feeling of invulnerability at his own uniqueness. It was aloneness, and it was completeness, one and the other without the separation of distance or the constraints of being.

She wasn't any woman. Tommy had had so many. She was the right woman. If yesterday he didn't think of her, or the day before, he wasn't looking for another. She consummated all the human desires he had. He could feel the subtleties of her vagina, the straining depth of her heavings, and the substance of her heart as she tightened and pulled him in her with each thrust. There was no other meaning to the world, no other place to be or to go. Moving his knees closer to her ass, she pulled her beautiful legs forward and put them on his shoulders.

With quickened movements, Tommy felt himself tense inside, preparing, ready to strike, and he could not control nor want to control the intensity as it built to a crescendo until, with a sudden explosion, he came inside her, watching and being watched in the strength of her arms.

* * *

"I'm not coming back to Tampa except to move," Tommy said, coming out of the apartment bathroom. "There isn't anything here for me. I want you to come with me, but I don't know where it's going. So no promises."

"Why are you always the tough guy? You don't have to prove anything to me."

"Look, it's time to move on. I was a boy in Tampa. I don't want to stay in these stupid kid games. Not when they're senseless like Sal's death. I want you to be with me because we'll both enjoy the highs and lows better. I love waking up next to you; I feel like I'm in heaven."

She looked defiantly at him. "So now you're making me a gracious offer. That's better. And if I come, what's my cut?"

He flashed a surprised grin. "Now you're understanding. We're partners. You get a piece of whatever I do and whatever we can steal. Let's see how nasty we can be."

She smiled insolently. "You think you're so damn smart."

He ran across the room and dove into bed with her. "Yeah, I'm smart, and so are you. That's what makes life so interesting for both of us."

Grabbing his shoulder, she held on as he tried to pry her off. Turning into a squirming collection of arms and legs, she fought against him. Finally, exhausted, she went limp. Tommy nodded in triumph, then collapsed next to her. They made love again.

Chapter 14

BACK IN ATLANTA, HARRY WAS sitting in his captain's chair at the dining room table when Tommy arrived. He had called ahead because he wanted Harry to be ready. The antics in Colombia were stupid and unnecessary. It could have gotten them busted. And he needed to clear up the situation with Kippi. The next time they went to Bogotá, Tommy would have firmer control. Robbing a casino was a bitch of a way to get nailed when they didn't do it. He would try to plan around accidents as well.

There was more to the Puerto Rico story than Harry had revealed. Harry said that when they picked him up, they were certain he was their man—how many men his size were in Puerto Rico?

Harry told them that when they arrived, he had noticed a pair who'd looked like Mexicans, and one was huge. So Puerto Rican police weren't going to believe him, but Harry, being Harry, had an ace up his sleeve. He gave the PR detective a card—a contact—he told them to call for verification as to who he was. Meanwhile, watch the airport.

Well, sure enough, a pair of Mexicans, one almost as big as Harry, were trying to leave the country. Harry's government contact verified who he was. Only one day in jail and the Puerto Rican cops were thanking Harry. He was the hero.

Tommy found it hard to believe the day in a muggy cell was good for Harry's coked-out nose. What bothered Tommy most was the mysterious call. Who bailed Harry out? Tommy assumed it was a cop but hadn't imagined Harry had those connections. He had underestimated the man and increased his caution.

"Forget your way here, or is this city just too big for you?" Harry spoke loudly, deliberately, and slowly.

Tommy walked to the table and sat opposite. Elsie, who was next to Harry, began to mouth a warning to Tommy like a sister trying to protect her baby brother from their father's wrath. Tommy smiled at her naiveté. He wasn't beholden to Harry.

"Where have you been?" Harry demanded.

"With you and that gorilla living here, we stopped to get something to eat." He continued, "Where is the pervert?"

"What the fuck are you talking about?"

"Don't give me that shit. It's wrong, Harry. Elsie, you should put a stop to it."

"Wrong my ass."

"You can't pimp out your daughter, asshole."

"Stop. What—what the fuck is your dirty mind thinking?"

"I'm not thinking. And you know exactly what I'm talking about. Keep that gorilla away from Kippi."

"Elsie, get Kippi," Harry ordered.

She slid off the chair and disappeared to the family room as Harry locked Tommy in a stare.

Kippi was dressed in pink shorts and a t-shirt with a butterfly on it. Her hair looked as if it hadn't been washed in days. She walked dutifully as if she was being called into the principal's office.

"Kippi, did George do anything to you?" Harry's voice was deep and stern.

"No," she said, looking directly at him.

"There." Harry turned to Tommy.

"What do you do with George?" Tommy asked. She looked at him and then back to Harry, who nodded.

"He plays games with me. He's good at games."

"What games?"

She hesitated and again looked at Harry, whose gaze was firm. She shifted her weight and dug her toe into the carpet. "Parcheesi." Harry smiled with satisfaction.

"Good girl. Now you can go back and watch cartoons."

Tommy was furious, but there was nothing he could do. Such total bullshit, like a trained animal. He could sense the fear in her, like the fear he felt when Father Byrne ordered him to help him bring vestments to the rectory. He could see what was going on. Harry was buying George's loyalty with the little girl, and it was wrong.

"Where the hell is my coke?" Harry raised his voice.

Harry was attacking, and Tommy leaned back in the chair to let the giant wind pass. He had to figure out his next move. He couldn't tell Harry about Tampa because the fat man would come down on him. Sal's death still hung around his life like an old woman's perfume. He wanted to tell, to make excuses, but the secret was better kept. If only Harry was aware of the vulnerability that Tommy was suppressing. Get fried, southern fried.

"How much heat are you drawing since your San Juan caper?" Tommy decided to try to turn the conversation back to Harry. "And who was the cop that bailed you out?"

"You're getting spunky, kid. A little too spunky," Harry rumbled warningly from deep in his throat. Tommy planted his feet as George entered the room. He met Harry's challenge, looking at him squarely. What could Harry do? Then Tommy smiled a wider grin.

"The expression on your face when those spic cops busted you must be worth a million bucks. How about it, Elsie? Funny, isn't it? Robbing a casino. And for the first time in your life, you were innocent. Shit." Tommy shook his head, but Harry didn't smile. Tommy dropped six bags of coke on the table and stacks of hundred-dollar bills. "That's your share of what I got rid of. I should have taken a commission."

Since coming back to the States, Harry had become more se-cretive, almost paranoid. He didn't want to talk on the phone, but Tommy didn't either. He was more concerned about the money than making the deal. "I can move the rest and give you the money, or you can come down and pick it up and move it yourself." Tommy thought Harry would want the cash, and by stepping on it again, Tommy would clear a nice profit.

"Fine, fine. Get rid of it and give me the cash. It's time to set up a bigger score." The hardness hadn't left his eyes.

If Tommy was taking the risks, he wanted the money. Harry was riding the top of the wave, hoping it would go on forever. Tommy wasn't working to support anyone he didn't want to support. Sandy came first. He was right all the way down the line. The Tampa scene was heavy and messy; he saw the rate of failure. And he was scared in the deepest parts of his bowels. Holding it down by will, with great pain and determination, he would succeed in making fear conform to his will. He was going to protect Sandy, make another big deal, and leave Harry in the rearview mirror.

"I stashed the rest in Tampa. I'll give you a call when the cake is done." He would only call from a pay phone. Tommy bristled and could no longer hold it in.

"It's wrong." He almost spat the words, feeling the blood rush to his head. "You can't pimp your daughter to that ape."

Harry rolled his eyes. "It's none of your business."

"It's wrong, and I can make it my business."

"She's a whore in training. They're all whores; it's just a matter of time and price."

"You can't do that to a kid. Your own daughter?"

"Who said she's my daughter?"

"She thinks so."

Harry dropped his gaze to the coke and opened the bag. "You're gonna fuck up." His voice was thick with ominous rumbles. "You do know that. You've gone too far too fast. If you stick your nose in where it doesn't belong, your dreams may outrun your ability. Be careful, grasshopper."

"What makes you so fucking smart? Who do you think you are? You don't tell me what to do and don't expect me to jump to your orders. If I fuck up, it's my life. I don't need you or anyone fucking it up for me. I will do it on my own terms." He stepped away from the table, looking again into the den, where George and Kippi were sitting on the couch.

"George, been to Tampa lately?"

George scratched his head and turned directly to Tommy. "Don't recall goin' there." He smiled.

"Fuck you don't," Tommy said. He wasn't going to let it pass. He turned back to Harry with more venom in his voice. "What makes you so smart? Money? I'm twenty-four, and I'm doing fine. It's my life, and I'm going to do what I want. If I get killed, so what? Bang, bang—I'm dead. Then I can't lose. It's over."

"You're talking big, but what do you think you know? You're where you are because of beginner's luck. You'll fail. Everyone fails. And then you'll pay. Then, then grasshopper, we'll see what you're made of."

"What are you made of, Harry? Unfulfilled dreams? You wish you were me because I'm not a sideshow attraction like you?"

"Yeah, kid," Harry's fat lips arched upward, "you'll pay your dues. Your fall is going to be a hard one since you're so cocky. I know that much."

"That's bullshit. This isn't a contest. I'm not playing anyone's game; there are no rules. We make them up as we go along. Right now, we're partners. People would piss in their pants if they saw this much pure coke."

Harry broke into a deep rumble of laughter. Tommy stopped speaking. "You have a disagreeable disposition sometimes, grasshopper. It must be the New York in you. You'll argue about anything. At least you got here with my lady."

"Our lady. If we're partners, we're partners."

"Yeah, kid, but you're cruising for some learning."

Harry looked up from the coke and examined Tommy with his silver-dollar-size eyeballs. He shrugged and began chopping the coke with a single-edged razor. He smiled with satisfaction as if he had won the argument. Tommy fought to contain his need to talk about Tampa. This wasn't the time. As if she had felt his thoughts, Sandy came to his side. Better to carry the pain and keep his secrets. Sandy squeezed his hand.

"Your boyfriend is heading for disaster. He needs to learn more respect. If I were you, I'd use my influence to get him straight before he runs into a bridge abutment. I'd hate to see little pieces of him along the highway."

"Harry, that's ugly. You shouldn't say those kinds of things."

"He's ugly. Don't mind him." Tommy smiled. "Let's get some dinner. What do you say, Harry? Let's spend some cash on some old-time homemade Southern cooking."

"You kids go. I've got dinner made," Harry said, eyeing the mirror in front of him. "On your way back, stop by the Varsity and get a dozen burgers."

* * *

When Tommy returned after two weeks, Harry was on the large black leather sofa; his arms spread like tentacles of a giant species of hairy squid. His head was curled into his neck like a turtle resting in place. His eyes were closed, and his breath rumbled deep inside him.

Tommy was tired as well. He had turned his part of the coke but now had to collect from Harry. He sat in the rocking chair and turned the television to the Braves game. He always liked baseball. New York baseball: the Yankees. Stay with a winner. They dominated with Mantle and Maris. Since moving South, he didn't get to see games on TV except in Atlanta, and it was National League ball.

The shouts from the television got louder. Harry opened his eyes and extended his neck. He peered around the room like an owl surveying the field without moving its head.

"How long have you been here?"

"Too long." Tommy hated the darkness of the house. Harry kept all the drapes closed tight. "Let's settle up, and I'll be gone."

"What's to settle? I trust you." Harry's head emerged from the rings of flesh on his neck, and he angled it left and right to the sound of cracking bones.

"Fuck you do. You owe me money." Tommy wasn't in a fighting mood. He wanted to get back to Sandy and sleep for a few days.

"I do? How do you figure that?"

"Right. *Partners*—equal partners. We split the shipment in half, except you took two ounces off the top for yourself. So pay me for one."

Harry rolled his head in a circle. "Has to be some for the house."

"So the house gets a good deal, two for the price of one. Let's not fuck around. I'm too tired to argue." Tommy took the Smith & Wesson out of his pants and put it on the table.

"You still carrying that old piece?" Harry waved at the gun. "I've got a present for you."

"Kippi, Kippi." His loud bellow filled the room. "Kippi, Kippi." Small footsteps came down the center hall stair.

"What, Daddy?" she asked. Seeing Tommy, she danced over and responded to him with a hard high five.

"Way to go." Tommy smiled.

"Kippi, go into my bedroom. On the floor in my closet is a metal case. Bring it to me."

As the little girl skipped from the room, Harry cracked the knuckles on each hand one by one. Tommy felt goosebumps develop on his arms. He had always hated the sound.

"It's heavy," Kippi said, leaning hard to the left as she put the box on the table in front of Harry.

Waving his hands in the air, so the sleeves on his shirt fell to his elbows, Harry produced the key, which opened the metal box. "It's a beauty. A real work of art," he said.

"Harry, I'm too tired for the show. What the fuck are you talking about?"

"It's a beauty. A work of genius with the finest craftsmanship." He held a sleek, black automatic pistol up. He moved the gun from hand to hand before he ejected the clip. "So light, so smooth." He turned the handle to Tommy.

Tommy was surprised. It was lightweight. It felt like a toy gun. "Is this thing real?"

"Isn't it a gem?"

"Can I see?" Kippi was leaning over Tommy's chair.

"Sure, little princess," he said, ejecting the clip before handing the gun to her.

"Bang, bang," she said, pointing the gun at the wall. "Bang, bang." Now to the front door. "Can I have one?"

"It's not a toy. It's a Beretta Cheetah, imported from Italy. I have a friend who has the dealership for the whole country. Barely known in this country. It's the James Bond gun."

"It's sweet," Tommy said, turning the handle back to Harry.

"No, no." Harry held up his hands. "It's a present for you. Classy, stylish, and brand new."

Tommy picked up the Smith & Wesson in one hand and the Beretta in the other. He had to admit it felt like a better gun. And a nine-shot clip instead of five. He'd take it out to the range and see how it fired. "And... what makes me so lucky?"

Harry smiled and pushed over a small bag of coke. "I may have been out of line. Let's call it even." He was slick.

Tommy chuckled. "You had it all figured out before I ever got here. You are a slimy son of a bitch."

"To be the master, you have to be masterful." Harry let a deep rumble emerge from his belly.

Chapter 15

WHEN TOMMY OPENED THE DOOR, Harry was ready for him. Two months had passed since they'd returned from Colombia, and they had sold all the coke. It was time to pitch the big deal, the one Tommy was waiting for. It was going to be simpler than the last time, and a much bigger score. He believed Tommy wanted to gamble, and now he had the shipping case. Always use other people's money.

"Hey, big man." Tommy was dressed in a silk shirt and tight jeans.

"So grasshopper, ready to go to the next level?" Harry could tell that Tommy was fed up with the name, but it gave Harry an edge—not much of one, but enough.

"Fuck you. You said it was urgent. So what's the big deal?"

Harry slowly finished the last piece of chicken from the KFC bucket in front of him, knowing how Tommy hated to watch him eat. He picked his teeth slowly, eyeing the kid. He needed to keep Tommy engaged. "Are you ready to double down?"

"On what? I do all the work, and you collect your share. You need me to move the stuff."

Harry elevated his top lip, pressing it against his nose so that he almost formed a trunk. He waited to respond, watching Tommy rock on the balls of his feet. "I have a new plan."

"Two racks of ribs and four sides of potatoes." Tommy laughed at his own joke. "Is that what's so urgent?"

"Can you be ready in three weeks? It'll take two hundred grand from you this time. Can you do that?" Harry let out a belch. "That chicken was good."

"Ready for what in three weeks? Be specific if you have something to interest me." Tommy turned the chair backward, straddling the seat and leaning over the back.

"Four weeks, Bogotá, twenty keys. How does that sound?"

Tommy's left eyebrow raised a quarter inch. Harry had the hook in. "Doesn't sound like a plan," Tommy said.

"Are you in? Then I can share details." Harry knew the answer: Tommy wanted money. "It'll make you that million."

"I'm in if I like the details."

"Dr. Ollie."

"Who?"

"The crazy dentist. I told you about him when the submarine interrupted that other operation. We have a perfect cover. We can meet him and work out the details." Tommy stood and began pacing. "The plan is very simple, the timing is good, but we have to act fact. Let's go see the doc."

* * *

Harry mounted his big bike Zorro and gunned the engine in the garage. Tommy was on a Honda 750. The freedom and exhilaration of the bike gradually took over his body as he glided smoothly down the road. Harry felt free and weightless on the powerful machine. The trick was riding with guts. With balls and some skill, he could outrun any cop in the world. Biking was an end in itself—he didn't need to look anywhere to justify it. He was biking without a helmet, the air rushing through his hair as he melted into pure energy at one hundred miles per hour. Could the kid keep up with him? Harry glanced back, slowing the bike until Tommy came into view. He had to give Tommy enough lead but had to keep him on the line. Money was the means, the ticket, the invitation. Without freedom, it was useless. Harry wasn't going to give up his freedom. As Tommy pulled aside, Harry held up two fingers, then three. A race to exit 23. Let's see if the kid still has any color left.

With a quick twist of the wrist, Harry shot ahead, cutting through traffic like a pro running back playing with high schoolers. The bikes strained at their casings, responding smoothly to the changes in acceleration. Harry sat back on the big black bike, his black leather jacket giving him the appearance of oneness with the machine to the other drivers as he knifed effortlessly through the Atlanta cars and trucks. He made the exit first.

Entering a medical complex, Harry rode onto the lawn and into a courtyard with Tommy following. They parked the bikes next to a door that read *Dr. Ollie Bentley, DDS*. Harry knocked three times on the door. Three knocks returned. Harry knocked four times, shaking his head and rolling his eyes at Tommy.

"Who is it?" a deep voice asked.

"Open the fucking door, Ollie, or I'm going to open it," Harry said. As the door cracked an inch, Harry leaned his body into the door, smashing it open. Harry hated the smell of antiseptics and cleaning fluids in the office.

"Harry, Harry. Sorry. Can't be too careful in this business," Ollie said. He was medium height, with a full head of greying black hair and a pencil-thin mustache. He had a square-cut jaw like a second-tier movie star. When Tommy followed Harry into the office, the dentist quickly hid behind Harry. "Who is that?" the doctor said in a voice made for radio.

"Ollie, this is Tommy, my partner. I told you about him."

Ollie smiled a quick smile and walked over to Tommy. "I am happy to make your acquaintance," he said with a country club formality.

"Likewise, I'm sure."

"I told you he'd be cool." Harry was enjoying the interaction because Tommy looked impressed. Let him focus some attention on Ollie. The plan could work with big profits and little risk—at least for him.

Dr. Bentley again checked the locks on the window and door. "You got it, don't you, Harry?" The doc moved close to Harry, clicking a retractable pen in his hand. "Do you have it?" He turned to Tommy. Click, click, click.

"Be mellow, doc," Harry said and belched loudly, causing the doctor to retreat. The acrid odor of the office reminded Harry how much he hated dentists. As a kid, his dentist didn't believe in Novocain. In fact, Harry didn't know it existed until he was eleven. He hated the idea of a man with a drill.

"Don't you ever air this place out?" he said disgustedly.

"It's all climate controlled. The air is constantly circulating without any types of drafts." Dr. Ollie walked to the wall vents, then to the thermostat, clicking his pen. "This system was designed by…"

"I don't give a fuck who designed it," Harry said as he occupied the entire couch. On the table were copies of *Reader's Digest*, *Better Homes and Gardens*, *Rolling Stone*, and some *Zap* comics. Harry had left the comics on his last visit to add variety to the reading material.

A car pulled up to the parking lot outside, and Dr. Ollie slid to the window, drawing a .357 magnum from beneath his white lab coat. He slowly peeked out the window with his gun ready.

"What's going on?" Tommy asked, looking for a back door.

"Ollie, put that fucking thing away." Harry's voice was loud but filled with the exasperation of a tired father. "You're a professional man; you shouldn't be playing with guns."

Dr. Ollie turned slowly, facing them. His left hand was shaking slightly as he pointed the gun to the floor. "There have been some robberies lately. I can't be too careful."

Tommy walked to the window and peeked through the Venetian blinds. "Nothing there," he said. "Plus, we have enough firepower." He pulled out his Smith & Wesson.

The dentist's eyes darted nervously around the room while avoiding Tommy's stare. Even the lab coat seemed to be trembling.

"Get mellow. Tommy will protect you as long as you don't do anything stupid like pulling a gun."

"No, no…" The doctor turned with a slight bow. "Listen, Tommy… I really didn't mean to…"

Harry rolled his eyes, burped, and then coughed once. "I came here to do business, not give you elementary school lessons."

"You're right, Harry. It won't happen again. You have my word on it."

"Doctor, sit down and get mellow." Harry took a flat, carved, wooden hash pipe and lit it. He offered it to Ollie, who began to refuse but then took hits, breathing a plume of smoke into the air.

"I'm just careful," Dr. Ollie began. "In my position, you can't be too careful. Each of us has certain failures in judgment from time to time. It's part of the human predicament. The whole of mankind…"

"I don't give a fuck about the whole of anything—that's your line of work," Tommy said.

"All I was going to say…"

Peter S. Rush

"Say what you mean the first time, and we won't have any problems." Tommy lowered his voice to make Doc Ollie lean closer. "Understand?"

"Yes."

"Harry, this guy shows promise of a brain after all."

"He is actually an educated man. Just no common sense."

"It's a problem for some people." Tommy and Harry were playing as the doctor crossed and uncrossed his legs several times before launching himself from the chair. Harry roared with laughter, which only caused the doctor to click his pen faster.

"What are you doing? You aren't fucking me over, are you, Harry? You wouldn't do that, would you? Not to me. I know too much… I mean, we've known each other for a long time. No, no. Listen, you brought the stuff? You know I know a lot of people—can move a lot of weight. My people, doctors, lawyers, they love coke, and your stuff is really good. You did bring it, didn't you?

"Harry, did you bring it or not? You haven't told me yet, and I want to know." At the last word, the doctor raised an eyebrow.

"So what?"

"But… But… You promised. I mean, if you won't keep your word… I promised people I would… You gave me your word."

"Can't cope, doc," Tommy said.

Harry straightened himself up, puffing out his massive stomach, and the dentist flattened himself against the table. He was dwarfed and suddenly shifted to a defensive, inoffensive posture. Harry could see Tommy trying to contain his laughter.

"The problem with you people, Ollie, is that you don't understand that you must be polite. If you aren't, it might be a capital offense. You do understand?" Harry contracted his nose, forming six ridges of fat, and wiggled the entire appendage like a rabbit.

To Harry, the show was an important part of life. That, fucking, and doing coke, with the latter coming up strong on the outside. The show was the one aspect of life that made the others work. "Let's talk about the plan first, then the reward."

Ollie said he was presenting a paper at the International Association of Dentistry for the Americas in Bogotá. As part of the program, there was a trade show where he had agreed to demonstrate a new machine. It would be shipped from his office to the trade show and then back. All very legitimate. He showed Harry and Tommy the new machine. Harry explained that the base of the machine could be removed, and the center was hollow. A perfect spot. Harry nodded to Tommy, who looked around the base and the screws.

"Won't it look tampered with?" Tommy asked Harry.

"We'll use machine screws. They'll be a perfect match, and we'll seal them, so it looks factory fresh." Harry smiled. If it got busted at customs, everyone could disavow any knowledge. They'd lose the coke and the cash, but that was it—and there was little risk for Harry Burr.

With Dr. Bentley more than an arm's distance away, again engaged with his pen, Harry slowly unbuttoned his shirt, exposing the soft, hairy white flesh. Harry grinned widely at Tommy before he reached into the third fold of fat from his belt. He produced a foil package of cocaine.

"It's the best stash in the world. No one looks," he gloated, a magician of modern civilization. Harry only used the stash when he rode the bike because the cops hated to search him. It kinda hurt his feelings that cops felt so repulsed, but it had saved his ass more than once.

"It's only a taste," Dr. Ollie whined.

"You refused to give a deposit. If there is any left, you can bid against my other customers. I told you a deposit was necessary this time."

Harry could see Tommy following how he was playing Bentley. The dentist would pay above the street price for good stuff. He was part of the country club set.

Dr. Bentley took the tin foil and opened it on the glass table. Shining the light on the coke, he held it up to the light. Inositol was a kind cut. Dipping his dry finger in it, Dr. Bentley rubbed some on his gums to test the numbing effect. Suddenly he stood up and walked into his office. Harry could hear the sound of pouring liquid. Dr. Bentley returned with a graduated cylinder filled with bleach. He studied chemistry.

The dentist dipped a matchbook cover into the bag with a clumsy wrist, then dropped the contents into the beaker. The coke plummeted to the bottom of the liquid and began to disintegrate before it reached the bottom.

"Harry, doesn't this guy know anything?" Tommy walked to the table. "Bleach only tests for sugars. So does the burn test. Here's an easier one."

Tommy placed a tiny bit of the mixture on the skin between his thumb and forefinger. With a smooth, circular motion, he rubbed the white powder, and it disappeared instantly. Holding his hand up to Dr. Bentley's face, he said, "What's left is the cut."

The doctor nodded in agreement. He went into his surgical cabinet and brought out a sterilized instrument plate and a scalpel to chop the coke. The doc went first class. He popped with the best works in town.

With the precision of a skilled hand, Dr. Bentley chopped the coke. "Cocaine is the most misunderstood drug in the world. I suppose most of it is racial prejudice, but no one wants to talk about that. At every level, it is fear of the unwashed." He assumed a scholarly pose.

"You are familiar with the work Freud did with cocaine after it was discovered as a wonder drug. He prescribed it to his opium-addicted patients. He substituted the addiction. He was off the wall with the prescription. But as a stimulant, it has no equal. The French bottled Veloz-Coca for their bicycle team to win in the Alps. We are afraid of our human weakness.

"People like you and Harry keep the market supplied. Coca was the divine plant of the Incas. Someday it will be the divine plant of Western society—not an oil economy but a cocaine society." Dr. Bentley did two lines, then two more, then two more. "It's great, Harry. Best you've ever brought me. Stupendous. How much is left?"

"Six ounces."

"I'll take them."

"You haven't heard the price."

"For this quality, price is not the object. How much? Seventeen, eighteen, nineteen?"

"Nineteen hundred dollars," Harry said. "Since you are doing all six, eleven thousand."

"I've got twenty-five hundred here. The rest on delivery. How soon can you have it here?"

"Let's make it tonight, right here. Be alone," Harry said.

"You can count on me. You know that. The money will be here, Harry. I can't wait. Harry, you make me a happy man."

"Doc, you're a derelict. Why they let you have a license, I'll never know. If your classmates at Georgia could see you now." Harry laughed roundly. "Be ready with the cash."

It was time to do this trip. "Are you ready for it, kid?" Harry asked as they mounted their bikes. He had the kid where he wanted him. The plan was simple; the money would be great. He could see Tommy thinking through his options. He liked the kid, but then, he always liked his partners till he didn't. This wasn't any different, just maybe more amusing. There would be time to deal with him when this deal was done. Tommy would have to go back to Tampa tonight and put his end into gear. He was alone with Sal dead. Did George enjoy that one? One more detail before the next trip to Colombia.

Chapter 16

George couldn't stop talking from the time Tommy glided the rented fishing cruiser out of Dunedin past Caladesi Island and into the Gulf of Mexico. George talked like he knew everything. He was an expert on sailfish, marlin, red snapper, and mackerel. Every time he went fishing, he always caught the most, the biggest, the best. Tommy steered the boat west, wanting to get a good two hours from shore so that the water would be deep and the tides wouldn't regurgitate his deed.

It was time. Tommy saw no other option. George had killed Sal; he was sure of that—but on Harry's orders? He wasn't as certain. George was a hitman who hid behind that Georgia country boy front. And Harry paid him with money and little girls, including his own. Sick. There was no cure for that. It was terminal, and this would be terminal. He eased off the throttle, and the silence of the ocean was broken by the gentle lapping of the water against the side of the boat.

"We can cast here," Tommy said. "There are some more spots farther out." He adjusted his cap and sunglasses.

"Why not," George said, opening another can of beer.

When George saw the gun, he started to move forward to crush Tommy with his bare hands. Tommy had thought he was going to explain to George why he would die, like in the movies, explaining his sins and transgressions. He couldn't wait to talk, because if the gorilla grabbed him, Tommy would be dead instead. He had thought his plan was tight, but it being his first time, Tommy had imagined there might be problems—but not this one. There was fear in George's eyes as he understood that he was going to die.

Tommy's one shot was clean into the forehead. When the big man fell, he nearly capsized the boat.

Tommy's challenge was dumping the big man without tipping the boat. He was already sweating profusely in the Florida sun from moving three hundred pounds of dead weight to the rear of the boat. He should have had him sitting in the stern when he shot him.

He still wasn't sure how he would get him over the side. Taking off the dead man's shoes, he felt he wasn't strong enough to lift him up. He took his fourteen-inch Buck fish knife and sliced George's shorts and the Hawaiian shirt until the corpse was naked.

Reaching down to the scrotum, he used the knife to amputate the balls and penis, which he threw over the side as chum. "No last time for you, motherfucker."

He laid each hand on the fish board and cut the fingers off, dropping them over the side—it made the corpse harder to identify. Now for the hard part. He wrapped some jute rope tightly around the legs. Worried that it might slip off, he created a harness over the shoulders and around George's boulder of a head. He used a slipknot to fasten the head to the bulkhead, then retrieved four cement blocks from below and carefully laced them together before tying them to the legs, leaving fifteen feet of rope so that he could lift the body into the water before he let the blocks bring it to the bottom.

He propped the body up over the stern, the head and arms over the rear, the stumps oozing blood into the blue Gulf of Mexico. He looked at the layers of white flesh folded like a walrus with a farmer's tan. The gorilla deserved to die. There was no other way to stop him, just like no one stopped the priests. It was jail or death, and there was no way Tommy was getting the cops involved. He decided to inch the body over the stern like a giant white slug crawling to the sea. It would take some time, and he rocked the body from side to side to move it.

He could feel the sun on his neck and back. Using his legs, he was squat lifting more than double his own weight. When he reached the tipping point, the giant head would lead the slug into the ocean to become fresh food for the deep.

He wished he had brought some coke. He could use a line or two now as the pain of exertion began to tighten his muscles. He should have made a better plan, but he was more worried about getting George on the boat and fifty miles out into the Gulf.

He stopped and took a long drink of water from the cooler. George's enormous white ass was giving him the moon from the back of the boat. *Yeah, that should be the last thing I see of you, that giant white ass waiting to be torn apart by sharks, barracuda, and thousands of small fish gorging on the whale's carcass.*

Once the midsection was up on the railing, Tommy leaned down, putting his shoulder under the ass, and pushed with his legs to lift the body into the ocean. Once, twice—soft shit covered Tommy's shoulder. He bent again. Once, twice—the body moved forward.

Once, twice—it inched forward again. He pushed harder, his breath coming more quickly. Once, twice—it moved forward, slowly creeping its way toward the sea. Tommy picked up one leg and pressed it over his head, adding more momentum to the carcass. It began picking up speed, and the lumbering flesh began a dive into the water.

Tommy turned quickly to avoid the cement blocks as they galloped to the stern, stopping at the gunwale. He exhaled deeply before jumping overboard with the body. Buck knife in hand, he sunk it deep into the body next to the belly button and cut a ten-inch gap in the stomach. He thought about gutting George like a giant tuna but didn't have the time. The hole was large enough so gases wouldn't build up and float the body, and the fish would enjoy the tasty entrails. Now the gorilla could atone for his sins.

He stripped off his t-shirt and washed his shoulder and hands in the salty water. He felt cleaner, clearer. What had to be done was done. No one would know—there was no one he could tell. Now it was between him and the fishes. The memories flooded back to him, the smells of stale tobacco and cheap church wine. The priest with his holy moly—how Tommy would be saved if he submitted; if he didn't tell. It was God's will. He ducked his head under the water and let go, just floating, sinking several feet as his lungs began to shout for air at the surface. He held, letting his memories marinate in the warm water. With a swift kick, his head broke the surface, and he gulped clean, warm oxygen. It was done. He had to get on with his life. One bad deed deserves another.

He dropped the blocks one by one into the ocean and was ready to go home. He gutted three king mackerel that he had bought at the dock, dumping their entrails on the deck, comingling their blood with George's. He threw bucket after bucket of seawater on the deck, diluting the oozy mess. He would scrub the boat clean when he got back to Clearwater.

Turning the boat east, he put it into an easy cruising speed. The Gulf was calm, as was he. He would get back before dark, too, which had been one of his goals for the day. Becoming a murderer wasn't his plan when he left high school for Tampa. It had happened too fast. Another trip to Colombia, and he would get out of the business.

He took a small joint from the tackle box and lit it, inhaling deeply. It would be a nice sunset—or would they always remind him of today?

Chapter 17

TOMMY COULD FEEL THE HOLES in his armor of self-esteem were getting larger before they got off the plane in Bogotá. Since he did George, he was straining more with his bravado, forcing more of his wisecracks, snorting more of his own cocaine. He would live with what he did, but he had to stop thinking about it. George's face came back to him, but he had to shake it off. He thought of Kippi and how she didn't have to deal with him anymore. George was dead and now was where he had to be.

When he boarded the southbound flight in Miami, he had a hundred thousand in hundreds in his carry-on bag. He wasn't going to think about what he had done. Touching Sandy, just for certainty, he listened to the flight attendant explain the emergency exits. He questioned himself about allowing her to come this time. But she had begged, cajoled, and threatened.

Finally, in desperation, she used logic on him. She said he would be less obvious as part of a young couple on holiday. She would reduce suspicion. He was afraid he was putting her in danger. She brushed his argument aside. She was going to be with him in good times and bad.

As the plane rolled down the runway, gaining enough speed to lift off into the sky, Tommy felt himself running alongside it, his arms and legs pumping with desire. He failed to leave the ground. He wondered how close he was coming to the end of the runway. He saw

Sal lying on the black asphalt. He could smell George as the pieces of the body dropped into the ocean. But what if… if he could get off the ground? What could he have been if…

Tommy chose life; he didn't believe in promises. His father always promised, promised someday. Someday never came until Tommy went to Tampa. Now, the trip might be enough to put him over the top, be enough to get out. He touched Sandy's arm. How much more risk was it worth? He remembered Steve's remark: it always ends badly. With Harry, what did Harry know? Suspect about George? He'd gone missing before. That's the story. This time, Harry didn't have his muscle. Those old ladies of Fate had tangled his brain. Harry was struggling against the sticky, resilient strands of hope. Yet, was there hope? With Sandy here, there was no place else he desired to be.

* * *

In the noise of the car horns, rapid Spanish, and the mountains of cocaine, Tommy knew where he was. At El Dorado airport, the taxi driver was a Cuban from Miami who spoke good English. In his mid-forties, his slicked-back hair was greying at the temples. The taxi was a 1954 Hudson. Since he had no desire to go straight to the hotel, Tommy asked the driver to give them a short tour of the city.

Old cars—Studebakers, DeSotos, Packards, and Chevys—were crowded with people. The high, thin mountain air was thick with exhaust from the leaded gasoline. Buses made frequent stops along the two-lane road as women and men loaded with bundles converged on them. Old cars were shiny and polished like new. A host of small Renaults, Fiats, and Volkswagens darted between the larger, lumbering machines.

A collage of colors, objects, and people created a constant movement in the open-air stores along the road.

"Can I buy a pineapple?" Sandy asked the driver, pointing at a street vendor.

"*Sí*, it is very good. Fresh from the north." The driver pulled over to a young boy, no more than nine, holding an enameled basin full of fruit.

Tommy and Sandy each bought some pineapple slices and a piece of fresh coconut. Sitting back in the car, they touched fingers for strength.

"You can't get lost in Bogotá. It's all very logical. Carreras go North to South. This is Carrera 8," the driver said, turning left onto a wide avenue. "Calles go East-West. Look for the mountain. Anything you want is simple to find. If it's Carrera 0 #32-1, it means on Carrera 10 between Calle 32 and 33, building 12. Logical. No one can get lost, not even Indians. Not like Miami."

Neither Tommy nor Sandy wanted to speak. It was better to just sit back and sightsee. Tommy didn't want to think about the next deal, about Harry. Now, it was better to just absorb the strange world.

They passed the San Carlos Palace, the home of the Colombian president; the Museo del 20 julio, with its rich Spanish colonial architecture; and the Plaza de Toros de Santamaría, where the bullfights were held. The Museo del Oro fascinated Tommy. A museum of gold, the driver said, with over eight thousand items, including bracelets, rings, crowns, bowls, and even gold weapons. Most were from the Incas. And the four largest emeralds in the world were located there.

The informal tour lasted an hour. By the time they arrived at the hotel, they both had headaches from the air. Tommy gave the driver a fifty-dollar tip, and the driver gave him a card with his number if he ever needed a taxi. Tommy took it as insurance.

They had returned to Hotel Cardinal because it was small and in a residential area. Harry, Elsie, Kippi, and Quintana had checked in.

They had three rooms, taking up one floor of the five-story hotel that catered to a family clientele. Tommy was happy to be out of the public eye. The first week, they consumed an entire ounce of uncut flake, freshly brewed Colombian cocaine, with cup after cup of thick *tinto*, the demitasse coffee topped with bottles of aguardiente and slices of oranges.

Time was unable to enter their rooms. Games kept going, dreams dreaming, laughs laughing. Florida was no longer alive. It was as far away as grade school. The coke kept them up for twenty-four hours. Tommy and Sandy built tents, had pillow fights, made love, invented games, and were happy. Their laughter continued through the days and nights with the innocence of children. Kippi often played with them.

After a week, the magic began tearing like old crepe paper. Tommy needed a larger world, and Sandy wanted to explore. Going in and out of the lobby, Tommy began to recognize the regulars. The hotel was better than the Tequendama but still not as invisible as it should be. Tommy decided they should rent an apartment. A six-month lease wouldn't raise as many suspicions as something shorter.

In the northern section of town, Tommy found a four-bedroom apartment with private security and a garage under the apartment. There were six apartments in the building. The door was made of heavy steel with thick steel deadbolts like the inside of a castle. A wide terrace with large concrete planters filled with lush foliage protected the glass doors from most outside observation. The terrace extended on two sides of the apartment, facing the street.

The rooms had twelve-foot ceilings and a wide doorway that allowed Harry to fit through. The formal oak dining room seated twenty. The master bath was the size of Tommy's first apartment in Tampa. The interior was hardwood, spacious, and elegant. A large crystal chandelier hung over the dining room table and bathed the room in the refracted spectrum of color. Harry found that the wide, leather easy chair in the living room fit him perfectly. It became his throne.

The plan was simple: twenty keys of coke shipped back to the States in Dr. Ollie's machine, which he was sending down for the dental convention at the end of the month. All the trade show material would ship back together, so there should be little screening.

Tommy needed to get the best product and the best price. He didn't want to be in a hurry like last time; they needed higher caliber suppliers. He and Sandy set about to explore the clubs in Bogotá. Tommy needed to feel the energy of the city, and he was beginning to learn the language. He had learned to count and say the time of day last time. He listened more closely, trying to remember his high school Spanish. With a little toot, Spanish became a game for him, a way to use his mental energy.

After exploring El Barril de Diógenes and La Manzana de Eve, they stayed at Unicornis, a mosaic of music, gambling, and beautiful people. Tommy met Miguel Marqueza, a young Colombian from Cali. Miguel was the first high-class connection Tommy had made. They discussed the disco business and the cocaine business. It struck Tommy as odd that this thin-lipped Latin should speak such excellent English. It made the negotiations easier. Tommy invited him to dinner at the apartment.

Harry was getting very strung out on coke. He was making a wall of games, having Quintana bring dealers to him. He was seated like an emperor in his large leather chair, a deck of cards in his hands, his fingers jeweled, the glistening Enterprise, and the teardrop pendant on his chest. The street dealers were envious but intimidated more at his size than his wealth.

When Miguel entered the living room, the afternoon sun was fading into the flitting lights of Bogotá. Miguel wore his hair slicked back in the Italian fashion, and his suit was European cut. Tommy noticed his dirty fingernails.

Miguel was twenty-three and acted like a mature man of the world. He told them his father was a fighter for the Fermin, in the early sixties. His grandfather was killed in *La Violence*, the ten-year period where politics was a deadly profession. Feuding political parties had roving bands of enforcers. Tommy thought they were like the New Left, but with automatic weapons and safe sanctuaries. Colombians were more passionate about politics because it was the game of money.

Hatred between groups and party factions ran like family feuds among mountain people. Vengeance becomes a way of life, a point of honor. The killings in the nineteen-fifties were a further testimony to the ferocity of the human animal when released from moral taboos. Miguel told Tommy of the common methods of torture and death. They included the skilled art of *pica para tamale*, where the body of the living victim was cut into small pieces bit by bit. Or *bocachiquiar*, where the victim was tied, and hundreds of small holes were made in his helpless body so he would bleed to death.

Miguel said such quartering and beheading techniques were invented such as *corte de mica*, *corte de franela*, and *corte de corbata*. Villages were dotted with crucifixions and lynchings. Schoolchildren were raped en masse, babies bayonetted, ears cut off, tongues cut out to silence the opposition. In warning to opponents, unborn fetuses were removed by a crude Caesarian section and replaced with roosters.

Miguel considered himself better than most Colombians. He wanted upper-class American connections. He had traveled to Houston, San Antonio, and Miami. From the beautiful city of Cali, Miguel enjoyed the upward mobility of Bogotá and the gringo dollars for cocaine.

Harry had a deck of playing cards in his left hand. Casually, he cut the deck between his meaty fingers, making aces appear and disappear. "I'll play high card with you," Harry said, challenging the Colombian's machismo. "In fact, I'll give you two-to-one odds on your money. Say, on one hundred dollars." Harry pulled a hundred-dollar bill from the air. Harry had learned about counterfeit money—*mallo* money. Colombians printed the best counterfeit American dollars.

"No, Señor Harry. I don't play cards with a magic man." His thin lips broke into a smile. "But for that bill, I will let you have this." Miguel unwrapped a solid rock of cocaine the size of a golf ball. Harry flailed his nostrils, trying to suck it across the table.

"Cut me a piece of that pie. Let me see if it's the real thing." He pulled a mirror and razor from a large carved oak box on the coffee table and picked up his jeweled space snorter. The diamonds and gold made Miguel's eyes wide. Tommy could see the Colombian wanted it.

Harry did the line, laid down the hundred, and took the rock. "Do you have an ounce as good as this?" He snorted, sending waves of flesh in motion with a suppressed sneeze. Miguel brought a thirty-gram bag out of an inner pocket of his coat. He laid it on the table. Harry smiled, nodding in agreement. "This calls for drinks. Elsie," he thundered.

Elsie appeared at the door dressed in blue jean shorts cut to her crotch and a sheer white halter that outlined her broad, round nipples. Her eyes had an animal glean. Miguel leaned forward in his chair, his eyes wide. Harry smiled in satisfaction like he had the Colombian hooked. "Get us some more scotch."

She walked across the room, smiling at Miguel, who leaned back in his chair, assuming a disinterested European movie pose. "Do you know where the mountain *Surratee* is?" she asked in her squeaky voice.

"Oh, *si*. Of course." He looked surprised.

"I told you, Harry. You said it was in France. I want to go."

"When you can get someone to take you, you can go," Harry said, opening the bag of coke onto the mirror.

"If you want, I can take you. There is a cable car. It is very high," Miguel jumped in.

"Oh, could you?" Elsie cooed. "Where is it? Can I see it from here?" She ran out to the balcony.

Miguel followed her outside. Harry took two plain brown plastic bottles from the oak box. He filled the first with nearly half of Miguel's coke. He then dumped a white powder, lidocaine, a close relative of coke, into Miguel's bag and mixed it up. The cut wouldn't show up for days.

Elsie detained Miguel for a few more minutes with oohs and giggles.

"I'm not going to take this today. If you can do some weight, we might be interested," Harry said. Miguel didn't look disappointed. He had a date with Elsie.

After Miguel left, Tommy said, "Was it worth it, Harry? Was it worth fucking up a good connection to beat the man out of a thousand dollars?" He turned to leave. "You can't fuck with these people. This is their country. And the cops don't fool around."

"Ah, these spics, they're all alike. Show 'em a piece of blond ass, they drool like one of George's hound dogs. He wants to fuck me. I'm just fucking him first."

"This ain't Atlanta. You haven't been outside. Life is cheap here. I hear you can hire a killer for five dollars plus, the cost of the weapon."

"Right, grasshopper. You believe it." Harry sipped his scotch. "I got the better end of that deal. Don't forget it. It's who comes out on top each time."

In the next week, Harry used an assortment of card tricks, cons, and Elsie to hustle a procession of street dealers that Quintana brought to the apartment. Harry fucked with people, always playing a game. It drove the Colombians nuts because they didn't know what was real. As the coke started taking hold, Harry started to play games with Tommy.

"Don't do it," Tommy said. Harry became defensive. Tommy got up during Harry's tasting ritual with a new pusher and left the room.

Tommy didn't care what games Harry played as long as it didn't affect him. Miguel had the quality they needed. Tommy was ready for the big score, and Miguel said he could do the weight with good quality.

* * *

Miguel was ready to do a deal, but Tommy needed to straighten Harry up. They were seriously outgunned in Bogotá. Tommy had purchased three revolvers from Miguel. Looking at the street, the M-16 seemed to be the smallest weapon the police used. He debated where the exchange should take place—in the open or at the apartment. They both had drawbacks.

Tommy and Quintana scouted for restaurants or other open venues, but Tommy always felt he was being watched—and with Harry present, they would definitely stand out. The apartment would have to do, even if they might be trapped. It was safer.

The dried-out Harry was becoming belligerent, so Tommy made certain there was plenty of food: sausages, fresh pineapples, papaya, bananas, and lots of chicken with rice.

Miguel would arrive that night. Tommy already had Quintana primed. They would make the exchange and get the stuff out the back door of the hotel as soon as Miguel left. He didn't want to give them time to make a move to reclaim it.

He guessed the Colombians would be armed—and so would they. No rip-offs, but if either side smelled trouble, the situation could go south quickly. Harry would have one pistol, Tommy the second, but who should have the last was a question. Quintana was too nervous to be trusted with it. Maybe he should have killed George after this trip. They could have used the muscle now. So it left Sandy. Was she ready for it? Was it fair to her, to put her in that position, to have to make that decision—if there was a decision to be made?

Tommy walked around the four-bedroom apartment. It had only one entrance and exit. They were on the third floor, so the windows were not a good option. He went over the setup in his head. Harry would sit at the table. Quintana would answer the door. Tommy would do the deal but face the door just in case. Sandy would stay in the first bedroom with the pistol ready—ready for what? The tightness crept up his back like an itch he couldn't scratch. He tried to relax his muscles, to clear his mind, to be ready, but the knot tightened. It was all his money—two years of deals. He wasn't going to lose it.

Tommy kept watching the front of the hotel from the window until a car pulled up. Harry sat doing card tricks. Tommy could tell he wanted more cocaine. There was a basket of fruit on the table that he picked at.

When the knock came, Tommy was prepared. Quintana opened it and moved to the side. Miguel entered with a thick, round-faced man who carried a suitcase. Miguel nodded to Tommy.

"Are you ready for business?" Harry's voice boomed, breaking the tension in the room.

Tommy moved slowly to the table, keeping some distance between him and the man with the suitcase. Tommy could see he was packing.

"No problems, señor. Just business tonight." Miguel smiled as he smoothed his hair.

Once the suitcase was opened, Harry cut into each block for a taste. Tommy tested each one with blood. The merchandise was excellent. Tommy reached under the table, and the suitcase-carrying man froze. Tommy held up his hands and slowly reached down to show a briefcase. He opened it slowly to reveal the money.

Miguel counted it quickly, testing some of the hundreds for authenticity. Tommy weighed each brick. Satisfied, he nodded. Harry moved closer to the suitcase. Tommy could tell that he wanted more than a taste. It would have to wait. As Miguel went around the room to shake hands with Tommy, Harry, and Quintana, Tommy could feel some weight ease from his mind. One step closer to a million. There was more to do tonight. This was just step one.

When the door closed, Tommy went to the window to watch them exit the building. He waited to see if anyone was following or entering.

"Come on. Time to taste." Harry had picked up a packet and was ready to party. Tommy clamped hard on his hand. "We got to move it now. I don't trust them."

"Fuck them. We did the deal."

"They will fuck us. I'm moving it now." Tommy closed the suitcase and motioned to Quintana. "Let's get out the back door."

"Leave me some," Harry said, coming toward Tommy.

"Sit," Tommy said as he turned on Harry, the gun drawn. "We can score some shit for you later. I'm not taking any chances with this load."

Harry's face turned red. He began to move closer, but Tommy cocked the pistol.

"I didn't come this far for you to fuck it up. And..." Tommy couldn't find the words, but he knew he would shoot. He would, just like he had with George. Where had his mind gone? Sandy stood in the doorway, her face ashen, the pistol hanging by her side.

He shook his head. "Let's go," he said to Quintana and resolved not to stop until they got to the dental trade show, and he could stash the coke.

At the trade show, Tommy found Dr. Bentley's booth. With ratchet wrenches they had shipped with the booth, he took off the bottom and quickly packed the contents, putting the insulation back around the bottom of the machine. He dirtied the bottom with some sawdust and reset it in the exhibition. He looked around the small show. Twenty booths displayed x-ray machines, dentures, braces, and other tools of the trade. Tommy thought how much he hated to go to the dentist.

Looking around, he was convinced the load was safe—or at least it was packed. What else could he do? Two hundred thousand dollars of his money was now sitting on the floor of this hotel ballroom. Fuck, what was he thinking?

In the taxi back to the apartment, Tommy exhaled. It was done. Tomorrow the trade show packed up, and the exhibit would go back to the States. Harry couldn't touch the stuff, and it was out of the apartment. When he returned to the States, it would be waiting… All good?

* * *

It was early morning a day later when Tommy heard a rustle coming from the balcony. He sprang awake immediately and listened. Bogotá was known for its burglars and thieves, and so he grabbed a gun he had bought from Miguel and pulled on his pants. Sliding along the floor into the living room, he peered quickly through the drapes.

A shot of adrenaline exploded through his body in a high-voltage charge of fear. An armed soldier in combat gear was looking for a way to get in. The street below was filled with troops getting out of trucks and pointing weapons at the apartment.

Tearing into the bedroom, Tommy shouted at Sandy, "Get dressed *now*." She sat up quickly, her eyes still covered in sleep.

"What's the matter?"

"Cops! Soldiers!" He ran to Harry's room as a loud pounding came at the steel front door.

"We're fucked, man. Clean out any of your personal stash. There are a thousand soldiers around the building. Move!"

"Go away. It's too early," Harry groaned.

Tommy threw a glass of water on Harry. Elsie sat up, the nipples on her naked breasts erect from the cold water. The door would hold them for a half-hour unless they had a bazooka. Tommy scoured the room for coke, flushing it down the toilet.

Harry began moving, but his look of terror caused him to move in slow motion. Quintana jumped as Tommy barked commands. Sandy cleaned up the pot that Harry had left all over the living room. The banging on the door grew louder. Quintana wanted to open the door. Harry wanted to open the door, to cooperate. Kippi was crying.

Tommy tried to remember where the rest of the cash was. He had stored some in the books in the library. He grabbed the twenty thousand he had in the top drawer of his nightstand and ducked into the laundry room. He climbed up on the table and reached as far up as he could in the narrow, damp ventilation shaft. He taped the envelope around the bend in the vent stack. He could hear the banging stop. He stuffed all his pesos into his socks.

When he returned to the living room, everyone was sitting on the couch, fear infesting their spirits. Tommy stepped on his fear with both feet as he jauntily approached the captain. "*Buenos dias*. What is this all about?" Tommy asked.

The short, thick officer barked a rapid command, his eyes looking pious under the stiff brim of the uniform cap. Two young soldiers grabbed Tommy's arms and tried to pull him to the couch. He shook them off. They backed away and leveled their carbines, motioning him to sit. Tommy smiled at them and sat next to Sandy.

The captain castigated them in Spanish, aiming most of his words at Tommy and Harry. Tommy caught some of their crude jokes about Harry and animals.

The soldiers tore the room apart, emptying the drawers onto the floor, and then proceeded to the bedrooms. Tommy counted twelve of them, but he guessed there were more outside. The captain didn't seem to speak any English.

"What are those buggers saying?" Harry asked quietly.

Tommy shrugged. "Something about you and a horse getting it on."

The search continued for over an hour until two soldiers let out wild cries of joy from Harry's room. They found the money in the books and began tearing them apart. There was fifteen thousand in American currency.

The captain returned to the living room, his chest and pockets filled with his triumph. He also had all the jewelry—Sandy's, Tommy's, and Harry's diamond rings, including the Enterprise.

A thin lieutenant arrived with a briefcase stuffed with papers. His black horn-rimmed glasses and white complexion made him look sickly next to the shorter, robust captain. He put some papers on the table in front of Tommy and Harry, pointed to the bottom line, and handed them pens. Tommy tried to read the legal document but could only understand a few words. The Colombian pointed insistently with his finger and motioned him to sign.

"I've got to read it first," Tommy said.

The lieutenant insisted that he sign, but Tommy argued with him loudly before saying, "I won't sign it."

Tommy wasn't signing anything until he could read what it was. He put the pen down. Harry signed his copy. The two officers immediately began a discussion. Tommy let his eyes scan the documents again. He didn't understand most of the words, but *esmeraldas*—emeralds—kept coming up. Were they being busted for trafficking in emeralds?

"What's this about emeralds? *Por favor, porque* emeralds?"

The two officers stopped for a moment and laughed. "*Porque Americano?*" The captain touched his pocket again and laugher even harder. Tommy got the idea. The army confiscates the proceeds. The money was gone, but he hoped they could recover some of the jewelry. The lieutenant shuffled the papers, annoyed that they weren't in order.

"Don't annoy them. Can't we get a lawyer?" Sandy whispered, her face still pale with fright. Tommy hurt for her, but there was nothing to be done. She had to face her fear. This was the reality of life—danger, the thrill, the horror. He looked with longing at her, and she was hiding behind a little girl's wall of innocence. He touched her hand.

The captain ordered Tommy to come over. Tommy understood but decided to play dumb. No sense in making this robbery any easier than it was. Shit, he should be a cop in this town.

A big country soldier, not more than eighteen, nudged Tommy with his rifle, indicating that he was to get up. Tommy shook his head no, confusing the soldier. The captain yelled the order again, and the confused soldier nudged Tommy harder with the point of his rifle. Tommy wasn't going to fight, but he felt satisfaction from the obstruction.

Tommy followed the captain into the dining room. The captain put the papers on the huge dining room table and began to explain in slow Spanish that Tommy had to sign the papers.

"English," Tommy said.

"Take your hands off me!" Sandy shouted.

Tommy pushed past the two soldiers and knocked the hand of the sickly lieutenant from Sandy's arm. The lieutenant drew his pistol, waving Tommy away. Sandy hid behind Tommy. Harry moved farther away, almost detached from the world. Elsie and Kippi were huddled together on the far couch.

The captain rushed over, shouting at the two soldiers, who quickly grabbed Tommy as the lieutenant lowered his gun. Tommy did not move. The captain demanded Tommy sign the papers, but he refused. The captain smiled menacingly, then ordered the two soldiers to take Sandy into the bedroom. As they came forward, Sandy blanched in horror. Tommy felt the strong fingers of the peasant soldier holding tight against his biceps. He wasn't going to let the captain touch Sandy.

The swarthy captain grinned a yellow smile at her, then again pointed to the paper. Tommy shook his head; he would not sign. The captain barked, and two soldiers grabbed Sandy and pulled her to her feet. Her eyes pleaded for help.

"Okay, Captain," Tommy said. He looked at the piece of paper, ready to sign, then switched the pen to his left hand and scribbled on the page. He could easily deny the signature. "Now, let the girl go," he said.

"*Si, si*," the captain said, folding the paper and putting it into his jacket. Two soldiers grabbed Tommy by the arms and stood him up. The captain ordered his troops to bring Sandy to the bedroom.

"Captain, I signed what you wanted. Leave her alone. She's not a part of anything." Tommy's stomach tightened as he realized he had no control over the situation. He had to protect her. Why did he bring her? "Captain, please, leave her alone…"

The captain bared his yellow teeth at Tommy and laughed a sinister laugh from deep in his throat as he bit the end of a small cigar.

With a downward explosion of his arms, Tommy broke the grip of the two men holding him. In the same motion, he brought his right elbow crashing into the solar plexus of the guard on his right, dropping the man instantly to the floor. With a quick sidestep, he swept the legs out from under the corporal who was holding Sandy's left arm. Shooting the palm of his right hand to the sternum of the other guard, Tommy freed Sandy. He backed her against the corner, putting himself between her and the Colombian soldiers. Now if they could get to the door, she could get to the street, where people would be.

"Tommy, no…" she cried as the soldiers pointed their guns, ready to fire. Tommy raised his hands. The captain, red-faced with rage, ordered him handcuffed. Some of the Colombians exhaled when it was accomplished. Tommy felt exhilaration as well as the cold steel of the cuffs. With two soldiers holding him against the wall, the captain shouted from six inches away, drill sergeant style. His breath smelled of onions and tobacco. He spit in Tommy's face and motioned his men to bring Sandy to the bedroom.

"*Capitano, uno momento…*" Tommy said loudly.

The captain stopped and returned to Tommy. He blew cigar smoke in his face.

"*Si, gringo.*"

"Just wanted to wish you good luck." Tommy smiled and rammed a front snap kick to the captain's balls, driving his testicles toward his stomach. The captain's eyes popped with the intensity of the pain. The cigar hit the floor at the same time as the captain's body. Agilely, Tommy dropped into a crouch, swinging himself loose from his guards. He caught the first with an elbow to the throat, putting the man on the floor. The big peasant boy crossed toward him, aiming his rifle butt at Tommy's head. Tommy whirled, kicking him in the chest with the heel of his left foot.

He shouted to Sandy to run for the door. She stood petrified at the violence and confusion.

Two soldiers rushed him. Tommy deflected the blow from one rifle with a high block, but the second one caught him on the collarbone, sending shocks of pain through his arms. The shouting and noise brought six more soldiers in from outside. Trying to find a way out, Tommy threw chairs and kicks at the horde, but there were too many. A rifle butt caught his ribs, knocking him off balance before the stabbing pain of a butt in the kidneys dropped him to a knee.

Covering his head, retreating to a fetal position, only pain remained in his mind. Somewhere, he heard Sandy's muffled cries, but the fierce flamenco of the soldiers' boots pierced his brain. The purpled-faced captain, cringing in pain, shouted encouragement in a high-pitched, trembling voice.

He was going to get to his feet. He was going to walk out, but he could no longer feel anything below his waist. His eyes were rolling into his head, and he wanted to sleep for a while. He wanted some coke—coke so he could be high and away from the pain. This wasn't the life he wanted. He wanted the comfort of Sandy's body, the perfume of her soul in his nostrils. He wasn't going to die—no, not like Sal. He wasn't born for that. The ladies of Fate had to like him for just a bit longer.

He always had a way with the ladies. A wink. A little wink. That'll keep them happy for a while longer. Just a while longer. His body could no longer contain the pain; it could no longer absorb the shock. Without retreating, his mind began to disappear into the peaceful darkness. But he could hear Harry's deep voice.

A colonel entered the room, and the soldiers snapped to attention. With a few quick orders, the captain was carried outside.

"This is a terrible misunderstanding," Harry said to the colonel, palming two hundred-dollar bills to the officer. He licked his lips with his thick tongue. "My friends can vouch for me as a legitimate businessman." He bent forward and wrote something on the piece of paper and gave it to the colonel.

"*Si, si,*" the colonel said as he looked at the paper. "We will investigate." He pointed to Tommy.

"He is just a business associate, that's all. I didn't know that he was doing illegal activities," Harry said without looking back at Tommy. "There is someone you should call. Very influential." He handed the colonel a business card.

"*Si, si.*" The colonel nodded.

Chapter 18

WATCHING TOMMY GO DOWN, SANDY screamed in terror as the soldiers continued to stomp and beat him with their rifles. She rushed at them, pummeling their backs with her fists until one soldier knocked her to the floor with his fist. She sat stunned for a moment, forgetting where she was.

The tall peasant boy, still grimacing in pain, pulled her roughly to her feet. Tommy was on the floor with a stream of blood oozing from the corner of his mouth. *Dead!* The explanation was an artillery barrage of reality, forcing Sandy to consider the world alone. If they killed Tommy, what would they do to her?

"Stop it, stop it," she cried, pleading in her heart for Harry to help. He sat on the sofa, impassive to the drama of Tommy and Sandy. He looked as if he was in his own world without feeling or communication with her pain. She hated him—loathed his face and contemptuous detachment. Tommy was defending all of them, trying at least to keep them free. Harry was still as a stone Buddha, breathing in the violence in abstraction. Would he even have moved to protect Elsie or Kippi? No. It was only about Harry.

With Tommy crushed like an insect against the floor, all life seemed meaningless to her. There wasn't anywhere she could flee for comfort. Tommy was gone, and she wasn't going to resist. None of the horror made any sense to her. She wanted to be on the beach, soaking up the rays, getting high, and making love to him. That was where she was going this afternoon. It didn't matter what these foreigners had to say. There were laws, and her father could call in favors.

The peasant boy grabbed her arm and pushed her roughly to the door and down the stairs. Elsie and Kippi were already huddled in the police van. The door closed with Tommy dead. She could only cry. Only cry—nothing to be done. In bitter memory, in vindictive hatred, she cried for him, and her mind began to numb. She didn't care about the ass pinching the peasant boy did as he hustled her outside. She didn't react when the captain squeezed her breasts as she entered the van. She wouldn't feel. There were no senses in the outer layer of her skin. She had retreated behind her own wall, away from the gross physical world. She was alone inside, mourning Tommy, wishing he would come to save her. He was her prince; she wished for her champion to resue her. He had tried. Now she was imprisoned, and she withdrew her feeling to make way for the defense.

* * *

The interrogation room at DAS headquarters, a monolithic concrete structure, was built with American assistance. DAS, the Colombian internal security police, was equally divided between dedicated Catholic anti-communists, still fighting wars against heretics like the renegade priest Camilo Torres and skilled military extortionists. DAS was effective in the cities but never ventured too far into the countryside.

The institutional grey walls had blotches of dried blood near the floor. There was a wooden bench, wooden desk, and a straight-back chair. Sandy sat alone on the chair. Elsie and Kippi were taken to the next room. Sandy could hear Kippi's crying growing fainter. Then Elsie screamed before there was silence.

The room teemed with unhappy spirits, misery, and death. She didn't want to stay in this cold place. She didn't believe any of this was happening to her. Soon she would wake, and the entire nightmare would be gone. Tommy would come running down the beach, and her cat would purr gently on her breast. Sitting straight on the chair, she curled her feet under her and pulled her arms tight around her chest. She wished Tommy was there and began to cry again.

A tall officer with slightly stooped shoulders, greying hair, and high Spanish cheeks walked briskly into the room and sat at the small desk. He put down several manila folders and looked harshly at Sandy before turning and barking orders at the door. He flipped through the folders impatiently, not looking at Sandy but not reading the papers.

She sat back on the small chair, trying to be invisible. In the windowless room, with only one door, there was no one to help her. No one. If only they would give her a phone call. If her father knew, if she could get word to him... the officer just sat, turning pages.

She had to ask. Tommy would. Tommy, was he alive? Of course, but it wasn't good to think about him. What was going to happen was going to happen. She shivered with fear and tightened her arms.

This time, when the door opened, a short, dark woman entered. She had an oval face and leather complexion and wore a uniform. Carrying a teacher's caning rod, she walked with the gait of a sturdy peasant, her long black hair tied down her back.

She saluted the colonel, who nodded at Sandy. "Search her," he ordered.

"Get up," the woman ordered Sandy in English. Sandy suddenly realized what was happening. The matron motioned with her stick for Sandy to take off her blue crew shirt. The man was now watching her. Her main desire was to run, but if there was going to be a strip show, she wanted to get it over with. As if she were a piece of meat on a rack, she quickly stripped.

The matron told her to bend over then stepped back to allow the colonel to come around his desk. Sandy tried to blank her mind, to not think about what was going on. When the man touched her shoulder with his rough hand, her belly cringed inward under her heart, and she wanted to die.

When he inserted his finger into her vagina, the pain began tearing a hole in her lungs. She wanted to scream but wouldn't give them the satisfaction. If she could think of somewhere else… The loathing was building, bitter and violent. She wanted to kill the man. His probing finger was painful and unwanted. This was what men were after—cheap thrills. This was how men suppressed women—with sexual terrorism.

When the search was complete, Sandy was led naked into the next room. It was a cell with a solid wooden door and a hinged peephole for the guard. The cell had a concrete slab, a thin grey blanket, and a pot. The woman gave her a thick grey cotton dress but no underwear. She sat on the edge of the slab, dazed and confused, her inner organs screaming in rage. She wanted to watch television for a while. And she was hungry. She had not eaten since last night and had no way of knowing what time it was. She wasn't quite certain of the day. There were no windows in the cell, only the grey of cement blocks now containing her body as well as her spirit. She pushed against the door; it was locked.

Her father said she would get in trouble if she went to Colombia with Tommy. He didn't like Tommy and called him a wild kid when she brought him home to meet them. He never seemed to like any of the boys she brought home unless they came from the country club.

Tommy, with his New York accent and silk shirt, was the most differ-ent. They had fought about it. But there was no way her father could stop her. Tommy had enough money. She didn't need any money from her father. She refused the money from her mother as well. It was a heavy scene. She was certain she would prove them wrong about Tommy and herself. If they could see her now... If only they realized where she was. If only she knew where she was. The thoughts of abandonment began mixing with her dread of the absolute still-ness of the cell. There was no longer any other world except that which, by the force of her memory and strength of her imagination, she could create. She had no idea what to do, so she fell into a light sleep to pass the time and relieve the fear.

The opening of the cell door shocked her into lucidity. Around her, she felt the malevolent spirit of authority. The crude rough-fingered colonel stood hunched at the door like a jackal waiting for a meal. Behind him was the squat captain from the house. They were both pantsless, their cocks hanging limply under the fronts of their shirts.

Sandy screamed a high, piercing shriek, but it was cut off by a hard slap to her face from the colonel. Her hatred boiled, and she swung back at the tall man. He hit her again, but this time, she was better prepared for it, blocking part of the blow. The captain rushed toward her, grabbing her shoulders and pushing her back to the slab bed. His thick, tobacco-laden breath and stained teeth were kissing and groping for her mouth. Sandy squirmed to avoid him, ready to vomit, wanting to kill.

As he forced her legs apart with his left knee, she slid to the side and launched a pointed foot at the man's balls. He curled in red-faced pain, his face and mouth distorted in surprise. Falling limply to the hard slab, she wanted her mind to leave forever. The satisfaction of getting one of them, of preventing one of them from getting anything but pain from touching her was a momentary though shallow victory.

She had no more strength to fight. If she was a piece of meat, then she was. If he tried to put his prick in her mouth, she would bite it off. Of that she was certain, she thought as the heaving of the body on top of her ceased, and another smelly form arrived. She would not open her eyes—she did not want to see. She was mindful of the humiliation she was feeling, deadly within, with no place to let out the tears. The pain of their abuse, the repulsive slime of the grunting males, was oppressively real, and she tried to find a haven of sweetness. Sandy Carlton went back to Atlanta. Only her body remained in the cell.

Sandy Carlton was playing tennis in cut-offs and a halter top with friends at the country club. Sandy was coked-out and smoked up at Tommy's apartment, listening to the Rolling Stones. Sandy ignored the pain in her body, the sweat on her skin, the darkness of the cell. She was cheering at football games and going to parties. She had no need for this experience; she didn't want it. The ugliness was too great. In her moment of fear, she opened her eyes as the Colombians lit cigarettes and exchanged coarse jokes. At that moment, Sandy understood what had been done. She knew, and from that recognition, she realized the ferocity of life and her vulnerability to violence. As she curled into a fetal position, again alone in the cold silence of the cell, she was afraid that life could be this forever. She feared that she would never be found, never see the ocean or the sun. And with that fever of hysteria, she wept bitterly and cried to be saved.

Chapter 19

AFTER THE SOLDIERS TOOK THE women out of the apartment, Tommy was lifted into the large leather chair. Dazed and in intense pain, the language sounded as blurry as their faces. The soldiers were now acting tough, reasserting their injured masculinity. They pointed and pushed with their rifles as they escorted Quintana to the waiting van. Three soldiers dragged Tommy out by the handcuffs, inflicting maximum pain.

At DAS headquarters, Tommy was separated from the other prisoners and brought into an office with fourteen-foot ceilings, institutional grey walls, and photos of Alphonso López, the president, and Simón Bolívar, the George Washington of South America. The floor was concrete with a thin wool area rug.

Tommy's wrists were bloody pulps; the skin scraped clean by the handcuffs. The throbbing pain throughout his body dulled his sense of reality. His left eye was swollen, making it difficult to focus with any depth perception. The room was a flat piece of cardboard, and each of the uniformed guards—ribbon-chested and stern—appeared as two-dimensional cutouts. He didn't know what would come next as he sat in the chair, tilting his head back to let the seeping blood run down his throat.

"*Muy peligroso?*" He heard the short captain tell the presiding colonel. The captain looked the worse for the battle. Tommy wanted to smile, but his body was unable to respond.

Tommy expected more torture, but they kept him in a windowless cell. Once a day, a bowl of grey gruel was pushed through the hole at the bottom of the door. *This is the end*, he thought. Disappeared into the bowels of DAS. For what purpose? He wasn't a big fish—hell, he wasn't even a fish. What did they want from him? Did they know anything? They didn't know about George—not even Harry knew. But what did he know? Why the raid on the apartment? The silence allowed him to heal, and he concentrated his mind on healing his body. Will it. Will it. There was nothing else he could do. Tommy tried to surmount the pain and exhaustion and slept fitfully.

In the morning, the captain said, "*La Modelo*." Tommy had heard of the prison and didn't know what or when he'd have another chance to act. He needed to get word out because he couldn't save Sandy. Her father had the money and the influence to get the American embassy involved. He still had some pesos in his sock; would it be enough to get a guard to cooperate? He decided it couldn't be just a guard; it had to be an officer. Reaching into his sock, he took two thousand pesos and moved next to the captain.

"*Por favor*?" Tommy said, showing he had some money. He made a sign that he wanted to write something. The captain looked around for a moment before taking a piece of paper and pencil from the processing desk near the door. Tommy quickly wrote the note to Sandy's father, folded it, and on the outside wrote: *American Embassy*. Handing it to the captain, he caught the man's eyes. "Important. *Muy* important, big man." He nodded to the captain as if he was letting him in on a secret and a potentially bigger payday.

"*Si, si*," the captain said as he put the note and the money in the pocket of his uniform.

The police loaded a van with Tommy and other prisoners for the trip to La Modelo. After processing, Tommy was taken to a cell on

Patio 4. He carefully scouted out the patio, the open area where the prisoners could congregate and exercise. The cells opened onto the space, and the railings were covered with articles of clothing and bedding hanging out to dry. At the far end was the work area. He saw that a tall, dark man sat in a canvas director's chair. The man was wearing a suit, jewelry, and a Davy Crockett hat. Tommy figured the man had to be important, looking at the rags most prisoners on the patio were wearing.

His cellmate, Pepe, told him that the man was called Al Caponi. He was from Medellín and had been involved in several criminal gangs in Bogotá. He was in for killing three police in a shootout after a bank robbery. Tommy watched as inmates approached him as they would a ruler, asking for favors.

Tommy's mind drifted to Sandy. He had to find a way of getting her out. If only he had some of the money he stashed. A hundred dollars would go a long way in this prison. Now he was almost a penniless gringo—almost as penniless as a *gamine*. The few hundred pesos he still had wasn't going to do it. The only way to get a message out was to pay a guard. If he was going to pay, he had to play. Looking down at the courtyard filled with penny *caspedis* that sold pens, combs, blankets, and toothbrushes, he looked to see who ran the monopoly.

Slowly, he ambled along the stone floor to where Caponi sat securely behind dark glasses. It was time to step up. He cranked up his spirit—never let them know what you were thinking or capable of. He had learned that early in dealing. The other side was just as nervous as you were. Use it.

"Gringo, you come to talk to Al Caponi? Maybe you want to work for me?" His dark eyebrows were knitted, and his accented English was thick and guttural. Two men stepped to either side of Tommy—giants among midgets—but they were street toughs.

Tommy held the man's gaze. The only way to survive in prison was fear. And now Tommy had nothing to fear and nothing to lose. He wanted to get out, but he had decided he would win or die.

With a sharp move, he brought the man on his right to his knees with an elbow to his solar plexus. Turning left, he blocked the man's descending fist, ducking under his arm as he twisted him to the ground, giving him a kick to the groin. The first man staggered to his feet, but a quick snap kick put him back on the ground. Several other men from Caponi's gang cautiously approached Tommy as Caponi raised his hand.

"I don't work for anybody," Tommy said, his eyes darting back and forth, looking for the next enforcer. He was ready to kill or die, and a numbness had enveloped him like a morning fog, thick with moisture obscuring the detail. If it ended now, Sandy would cry, but would anyone else? His blue eyes were cold. He'd trained them not to blink.

"Gringo, you are good. We can do business," Caponi said, lighting a cigar. A scar across the side of his neck was like a raised red stream—he had survived an attempt on his life, according to Pepe.

"Aren't foreigners on Patio 5?" Tommy gestured to the high wall at the end of the block. "They have money. You have anything to sell?" he asked, not knowing if Harry was there or anywhere.

As Caponi stood, several prisoners jumped to their feet. Tommy tensed, but Caponi raised his hand like a priest and his troops relaxed. He led Tommy to his cell, which had curtains covering the bars so that no one could peer in it. In several trunks, he had food, watches, clothes, and cocaine. He told Tommy he paid the guards to smuggle liquor and drugs into the prison. The food came from the weekly family visits. It wasn't hard. Just about money. Caponi still ran a protection business on the outside as well.

"How about Patio 5? Any of this stuff sell up there?" Tommy asked.

"*Si*, good money there. But you have to have connections."

"I'll take care of that."

"*Si*, they have the little stuff, but here is what they want." Caponi held up small, folded aluminum foil packets. "The coca."

Tommy smiled. It was the same in here as outside.

"How do I get to Patio 5?" Tommy asked. Now to make the man part of the solution.

Caponi said it was difficult, but he would pay the guards to look the other way. That night, Caponi fronted Tommy ten packets of coke. Why not; where was he going to go? Tommy scaled the ten-foot wall using small finger holes in the concrete. He walked along a narrow ledge that led to a twenty-foot drop on the other side. Skillfully, he put one foot in front of the other, a high-wire artist performing without a net. He tightened his stomach to ease the pain from his bruised ribs. He had to make it. As he landed on the other patio, instantly, he could see the difference. Every cell had a mattress, and some were private cells. There were food and cigarettes and the sound of English. He found an American holding court with a deck of cards.

"Whoa, what do we have here? A visitor from another planet?" The long-haired American had a Southern drawl.

"Who's in charge here?" Tommy asked, his eyes surveying for threats as a number of people began to assemble around him.

"I'm the mayor, Bobby Joe McGrath. McGrath from Arkansas." The man held out his hand.

"Tommy Logan. You have a place we can do business?" In McGrath's private cell, Tommy found out he was a pilot hiding out in Modelo on bullshit charges while his suppliers looked everywhere else for him. Seems a planeload of pot disappeared, and some of the suppliers figured McGrath had a part in it. He only smiled when Tommy asked if it was true.

Tommy sold him the coke for twenty thousand pesos. He slipped back over the wall richer—but more importantly—with the names of guards he could bribe, and a lawyer who could spring him.

* * *

The cryptic message Tommy sent with the captain should have been good enough to get Sandy's father in gear. There wasn't anything more he could do from inside but wait and see if he could be moved to Patio 5, where the smell of shit from the cement showers wasn't so nauseating. There was one bathroom per patio—shit, shower, and shave all in the same large concrete room. At the end of the day, the human excrement was washed down the narrow, clogged drains in the center of the room. A pair of flip-flops was a necessity.

The alliance with Caponi made him a rich man by patio standards. And Caponi got a great markup on the coke. By doing business with Caponi, Tommy bought himself a measure of protection, which was good for Caponi and him. He had to get out, and McGrath's information gave him the opening. He had to get to the lawyer. It was the only way out.

Alone in his cell, Tommy fought the fear that wanted to envelop him. He could show no fear. He had to be, act, and perform like a rich, powerful gringo. It was an edge he had to maintain, or he would be abused and destroyed like the street kids.

For dinner, the prisoners were herded into the *aborista*, which was a cafeteria with rows and rows of concrete tables and benches. The benches were too slimy to sit on, so the prisoners either squatted or stood while eating. Dinner consisted of rice, beans, potato, a small piece of fat, and *aguapanela*—sugar water. As the prisoners were done eating, the plastic bowls were brought to the front and piled in stacks.

They weren't washed or even rinsed before they were reused because there weren't enough bowls for all the prisoners. Everyone ate with their hands, licking the bowls, the table, everything. It was sickening, almost as sickening as the food. Because he was rich, he could buy food on Patio 5.

A shout went up from the middle of the hall as two *maricas*, two Colombian gays, got up onto a table. Doing a little waddle, they drew a torrent of whistles and shouts as they put on their show for more food. Prisoners tried to entice them with their bowls of rice slop. One thick-set *marica* was God-awful ugly. His eyebrows were shaved off and drawn back on with pencil. Tommy learned later that the *maricas* taped razor blades between their fingers so they could cut like cats in a fight.

By the second week, the horror and fear had subsided a bit. He wasn't ready to die. As he walked around the prison, he realized that it was the same violent Colombian society contained within the walls of one place. Once a week was visitor's day. Wives, relatives, and a selection of diseased whores came calling. Prison was the same as the outside world: everyone had to make a living or perish. Nothing was provided; the prisoner had to buy everything.

The *gamines* had it the worst. With no skills, no connections, and no money, they were killers for hire. Five hundred pesos, and the dude was wasted. Ten or twelve of these little geeks in hunting parties would converge on their victim with homemade daggers, and it was over. With five hundred pesos, they could live a month without being hungry.

After speaking with Caponi, Tommy bribed the captain of the guard to move him to Patio 5 with the other Americans. Tommy would be the inside man there, and Caponi could keep up his lucrative business. Tommy figured the system was the same. Everyone had a price.

Sandy was on his mind. How was she holding up? Where was she? What was happening to her? The thoughts of guards touching her brought streams of anger to the blood vessels of his neck and temple. He forced himself not to think of it. Yet he was worried. He sent another message to her father, this time direct. If only he had the money he had hid in the apartment. Then the worry began to set in. Was it still there? Did the police find it during the search? And did the coke get through with Dr. Bentley? The dental chair was to be held in storage, so neither the doctor nor Harry could get at it—but did it get through? Or could they get to it?

He had to find a way out. The charges were bullshit, and somehow, Harry wasn't here. So he must have cut a deal already. He wouldn't leave him here, would he? Tommy was certain that Harry was out for Harry, so if there was any risk… He had to move because if Harry got to the coke first, he'd never see a dime.

McGrath smiled; his front teeth yellowed from his time in Colombia. "Got to have friends."

Tommy ran his hand across the new fuzz on his shaved head. *The big turd left me out to dry.* A panic began to rise from his stomach. *I trusted the fucking Buddha turd, and he sold me down the river. He made some sort of fucking deal and didn't cut me in.* Tommy paced in front of an empty cell. The smell of offal from the cistern was thick in the air. Two boys watched him but did not approach. No doubt Harry was snitching on the connections they had made down here— anything to save his fat ass. But he could have made the deal for both of them. Fuck him. Fuck me.

Tommy should have been smarter. He should've made the deal at the apartment. He was angry and lost it when they went to touch Sandy. He could have made a deal for both of them. Offered some money. Fuck him. How stupid he could be. Now he had to get out—

out before they could check out Harry's stories. Out of the prison and out of the fucking country.

McGrath could help. The planeload of pot had set him up for life if he lived long enough to enjoy it. He knew a lawyer who could get him out. Caponi had a number of *gemmies* working for him who, after they scaled the wall, found Tommy. He took care of the action on Patio 5. Tommy had enough money for a visit from the lawyer and by Saturday he'd have enough money for the fee. Harry left him here, so he was on his own.

Tommy wanted to get away—away from society, from people. Some desert island with Sandy, drinking piña coladas and listening to music under the stars. It all seemed a dream. Even Sandy was beginning to sound like a dream. Where would he go? Who would help him? DAS had his passport, so even if he got out, what could he do? Was he part of Harry's deal? No. They already had him, so he was of no value. What next? Where?

In his cell that night, Tommy listened to the ebbing and flowing sounds of human suffering coming from the concrete corridors of the jail. He was there for his own arrogance, stupidity... He wouldn't make that mistake again. Or was it Harry? He owed more to Sandy, and he would make it up to her when he got back. He hoped she was home in Atlanta, safe, sipping a margarita.

He looked around the small cell and curled onto the thin mattress, and once again, Tommy felt tears forming in his eyes. He had to be strong. It wasn't over. He had to get back to Sandy and make it right. Why did he bring her? He fought the clouds of doubt as he fell into a fitful sleep.

Chapter 20

McGrath's lawyer was good, and Tommy was out on bail by Sunday. He had to act fast. The lawyer, Lopez, wanted money to have Tommy's case transferred to his cousin's court in an outlying district. It would only cost two thousand dollars to quietly dismiss the case. It had to be done quickly. DAS had the keys to the apartment, and the apartment had his money.

Back on the street again, Tommy felt the burden of his problems. The money in the apartment weighed on him. Was it still there? It would be his salvation, but how to get it? And Sandy. Where was she? Did his messages get through to her father? He needed to resolve that to clear his mind.

When he called the house in Atlanta, her mother cried. "Let her come home. Let her come home." It took a few minutes before she told him that Sandy was in a hotel in Bogotá. Her mother said she was safe but that when Sandy found out Tommy was in prison, she refused to leave Bogotá without him. Her mother pleaded with Tommy, "Get her out of there. Get her home." Tears swelled in his eyes as he put down the phone at the post office. She hadn't left him.

He called from the front desk of the small hotel where she had a room, not wanting to scare her with another knock on the door. She wanted to spring down the stairs, but Tommy told her to wait in the room. He took the dark emergency stairs to the third floor, not wanting to be confined in the tiny elevator. Softly tapping on the door, he thought he could smell her through the door as the deadbolt turned. He quickly pushed her into the room, bolting the door behind him.

She was tears and kisses, and Tommy released his fear with a passion. He held her close to never let her go, burying his tongue with hers as they stripped off their clothes. He carried her to the single bed, banishing all thoughts from his mind except her, the moment, and they hugged each other until they fell asleep.

The room was dark when Tommy awoke. Sandy was breathing beside him. What time was it? He was on a deadline. Sandy had brought him back to the living, but now he had to move quickly. He had to get back into the apartment.

Right now, Tommy had to find a printer named Enrique, who McGrath said ran a passport business. Without papers, he did not exist. Without papers, the government could gobble him up off the street. Without a passport, he couldn't leave. He was going to survive. He left a down payment of a thousand pesos, and Enrique told him to return in three days with ten thousand pesos for the product. He then bought a .32 from an Ecuadorian friend of Caponi's. With it in his pocket, he finally felt comfortable and free. This time, he was going to stay that way. When Sandy saw the pistol, pain and panic darkened her face.

"Are we going to need that?" She pulled herself close to him.

"I hope not. From what I've seen of this country, I want to feel safe." He put his arm around her and pulled her to his chest. He had to get the twenty thousand dollars he had hidden in the apartment. Hopefully, it was still there. With that in his pocket, they could be out of the country in days. DAS had refused to give Lopez the key to the apartment. Evidence, they said. Tommy wasn't going to fight about it either—one tour was enough. And Lopez wasn't going to try harder until he had his money. Catch-22. He would break-in.

Sandy rented a small Renault. Tommy drove past the place twice. Not seeing any guards, he parked the car two blocks away. Both of them were dressed in black. Tommy carried the .32, a glasscutter, a knife, and a flashlight. Sandy had twenty feet of nylon rope in her large purse.

Tommy climbed the eight-foot wall easily and pulled Sandy up behind him. Inside the courtyard, he lifted Sandy to his shoulders and pressed her overhead until she reached the balcony. She dropped the rope for Tommy to climb. On the balcony, Tommy cut the glass on the door and tapped it clear so he could unlock the deadbolt. The alarm didn't go off; the police hadn't reengaged it when they left. Tommy flashed his light on the sidebar and at both doors. Hoping there were no guards inside, he crept toward the kitchen. Sandy, a step behind, was straining to hear any sound with the confidence of a young fawn. Tommy reassured her with his hand.

"Relax. We did pay rent for six months."

His eyes adjusted to the dark as he looked into the laundry room. Nothing seemed to have been disturbed.

"Take this and stand over by the door where you can see both corridors." He pointed to the kitchen entrance. From there, she could see the front door and balcony.

Tommy wedged himself up into the ventilation shaft. He rounded his shoulders as he wiggled into the tiny space, extending his arm outward, feeling for the package. They could have gotten it. The thought went through his mind. If they had done a thorough search—but did they come back after that night? Tommy patted the sides of the sheet metal duct. Shit, where was it? He inched further into the space—bottom, side, side, top—until his fingers rested upon the envelope. Salvation.

Almost giddy, like after a first date, he slithered back out of the duct with the prize in hand.

"Let's go see if they left any clothes." Tommy's voice startled her. "Did you get it?"

"Get what? I was taking a shit."

"Tommy." She giggled as he swept her into his arms.

"Right where I left it." With the money in his pocket and Sandy in his arms, the world felt beautiful again.

They hibernated for the day in Sandy's little hotel room. They experienced a rebirth of beauty and tenderness in their heightened excitement of tension and danger. Sandy turned gently into his hands, wrapping her legs around his torso—the smells of the cold concrete were lost in the sweetness of her scent. They touched, trying to heal the bruises.

At a neighborhood restaurant, they ordered a meal of onion soup; avocado with lime; filet mignon; cold broccoli with garlic, onion, and lemon; and ice cream for dessert. They savored the finest moments they had spent in months. Having discovered the money, the green American paper, they sang and drank until they fell asleep happy.

It took two weeks for the lawyer to move the case to a cousin who was a judge, where the charges were dropped. With his real passport back in his hand, he wanted to get out immediately, but it took another day to find an open flight. When they stepped into the crowded airport from the taxi, each with a suitcase and a small travel bag, it was their break for freedom. Tommy tore the picture page from the false passport, ripped the page, and tossed the pieces into several trash bins. He didn't want to get stopped with bad papers. He thought of being on the plane, sitting in first class, lifting off from this fucking country. He was holding his emotions together with string and masking tape. He couldn't let them see inside. He would be cool, correct, business direct.

* * *

Sandy's heart was pounding the reality of life into every vein in her body. At the apartment, when Tommy disappeared into the room, she wished she could see his face, to know what he was doing. She had gripped the pistol more tightly. Though fear had careened through her nervous system like a pinball, she had been detached enough to function. The memory of the police had stirred as she faced the steel door. This time, she wasn't leaving the apartment without Tommy. Moments in the darkness had twisted her mind to the face of the captain, the smell of tobacco oozing in yellow spittle from his mouth. If soldiers had come, she wouldn't go back with them. Not while she had the gun.

Waiting to be processed through customs, she could feel her heart pounding. Before she had left Atlanta, her mother had told her to sharpen her claws. They had been in her mother's rose garden.

"You're a willful and uninformed young lady. I know nothing I say will change your mind." Her graceful mother stepped closer, tears in her mascaraed eyes. She was holding two clipped roses in her gloved hand. "Sandy, you're so young, and you are very beautiful. It's difficult to be a beautiful woman. Please take my advice; at least think about it. You need some thorns to protect you." She carefully presented the flowers. "You're a fool to put your trust in a man the way you are. You better learn to use your claws."

"I can take care of myself, Mother," Sandy had said. Now she had lived through the difference. Now she knew. A year ago, she would have never survived. The events of the last year had brought her power that carried her beyond her mental limitations. Tommy propelled her into living dreams that never could have been. She was certain that this insanity was now hers. She knew of nowhere to put her newfound knowledge.

* * *

Tommy touched her hand lightly as he approached customs. The ticket was in order and matched the passport. She was still with him, having survived an initiation of violence and pain, and chose to stay. She was not only his woman but was an incredible person, strong and alive.

The agent took the passport and tickets through the little slit in the glass. He looked down at the papers without looking up at either of them. Tommy compressed the air in his stomach. There was nowhere to run. The crunching of the stamp on the paper was the most welcome sound Tommy thought he had ever heard.

He calibrated his breath as he collected their passports, and he allowed Sandy to pass in front of him to freedom. As the plane lifted off, only blotches of orange and blue were left in the Western sky over the dirty city nestled in the mountains below.

* * *

In Atlanta, Tommy sat on the sofa in an extended-stay motel, still turning over his thoughts from the plane trip home. Why had Harry left him? The partnership was dead, but Tommy needed to know. Where was the coke? Did it make it? Did Harry take off with it—or snort it? What would it have taken for another phone call? Harry was about Harry. Tommy was under no illusions about being a partner, and Tommy was still holding Harry's diamonds. He drank black coffee, rolling around his next move. Sandy was getting back to normal now that she was home. She asked her mother to lunch. Tommy smiled. It was good for her. Now he had to act.

Later in the day, he pulled his car to the curb behind Quintana's black Mustang. Quintana had gotten out of Colombia ahead of them and had been laying low since then. As he reached the door, Quintana stormed out, almost knocking into him.

"Whoa! *Que pasa?*" Tommy asked.

Quintana's face was red, and his eyes were darted with cocaine lights.

"Tommy. Man, glad to see you. That Harry is sick. He thinks he can treat me like some poor peon."

"What's the matter?"

"He fucked me in Colombia—he never paid for the second batch with a street dealer. These guys start coming after me, and I had to fucking hide in a garbage bin. I was a dead man if they caught me. So these guys here know each other. I think that is why we got busted. And now, now he wants me to sell the cut shit while he takes the profit. Ain't gonna do it. Big old Harry can go down the ghetto and sell that shit himself. Not me."

"Okay, okay. Be cool. I'll see what I can do."

"Yeah man, sure." Quintana's shoulders twitched twice. "You do that, but I'm done. He ain't setting me up for no one."

Tommy watched him accelerate down the walkway. He could still feel Quintana's anger.

All the lights were on in the house as Tommy entered. Harry was sitting in his captain's chair, the sleeves of his yellow cotton shirt rolled up to his biceps. His huge head was in constant motion like a large reptile, his tongue darting. Thin black hairs stretched to cover the tiers of flesh on his white face. On the table in front of him was a small mirror, a glass of water, and a half-empty bottle of Johnnie Walker.

"Good to see you up and around, kid." Harry was very high. His words poured out of his mouth, thick with saliva around his tongue. "Did you see Quintana on your way in? He was just here. Brought me this." Harry held up a piece of tin foil. "But now I have my lucky lady back, and I must get acquainted." He began unwrapping the foil.

"He wasn't very happy with you."

"Dumb spic. He needs to learn his place and do what he's told."

Tommy wanted to take the Beretta and put two bullets through that fat head. *Like nothing fucking happened? Just sit there like a giant turd and think I don't remember or care. Fucking insane.*

"Want to do some business?" Harry was trying to make lines with the edge of a playing card. "Quintana says he knows someone who wants to do some business. Some higher class of dumb spic."

"Where's the coke?" Tommy wasn't in the mood for games. He wanted an explanation about Bogotá, but first, business—he had $250,000 invested in the bottom of a dentist's chair.

"It's safe," Harry said, raising his eyebrows.

"I'm not fucking around. Where is it? I want to move some and turn it into cash before it goes up your nose."

"Grasshopper, you offend me." Harry put his hand to his chest. "I have everything under control."

"With that fruitcake dentist. I want my share now." Tommy moved to the table and leaned in Harry's face. "I know you fucked me in Bogotá. You ain't gonna fuck me here. So where is mine?" Tommy could feel the adrenaline rising in his blood. *Keep it under control. Seem angry; don't be angry.* He wanted to get back to Tampa, unload, and retire. It would be a million for his share.

Harry slowly rose from his chair; the caftan draped around his body fell to his knees. Tommy noticed plates and pots piled in the kitchen—where were Elsie and Kippi? He didn't like the vibe. Harry led him to the cellar stairs, which he descended, holding on to the railing. The cellar was unfinished, with pipes overhead and boxes around the edges. Tommy wasn't sure if they were going for a ride on the bikes. Harry unlocked a door that led to the heating unit. Next to it was a large metal tank that stored heating oil. Harry went to the back of the tank and opened a hatch.

"I converted the heat to gas a number of years ago—much more environmentally friendly," Harry said with a wave of his hand. "When they told me how much to remove this tank, I thought, now I could use it. You can't even tell this hatch is here unless you know where to look for it."

Tommy was impressed. It would take someone a long time to figure it out. Harry took out four packages of coke, still wrapped as Tommy had seen them in Colombia.

"I get six; you get four. My cash," Tommy said.

"For the risk I took, we should split it fifty-fifty," Harry said.

"My ass. It was sixty-forty. I'm not renegotiating. My money, my risk, my coke."

Harry shrugged his large shoulders and put two more packages on the table. The second one didn't look right. It had been opened. Tommy figured it was light, probably with some cut in it. Was it worth the fight right now? He wasn't ready for one. He needed to move this powder and turn it into dollars.

"Harry, you're a shitty partner. Is that my coke you were snorting upstairs?" He picked up the repackaged coke and turned it around in his hand. "You're such a jackass. If it's light, I'm coming back to you."

"You do that, Tommy boy," he said as he walked to the door. "You do that."

* * *

It was time to settle up with Harry. No more deals, no more cons. He was out before Harry really fucked up. He wasn't the big time; he was just a ton of shit pretending to be someone. Tommy sat in the side chair. Harry was drunk, stoned, and filled with self-pity and emanating a loathing, contagious disease that could be transmitted from human to human.

"What a pigsty. Where are Elsie and Kippi?" The kitchen was full of plates and bags from take-out places.

"They went to see her cousin get married, or whatever those people do up in the mountains," Harry said. "I'll fuck her up if she doesn't get back here soon."

"Always fucking somebody, Harry. What comes around goes around, as you say?" Tommy didn't move.

"Fucking, my father taught me all about fucking people. He turned me into the cops for stealing a car when I was seventeen. He went out of his way to fuck me. I learned to love fucking. Fucking people. It's a high, a rush like hitting with the lady. You know it 'cause you've done it. I've fucked everyone I ever knew. It's the game. I had to. Bending them over and sticking my huge hard-on up their tight asses. That's like no other feeling. Unique like coke." His head was weaving, and his tongue darted in and out of his thick lips like a snake in a stone wall.

Harry continued, "You and your heroism. Heroism is useless: This isn't the movies. The hero is the fool. Save your own ass, kid.

'Cause you're in tough shape. Two strikes against you. You're fucked like the rest of us. You're not any better like you think you are." Harry shuddered. "I fucked you, kid. I did it. Nobody else." He closed his eyes as the flesh of his cheeks rolled in slow waves.

"Why the fuck? What did it do for you?" Tommy wasn't going to forgive or forget, but nothing was going to be resolved tonight. He had to make a decision about the business and Sandy. He had enough to get by—maybe now he would join the country club set and be part of Sandy's world.

Bogotá had scared the shit out of both of them. They were lucky to get out. And he was even luckier to still have Sandy. He could have thrown it all away. Harry was shit. He admitted it—he fucked him. And he would do it again. So this was the end. End with a whimper, not a bang.

He closed the front door.

Tommy spent the next two weeks cutting the coke and distributing it in Tampa. It was more than his usual amount, so he had to take some risks with new customers. He didn't like to do anything big with people he didn't know; there was too much risk of informants or guys trying to make a deal with the man. He counted the cash with Sandy—$800,000—and they went to her father's bank and rented a new safety deposit box. He was ready to retire.

* * *

As he left his apartment in Tampa, a green Plymouth Fury followed him. Tommy noticed it as he entered I-285—they looked like cops. Unzipping his suede jacket, he slipped off the shoulder holster with the Beretta and put it in the glove compartment, then locked it. Looking at the speedometer, he stayed just at the speed limit. The Plymouth did the same two cars behind.

He told himself to be cool, but the adrenaline was galloping along the inner walls of his stomach, causing it to skip and jump. He had to act calm, show no facial emotions. If he acted scared, they would know it, just like animals.

There was nothing in the car; he had to keep that mindset. Nothing. There was no reason for the police to stop him. He was Mr. Average Q Public. Play dumb. *Who, me?* At least he was straight. If he had been snorting, he might never have noticed the lights in his mirror. Maybe he could stop at a mall. The parking lot would be large enough to lose the tail. That would be easy.

A Tampa patrol car came up fast on the outside as they approached Exit 3. When Tommy started to exit, the cop hit his lights and followed him down the ramp.

With lumps in his gut, terror swept his mind. He wanted to run, to disappear, to move faster than… The Man was all around him, and there wasn't any escape.

Another patrol car appeared at the bottom of the ramp. If only he had a bike, he could go over the embankment. They'd never catch him. He pulled the car off to the side of the ramp. Might as well choose a difficult place.

What did they know? They must know something or why so many cars. Maybe it was the car, the Monte Carlo. It was registered in his name with Florida plates. Did they want to question him about Sal's death, or did they find pieces of George? Were the cops watching Harry's house since he came back? Why stop him now?

Perspiration dripped in his armpits as his fingers turned cold against the wheel. Two troopers, with guns drawn, approached from the front and two from the rear. This time, it was for real.

"Turn off the car and get our slowly with your hands in the air," growled the Tampa lieutenant. His sideburns had been shaved over the tops of his ears. The tall man had a military bearing and held a .357 magnum leveled at Tommy's head.

"Whatever you say, Officer." Tommy's voice was obsequious. "I don't know what this is all about. That gun makes me nervous." He had to keep control of his running blood. Keep talking, keep the mouth and mind working. Hatred for the man pointing the gun at his face flashed violently in his mind. He wanted to take it away from the pig, a quick crescent kick as he got out of the car. What right did he have to threaten? Tommy was innocent, so he could...

"Shut up. Turn around and put your hands on the car," the officer ordered without lowering his weapon. Two other cops roughly frisked him.

"He's clean, lieutenant," a thick-set, beer-bellied cop with a flat, vacant face said.

"Get the keys, boys. Search the car."

"What's this all about, sir? What was I stopped for?" Tommy continued as they handcuffed his hands behind his back.

"Shut your mouth, boy. Don't go making it worse for yourself. Fucking Yankees think y'all can come down here and push your drugs. You're scum." The man launched a line of yellow spit that hit Tommy in the leg.

His anger nearly broke; Tommy took a half step toward the cop who had a black wart on his left temple. Tommy measured the distance for a kick. Two troopers pushed him hard against the car.

"Am I under arrest? Why was I stopped?"

The swine-faced cop stuck his stick hard into Tommy's side. "Shut your mouth, boy. You heard the lieutenant; he doesn't want to hear nothing from scum."

The lieutenant walked slowly to the green Plymouth, which contained two men in business suits. Tommy could only see half shadows as he strained for a better view. The profiles were clean and neat, with a federal government-look about them. As the door opened, the light illuminated the red hair of the driver. Tommy was certain he had seen him before.

"Can I get a light from you?" Tommy tried to make a connection with the skinny young cop at his side. The fat one was tearing up the inside of his car. "Do you have any idea what this is about?"

"Whooeee," the fat one squealed from the other side of the car, holding up the shoulder holster and the Beretta. "Lookee what we got here, Lieutenant. This here looks like some artillery." The cop swaggered around the car to Tommy. "So you're the tough guy from New York. Maybe we'll just take you coon hunting on the way back to town. We'd save the courts lots of money."

"Anything else in that car," the fat cop barked.

"No, sir. This here gun is all I could find. I tore the whole thing apart."

"Look under the hood, under the fenders," the lieutenant said as he walked over to the fat cop. "There has to be more."

Tommy didn't like it. The fear was slowing as he began accepting what the reality of the situation really was. He was their prisoner. He had no choice. The search was illegal. They didn't stop him for anything, and they never asked his permission to search the car. The lieutenant nodded to the Plymouth as he pointed the fat cop to the back bumper. The cop produced a plastic bag with white powder in it. Tommy shook his head. Fucked. They planted fucking shit.

"You planted that shit. It ain't mine," Tommy said, straining for concentration as he watched the fat cop come charging at him, spittle gathering in his mouth. As he let it fly, Tommy snapped his head to the side, causing it to miss. The cop dug his stick into Tommy's kidneys, bringing him to his knees. It was hard to hold the fear in his stomach. He wanted to fight, to change reality.

"You're scum. Animals like you should be shot in the streets." The lieutenant sank the toe of his boot into Tommy's ribs. Tommy curled into a fetal position, protecting his head and face. If he could only fight them one at a time. Even two at once.

The cops began a primitive stomping dance using Tommy's body until the men in the Plymouth finally stopped it.

Numbness of the brain called out to him, but with whitened knuckles, Tommy fought against the blackness. He could see Sandy bending over him with a cool, clean cloth, and he gripped her hands while shaking his brain clear. He wasn't going to lose; he wasn't going to give them that satisfaction.

Pulling himself to his feet, Tommy staggered to the car under his own power, his eyes set and firm, looking beyond the pain to getting to the seat. He had to get there. One more step. One more time. They weren't tougher than the Colombians, and they didn't break him. He was past the pain of the marathon run; he could keep going on. As he sunk into the backseat, clouds of exhaustion fumigated his mind. A satisfied, amused smile arrived on his face with sufficient insolence to enrage the lieutenant. Tommy was slapped in the face, but the clouds of exhaustion refused to dissipate. The smile remained. One of the Feds escorted the cops to headquarters.

Chapter 21

CHARGED WITH POSSESSION, TOMMY WAS confident the stop was illegal. Sandy arranged a lawyer. The judge set bail at ten thousand dollars. The police arrived at the apartment with a search warrant that included a specific reference to a safety deposit box in Atlanta's Second National Bank that only a few people knew Tommy had. In it were Harry's diamonds—the collateral for a rainy day.

Two days later, Tommy was arrested again. This time, the charge was first-degree murder. Tommy was guilty—they had found George, or parts of George had somehow washed up on a beach. He thought he had been living on borrowed time. What was the evidence? He sat in the small cell in Tampa, trying to piece together the evidence. Why the search warrants? There was nothing in his apartment or the safety deposit box.

Sandy was crying during her first visit, done through the glass with those stupid telephones. What the fuck were they thinking? Everything would be fine, and they could live happily ever after? He wanted it to be that way with Sandy. The key now was to get a good criminal attorney. The first arrest was illegal, and maybe that would taint the entire prosecution. He didn't know, but that's how it was done on television.

While he was awaiting arraignment, Tommy was told he was being charged with murder. He could still see the confusion mixed with rage on George's face as he tried to get to Tommy before the bullet penetrated his head. He could smell the odor of the flesh as he pushed him into the ocean. But murder, that was a state charge. Were they holding him for extradition to Florida? Then he read the charge: the murder of a jewelry dealer named Isaac Greenburg in Miami two years ago during an armed robbery. Tommy was stunned. What did this have to do with him? He didn't know any jewelry dealers, and he certainly never robbed one. It had to be a mistake.

At the bail hearing, Tommy was painted as a career criminal who would flee the country if released on bail. Tommy's lawyer, Garry Weisman, was a second-generation Tampa attorney who specialized in criminal defense. He demanded ten thousand dollars up-front before he would even look at the case, and another ten thousand if it went to trial. After some stiff fast-talking, Weisman settled for five thousand cash and two ounces of coke. If it went to trial, they would negotiate again. Weisman objected to the half-million-dollar bail. "My client has no criminal record," he argued. "And has ties to the community."

Weisman was certain the charges would be thrown out before it got to trial. Illegal search and no evidence tying Tommy to the crime. The lawyer motioned for evidence to be suppressed. Tommy was released on two hundred fifty thousand dollars bail.

* * *

Sandy was panicked. Barely over the Bogotá experience, she found herself alone again. She tried to reach Harry, but he was nowhere to be found. It didn't make sense to her. Tommy wasn't a killer. He certainly didn't kill some jewelry salesman in Miami—she didn't think Tommy had ever been to Miami. Her parents told her to keep her distance. After a violent argument with them at the club, Sandy felt even more isolated. Where was she going to get help? Who would help Tommy?

For three months, the legal formalities continued: arraignment, pleadings, delays, delays, pre-trial hearing, formal indictment, delays, and finally a trial date set. The district attorney wanted a plea—twenty-five to life—so he wouldn't seek the death penalty. "Fuck no," Tommy said. He was innocent, but how was he going to show it?

The discovery phase was more of a revelation than a legal proceeding. Tommy sat with Weisman reading the documents. It wasn't real—it couldn't be real. The bullet that killed the salesman came from the Beretta—the fucking Beretta Harry had given him. And among the prosecution witnesses was one Harry Burr. That fat piece of shit.

What kind of deal did he cut to get his ass out of jail? Tommy turned the facts over in his mind. Two years ago was right after they first met. Harry was running him, using him from day one. Tommy wanted to put the fucking Beretta in Harry's mouth and blow his brains out. Partner? Fuck, he went out of his way to save his ass in Colombia to come back to this? He clenched and unclenched his jaw. He railed at the lawyer, "What bullshit! I had nothing to do with this! It's all Harry Burr."

At his office, Weisman tried to calm Tommy down. There were the police reports, the search of the safety deposit box with the loose diamonds, the gun, and whatever Harry was selling. He would see what he could do, but it didn't look good.

Judge Thaddeus Mathews had refused to dismiss the charges or suppress any evidence. When the thin, bespectacled man set the trial date, Tommy thought he saw a spark of glee in the old man's eyes. The short prosecutor was prematurely fat and bald, with a slow Southern drawl.

Weisman told Tommy that Mathews had been a judge for thirty years. He was appointed from a small town near Bradford when it was a hip-pocket Democratic town. The solemn cypress-lined court-room reeked of nineteenth-century morality and ruling class notions of the majesty of the law in keeping certain elements of society under control. Behind the majesty of the room, Tommy saw every poor sucker who was railroaded into chain gangs. It had the same hollow formalness of a coffin with satin and silk. This was the place of the grand inquisition disguised as the bastion of noble justice. The dungeons were concealed far from the formalities of the law.

Tommy had to look twice at Steve when he arrived at the lawyer's office. His hair was cut with some style, and his beard was neatly trimmed against his face. He was dressed in grey dress slacks with a cream shirt and tie. Tommy couldn't remember when he last saw his big brother this dressed up.

"Heard you could use a little help," Steve said, shaking his head slowly.

"Yeah, I'm in a little shit," Tommy said. "How'd you get here?"

"Drove," Steve smiled.

"Shit." Tommy smiled back, relieved of his tension for a second. "How, why?"

"Sandy found me. I spoke to your lawyer. I think you need an investigator on this case. Things don't add up."

"Fuck they don't. That fat turd set me up." The vein on the left side of Tommy's neck began to throb. "He's made some kind of deal to get himself out."

"No doubt." Steve made some notes on the reporter's notebook he took from his back pocket. "You have to think through the whole timeline with the Burr guy. From the first time you met him. Between you and Sandy, we have to reconstruct where you were when this murder occurred."

"Shit, it's just not true. I'll take the stand and tell them myself."

"That's between you and your lawyer if you testify or not. Right now, I'm just trying to be a good cop and put all the pieces of the puzzle on the table. We'll figure out how they fit together later."

"Man, I owe you." Tommy stood and hugged him.

"Sure. Let's concentrate on getting you out. I'll be seeing you, brother."

Tommy traced the timeline with Weisman. He had first met Harry about the same time the jeweler was murdered. It was after they first met and after Harry gave him the diamonds as collateral. Shit, to make him a fall guy. Harry was cash poor until he fenced the diamonds from the robbery. It all made sense to him.

Steve went through the police report of the robbery. Piss-poor crime scene work. They dusted for fingerprints on the case and the door but not on any of the other surfaces. The prints did not match Tommy's. Harry said he was there but was wearing gloves. The ballistic report showed that the bullets that killed the jeweler matched the ones from the Beretta that Tommy had in his possession. How to prove that the gun wasn't Tommy's? The rest of the case rested on Harry's testimony. Pretty thin, but maybe enough to convict in Florida.

"These other prints," Steve asked. "Any idea who else was tight with Harry?"

"George." Tommy shook his head.

"He probably has prints on file. I'll run them. Any idea where I can find him?"

Tommy couldn't say anything. "He took some job in Asia, last I heard." He could see the wide eyes and the smell. The smell would never leave him.

"Okay, so we focus on the prints. I'll talk with this Elsie, see if she knows anything more," Steve said.

"Is Harry out on bail?" Steve asked Weisman. The lawyer shifted a stack of papers from one side of the desk to the other to give himself room to write.

Tommy leaned back in his chair, happy his brother was here. He needed someone on the outside he could trust.

"Yes, he's got some protection from the Feds. I won't know the details until I do the deposition."

Steve walked around the small office. "Harry is running some deal. Trading you for immunity. I can feel it. Have you spoken to the prosecutor? I don't like the smell of it—it may be my instincts from my police days. What about the gun?"

"The report says it's the murder weapon."

"Yeah, but Tommy said Harry gave it to him."

"How do we prove it?"

"I'll do some investigation," Steve said. "It looks like you're overwhelmed, and I've got some experience." Tommy looked at the disarray of the office and thought that the lawyer needed his brother's help.

"Steve, good idea. Thanks," Tommy said, nodding to the lawyer.

At the next meeting in the lawyer's office, Weisman dropped a manila folder on the table. "Their witness list," he said.

"Fuck, I knew it," Tommy said, standing and kicking the chair to the floor. Steve looked at the folder.

"He made a deal. You for him," Steve said, shaking his head. Sandy was livid and started to cry when she saw Harry was the state's chief witness. Steve and Weisman calmed her down. They would need a plan.

As she regained her composure, Weisman was making notes on the list with Tommy and Steve looking over his shoulder.

"I'm going to call Children's Services," Sandy said through her tightly drawn lips.

* * *

After the months of preparation and discovery, Tommy was ready for the trial to begin. Sandy told Tommy that Harry and Elsie were deemed incapable of taking care of Kippi when Children's Services visited and found drug paraphernalia in the living room. Steve had found her in a foster home.

When the opening gavel pounded on the bench, Tommy quickly looked back at Sandy and Steve and smiled. Her face was nervously encouraging. She filled Tommy with another edge of belief and pride. He had too much to live for. When the evidence was heard, he would be cleared. He had confidence, at least, in that part of the American system. There were rules. Tommy understood that much. Rules made by some people for their own benefit. Rich people make the laws against stealing; poor people don't.

Weisman's curly dark hair and olive complexion stood out against the clean-shaven rednecks in the courtroom. The jury of seven women and five men had an average age of forty-seven and an average education of ten years. Two stern housewives sat together at the end of the jury box. Tommy could almost hear them clucking their tongues as the prosecutor recited the charges.

"Premeditated murder, murder while committing an armed robbery, armed robbery with a firearm. The defendant knowingly, and with malice and foresight, take the life of Isaac Greenburg."

Everyone seemed indifferent to Weisman's presentation. The young lawyer's thick sideburns were in stark contrast to the crew cut of the prosecutor. But his voice was soothing and reasonable. Tommy and Sandy exchanged glances, looking for reassurance. The air in the courtroom was thick with irrationality and laced with the incense of morality. It was him alone, standing straight before the wooden, iron, concrete, and steel shackles, waiting for the system to be done with him, to digest him and spit him out again.

He sat quietly at the defense table in an English plaid three-piece suit, watching Lieutenant E.W. Walker describe the police action when they caught Tommy at the exit. Walker described in cool, rehearsed sentences the shoulder holster and pistol Tommy had and, of course, his attempt to elude capture, which required the use of force to subdue him.

Weisman objected to the introduction of evidence from the stop because of no probable cause.

"Objection overruled," Judge Mathews said each time Weisman raised an issue.

Officer Rogers, the pot-bellied one, recited almost the exact story for the jury, down to the same number of times they hit Tommy—five. Weisman tried to shake the testimony, but each time, Rogers repeated the story as if it had been recorded. The police lab technician testified that the Beretta recovered from Tommy's car matched the markings on the bullets in the murder.

On the second day, the state's star witness appeared. Harry paraded down the center aisle, taking up all of the space. He was dressed in a grey suit, his hair and beard trimmed. He wore no jewelry, but the open neck of his shirt allowed some renegade hairs to pop out. As they led him to the witness stand, there was some commotion with the prosecutor and the judge. The bailiffs scurried to move the witness chair and install a bench so Harry would fit in the box. Tommy smiled to himself. The fat turd was too big for the scales of justice.

Harry refused to look at Tommy. Tommy kept his eyes directly on him so that Harry knew how much hatred there was in the room. Harry answered questions in a monotone. It was Tommy's idea to rob the jeweler. It was Tommy who had the gun. It was Tommy who roughed the man up. It was Tommy who shot the man. Harry was just an innocent bystander. He thought they were going to buy jewels, not steal them. As Harry made the statements, his large lizard eyes rolled slowly left and right. His tongue darted out of his mouth as if trying to suck in oxygen. He gave a Harry performance without the card tricks.

Weisman led Harry down the list of his past crimes, including murder and armed robbery. He challenged Harry's timeline and his acquaintance with Tommy. He asked about any deal offered him by the prosecutor or other law enforcement agencies. Harry said there were none. Tommy knew that was a lie—Harry wasn't out on bail because of his good looks.

"That's a lie," Tommy whispered to Weisman.

"True and false. It's worded as contingent so he can deny having one during his testimony. Sleazy prosecution tactics."

At a recess, Tommy saw the red-haired guy from the Plymouth at the back of the courtroom. "Gary, that's the other cop. Can we put him on the stand?"

"Are you sure?" Weisman asked, nodding to Steve, who came up to the rail.

"I'm pretty sure. I wasn't seeing real good by the time we got to the station. I think he was in Puerto Rico too."

"I'll talk to him." Weisman walked to the back of the courtroom and exited with the Fed. They were gone fifteen minutes.

"His name is Inspector Patrick McCauley of Alcohol, Tobacco, and Firearms. He said he has never seen you and just stopped by the courtroom because he heard a first-degree murder trial was going on."

"Bullshit. I know he was there. He's Harry's handler." Tommy wanted to spit but realized it wouldn't look very good.

"I'll see what I can find," Steve said to the lawyer, "but let's not count on it."

The defense started with Sandy. Her pink blouse and blue pleated skirt made her look like she had just come from Sunday church. She looked like every mother's dream of a proper young lady. She testified about when she met Harry and how and when she introduced Tommy to him. The prosecution grilled her on her memory, her use of drugs, her trip to Colombia. She maintained a pleasant and proper demeanor.

Elsie was nervous from the moment she entered the courtroom. Her skirt was too short, and the yellow top she wore was too loud for the court. She only answered questions in mumbles and claimed to have forgotten almost anything she ever knew. Tommy shook his head at the table. This wasn't good.

Steve had tracked down the salesman who testified that he sold a Beretta to Harry for some coke—who could forget someone that big. The product wasn't on the market yet, but Harry promised to introduce it to some of his friends at the Federal level, so he thought it was a good investment.

Kippi, now twelve, seemed to be composed as she took the oath to tell the truth. Weisman led her carefully through meeting Tommy and her life at Harry's house.

"What is your name?"

"Kippi Watson."

"I thought it was Kippi Burr."

"I did too, but it's not my real name." She put her head down, answering very quietly.

"Do you know Harry Burr?" Weisman stepped closer but didn't want to invade her space.

"Yes. Yes, I did…" she whispered.

"Who is he? It's okay, dear. Take your time." Weisman smiled, touching his sideburns.

"He was my daddy. Or I thought he was my daddy. I used to live with him." She looked over at the defense table. Tommy smiled at her. The side of her mouth turned up slightly.

"Did you ever see any diamonds at the house where you lived with Mr. Burr?" Weisman asked.

"Harry always had them. He had a big bag locked in his bedroom. He wouldn't let me play with them." The side of her lips turned down.

"Do you remember, did he ever give any to Tommy?"

She scratched her head a moment. "Yes, yes, I remember. Harry told me to get the case, and he gave some to Tommy. He wouldn't give me any," she pouted.

"And about this gun." Weisman brought the Beretta over to Kippi and ejected the empty magazine. "Did you ever see this before?"

She brightened, taking the gun from the lawyer and turning it over in her hand. "It's so light. It was Harry's. He kept it in a metal box in his closet. I couldn't play with it, but I wanted to," she said.

"Did Harry give it to Tommy?"

She put her finger to her chin and cocked her head, thinking. "Yes, he made me get the box. I was sad because I wanted it. It's like a toy."

Weisman walked back to the defense bench and picked up his notepad. "Did anything bad happen to you at the house where you lived with Mr. Burr?"

She put her head down, shaking it from side to side. Little tears began rolling down her cheeks. Weisman waited, giving her time to cry.

"It's okay, sweetheart. You're safe now."

"Yes," she said.

"Did Mr. Burr know about it?"

She nodded yes.

"Who did these bad things to you?"

"Uncle George." Her body began to shake with her sobs.

"Fifteen-minute recess," the judge ordered. His gavel broke the spell of the courtroom.

After Kippi's testimony, Weisman put a woman from Children's Services on the stand who read a report on the abuse Kippi described at the Burr house and in Colombia. Tommy's eyes were wet, realizing he could have stopped it sooner. George would never do it again, which was more than the court knew. The prosecutor said that George had fled the country.

When the jury filed back into the courtroom after five hours of deliberation, Tommy could feel the wetness under his arms expand. The stern group was led by the two ladies at the end. He was guilty, but not of this crime. He should be punished, but Harry was the one who should have been on trial. The slimy bastard made a deal, but the devil would be out to get him now. It wasn't right, but it was the best he could do. Maybe next time, he would be a better man. He looked back at Sandy, who held Steve's hand. She smiled and nodded at him.

How stupid had he been not to see all that love before? He would make it right. He would find a better way for them—for her. She deserved it.

Tommy stood and faced the jury. He couldn't see into their hearts, but he wanted to tell them how sorry he was for everything he had done. "Not guilty" was said to each of the charges. Tommy could feel the tears leak out of his eyes as he stood erect, pushing his shoulders back. "Not guilty" registered in his mind. He had another chance. He wouldn't fuck it up. He hugged Weisman and turned to Sandy when the judge dismissed him. Released from hell, released from hell with a chance for a do-over.

He gripped her so hard, trying to pull her into him, to make them one. Their lives were here, now, immediately, as he felt her heart beating and warm flesh against him. She was the only why he would ever understand. She was the only reason sanity was worth the fight. He wouldn't let her ever get away.

The weeks passed quietly as Tommy and Sandy settled into a peaceful suburban life. Tommy was going to karate five times a week and taking two courses at community college with Sandy. She was seeing her parents again and even took Tommy to the club for a swim. He thought he might take up golf so he could play with her father. He started thinking about business, realizing he missed the thrill of the deal. There had to be something else he could do.

Quintana's call came early in the morning. Tommy was still half-asleep.

"No more," Quintana said.

"What?" Tommy said. "Who?"

"No more," Quintana said. "He ripped off one too many, and they gave him what he deserved."

"No, they didn't…" Tommy remembered that the Colombians could be brutal.

"It will probably be reported as an overdose, but I wanted you to know better."

Tommy let the phone hang, one foot over the edge of the bed, ready to get up. Looking at the receiver, he put it back into its cradle. It could have been him.

He moved Sandy's hair over her ear so he could see her face. He kissed her gently and spooned closer to her.

www.ingramcontent.com/pod-product-compliance
Lightning Source LLC
Chambersburg PA
CBHW021203250626
47155CB00008B/2650